THE SECRETS AMONGST THE CYPRESS

THE HOUSE OF CRIMSON & CLOVER VOLUME X

SARAH M. CRADIT

Cover Design by Sarah M. Cradit
Editing by Kathy Lapeyre

First Edition
ISBN-10: 1539461971
ISBN-13: 978-1539461975

Publisher Contact:
sarah@sarahmcradit.com
www.sarahmcradit.com

ALSO BY SARAH M. CRADIT

KINGDOM OF THE WHITE SEA

<u>Kingdom of the White Sea Trilogy</u>

The Kingless Crown

The Broken Realm

The Hidden Kingdom

<u>The Book of All Things</u>

The Raven and the Rush

The Sylvan and the Sand

The Altruist and the Assassin

The Melody and the Master

The Claw and the Crowned

THE SAGA OF CRIMSON & CLOVER

<u>The House of Crimson and Clover Series</u>

The Storm and the Darkness

Shattered

The Illusions of Eventide

Bound

Midnight Dynasty

Asunder

Empire of Shadows

Myths of Midwinter

The Hinterland Veil

The Secrets Amongst the Cypress

Within the Garden of Twilight

House of Dusk, House of Dawn

Midnight Dynasty Series

A Tempest of Discovery

A Storm of Revelations

A Torrent of Deceit

The Seven Series

1970

1972

1973

1974

1975

1976

1980

Vampires of the Merovingi Series

The Island

and more

The Dusk Trilogy

St. Charles at Dusk: The Story of Oz and Adrienne

Flourish: The Story of Anne Fontaine

Banshee: The Story of Giselle Deschanel

Crimson & Clover Stories

Surrender: The Story of Oz and Ana

Shame: The Story of Jonathan St. Andrews

Fire & Ice: The Story of Remy & Fleur

Dark Blessing: The Landry Triplets

Pandora's Box: The Story of Jasper & Pandora

The Menagerie: Oriana's Den of Iniquities

A Band of Heather: The Story of Colleen and Noah

The Ephemeral: The Story of Autumn & Gabriel

Bayou's Edge: The Landry Triplets

For more information, and exciting bonus material, visit www.sarahmcradit.com

You can find a complete list of content warnings on my website: sarahmcradit.com

For Holly
My Muse

"It's no use going back to yesterday, because I was a different person then."

"He was part of my dream, of course -- but then I was part of his dream, too."

Lewis Carroll

THE WHEEL

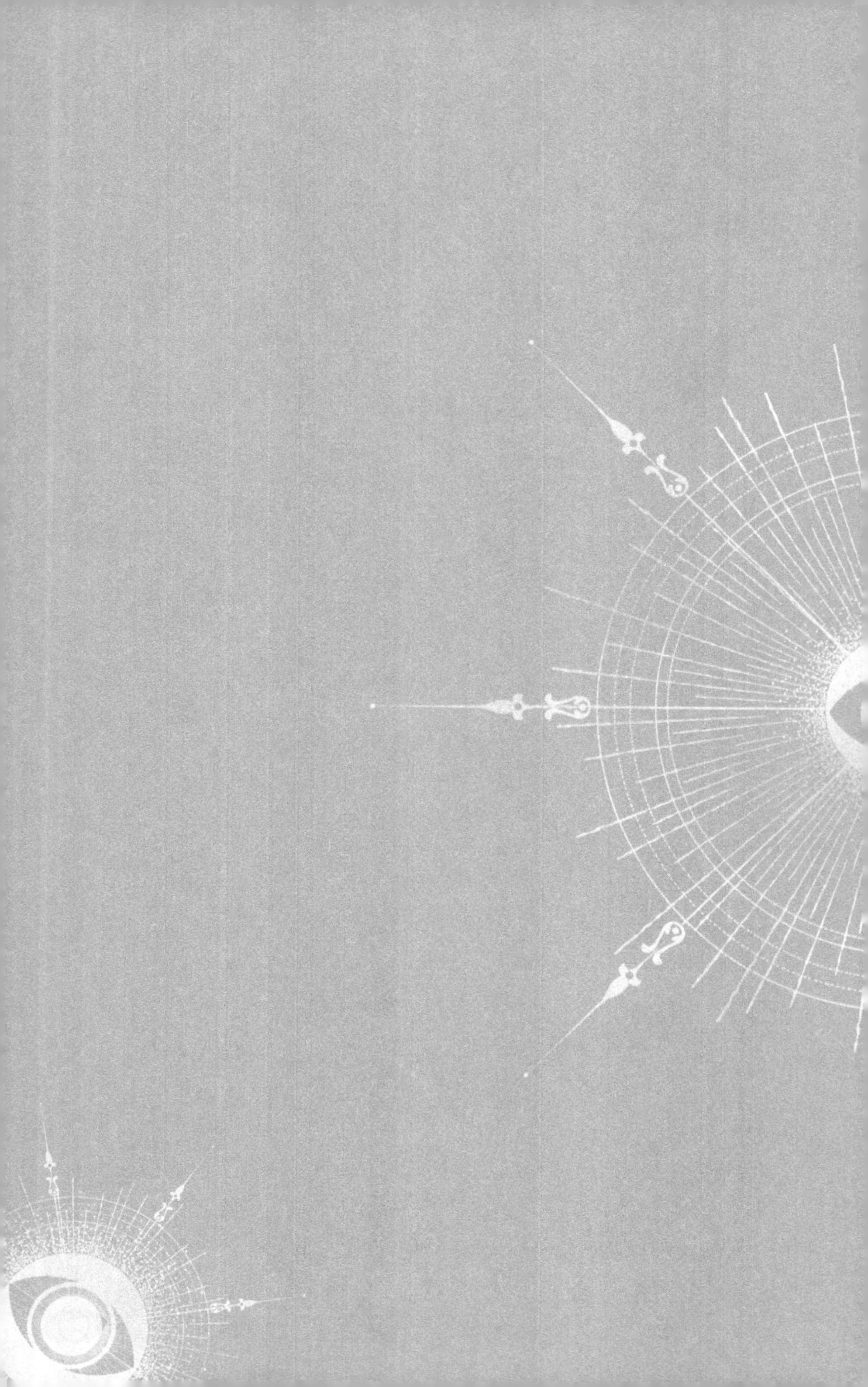

PROLOGUE

Amelia

Outside the safe house, screams escalated, filling the air with terror. The smell of burning—bitter, not the comforting scent of a camp fire—traveled toward them, though their eyes couldn't see the source of the flames.

Farjhem is burning, Amelia realized, pressing her face into Jacob's chest as he focused on pulling them out of the danger. She prayed Holger would find his own escape, and forgive them for not keeping their promise and staying.

"Hold on," Jacob whispered, as his grip tightened and the air around them went from still and pungent to the sensation of being whirled through a vacuum canister. Her skin stretched tight against her bones, as if it might peel from her frame if the gust grew any stronger.

Amelia dared not open her eyes. What remained of her lucidity might float away with the swirling wind.

The gust stopped. The smell of fire faded to the pleasant scent of saffron and other exotic spices.

"Open your eyes. *Blanca.* Look!"

Amelia did as Jacob asked. She backed slowly away from his arms, taking in the sweeping view of *Ophélie* from Brigitte's Garden. The topiary and flora were low to the ground.

"I don't know how, but I got us home," Jacob said in awe as he knelt down, taking a handful of earth in his hand. The dirt sifted through his fingers.

Amelia frowned, glancing toward the Big House, and the missing Belvedere. It was a feature added later, not built with the house. Turning left, she saw the fresh coat of ivory paint on the newly constructed *garçonierre.*

"Not... exactly," she replied, as she added together the visual cues. "Jacob, I think—"

"The birthday festivities are starting!" a young blonde woman in a low-necked, corseted evening dress declared, sashaying toward them. Her skirt rustled over the top of the cage underneath.

Standing before them, the young girl scrunched her browse in perplexed study. "Why, look at you. Are you a guest of my father's?"

Jacob gaped, speechless, his gaze traveling between both women.

"Ah... uh, yes," Amelia asserted, tucking her shaking hand behind her. "We—"

The woman's face lit up. She clasped her hands together. "Oh! You must be from London!" She artlessly fingered the stitching on Amelia's riding coat. "Tell me, is *this* the current fashion for ladies?" Not waiting for a response, her words continued to rush forth in an excited gale. "My brothers brought me the finest corsets from Paris when they went on their Grand Tour. They completely neglected London!"

"A shame," Amelia said with a polite smile, biting her tongue to hide her disorientation... and her decidedly different accent. She hadn't realized how much the dialect had changed over the last century-and-a-half.

"Come, gather inside! You can tell me all about London after the dance, when the men break for cigars and brandy."

"Yes, thank you," Amelia said pleasantly. Then the young girl turned, with a practiced motion, lifting her skirts as she made her way back toward the Big House.

"Don't recognize her?" Amelia asked her husband, still staring down the path toward the house. "I thought you were an expert on the Deschanels."

"It can't be." His jaw went slowly slack.

"Oh, it is. That's Ophélie, and today is apparently her birthday. The place isn't crawling with Union soldiers so I'd guess this is before the war... which puts us around 1859 or 1860, judging from her age."

"Jesus," Jacob whispered, rubbing his face with the edge of his palms.

"Actually, I think it's the goddess you should be appealing to right about now," Amelia mumbled with a half-smile. Her face creased in concentration as her mind struggled to catch up with everything around them.

Jacob was too stunned to tease back. "What do we do?"

"When you closed your eyes and asked for the help getting us here, did you specifically wish to take us home?"

"Not really. What I asked was to get us out of danger." He scratched his head. "I didn't think that far ahead. I should have focused on somewhere specific. Should we try again?"

Amelia looked toward her family's plantation and beyond, toward the river, teeming with commerce. Brimming with life full of hope, before war would tear it apart.

With all her heart, she wished she could go back to her own moments of peace, before her world was torn in two.

But her scars were her own, as Ophelie's would be hers. All Amelia's family owned their hurts, bravely and with a resolve that defined them.

"No. We were sent here for a reason," she said after a considerate pause. *Everything that happened up to this point has been for a reason. From the moment we stepped on to the plane, to the child I refused to have but was given anyway, despite our precautions. Given, and then taken. Even Baldur's vicious attack has significance.*

"What could be the bloody reason for *this*?" Jacob's incredulous eyes scanned the garden and the slave cabins in the distance, still inhabited by those they were built for.

"Hell if I know, Donnelly," Amelia replied, her sigh as confused as her thoughts. "But I suppose we'll find out."

She held her arm out and Jacob took it, with a lazy, slow smile. "The situations we find ourselves in, *Blanca*."

Indeed. Things great and terrible, Amelia thought. *But at least together.*

"*Síoraíocht, Mo mhíle stór*," Jacob whispered, as they made their way toward the future past.

Finnegan
One Week Later

ANASOFIYA'S HEART WAS A SERIES OF DARK TUNNELS, DESPAIR PAINTING the walls in haphazard patterns. Finn would meander those halls for the rest of his days, scrub clean the pain, warming her from the inside out.

As she stood before him, hand laced with her son's, ready for their next adventure, Finn no longer feared the road ahead or the forks in it. The past might haunt her, but he would be her light in the yawning darkness.

"Are we ready?" Finn asked his son and wife, linking his hands in theirs to complete the circle.

"We are," Ana replied.

"Affirmative," Aleksandr chimed in.

Finn smiled thinking about the two halves of his heart, the only true purpose he'd ever known other than navigating the endless sea. Around him, they stood, and would always stand. "I have no guarantee this will work, but this is Aleksei's idea, so it has to be a good one, right?" He winked at his son.

Aleksandr blushed and lowered his gaze. "Amelia and Jacob have been gone for, what, a week or two? They could be anywhere, even if they came here first."

"We'll keep trying until we find them," Anasofiya said with confidence. "However long that may be. A vow is a vow. And Amelia is my cousin."

Forbia barked and circled their feet. For the first time since his reunion with Ana, Finn felt the knot in his heart re-form. "I'm so sorry, girl. Wolves don't really blend in. We'll be back soon, I promise. Jon will watch over you."

At the mention of Jon, Ana flinched but said nothing. Whatever she was thinking—whatever Finn, too, was considering about that matter—would need to wait until their return.

For now, they had a more pressing matter.

Finn's eyes closed.

He couldn't remember meeting Jacob more than briefly, but Amelia's was a face he could never forget, proof of the strength in the Deschanel genetics; it was Ana's face, painted with less pain and framed with a halo of white gold.

All right, Goddess. You brought us here, and these are your guiding words. So show me the way. Wherever Amelia and Jacob are, we need to be there as well.

THE WORLD LAUNCHED INTO A DOZEN SOMERSAULTS.

PERPETUAL MOTION CARRIED ALEKSANDR FORWARD, KNOCKING BOTH his parents over onto their backs. They landed in grass. Overhead, the sky was edged in purple, welcoming the first whispers of dusk.

"Sorry," Aleksandr said with a shy grin and rolling off to the ground. "That happened faster than last time."

Finn sat up to gather his bearings. Anasofiya was a step ahead of him, both in maneuvering off the turf and in her recognition of the surroundings.

"It can't be..."

Aleksandr's eyes brightened, and he sprang to his feet. "No *way*!"

Finn's vision cleared, and he examined his surroundings. The looming Big House came into view. All around them the familiar live oaks stood sentry, though they appeared smaller, or perhaps trimmed.

"*Ophélie*," he mused, pushing himself off the ground. "I'll be damned. We came home."

"Not exactly," Ana replied in wonder, meandering off ahead. "This is *Ophélie*, yes, but look at the height of the levee. You can see the river at ground level. Usually, we can only see it from the third floor. And the oaks, Finn, see how much smaller they are? They've only recently been planted. The grass hasn't even grown around the roots yet."

"Check out the size of those boats!" Aleksandr pointed

toward the Mississippi, where two steamships passed in transit.

"What year is this do you think?" Finn asked, gaping wide-mouthed at the fresh white paint on the plantation home. And that *garçonierre*... still bore the shine of new construction.

"Before the war, maybe," Ana replied, lost in thought. "I guess it depends on who opens the door when we knock, right?"

"You really think that's a good idea?"

"I don't believe we came here to be spectators," she answered.

Aleksandr studied his clothes and grimaced. "We're really not dressed for this. Like, at all."

"We'll say we're cousins from the Low Countries," Ana said. "Or descendants of the Habsburgs. They had their hands in every house of Europe. It would take years to disprove us."

"You're enjoying this when you should be crapping your pants," Finn accused.

"If the alternative to enjoyment is shitting myself, I'll choose a good time any day, thank you," she teased.

God, how he wanted to take her in his arms and crush her in a never-ending hug. To see her smile, her lips tilted at the corners on the verge of a laugh... he could admit it now since she was back and safe. He had half expected to never see either again.

"Earth to Poseidon," Ana said. "We doing this?"

"I love you," Finn said, unable to help himself. "Both of you. So damn much."

Ana regarded him from the short distance, and she was, for a moment, the beautiful mystery girl living next door on the island in Maine with the shy, unsure smile as she ran toward him down the coastline, book clutched to her chest.

And then she was in his arms, Aleksandr right behind her.

All was right. All was okay. The world had stitched the broken seams, and the fabric had its stretch back.

"This is love," she whispered, pressing her lips against his neck.

"This, right here," Finn replied, planting his feet firmly in the soil.

DAY ONE

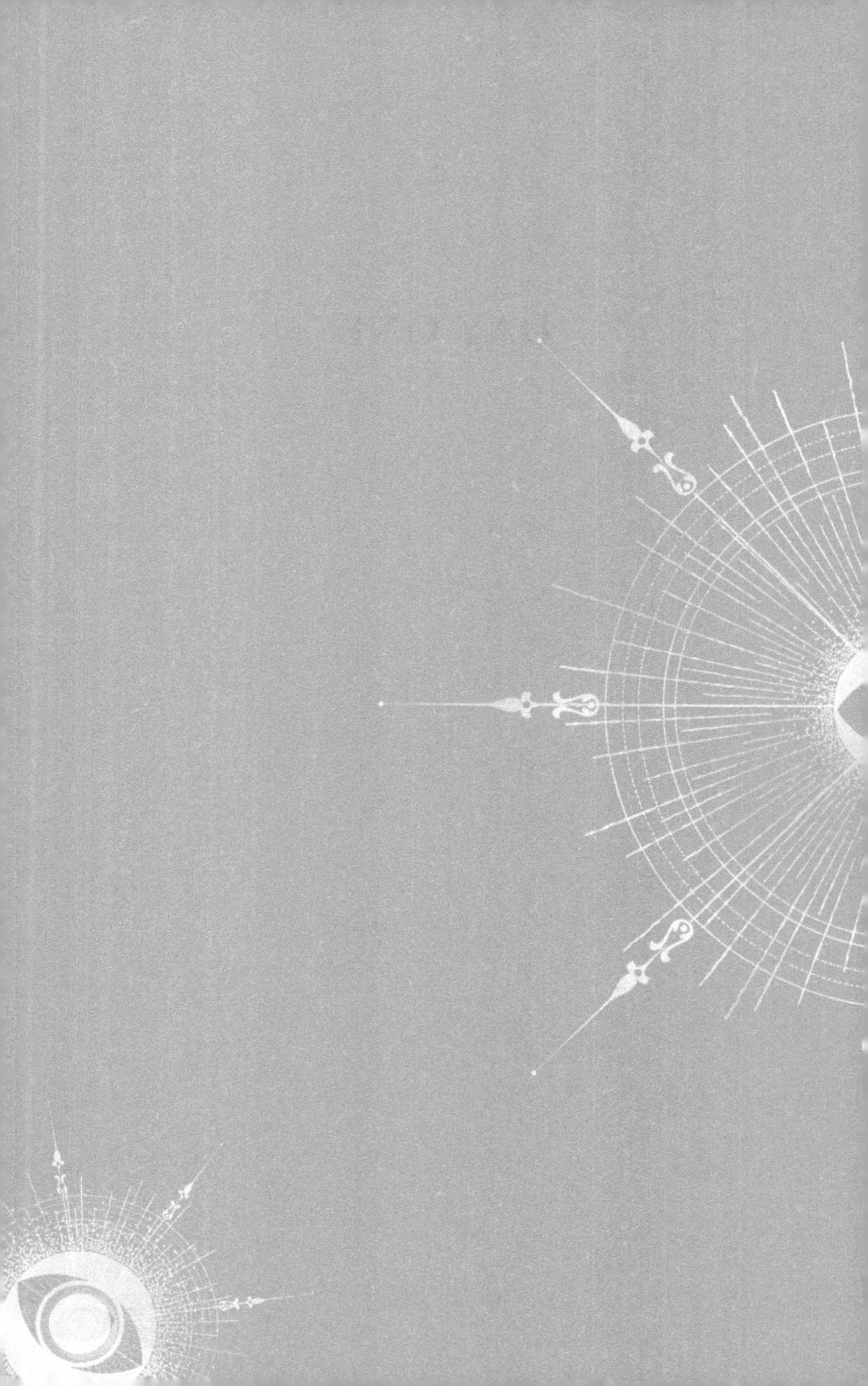

1
JACOB

Amelia and Jacob followed Ophélie Deschanel across the freshly seeded, sprawling grassland of the property bearing her name, in a century not their own, toward a future they could not predict.

Jacob hadn't had the luxury of time to think through the consequences or results of time dancing, any more than he'd had when he joined form with the bear, recognizing the creature's own beastly vigor roar and rip through him as he quite certainly saved his wife's life. Jacob still didn't even know how he'd done it. He didn't quite remember the exact moment he'd been stripped of his own mortal skin and thrust into the warm, vital flesh of the bear, becoming one. Could he replicate it? He didn't know that, either. This gift of warging emerged only in times of great need, which was true of all his gifts, according to Padraig.

He may have saved Amelia, but the world remaining for her offered a fate perhaps worse than death. What happened in Ireland had changed them both, but no one more so than his wife, who had endured horrors neither of them could even speak of.

Then they had made it even riskier by entering Farjhem in turmoil. This trek was more than a gamble in Jacob's estimation, and it left them with few choices and even fewer minutes to make them. Always quick on his feet when his back was up against the wall, he searched for the answer, and it appeared. Once he decided, there was no un-deciding: The couple had to do more than leave the *where.* They had to leave their *when.*

He couldn't say why that, of all solutions, had popped into his head, only that he couldn't bear his broken wife's wide eyes surveying the landscape like a cornered animal.

Are you sure? Amelia had asked, putting all her faith, all her hope, in him, despite her obvious doubt. *How can you be so sure? How do you know this* when *is any better than the last one?*

"I'm not," he mumbled, under his breath at a volume neither his wife nor the historical figure ahead of them could hear. "Not sure of anything anymore."

"You've brought your appetite with you, I hope?" the young woman called over her shoulder as they meandered toward the dusty drive leading to the front door. She lifted her skirt and bustle as she prepared to ascend the stairs. A few men in dusters and frock coats leaned against a nearby column, a cloud of smoke swirling the air around them as they engaged in animated discourse.

Several young black men worked to calm and corral a handful of horses with a carriage attached. Jacob's stomach tightened. He was witnessing slavery in action. Amelia offered him a cheerless smile from his peripheral. They would see more before their time here was at an end, he knew, and it would take tremendous willpower not to act on it. Only the two of them possessed the hindsight of a past never lived through.

"Famished," Amelia answered when Jacob did not.

A cacophony of deep voices followed a strong wind carrying cigar smoke, pouring from inside the Big House of the plantation. He grimaced. *More people. Lots more.* Later, he might find himself in the mental shape to appreciate that they stood on the lower gallery of one of the finest homes in Louisiana, at the height of its prime. For now, much of him existed in suspended animation, a place where he wasn't quite convinced they weren't still stuck outside of Farjhem almost two centuries later.

"The men retired to the parlor early," Ophélie explained with a light cluck of disapproval. "They never can wait!" She paused at the door, lowering her skirts, leveling her gaze at Jacob. "Would you like me to introduce you to Papa, so you may join them?"

Jacob shook his head a little too emphatically. In his peripheral he saw Amelia look away, biting back amusement.

"No, I suppose you brought manners with you across the sea," Ophélie decided, then blushed at her own forwardness.

As if answering an unspoken command, the double doors yawned open, revealing a bustling hall filled with a half-dozen brightly colored hooped skirts swishing across gleaming cypress boards. The high lilt of excited young debutantes competed for volume against the men congregated in the nearby parlor. A young butler offered mint juleps from a silver tray.

Jacob's breath caught. He blinked hard to bring himself into the moment. Surely, he'd stumbled into the ballroom scene at Twelve Oaks. Ashley Wilkes would descend the staircase any moment.

A cluster of ladies ceased their animated chatter, running

their eyes over he and Amelia, not disguising their appraising looks. Where Ophélie had latched on to them being from England to explain their strangeness, these ladies didn't know what to make of the sight before them. The gossip later would be interesting, to say the least.

Jacob caught some of the excited whispers. They seemed especially scandalized by Amelia wearing pants.

"I will see you to your quarters so you can dress for dinner. I expect us to be called shortly and do hope Clara hasn't assigned all the guest rooms yet," Ophélie commented to herself, boldly separating the gathered girls in two with outstretched arms. They parted, and as they did, their judgmental curiosity faded to silent reverence as the beautiful young mistress of the house ascended the staircase.

She paused at the top, whirling. "Why, forgive me, but I'm not sure if you two are..." her gaze fell to the diamond on Amelia's left hand and her eyes expanded to saucers. "Well! You know how to treat a lady in England," she exclaimed in a breathy whisper, her earlier question apparently answered.

Jacob glanced between both women, flushing. Diamond rings were a more recent trend. The women in this period would be wearing plain bands.

If they weren't careful, it would be the small details that did them in. "Aye," he answered. "I'll not have my wife in anything but the best."

Amelia hid an eye roll, but Ophélie blushed, clearly smitten. "I daresay we neglected to bring along some of the finer traditions when we created this great nation," she declared in a fluster, then turned to continue up the stairs. "I've never heard accents quite like yours. Of course, I've never been across the ocean. My brother, Jean, has been on his Grand Tours of Europe, as I said, and my youngest brother will be along on his soon, but it isn't proper for the women."

"Colonists," Jacob muttered with a shrug, falling into character. Amelia elbowed him.

"How rude of me. I haven't asked your names!"

Amelia went rigid, paling. She wasn't in the frame of mind for these rapid fire, on-the-spot answers, so the bulk of creativity fell upon him. He saw no reason to lie. "My name is Lord Jacob Donnelly, and this is my wife, Lady Donnelly."

Amelia released a slight, disapproving sigh. *Now you've done it.*

Okay. Maybe a small lie.

"You're of the peerage, then!" Ophélie declared. Her hands crossed over her décolletage. She appeared positively star struck. "Papa never mentioned we had such distinguished cousins. He'll be so pleased to have you at our table this evening."

"You must be Charles' daughter, Ophélie," Jacob replied in his most charming tone. "We weren't aware we'd be arriving to help you celebrate. How old are you now?"

"Sixteen." She beamed. "Tonight, I'm to meet my betrothed."

"How lovely," Amelia said, her hand still latched tightly to Jacob's. She barely held it together. "Happy Birthday."

They stopped in front of a set of French doors leading to, in the future anyway, Lucienne's bedroom. Jacob didn't know who stayed there anymore. After Lucienne had died, he believed the room had remained empty until Nicolas turned the house into a refuge for Empyreans. "I do hope this will be suitable. I know it's not what you're used to in London, but—"

Jacob's smile stopped her in mid-sentence. "It's perfectly fine."

Ophélie sagged in relief. "Oh, wonderful. I do want you to be comfortable here. Where did you leave your trunks? I'll have Edwin bring them up straight away."

Amelia glanced away, her stiffness fading to slack. Jacob realized she was moments from a breakdown. "I'm afraid that's a long story. They didn't make it with us off the ship." He held his breath; he'd almost said *plane.*

Ophélie appeared genuinely mortified. "You poor dears. My brother, Jean, lost an entire trunk on his Grand Tour and never saw it again." Her hands wrung over her corseted waist. "Not to worry. Ruth can fit you for a new wardrobe later. There are sleeping garments already in the room. Though that doesn't help us for this evening's events, and what you're wearing won't do..."

Jacob reached out and laid his hand on Ophélie's delicate upper arm. She looked mildly scandalized. "If it isn't terribly rude, my wife and I could use some rest after the long journey. She doesn't fare well on the sea."

Ophélie skimmed Amelia's peaked countenance and shook her head. "Poor dear. Since you don't have a gown... why, perhaps it *is* best for you to retire for a short while. After the ball, we'll serve a late evening course. The young women and their chaperones will have departed by then so it will be the local gentry and their wives. Ruth can bring up something suitable for you to wear, and tomorrow we can see about a wardrobe. I won't be permitted to attend into the later hours, but perhaps Papa will allow me to join as a hostess. Shall I retrieve you then?"

Jacob nodded, feeling Amelia sway to his left.

"Very well. There's fresh water from the well on the serving table, and should you need anything, the servant's bell is on the left wall, near the windows."

"Thank you, Mademoiselle Deschanel. And happy birthday."

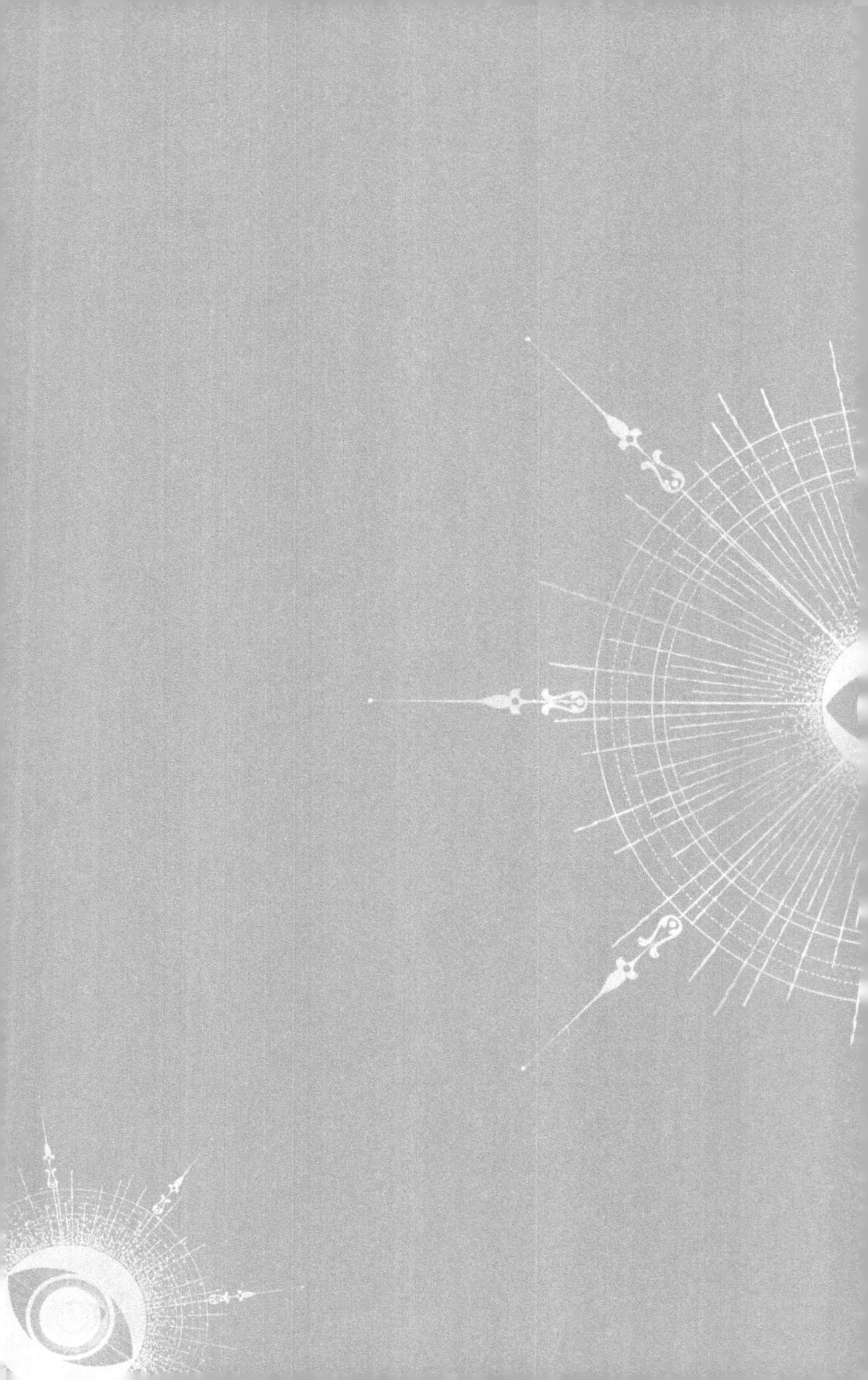

2
AMELIA

Amelia barely made it to the bed. She slumped forward over the quilt, face pressed into the fabric with her arms akimbo. Jacob was behind her at once, lifting his wife to situate her in the center of the mattress.

Jacob tripped over himself in a rush to get her water. He hoped whatever is in the pitcher was sanitized, because it was all they had. "I'm all right," she said, winded. A weight she couldn't see pressed tight into her forehead and constricted her chest. The sensation wasn't unlike when she'd been imperiled as an empath, except this time she was overwhelmed with no emotions other than her own.

"Clearly not, *Blanca,*" he replied. He placed one hand behind her head and tilted the glass toward her lips.

"I said I was fine," she asserted. Water dribbled out the left side of her mouth. She snapped her head away. "Stop. Please."

Jacob backed away but held tight to the glass in stubborn compromise. "You almost fainted on the carpet out there."

"You mean the plush scarlet carpet that's brand new and shouldn't be?"

Jacob shifted. He set the glass on the nightstand. "We should talk about this."

"Of course, *Lord Donnelly*," she said with a snicker, breaking her gaze away. Amelia didn't know why she was doing this, pushing him away; picking a fight. Fear and anger wrestled for placement within her, but all she could do was train it on the person who deserved it least.

She was sick with her own behavior, and they hadn't been here more than a quarter hour.

"Was the best I could come up with at the moment," he defended. "Are you mad I didn't think to make you a duchess? Because that would be more easily verifiable, should it come to that. They don't have Wikipedia, but Charles probably shares correspondence with King Edward's court from time to time."

Amelia grunted in response, a dismissive sound. She caught the small smile playing at the corner of his mouth and realized he'd been doing what he always did in tense situations, trying to lighten the mood.

"I'm sorry," Amelia said after a long and tense pause. "I know I wasn't much help out there."

"I don't know that anything I said was especially helpful, either."

She cast her eyes around the room. As a girl, she'd babysat Lucienne and Adrienne in those summers when they were still young, still playing with dolls. Lucienne's room had been an explosion of pink taffeta and ruffles, nothing at all like what she saw now, but she recognized the furniture. In the present, it was spread throughout the house. "This room has a very Parisian feel. Rococo and Louis XVI, if I know my styles."

Jacob smirked. "And do you?"

"Only what I've heard my mother tell tourists," she conceded. "Years ago, *Ophélie* was open to the public for limited tours, and my Aunt Cordelia showed no interest so

Mom would come out and run them, from time to time. I loved going with her." She pointed. "That painting there, above the mantle, is in a museum now, in our time. There's a fantastic story behind it."

Jacob followed where she pointed. A young, deeply rouged Frenchwoman with a low-necked carnelian-colored gown posed with an Oriental fan. Her blonde wig piled high on her head was ornamented with powder. The subject's wry grin spelled of intrigue and trouble. "I've definitely never seen that before."

"Marianne de Deschanel," she explained. Talking about things, knowing about them, brought her back to a sense of calm. Grounded her. "Charles' grandmother. She was a very young courtesan of Louis XVI, a favorite who was with them at the start of the French Revolution. Family rumor has it she helped sneak footmen into his room. He fancied the boys." She laughed. "Who knows if that's true. But she was definitely with them during the Flight of Varennes, when Louis and Marie Antoinette escaped from Paris. That's a matter of record. The story goes that she escaped any serious punishment because she was recalled in order to be married. But journals recounting her time at court were downright scandalous. Better than fiction."

"Why the hell is this in a museum and not still in the house?"

"My mother might tell you Uncle Charles donated it to the preservation society," Amelia replied with a slow grin. "Aunt Maureen would say that he lost it in a poker game with the French Ambassador."

"I need to start drinking with your Aunt Maureen."

Amelia slid over, opening a spot on the bed. Jacob crawled up, tentative, but his eagerness to be near her was written in his gaze.

He grimaced and shifted back and forth, settling in. “This is the most uncomfortable bed I’ve ever lain on.”

Amelia gestured up to the carved headboard, where an oak bar resembling a rolling pin was situated, below the tester. “That’s because the mattress is stuffed with Spanish moss and feathers. That pin there is rolled over the bed in the evening to smooth out the rough spots. They put it back in after and voila, you have a useful decoration.”

“Did you just make that up? If so, I disagree that you can’t contribute to our growing delinquency of lies.”

“Between playing tour assistant to my mother, and growing up here with my cousins, there’s not much I *don’t* know. And you’ll find these all up and down the River Road stretch, not just here. We still have the same beds in *Ophélie* today with more civilized mattresses.”

“I can’t believe we’re having a serious discussion about mattresses. We woke up in 2006 and now we’re in 1860.” Jacob released a thin whistling sound. It was barely audible over the din from the festivities downstairs, which felt like a taunt; a promise of a future they would inevitably be required to address. “Or 1861. I don’t know.”

“And it’s cold outside,” Amelia added. “That worries me.”

“Because we forgot to pack our frock coats?”

“Because Ophélie is sixteen. War was declared in January of 1861. For it to be this chilly, it would have to be December or January, right? We get maybe two cold months out of the whole year. So we’re either a year away from war or a month.”

Jacob gazed up at the satin folds of the half-tester. “We won’t be here long enough to worry about it.”

“Why do you say that?”

He laughed. “Come on. We can’t possibly stay here.”

Amelia propped herself on an elbow and turned to face him. “Jacob, we’re here for a reason.”

"Because I suck at time traveling."

"No," she went on. "Holger told you your abilities would surface when you most needed them. Padraig said that too, right? We could have landed in a battlefield in the Middle Ages, but instead, we're *here.*"

"I'm sorry, *Blanca,* but you're looking for signs where there are none," Jacob said carefully. He reached for her hand but paused, withdrawing. She picked the reason off the perimeter of his thoughts. Holding her close out in the world was as simple as an afterthought. In here, alone, it implied intimacy, and he feared anything that might place pressure on her.

Well, she feared it, too.

"We only know what we know, and what we *know* is your ability serves you more as a need than a want. The two of us needed to be here, we just don't know the reason yet."

"How long do you suggest we wait to figure that out?"

Amelia didn't have an answer.

Jacob gestured toward the door. "That nice young girl out there, your *ancestor*, is going to come get us in a couple hours. When she does, we're going to have to socialize with people who might be less quick to accept a vague story than she was."

"We need a story," she agreed, scrunching her face to push back a yawn. "And since we are apparently landed gentry, the pressure is *on*."

"I sense two eyes dying to roll," he said, working to discern what it meant that she was dithering between annoyance and passive disregard. She saw all of this like words on a page, his mind still wide open.

"Just tired is all. When we left Norway, it was night. And another century. My circadian rhythm is terribly confused," she replied, pressing her cheek deeper into the pillow. "Maybe in shock, too. Can we lock ourselves in this room until we're ready? Just close the world out? I don't know how to make sense of what we've gotten ourselves into. I don't think I'm ready to, either."

"Ready or not, we're here." Jacob intentionally softened his tone upon the realization he was annoyed at the growing disconnect between the two of them, and that he could find no easy blame or simple fix. Amelia loved Jacob for caring so much. She hated herself for not having the emotional energy to make it better for him. "And if you're right, and we need to stay and figure it out, we can't go down to dinner with stupid expressions and pretend we don't speak the language."

"Que?" Amelia flashed a drowsy smile. Her pale blue eyes fluttered, half-closed. *Jacob's heart melted. The small moments mattered more than they had before, somehow. He wished he could return to a time where he didn't need to count them.*

Amelia winced. She needed to get out of his head. Open to her or not, she didn't belong there. It hurt to be there.

He had never been so open to her, without even reciprocation. Maybe he *wanted* her to read his thoughts, in place of the words he couldn't find.

"Charles is going to want to know why we're here," Jacob said, pushing on and running his fingers down the outside length of her arm, "without any advance warning or invite. I don't know a whole lot about his temperament. Do you?"

"I know he let a bunch of Union soldiers rape his daughter to protect his own ass, then he killed her to cover it up," Amelia said with a sharp frown. "So I wouldn't expect much compassion."

Jacob blew out a breath. "Wow, okay. Yeah. There's that." His hand stopped. "Maybe Brigitte is our ally, then. Our way in. A woman's touch, and all that."

"I haven't heard many good things about her either," Amelia said amidst another consuming yawn. "Sorry."

"It's not your fault you aren't the expert on people you've never met."

"No. For being so tired and so unhelpful."

Jacob brushed his lips against her forehead. "You're right. You are probably in shock. I might be too. If we get asked tonight, we'll just say... I don't know... that we're interested in land along the river. And hopefully, we won't be here long enough to have to come up with anything better than that."

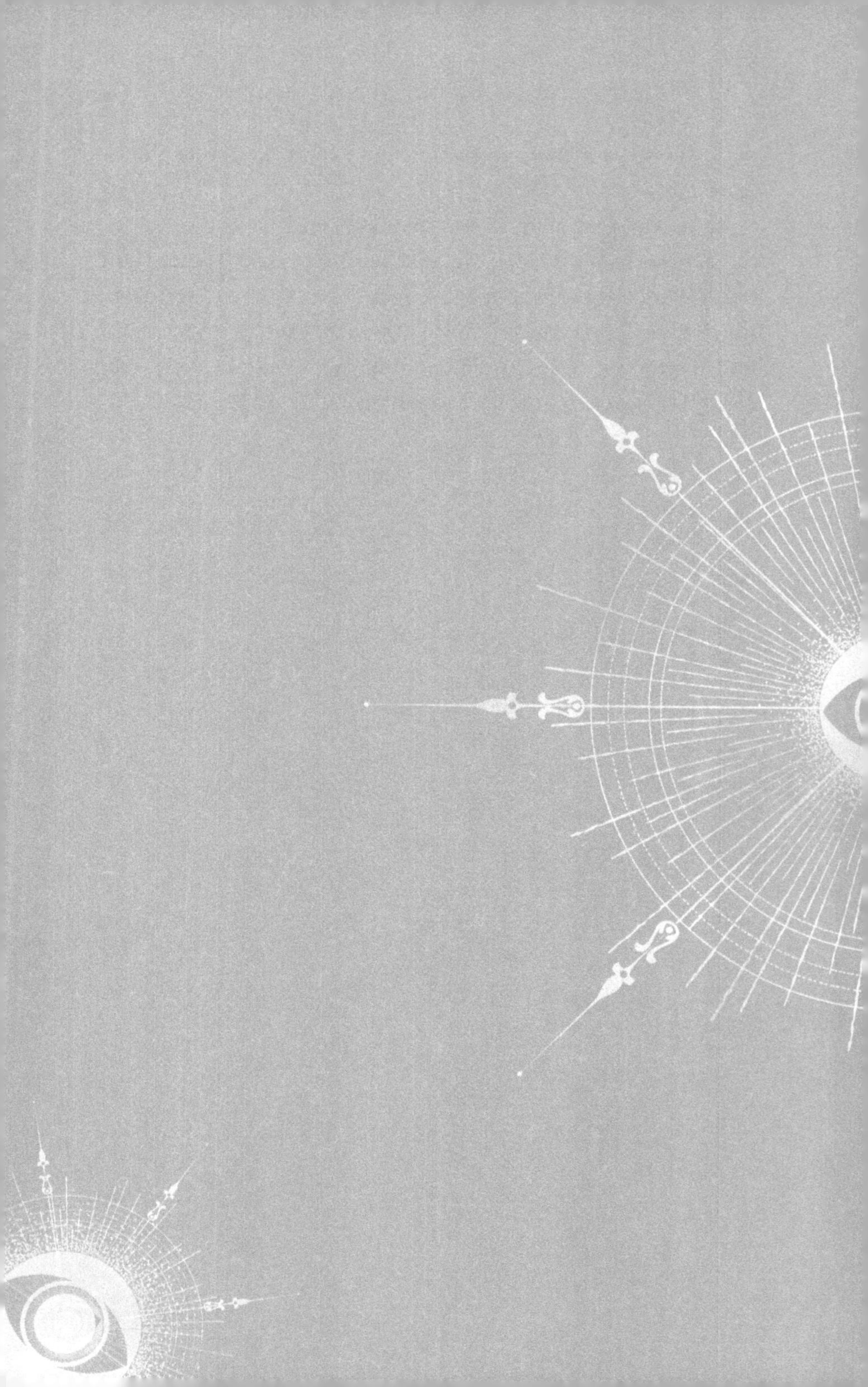

3
JACOB

Jacob didn't even doze. Instead, he watched his wife sleep, wondering if he'd inadvertently led them into worse danger than they'd escaped.

What was wrong with him, bringing her here? They weren't ready for this. *She* wasn't ready for *anything* after what she'd experienced.

Well, he hadn't been thinking. That was the long and short of it, and everything in between. He'd seen the risk, formed an idea, and ran with it.

And Amelia had been playing around in his head since they'd arrived at *Ophélie,* something he could have stopped but chose not to. Jacob welcomed it, letting his guard all the way down. He would do anything to bring her comfort, and if seeing his care for her, in the space of his private thoughts, helped in any way, she could spend the next eternity there as far as he was concerned.

But here? *Here* would be short-term. He'd managed to bring them without much trouble, so hopefully getting them home would be as easy.

. . .

OPHÉLIE APPEARED RIGHT ON SCHEDULE, MOMENTS AFTER CLARA departed from her torture session of stuffing Amelia into a dress and corset. She'd weathered it as well as any twenty-first-century woman used to the comfort of t-shirts and jeans might... grimacing and groaning all the way through. To her credit, she tried to smile pleasantly through the assault.

Jacob had never been so happy to be a man.

"Why, Lady Donnelly! What a delight you are!" Ophélie exclaimed, hands clutched to her mouth, wearing an expression that seemed as sincere as her ecstatic words. "The crimson is shocking with your white as snow hair. Not that we get much snow here."

Amelia smiled politely. Jacob wondered if their hostess could see his wife fighting for breath, courtesy of her new twenty-eight-inch waist.

Ophélie had also undergone a wardrobe change of her own, now in a lower cut emerald number that Jacob assumed was better suited for evening socializing.

"Is this your first time in the Americas?" she asked as she led them down the long upper hallway. Jacob nearly tripped as he eyed the portraits lining the walls, some familiar, others not. Charles, Brigitte, their children... those all still hung in the present-day plantation. But the others, oil likenesses of men and women in frilled blouses, rouged lips, and high, powdered hair, were clearly from France. Sometime between the nineteenth and twenty-first centuries, they'd been removed.

"Yes," Jacob said, scanning the pictures to memory.

"No," Amelia said in tandem.

They exchanged looks. *We need to get our damn stories straight, Donnelly,* Amelia shot him, opening a telepathic connection.

Well, we spent our alone time talking about mattresses and courtesans.

Your sarcasm is, for once, not welcome.

"Lady Donnelly is thinking of the time we visited Saint-Domingue," Jacob quickly explained, lowering a quick, satisfied grin at Amelia.

You realize we would have no reason to be in Haiti in the 1860s, right? The feudal system there was destroyed three-quarters of a century ago, and we are very much persona non gratis.

I realize that now, thanks.

"Oh?" Ophélie asked as they descended the staircase. The carved banister shone with fresh wax, catching the flickering light from oil lamps decorating the walls and tables. "We have relatives here tonight whose grandfather managed a plantation in *Cap Français,* but they were driven out when the slaves rose up. Maybe you've heard of them? The de Blancheforts? They own property all up and down this stretch of the river and are married into all the most prestigious families. The Romans, the Destrehans..."

Ophélie continued on her recitation of names and connections, but Jacob's focus was on his wife. Her cheeks had lost all color. He didn't know if it was the lack of oxygen, the stress, or a twisted combination of both.

"I'll find some water," he whispered out of the side of his mouth as they reached the bottom step. Ladies and gentlemen gathered around in small masses, the gaiety of the early afternoon having faded to more serious discussion. The women wore darker, richer fabrics. Even the overhead lighting had dimmed.

Amelia shook her head. "I just need to sit down. Maybe we can find a nice corner that also somehow makes us invisible until the evening can be over."

"You're looking for a wormhole. I'll keep my eyes peeled."

Her lips twisted. She gripped her waist in a desperate grab for comfort. "Water sounds good after all."

Ophélie knowingly sat them in the corner of the double parlor on a burgundy velvet Queen Anne sofa Jacob recognized. The room was near to overflowing with guests of all ages. Jacob had never seen both parlors opened in this combined way, and was shocked at the sheer size of what resembled a grand ballroom. Men in frocked waistcoats and women in low-necked gowns gathered from group to group, the lighter joyfulness of the afternoon replaced by a tone decidedly more mature.

"I don't suppose you know anyone here?" their hostess asked, lifting a blue Spode saucer of chicory coffee with dainty deliberateness. Her tiny sip was soundless.

Amelia nursed the water Clara had fetched her from the well, her gaze fixed on a French Renaissance-era Henry II buffet in the corner. It seemed familiar to Jacob, as well, though he remembered it from his own past in the orphanage, which had been filled with countless donated antiques.

How many other heirlooms would they recognize? "I can't say we do," Jacob replied for them both.

Ophélie's entire face lit up with purpose. "Why, I'll catch you right up, my lord." Her teacup was relegated to the rosewood candle stand to her right. Her posture straightened.

She gestured toward an older fellow with white tufts at his temples and a distinctive Roman nose. He held his sherry glass in an intentional manner, away from his body, suggesting he required continuous refills. "That right there is Duncan Kenner. He's the owner of Ashland, which Papa says was the old Linwood Plantation, but that was before our time here. He's a statesman in the legislature. His wife, Nanine, is the daughter of the master of L'Hermitage, Michel

Doradou Bringier. They say Kenner named his plantation after fellow horseman, Henry Clay. He has a fine racetrack, which I walked with Mama and some of the other ladies when we went there for the New Year's celebrations two years past. A walk like no other! My feet ached for days, and my shoes had to be re-soled. They say James Gallier Sr. designed the house, but Charles Dakin claims *he* did. Or so they say. Dakin has been gone nearly a decade, so no way to ask..."

Jacob was fascinated to hear Ophélie recite names he'd grown up reading in local history books. *You hear that,* Blanca? *We're looking at the dude they named the city of Kenner for.*

Amelia didn't respond, but she was listening.

Ophélie nodded next to the gentleman with hawk-like features in deep conversation with Kenner. "Msr. Rost married into the Destrehan family, and he's now the owner of their lands down in St. Charles Parish. The Destrehans are royalty in these parts, as much as the Aimes or the Romans or de Blancheforts. He's said to be a dinner guest of President Buchanan, which Papa thinks could be a benefit for us should we secede from the Union. That younger man to his left is Emile, his son." She frowned at the last mention, scrunching her nose briefly before moving on. "Papa began marriage negotiations for he and I a year ago, but they failed."

Jacob could see nothing wrong with Emile Rost, but Ophélie's tone made it clear she had no time for him.

"That, of course, is Judge Randolph, and the man he's talking to is John Andrews. They have quite the rivalry! Would you believe they built the largest homes along the river, side-by-side? Randolph is the master of Nottoway, and Andrews has Belle Grove. Papa says Nottoway blinds you when you travel upriver, the paint is so fresh. Those young men gathered by the hearth are their sons. Heaven knows why they come all the way out here to gossip together when they could do so in their own backyard."

Jacob had heard the story of the dueling plantations, but now only Nottoway remained in the present day. Belle Grove had been lost to a tragic fire. All that remained of the lost beauty were grainy black and white photos.

Ophélie straightened her spine and blushed. "And that," she said, pointing to a regal fellow sitting at the head of the table, a spot Jacob assumed should have been reserved for Charles. "If you can believe it, is Valcour Aime himself. Surely, you've heard of *him*, at least? They call him the Louis XVI of Louisiana." She implored Jacob for a sign of recognition, but he shook his head. He, of course, knew *of* the man, but he couldn't exactly confess how so it was safer to play dumb. "No? Why, you can hardly travel the River Road without stepping foot on one of his properties or meeting one of his brood. He married a Roman girl, Josephine. The Romans who own Oak Alley?"

Jacob knew who the Romans were, too, from his studies of Louisiana history as a child, but he wanted to hear what she would say next. The opportunity to see the past through her eyes was too much to pass up.

Ophélie eyed Jacob as if he might truly be hopeless. "Yes, well, Aime's wife is a Roman, and their four daughters are mistresses of their own plantations. His sugar plantation, St. James Refinery, down the parish is the sight to see. They call it *Le Petit Versailles* because he hired designers from King Louis' court to design the gardens. Aime might own half the river if you add it all up. The plantations closest to us, St. Joseph and Felicity, were gifts to his daughters, so we're surrounded by Aimes. Aimes, Destrehans, de Blancheforts, Romans. You could make a song about it!"

Amelia smiled politely when Ophélie leveled a concerned gaze on her. "I'm fine. Go on."

Ophélie paused in one more moment of measure and went on, eager to continue her education of the foreigners. "Aime knows more about sugar than the entirety of the West Indies. His girls, Edwige and Felicite, both married one of their Fortier cousins. Josephine married one of the Ferrys and Felice, of course, married back into the Romans. First cousins and all. Quite the scandal. But did you know, most of all, that Msr. Aime's being here is a miracle? The poor man lost his only son several years past, then his wife, and even one of his daughters. He very openly declared himself free of public life, so for Papa to have convinced him to come..."

Jacob realized their hostess was seeking confirmation of this blessed miracle so he opened his mouth in a wide O. "Your father must be something else," he said, knowing more about Charles Deschanel than his daughter could imagine.

Ophélie colored in a way that suggested she was responsible for the compliment. She rattled off a number of other names. The Bonaparties, whose daughter, Julianne, would later marry Ophélie's brother, Jean. Some Fortiers. More Romans. Other names Jacob had never heard before.

Jacob only paused to catch up when she indicated Victor and Elisabeth de Blanchefort, a couple no more than a few years older than Jacob and Amelia. Victor's raven hair held a shocking, preternatural shine that seemed impossible to achieve. Skin unblemished, too perfect. While he gave every indication of being enraptured by whatever means John Randolph used to regale him, his emerald eyes sparkled, fixed on Amelia with an intensity that stopped Jacob's heart.

He had an inexplicable urge to find the nearest wildlife and take the man down.

"Those are their young sons, Nathaniel and Lestan. Papa has secured my betrothal to Lestan, though the de Blancheforts are cousins, but not for some generations past so there won't be a scandal. Their lands sit in St. Charles Parish, near the Destrehans..."

She rambled on, oblivious, but Jacob saw or heard nothing but Victor de Blanchefort's silent but unmistaken claiming of his wife.

What is it? Amelia sensed the shift in him.

You've got a stalker.

Where?

Eleven o'clock. The black-haired dude cornered by Randolph. The devil hasn't stopped gawking at you for the past five minutes. Maybe longer, for all I know. I've got his number now.

I wasn't quite listening. That's de Blanchefort, right?

You're not listening now. I'm going to kick the dude's ass.

He's rather handsome...

You're making jokes about this, but I'm not playing. I don't think there's any bear around here, but I'm not above hijacking a nutria to take care of this problem.

And have to deal with those ugly orange fangs?

Temporary pain. I'm a problem solver.

Or being silly. De Blanchefort brought his wife and kids. This isn't exactly a meat market.

No. It's where you're supposed to reassure me you're not going to run off with him and leave me with all these eccentric millionaires.

He looks a little bit like you... his hair might be nicer, though. Who the hell is his stylist? And those eyes...

Feeling somewhat insecure over here.

I think we have bigger problems right now than an enigmatic, handsome, dreamy—

Glad to see you're feeling better.

Sarcasm intended?

Ophélie continued her recantations of the remaining guests, and when she finished, she began with those not present at the party, reciting the name and lineage of every River Road family from New Orleans to Natchez.

Long after Jacob and Amelia's eyes had glazed over, an imposing figure cast a long shadow over their small corner party. The gentleman looked down on them across his Grecian nose, the signature pale blue eyes of many Deschanels taking their measure.

Jacob needed no introduction. No less than five paintings of his image hung in present-day *Ophélie*.

Charles Deschanel extended both hands, clasping them over Jacob's right. "My daughter informed me we have members of the English peerage under our roof this eve. A fine surprise! You are most welcome here, Lord Donnelly. Lady Donnelly."

Amelia rose and affected a curtsey that wasn't fooling anyone. Jacob was never more grateful they had the excuse of being foreigners on their side.

"We appreciate the hospitality, Monsieur Deschanel. And the clothing. Our trunks were unfortunately lost at sea," Jacob answered.

"A shame this continues to happen," Charles said with a sympathetic cluck. He set his generous jaw into a tight scowl. "My son, Jean, lost one on his return from his Grand Tour. My daughter, I see, has assumed the role of hostess on my behalf. I apologize for not offering a finer greeting, my lord. Your notice of arrival must have been lost in the same manner as your trunk."

Jacob tensed. The words were delivered lighthearted enough, but he couldn't forget they were skating on thin ice. "We truly are sorry for any inconvenience. We can find other accommodations—"

"Nonsense," Charles boomed. Others in the room stopped their chatter and turned to look. "We're honored to receive you. And tomorrow, when the remnants of the party have scattered to their own homes, I can afford you a proper welcome."

"I'd like that," Jacob said. "We're here about land." Land... the word popped into his head in the same obtuse way time dancing had seemed a great idea.

"Land?" Charles asked, nodding in approval. "It's not only the French and Spanish anymore who see the value in the riverlands, then. Are you seeking to emigrate to the States, or is your interest investment minded?"

"Time will tell," Jacob answered, proud of the reaction he garnered from their host at this enigmatic response. Amelia flashed him a look he couldn't read, but the mystery was quickly solved. *Not bad, Donnelly.*

"I enjoy a man who leaves his options open!" Charles declared, accepting a refill on his wine. He tipped his glass toward Amelia. "Lady Donnelly, you are a delight. A glass of cool rosewater on a sweltering summer afternoon. How fortunate your husband is to have you on his arm. I'm reminded of the porcelain beauties of the French court, in your blessed presence."

Amelia smiled but said nothing.

Charles' gaze hung on her another uncomfortable moment, then he seemed to remember himself. Clearing his throat, he shifted to, "Have you met Madame Deschanel?"

On cue, a tiny, dark-featured woman appeared at his side. Madame Deschanel's hair was braided at the nape of her neck in a complicated plait. Her knowing, black eyes made Jacob more nervous than anything Charles had or had not said.

To his side, Amelia's entire body tensed. When he clasped her hand to his, it trembled.

What is it?

It... it's her, Jacob. My empathic senses have been muted since we arrived, but my God... she's... something's wrong. Very, very wrong.

I agree, about her. Are you okay?

Maybe for now, but I can't be around her. We need to figure out a way out. God, it's strong. She's just sent my empathic feelers into hyper drive.

Breathe, honey. I'll get us out.

"Ophélie, it's well past your retirement," Brigitte chided. Amelia had turned her head to the left, hiding breathing exercises. A sinking, hollow feeling filled Jacob's belly.

Ophélie flushed. "I was acting as hostess for our guests from across the sea."

"We really should—" Jacob started, but he and Amelia were seemingly forgotten in the tension.

"Nonetheless. When you're married, you may stay up with the other ladies as you please. For now, it is not proper, and I will not have tongues wagging that Madame Deschanel lets her daughter run as wild as the bayou beasts."

"Maman!"

"I'll see her upstairs," Charles said, flashing Ophélie a wink out of Brigitte's purview.

"No. Jean shall see her upstairs."

Charles frowned. "Jean, then. She's been a tremendous aid to me tonight while I entertained the throngs."

"Nonetheless," Brigitte repeated, glowering.

"Thank you for keeping us company this evening," Amelia said in a tone heavy with charm, bringing Ophélie's hand to her mouth for a brief kiss. She dropped into another curtsey, but Jacob sensed these actions were her way of maintaining control in the midst of her burgeoning fear. She carefully avoided looking at Brigitte. "You were a most gracious hostess, Mademoiselle Deschanel."

Ophélie blushed even darker, hiding a smile. "The honor was all mine, my lady."

Charles signaled his son, Jean, who rushed over. A fit, sturdy young man with a strong genetic resemblance appeared. Jacob startled at how familiar he was. Many of the male Deschanels in present day resembled him, including Amelia's brother, Ashley, and her cousin, Markus. Pale hair and eyes, high, drawn cheekbones. "See your sister to her room."

"Yes, Father," Jean said, holding his arm for Ophélie. She slipped her hand through the crook of his elbow, but her entire bearing had altered in her brother's presence. Ophélie slumped lower, and the radiant light of her face blinked out.

"Enjoy the rest of your evening," she murmured as her brother led her up the staircase.

Brigitte brightened, her knowing smile following the two children as they ascended.

Did you see that? Amelia asked.

I sure did. Now, let's go.

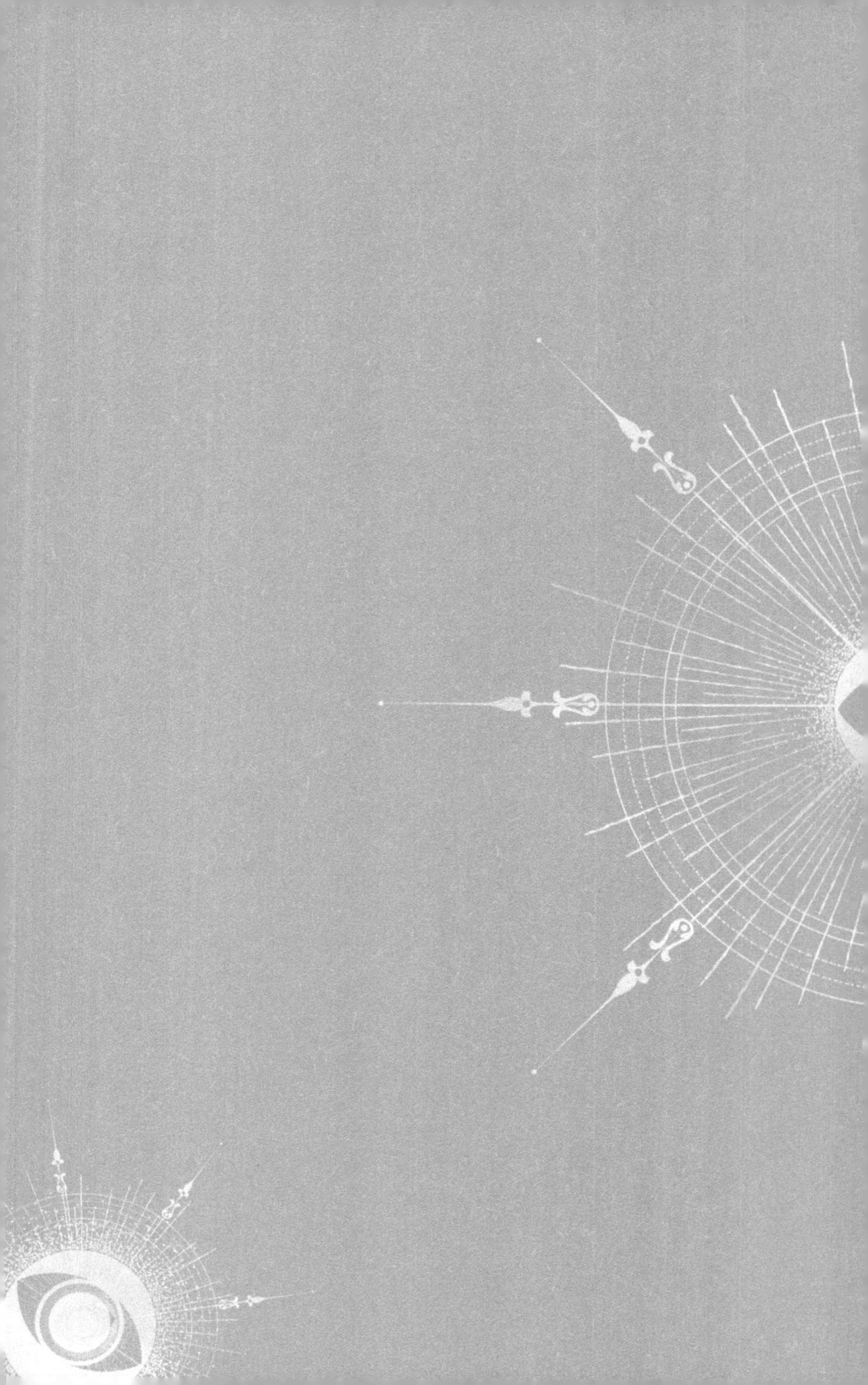

4
AMELIA

Amelia choked out several desperate breaths as Jacob released the stays of her corset. The color slowly returned to her cheeks.

"There has to be an alternative to that." Amelia sneered, pointing at the boned monstrosity lying in a heap in the corner. "Maybe that's why I was sent here. To invent one."

Jacob chuckled. "It's called *not giving a shit,* but you're right, that hasn't been invented yet. You're stuck."

"Just wait until they put you on a horse, Donnelly."

Joking seemed natural. It felt like *them.* At the same time, every word shared was a delicate dance, a careful choosing of each single syllable. Who would step over the line first? What were the consequences?

Jacob would be hurt to know she'd rather be wrapped up like a sausage, struggling to breathe, around strangers from another century, than alone with him.

It hurt her, too.

Jacob's brows stitched together, and for one horrifying

moment, Amelia feared she'd left her mind open to him. Then he said, "Where on earth are those pajamas they left for us?

Amelia exhaled slowly and pointed toward the rosewood armoire with the carved, angular frame. *Also, Louis XVI*, she thought, wondering at how easily the details were coming back. "Top drawer."

"Ahh. The ever-elusive dresser," he mumbled and yanked the nightclothes from the drawer.

She watched him. How he paused at the armoire as if considering the contents, when in fact, she knew he was thinking of her. Unlike earlier in the evening, his mind was not wide open. If Amelia wanted to add betrayal to her list of sins, she could sneak into his mind, undetected, and withdraw the exact contents. But she'd never done that before, not unless he'd left it open for her, and she wouldn't now. Amelia would always tell him. Not telling him would be akin to the offenses Baldur had committed on her.

"Interesting night," he offered as he slid out of his clothes, a much easier task than it had been for her. He tossed her a high-necked white lace gown.

"It's curious how almost no one talked to us. Don't you think?" Amelia returned, as Jacob quickly changed into his sleeping garments. He regarded her with curiosity when she only turned hers over in her hands. A look of tragic understanding passed over him, and he turned his back.

Her heart skipped, leaping into her throat. Had it really come to this? Was she so damaged she couldn't even disrobe before the person she trusted most in the world?

The answer wasn't welcome, but the result was the same. Quickly wriggling out of the remainder of her dressing clothes, she slipped into the gown.

"Yeah," Jacob said, pretending to look out the window into the darkness. He placed both hands against the glass, straining his gaze. "I guess I don't know much about what's customary, though. Maybe they were waiting for Charles to introduce us."

Amelia couldn't bring herself to say the words in her mind. *You can turn around now.* Further proof and implication of how she had changed. Instead, she signaled the same by crossing the room toward the pitcher of water. He caught her in his peripheral and turned.

"One day, that will be in a museum," he said, bemused, as she stood facing him. "With your great-great-great-whatever Grandmother, Marianne."

"Not if I burn it first." She was no longer thirsty, but since she'd made a show of coming for water, she poured a glass. "Maybe you're right about them waiting for Charles, so why didn't he?"

"I got the distinct impression Brigitte is the one wearing the pants here." Jacob watched Amelia for a reaction. "How are you feeling now? I was worried downstairs."

"Better that I'm not in her presence anymore," Amelia answered, swallowing the warm water, which was surprisingly okay. She remembered hearing that while some of *Ophélie's* water in the nineteenth century came from two working wells on the property, they "imported" the rest from Sabine's freshwater to impress their guests. "That's only happened to me a few times in my life, and each time it was for good reason. Something is *not* right with that woman. If I could tap fully into my empathic touch, I might have a better answer, but Aidrik's ward is intact, it seems."

"I forgot about that. Doesn't that mean Charles and his family are benign, then? The way Nicolas and his family were all those years?"

She shrugged. "I would say yes, but whatever abilities they were born with were more than likely completely fine in France, so I doubt the ward completely squashes them. It's probably more as it is for me, you know, where my ability still works, and it's just muted. That's often how I felt growing up, too, at Ophélie. As if I wasn't completely myself, but I never entirely lost it."

"Great. Now we get to find out what crazy shit *they* can do."

"Which could matter for us. I got the distinct sense Brigitte was sizing us up, preparing to place us in her crosshairs. I didn't like how she talked to Ophélie, either."

"You remember what your cousin Katja said. About how the Deschanels had inbred for years to avoid dilution of all your crazy abilities? And Brigitte being dead set on continuing this here in Louisiana."

Amelia nodded. "She also believed Brigitte cursed the family for Ophélie's death because it meant she failed. I don't know if *I* believe that, but it only matters what Brigitte thinks. Our views drive us."

"I believe it," Jacob said, firmly, not waiting for her response, or more likely, rebuttal. "And when she got weird about who escorted Ophélie to bed, I was never more convinced. Some *Flowers in the Attic* bullshit. She's clearly terrified of her brother."

Amelia's brow shot up. "The mother didn't push her children to fornicate in *Flowers.* She locked them in a damn attic, and they had to create their own sense of normalcy."

"Yet fornicate they did, Doctor." Jacob was unruffled by Amelia's light reprisal. "As I'm sure Ophélie and Jean have been doing."

"That's not fornication, that's *rape.*"

The color drained from his face as he realized his error. "I wasn't trying to make light of it, *Blanca.* I'm sorry."

"I know." She exhaled what felt like days of anguish. "Maybe that's why we're here. To help her."

"I thought we couldn't change the past?"

Amelia sank into a crimson plush armchair. "You're right, but... still. If we're not supposed to have any impact on the future, why else would we be here? To watch? What good is that for anyone?"

"Observing can leave a bigger impact than you think," Jacob answered, straddling a chair on the other side of the room, facing her. "Take that de Blanchefort fellow, for instance."

Amelia affected a slight eye roll. "Again? Really?"

"I'm not jealous," Jacob defended. When she pursed her lips at him, he conceded. "Okay, a little. But that's not really what got me. It was how *bold* the dude was. Like he didn't see me sitting right damn next to you, or worse, didn't care."

"So he's a jerk," Amelia said evenly. "What does that have to do with us?"

"I don't know."

"We don't live here. We won't be here forever, and, chances are, we won't see de Blanchefort again."

"I know."

"It isn't as if he can hop in a car and come over. Travel takes forever to get ten miles. They plan these types of visits for weeks."

"Yeah. I know."

"But you're still upset."

"Yes, I am." Jacob rose. He pivoted again in a fidgeting manner, the way one did when they'd just met someone and hadn't established a level of comfort or familiarity. Amelia supposed, in their case, there was some truth to the theory. She'd entered that cabin on the edge of the Quinlan forest as one person and emerged someone else entirely. So had he.

"If it makes you feel better, I saw de Blanchefort watching Ophélie the same way," she offered.

Jacob glanced up and shook his head. "It should make me

feel better that he was also undressing a teenager with his eyes?"

"I'm only pointing out that he seems to be an equal opportunity sleaze." She sighed.

"It's late. We should take advantage of all the sleep we can get in this crazy place."

"You said we needed to get our stories straight," Amelia said, wondering what provoked her to engage him in even more uncomfortable conversation. Pragmatism? Guilt?

"And we do. Let's try again after some sleep. I don't know about you, but I'm about to pass out where I stand. I'd love to see some studies on the coinciding natures of time travel and jet lag, and the offset to your circadian rhythm."

The words were all said with his most serious face, and she could see that, yes, he *was* too tired to banter. So was she, though time travel was only one offender on the list of blame.

"Tomorrow, then."

Amelia didn't come to bed right away. Her thoughts floated, watching her husband's fitful rest, his mouth parted in a half crescent. Were his dreams colored with nonsensical plots or was he plagued, as she was, with returning to the scene where their world had shifted off its axis?

The moon was near full and shined through a gap in a clouded sky, illuminating a path across the cypress floors. As a girl, she'd slept in almost every single suite, all the cousins piled in room after room on a hot afternoon following a family picnic. Twists of tiny bodies, no concerns worth caring, while the adults sipped mint juleps and streetcars in the double parlor or, when the river offered a breeze, the gallery. Sometimes drinking too many. Afternoon would fade to dusk and evening, and there might be as many as thirty Deschanels sleeping under one roof. Amelia's mother was known for saying those were the nights her heart sang the loudest.

With a dull smile, Amelia considered she was sleeping in the same house as five Deschanels... five that no one, not her mother, not anyone living in her contemporary life, could ever claim to have met.

Later, perhaps, this would mean more. The weight of what Amelia experienced here might or might not wake her in the middle of the night, or give her pause. She might wonder about it, maybe even study the phenomenon that brought them here. When Amelia traveled abroad, first as a girl and later as a student and adult, visiting Scotland or Morocco or any number of wondrous places, she believed only half of her was enmeshed in the experience; the other half wasn't capable of grasping everything her eyes translated to her brain. The full array of colors and sounds and sensations would come to her when she returned, sometimes all at once but usually in waves. Amelia considered the experience a gift.

Whether or not their visit home in another time would prove to play out the same way, she couldn't guess. But what she'd told Jacob was something she believed utterly: They were here for a reason. And this was not only a product of Jacob's abilities surfacing for their needs but also her own sixth or seventh or eighth sense as a Deschanel. She knew it inherently. Her fear was only that knowing, discovering, would bring more knowledge but not the peace she craved.

Amelia dreaded closing her eyes each night to the sharp cut of Baldur's nails on her skin as he bandied her around, torturing her for hours before the inevitable rape.

She feared Jacob's presence in this memory would forever tarnish the deep, abiding love she once believed could be torn asunder by nothing.

Most of all, she panicked at the complete loss of herself. She was afraid Baldur had won, at the cost of her soul.

Amelia climbed into the tall half-tester bed, one Lucienne would later sleep on for seventeen years. She tried to calm her rising pulse before waking Jacob. *Breathe. Slowly in. Slowly out.* Her throat throbbed wildly like a jackhammer, more anxious lying next to a man she'd lain beside for years than she had been her first time in bed with a man.

Jacob's breaths maintained the same sleepy consistency, but he couldn't hide his body tensing as she slid in beside him. *Bless him*, she thought. *He's pretending to sleep for my sake.*

Amelia turned away from him and, at once, he was behind her, his arm wrapping over her waist with a lazy, languid effort she recognized from almost every night of their relationship. Familiar. Terrifying.

His hand traveled across the small of her back, and the sharp cries of darker memories sounded out across her soul. Of Baldur, resting his hand there, a near gentleness to the touch, moments before he'd pressed the knife into her belly.

Please make it stop, she prayed, scrambling to the opposite edge of the bed, as far from Jacob and the memory of Baldur would carry her. *Please don't take everything from me. I love you so much,* she thought as she stared at her husband's back, but she didn't give voice to the words. Amelia couldn't risk him rotating again, and touching her, triggering another horrifying memory. This was the worst of all that had been taken from her.

She waited until his tension again faded to real sleep before attempting to find some for herself.

DAY TWO

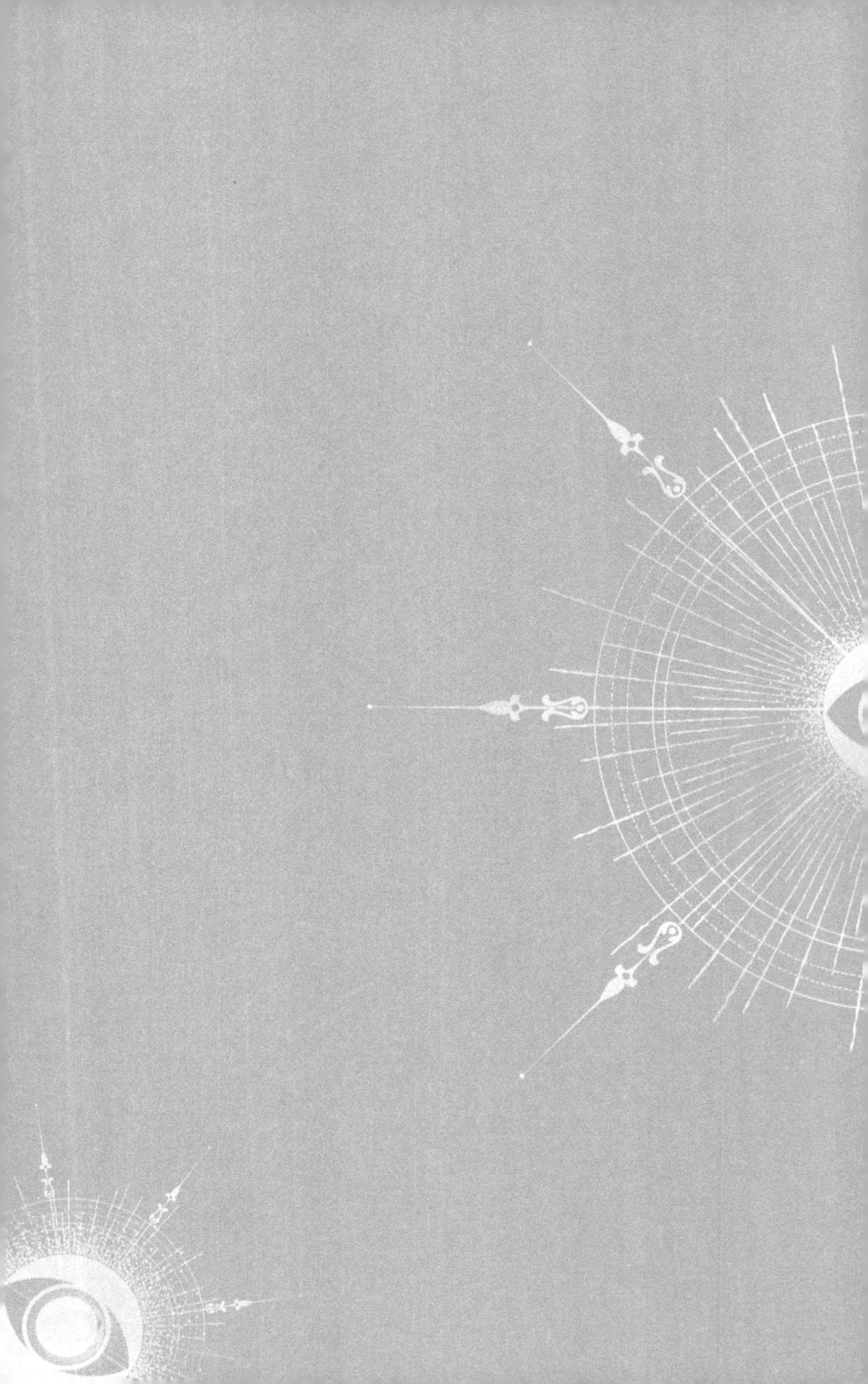

5
JACOB

The chorus of the bayou woke Jacob.

While pretending to sleep the night before, he'd considered the best use of his time. Amelia had it in her head she was searching for a sign, some signal to indicate what they were doing here and why they shouldn't take the next time travel train home to the present. That they both believed this reinforced to him, he should search for his own usefulness.

In the "win" category, they'd spent an evening in 1860 or 1861 Louisiana and woken in the same time without bursting into flames or going full-on event horizon. No one had died. The world hadn't exploded.

To his right, Amelia dozed. Whatever sleep she'd garnered through the night was never very consistent. Jacob had held her when she'd cried out, her mind fleeing a terror he understood but couldn't fix. He could have offered her so much more but she wasn't in a frame of mind to accept, and he knew better than to force it.

Charles had extended an invitation to speak with Jacob

today about their business there, and the sooner they had that discussion, hopefully, the less anxious he and Amelia would feel like outsiders. Without a timetable, Jacob wasn't comfortable tiptoeing around their host for an inestimable period.

The Big House already bustled with activity, from housemaids to cooks and governesses, moving to and fro with soundless energy. Slaves, all of them, though the ones in the house were well dressed in comparison to the men he'd seen in the fields the day before. A pit rose in his stomach that, for a single moment, he'd allowed their slightly improved circumstances to affect him, when, no matter how they were dressed, they enjoyed none of the basic rights as their masters. In fact, it was upon their backs in which this house and all the luxuries enjoyed within were built.

At least, Jacob took comfort in knowing the injustice would not last much longer, though the road ahead for freed slaves wouldn't be much easier for some time.

The house had two offices. One on the third floor, where the heir conducted private business. Then a larger one on the main floor, for all public commerce. Jacob wasn't comfortable venturing uninvited to the third floor, which also housed the heir's private suites, so he ventured down to the first floor. The pendulum on the oaken clock had chimed eight times, late morning for a planter, so it was a fair bet Charles had been up for a few hours already.

He stopped halfway down the staircase. At the bottom, a man inspected an oil rendering of the Deschanel's chateau in France. Jacob recognized the painting... and also the man.

Victor de Blanchefort.

As if called by name, de Blanchefort pivoted toward the new intruder and his face erupted in a warm, broad smile.

Jacob wasn't fooled.

"Lord Donnelly. I regret we did not receive a formal introduction last night." Victor moved toward the stairs. As he did, Jacob realized he had taken a step back.

"I'm sure you do," Jacob replied, eyeing the man's extended hand with acute distaste. He questioned his disgusted hesitation. *Why do I care this much? It isn't as if he's a real threat to my marriage. Just a nuisance.*

De Blanchefort missed Jacob's sarcasm, taking him at his word. "Allow me to remedy this. I am—"

"I know who you are."

"Last I found myself in England, a handshake was still customary." The man's eyes twinkled with a hint of controlled playfulness. Maybe not so obtuse, after all.

He saw no other choice. Refusing a pleasantry would be a great way to draw further suspicion to their already tenuous appearance.

Descending the staircase with an inward frown, Jacob took Victor's hand. It was soft and inviting, like a satin glove, as if he'd never touched a thing in his life. The effect was both unsettling and rather curious, as if coming across an artifact from another time or place.

"Now we are well met," de Blanchefort decided, returning his hand to settle upon his other, across his torso. "And where is Lady Donnelly?"

Wouldn't you like to know, Lord Byron? "Resting. It was a long journey."

"Understandable. I find it most important to protect the delicate constitutions of the gentler sex."

Jacob sighed, already exhausted trying to decipher what had been earnest comments from the man, and what was intended as sarcasm. "I'm looking for Monsieur Deschanel. Have you seen him?"

Victor smiled. "He's in his office with my father."

Jacob couldn't stop himself. "And you're here because..."

"My father's attendant. He's grown less than fond of travel in his elder years."

Jacob's nod was more reflex than interest, considering his options for extricating himself from the conversation. "I'll come back later, then, when he's not engaged."

Jacob recoiled when Victor's fingers wrapped around his shoulder. "I'll interrupt them on your behalf. They should be nearly finished."

"No, don't intrude. I'll come—"

"Lord Donnelly. I *insist.*"

His words—or not so much the exact ones de Blanchefort said, as much as the hollow, commanding tone in which they were delivered—gave Jacob pause long enough for Victor to rap twice on the office door and enter to announce himself before any invitation was extended. He then proceeded to insist Jacob should join their meeting, even though he had no compelling reason to be included.

Jacob couldn't fathom the testicular fortitude of this creature. The boldness at which the man had coveted his wife, openly, publicly, and now, barging in on a man doing private business in his own office with all the delicacy of a conquistador.

If he didn't perceive de Blanchefort as a nuisance—maybe even a threat—he might've found himself mildly enamored.

"Lord Donnelly is welcome to join us," Charles huffed, standing. He seemed less annoyed at the affront and more like an ornery parakeet whose feathers had been ruffled. "Though I cannot pretend to offer anything more engaging than the tedious negotiations of a betrothal."

"Unutterably dry," Victor agreed, only loud enough for Jacob to hear, as if they were secret conspirators.

"I would hate to interrupt," Jacob insisted, but the protestation was pointless. By now it was apparent, between Victor's boldness and the position the disruption had placed Charles in, that it mattered not if Jacob was intruding. Asking him to leave would be socially untenable.

"Nonsense. Have a seat," Charles said, gesturing toward the empty one to the right of his guest. From where Jacob stood, he could only see the elder de Blanchefort's back, though he was immediately struck by the old man's full head of black hair.

Jacob avoided catching a glimpse of Victor, both out of a desire to be rid of him and also for fear the man might think Jacob was thanking him for his behavior.

I just have to seek out something to make myself useful.

The heavy door clicked closed, and Charles settled again into his tall-backed chair behind the mahogany desk. Jacob took the seat offered moments earlier, and chanced a glance at de Blanchefort.

Jacob did a double take. The man was no older than his son! And he'd said this was his father? No, this must be his brother or a cousin; there was no other explanation. If Jacob owned a bar, and this man came in to order a drink, he would've carded him faster than lightning.

Where did the games start and end for Victor?

"I'm truly sorry to disturb your meeting," Jacob said, heart racing with an emotion he hadn't quite landed on.

Charles brushed aside the apology and instead aimed a hand at the man to Jacob's side. The gentleman clearly no older than he, maybe even younger.

"Lord Donnelly, allow me to offer a formal introduction to Marius de Blanchefort, master of *Coquillage* plantation down in St. Charles Parish. You've already met his son, Victor de Blanchefort."

Jacob reached a hand out, trying desperately not to stare at the creature with the pale, unlined skin and black hair… all pepper, no salt.

Marius ignored the gesture and affected a subtle nod, eyes closing briefly, like an exhausted old man who was up way past his bedtime. Jacob dropped his arm. Warmth flooded his cheeks. He realized he'd been holding his breath.

"De Blanchefort," Charles continued, relaxing back into his chair, "is a business partner of mine. His father's experience in coffee and indigo on the islands has proven invaluable, and, together, we run one of the only prosperous coffee and indigo productions in the region."

"That's great," Jacob offered weakly. He kept his eyes focused forward. If not, he would undoubtedly gape at Marius until he could make sense of the age discrepancy.

"On this day, however, we are here to discuss other business," Charles added with a weary sigh, as if already tired of catching up his guest. "The son of Victor, grandson of Marius, who goes by the name Lestan, is to be the husband of my Ophélie."

A hushed, chocolate voice filled the room. "Lestan is yet fourteen. On the eve of manhood, but not yet over the precipice." Marius also kept his eyes trained forward. "Charles wishes to see the ceremony complete by the commencement of summer, a rush he has chosen not to explain. In 1866, Lestan will be nineteen and a man prepared to be head of household."

This was not the face of a man in his twilight years, nor the voice. To the contrary, he was beautiful, in the way angels in Italian frescoes caught your eye and held your focus. Bewitching. Victor had the same look, though it had taken Jacob longer to this realization due to his distaste for the man.

Jacob had no idea what to make of any of it.

His mind rewound a few moments to Marius' last words. *In 1866, Lestan will be nineteen.* 1861, then. To Amelia's fear, they had landed in the year of the commencement of the Civil War. January, then, because if it were December, they wouldn't be troubled with betrothals anymore. War would be the only word on any tongue.

Charles' face wrinkled in disgust, but his eyes held a wild, panicked look. "And Ophélie will be twenty-one by that point! If your family were to choose to break our contract of betrothal, she would be left in a very precarious position. Her prospects would be much reduced from what they are now."

Marius remained stiff. "I've given no reason you should believe I am not to be taken at my word."

"And yet, we are bearing all the risk of this trust."

"By demanding we progress ahead of what is natural, you are asking me to bear the burden of your daughter in my home for the next five years."

Charles pulled back. His eyes narrowed, but then, regaining his composure, he smiled one he clearly did not mean. "I would be pleased to assume the cost of her upkeep. This increase would be accounted for in her dowry, with interest."

"You miss my point."

"My Jean will be taking the Bonapartie girl as his bride at sixteen," Charles emphasized the latter half of this proclamation, speaking slowly to ensure Marius understood. "Fitz, at thirteen, is set to take Montgomery Anderson's oldest daughter at an even earlier age. At *fifteen*."

"What you choose to do with your sons is no business of mine."

"We would send them into battle at thirteen, to die, but they are not yet man enough to take a woman to bed or run a household?" Charles scoffed.

Marius folded his hands over his lap and regarded his host with the same even expression. "We are no longer in the

Middle Ages, Charles. There is no benefit to living in the past. Our children will not die at the age of thirty."

Jacob's attentions traveled between the two men as they continued their discourse; Marius, using strong language but without visible fervor; Charles, who appeared on the verge of a frenzy and only avoiding one with extreme self-control. Jacob was by far no expert on marriage contracts of the nineteenth century, but even he was having trouble understanding Charles' anxiousness.

"What if the couple were to stay here at *Ophélie*?" Jacob suggested. Before either man could respond, he regretted inserting himself into this game of loggerheads.

Charles snapped his head in Jacob's direction. He opened his mouth to protest, stopped, tried again. The suggestion unsettled him, but, for whatever reason, he wasn't willing to share an explanation. "We are, of course, happy to take in Lestan, but such an arrangement would be highly unusual..." He turned to Marius for support, but Marius examined his fingernails.

"Here. There. Both would be unusual because Lestan needs to reach an appropriate age before assuming the burden of a family. I will not conceive to place him into such role until he is ready. I have already advised of my intention to build the couple a property of their own, near Dauphine, which as you know was a gift to my sister upon her marriage to Remy Destrehan."

"They could have separate suites..." Charles ran his hands over his hair, which was now as disheveled as his expression. He wanted Ophélie gone now. But why? He couldn't know she would be murdered by Union soldiers during the war... or could he? Charles was a Deschanel, and all Deschanels had a touch of something. Perhaps he had divined this and hoped to change it.

But unless Jacob and Amelia had landed in an alternate version of history, Ophélie *would* die, and within the next year.

Marius rose suddenly, though Charles was in mid-speech. "I wish for some air. I am old now, as you know."

Charles' eyebrow arched in marked skepticism.

"We have more to discuss," Charles insisted.

"On the subject of tobacco, yes. We can reconvene this evening. Regarding the betrothal, you have my word Lestan will live up to the terms of the contract—when he is nineteen," Marius said and excused himself before Charles could find a reason to compel him to stay.

Jacob shifted awkwardly as Charles huffed and sighed, twisting in his seat. He didn't know whether to stay or excuse himself.

Charles waved a hand in the air and squared his shoulders. A peacefulness seemed to come over him, and the man who had all but dropped to his knees and pleaded with his guest, was replaced by the figure Jacob had imagined when reading about the builder of this majestic, successful plantation.

"Please stay, Lord Donnelly. I'll send for coffee, and we can find ourselves better acquainted."

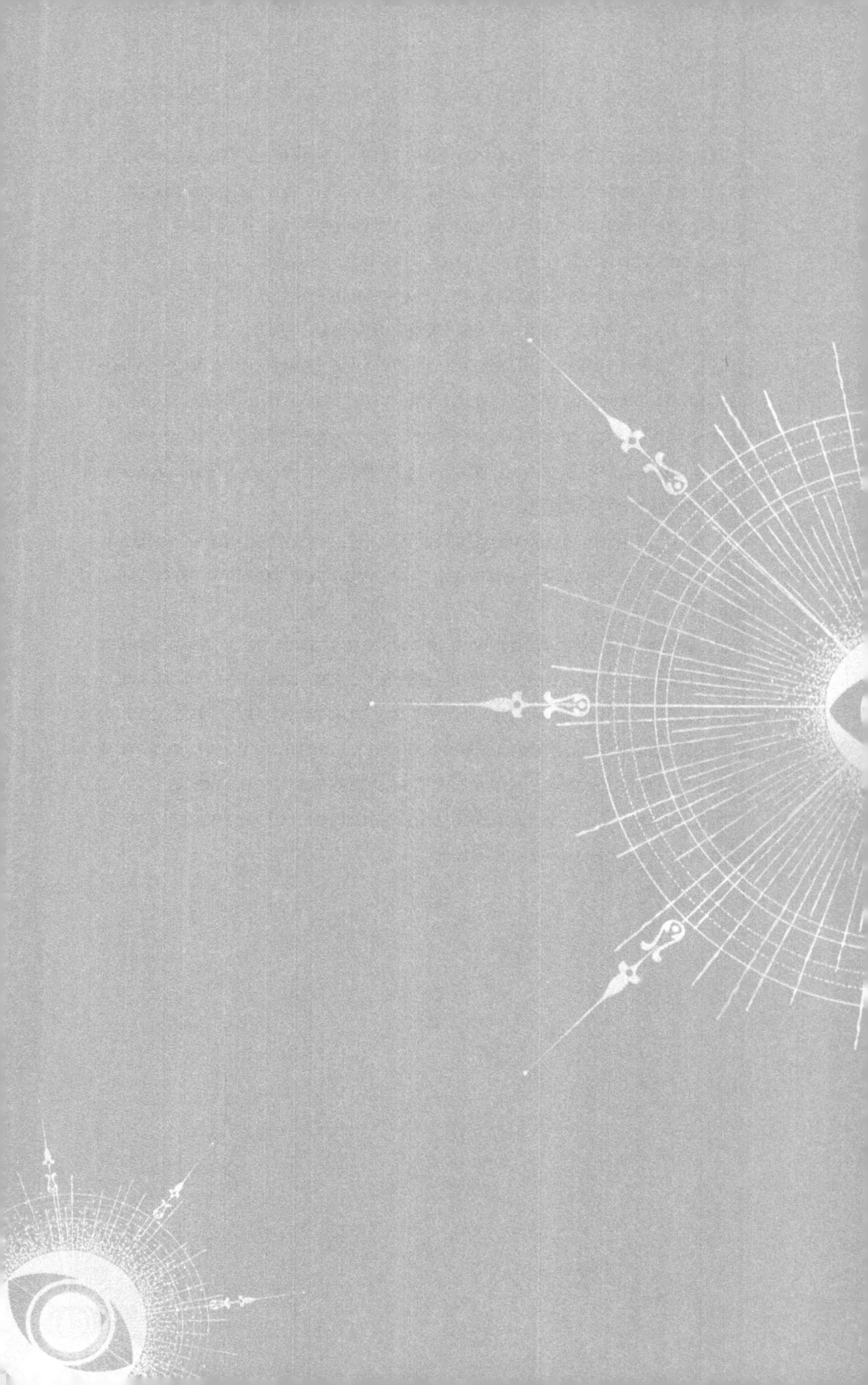

6

AMELIA

Amelia heard Jacob rise and leave, and she let him do these things despite being awake herself, despite that the sounds he took for sleep were contrivances.

She longed for his comfort, but the very thought of his touch made her skin crawl. Amelia had never hated herself more for these things. Baldur, the monster responsible, had turned her into another kind of monster, one who walked and talked and breathed but no longer knew what it meant to *live.*

Amelia didn't know why they had traveled to this particular time and place, but she held on to a tiny, secret hope that it would help her find her way back to who she was and wanted to be.

Even the thought was daunting.

Once she knew Jacob was gone, she slipped out of bed and dressed in one of the pieces the housemaid had left for her. It was decidedly less abhorrent than what she'd worn the night before, though it still left her grateful for having been born in a time where jeans were the norm.

Downstairs, occupants of the house were awake and alive, and she supposed she'd risen late, though she could always claim to be affected by the time change. Jet lag wasn't a thing yet, but surely they knew about different time zones, if not as a point of fact then at least in experience. Charles and Jean had both enjoyed Grand Tours of Europe. Fitz, Charles' youngest son, who must have been thirteen or fourteen at this point in history, would be along on his in short order as well.

She hadn't yet spotted Fitz on this trip. Like Ophélie, he was destined to die young, but not until he had a son of his own.

Ophélie perched at the bottom of the stairs, her expression welcoming.

"It's as if you've been waiting for me," Amelia teased, as she descended the final steps. Relief came over her to see a familiar face, and it occurred she had been thinking about seeking out Ophélie since leaving her room.

Ophélie blushed. "I saw Lord Donnelly come down to visit with my father and assumed you might be along."

"I've been tired from the journey, but I'm better now." It wasn't a lie. The time travel *had* exhausted her, in a way she couldn't verbalize. She had changed from Norway time to Louisiana time, yes, but skipping backward nearly a hundred and fifty years had an indescribably heavy effect on her. One she couldn't ever bring up in casual conversation.

She wondered if Jacob was feeling the same.

A month ago, she would have already known the answer.

Ophélie wrung her hands over her torso, brightening with excitement. "I hope one day my husband takes me to Europe."

Amelia returned the smile, only to realize Ophélie's enthusiasm rang false. The young woman's eyes were like the Rosetta Stone to her soul, either backing up or countering any spoken words. *She can't know what I know about her future. Can she?*

"I'm sure he will," Amelia replied, feeling only a twinge of guilt at the lie. All the information and knowledge she'd amassed about her family and this region during her lifetime would be of no use to those living here as contemporaries. One simply didn't tell a sixteen-year-old girl she would be dead within a year.

Even if she did settle on becoming the soothsayer of *Ophélie*, throwing down every last bit of historical intelligence she had on life here in the nineteenth century, it would most likely be received as witchcraft and unwelcome.

"I thought I might take you on a tour of the grounds of *Ophélie*," the young woman offered, the blush rising to the apples of her cheeks, this time, genuine. "That is if you aren't otherwise engaged. It may take us several hours, at a leisurely pace."

"I have nothing planned for today, so I would love that."

They passed Charles' office on their way out the door. Amelia's heart hitched when she saw Jacob seated inside. To his left, a young man turned to look at Jacob, and she caught his profile. He was familiar.

"That's Marius de Blanchefort," Ophélie explained, giving Amelia's arm a light tug to move them along. "I believe you may have seen Victor last night. His son."

"His... son?" Amelia stopped again, and Ophélie once again urged her along, evidently eager to be out of the house. "You mean to tell me you think Marius is Victor's father? That man in there, who can't be a day older than Victor?"

Ophélie passed her a grin and a slight eye roll. "You would not be the first to question it."

"I'm not *questioning* it. I'm saying it's biologically impossible!"

"I know it seems that way," her young host agreed. She visibly relaxed when they reached the gallery porch, spreading her arms to receive the wave of light heat. A pitcher of amber liquid sat on the wooden bench between two rockers. "But there are many who have conducted business with Marius de Blanchefort for more than sixty years who can bear witness. Would you believe the man is near eighty?"

"Only if you believe I have some oceanfront property in Arizona to sell you on the cheap."

"Arizona?"

Amelia halted and pivoted herself before Ophélie so they were face-to-face. Her hands rested on both shoulders. "There's no way on earth that man is eighty, no matter what anyone says. Some people age well, but no one subverts the process altogether."

Ophélie shrugged. It was clear she believed it. "All the de Blancheforts are like this. Some say it's because of their time in the islands."

"What do you mean?"

"Marius' father, Etienne, had a plantation on Saint Domingue. The family left when Marius was a boy, but they barely avoided a massacre when the slaves rose up and claimed the island. I've heard they have a mambo... a priestess of voudou... to whom Etienne sold his soul and the souls of his family in exchange for protection."

Amelia pursed her lips. "Even if they have a priestess in their corner, that doesn't explain the lack of any visible aging."

"There are other whispers, too," Ophélie said, lowering her voice with a glance around. "But we best not speak of them where ears can hear."

"Speak of what, my darling?"

They turned to see Brigitte exiting the house. The presence alone of the woman soured Amelia's spirits. Her empathic strength was muted under this roof, but what remained could not be doubted. She knew in her heart of hearts Brigitte Deschanel was evil. Not in the innate sense of a born psychopath but rather a very intentional malignancy. Everything about the woman was deliberate. Every word, every message sent in other ways.

"Maman, I only meant to bring our ladies' chatter far from the house so as not to disturb Papa and his guests," Ophélie replied, head bowed.

The petite woman's lips twisted in disdain. Brigitte leveled a hard gaze at her daughter. "You have not finished your needlework." The words were cased in accusation.

"I'm showing Lady Donnelly around the property," Ophélie countered in a timid voice. She shrank into Amelia's side.

"Which you may do when you are not laden with unfinished responsibilities."

When Amelia was a girl of Ophélie's age, an admonishment like this from her mother would have thrown her into a pout. Ophélie's reaction was curious. She was angry, that was clear, but the way her eyes narrowed, only briefly but long enough for Amelia to witness, seemed to indicate she was more suspicious of her mother than anything else.

Well, that makes two of us.

"It's okay, Ophélie, I'll wait for you to finish, and in the meantime, I promise not to receive a tour from anyone but you," Amelia promised, positioning herself between the two women so her back was to Brigitte. She didn't know what Ophélie was capable of as a Deschanel. While they all had talents, there was no written evidence of what their ancestors could do, at least not from this period. But Amelia focused all her energy to send the girl this: *I'm your ally. I'm here for you, for whatever you need.*

A flicker of shock registered across Ophélie's face, followed by the faintest trace of a smile. *I already know that, Lady Donnelly.*

She followed her mother back into the house, leaving Amelia disturbed by what she'd witnessed. Brigitte and Jean were both adversaries of the young girl. Where was Charles in this? From history, Amelia knew he overlooked many of the abuses heaped upon her during the war, but was that true? And what of Fitz?

"Are you awaiting a parcel?"

Amelia snapped out of her daze and turned to see the man from the night before, Victor de Blanchefort, standing on the top step, hands laced behind his back.

In the morning sun, the man was even more preternaturally dazzling. His dark hair took the light and from it bounced shades of purple and pure raven black. His green eyes matched the unusual forested emerald shade of his waistcoat, which was certainly fashionable but not for this century.

She remembered his "father" inside and was immediately suspicious.

"I was just going in," she replied and started up the steps in a near-sprint, not precisely ladylike. Regardless, something about this odd creature made her believe he didn't care about such things, and, in any case, his opinion was not her concern.

As she passed by him, his hand landed on her upper arm, and she was jolted to a stop.

"Your husband is otherwise occupied and may be for the next while. Please, walk with me." In contrast to his firm grasp, his words had a note of pleading.

Amelia jerked herself loose and backed up several steps. "Don't."

"My apologies, Lady Donnelly," Victor replied, dipping into the slightest of bows, "I sometimes don't realize my own strength. If I hurt you, it was not my intent."

"I'm fine," she mumbled, wondering why she felt it necessary to make him feel better.

"Will you, then? Humor a new friend, and walk with me?" Victor's bright green eyes were unlike any she'd seen on someone not wearing contacts, but those weren't an option in the 1860s. Closer to him now than she'd ever been, the gold flecks throughout the green—not simply a single shade, but several, competing hues of mossy undertones—could not possibly be real. A trick of light, maybe. Something.

"I'm not sure that's a good idea," Amelia replied after realizing she'd been caught staring. *For science.*

"The best moments in history began with terrible ideas," Victor replied and held out his crooked elbow. "It's too lovely a morning to let it go to waste."

Cautiously, and not without a strong suspicion she'd lost her damn mind, Amelia took the elbow of the peculiar man, briefly thinking of Alice in the moments before she consumed the *Drink Me* potion that sent her careening down the rabbit hole.

AMELIA LED THE WAY, HER INNATE KNOWLEDGE OF THE INTRICACIES OF the property guiding her through the fields and outbuildings that kept the plantation running. It was a shock to the system to see the farm in its prime, with dozens more working shops and kitchens than still stood in the present. A blacksmith toiled over a forge in an open wooden stand. Nearby, several women gathered around a large kiln, dipping in the steaming liquid bedding and clothing they stirred with a long pole. The plantation was a village, everyone working toward their own task, keeping the land alive and thriving.

Today's *Ophélie* was a shell of its former self, at least outside the Big House. Half the buildings had been demolished or burned down, the other half repurposed for storage or guests.

Victor, with a knowing smile, called her out on her confidence. "Are you certain this is your first visit to Louisiana, Lady Donnelly?"

Amelia faltered for a split second but recovered, hopefully before he noticed. "We wandered a bit yesterday," she said. "I have a strong memory."

His smile continued on, but he said nothing. He didn't need to. Victor's expression conveyed his skepticism clearly enough.

In a quick move, he lifted her up and over the root of an oak she hadn't seen and almost tripped over. Her breath faltered at the odd intimacy of the gesture, at how his hands came around her waist with a possessive firmness. *Turn around. Go back.*

"Let us speak of intentions," he said. "Yours interest me a great deal. For instance, the truth behind why you're here."

Amelia's lips parted, only to realize she and Jacob *still* had not conspired on a cohesive story. Undoubtedly, Charles was asking the same thing of Jacob at this very moment. "We're cousins of the Deschanels," she answered, hoping this was safe, praying it did not conflict with whatever Jacob had laid out for their host.

"The Deschanels undoubtedly have many cousins," Victor answered. "But it is a long and expensive voyage from England to come without purpose." He guided her away from the business of the outbuildings, through the rows of oaks. *Away from others,* she thought.

"Lord Donnelly has business with Charles Deschanel."

"Secret business, then?"

"Not secret." Her mouth felt full of cotton. She had never taken pleasure in lying, nor had she learned the skill to do it well. What had Jacob said to Charles in the ballroom? "Um... land. We're interested in land."

"So secret even Charles himself was unaware of it," Victor mused, ignoring her explanation. "You both voyage here, unannounced, toward aims you refuse to disclose." He leaned in close and whispered the next, "Ahh, perhaps you are spies for the British!"

"I just told you why we're here. We aren't at war with you," Amelia countered, falling into character. "We lost the Battle of New Orleans, as you may recall."

Victor's laugh rang across the oaks? "Me? No, I'm afraid not. That was nearly half a century past. My father does."

"You mean that man in the house? Marius?"

"I might suggest you refer to him as Monsieur de Blanchefort as a more socially amenable alternative," Victor teased.

Amelia sighed. "But we're talking about the same person? That young man inside? You are seriously going to try and convince me he is your father?"

"I wouldn't deign to convince you of something that's a recorded fact. He *is* my father."

"Bullshit."

"What a lady you are!"

"I'm no lady any more than that man in there is your damn father!"

Victor stopped at the base of one of the larger oaks, a behemoth with several branches sweeping the dewy grass like benches. He leaned into the tough bark. "Why are we talking about my family when your background is so much more interesting?"

Amelia's hands perched on her hips. She began to question her own motivation for following him, or, at a minimum, her judgment in doing so. It didn't feel at all like something she would do, and yet she'd done it with little prodding. "Why are we here, Victor?"

His grin spread even further, deepening the beds of his dimples. "Are we on a first name basis now, Amelia?"

She recoiled. "I never told you my name."

"To return to your question, I know a great deal about you," he said. "I know, for instance, you're not here on any business with Deschanel. I know you're not from England. And I know you are, quite certainly, no lady." When her face flushed red, he added, "Of the peerage, at least."

"You have no idea what you're talking about," she spat through clenched teeth. Her hands twitched, and she quickly linked them behind her back. Bad idea or not, walking away now, without resolving whatever strange and inexplicable suspicions Victor de Blanchefort possessed about the two of them, would leave them vulnerable. "Our business with Deschanel is our own."

"Truly, for even he lacks knowledge on the subject."

Amelia snorted, continuing on her quest of unladylike behavior. "And how would you know anything about it? Are you his business advisor? Are *you* the spy?"

"I know things in the way you know things when you should not," Victor answered, this time without any of the mocking from before. "I know who you are, and from where you come. Or should I say, *when*?"

It all happened so fast. Blood rushed to her head in one powerful, overwhelming burst. The sky flooded across her vision, passing by in a long, dramatic arc. Her feet flew off the grass and into the air.

She cried out, then felt nothing.

Slowly, the world around her returned to focus. Amelia looked up into Victor's concerned face. She leaned back against something. His arms.

"Are you all right?"

"What did you say? Before I passed out?" Amelia shook her

head and tugged at his arm, pulling herself back to standing on her own, a challenging feat in her constricted dress. She staggered into one of the long arm branches, and Victor was again at her side. She shoved him away. "Never mind, don't tell me. I need to get back to the house."

"You know what I said." The words flowed with the first kindness she'd heard from the man. "And now you know I know."

"I understand you're completely mad," she panted. "And we're done here." The weakness of moments before hadn't entirely fled, and she needed to be far, far away from this creature, who was taking something from her now as surely as Baldur had stripped her of everything in Ireland. It didn't matter what he thought, not right at this moment because she needed to be free of him before she completely lost her mind.

"You might convince yourself of that, to avoid the truth," he said. "An understandable self-deception. But you came here safe with the knowledge no one would know your truth. Naturally, you did not count on finding me. In all the countries, in all the cities, in all the world, there are so few like me, like us, that this assumption was a reasonable one. But you are here, from a time foreign to me, and I am here, awaiting you, and our meeting is not without purpose."

"I'm going back to the house," she said again, thinking of Jacob. Of what he might think when he realized she'd been off with the very man he'd considered a threat the night before. The man she now knew to be one, but for very different reasons.

"Your secret will remain safe in my keeping, Amelia." Victor closed in on her, effectively cornering her against the branch. His breath, a cloying, honeyed scent, burned her cheeks. "I'll tell no one. I'll make no demands on you. I am not your enemy."

Tears tickled her eyes. She sensed the danger in Victor, but it was the other emotion, the one she could not fully distinguish, that kept her rooted in place. “Then who *are* you?”

Victor kissed the corner of her mouth, a lingering act that was somehow both abhorrent and enticing. He backed away to afford her space. “Who I am is not nearly as interesting, or controversial, as who *you* are, my darling.”

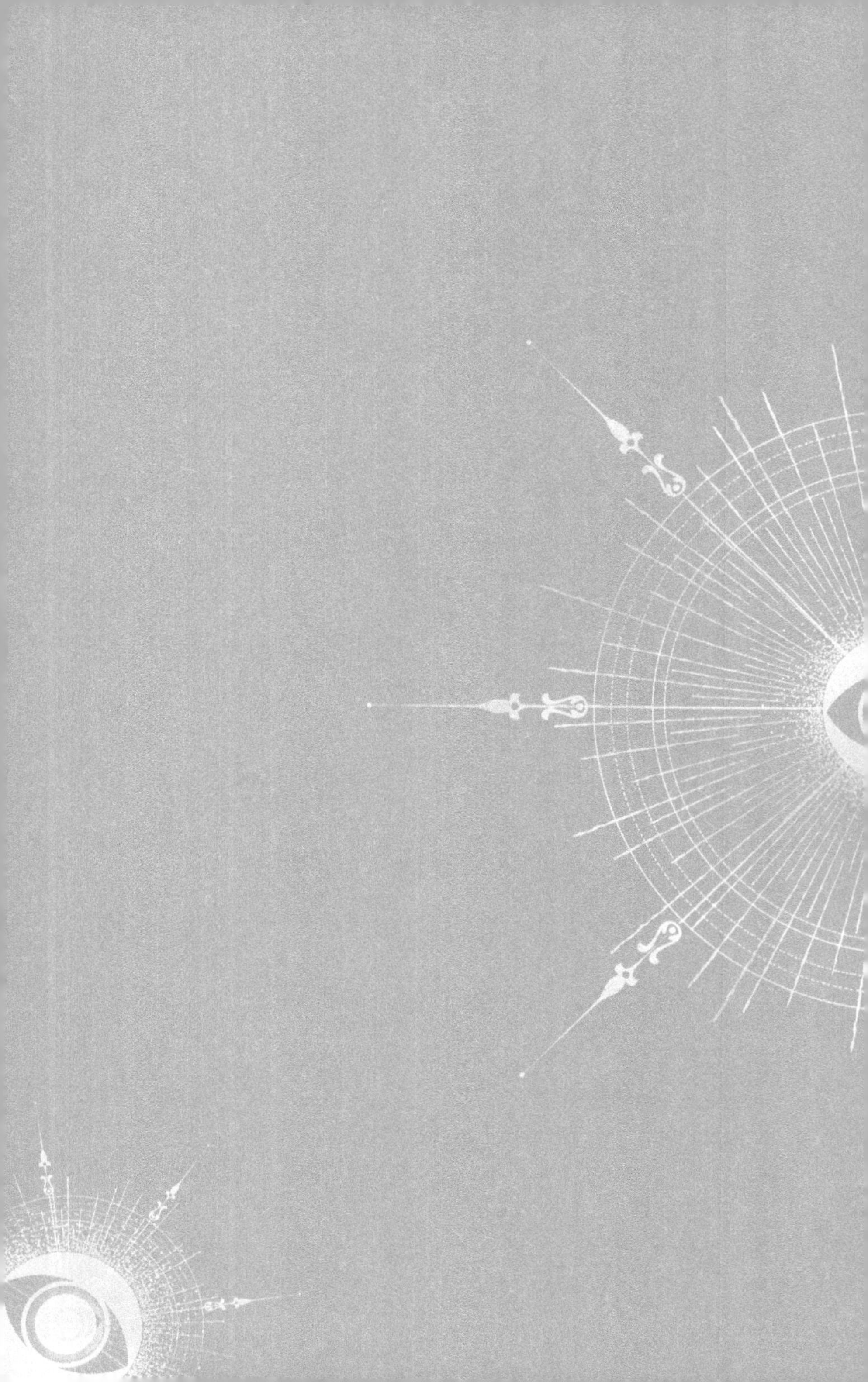

7
OPHÉLIE

The deep chime of the grandfather clock at the far end of the ladies' parlor was what finally brought her to the present. Her thoughts had been wandering to recent developments in her life, how dreams had shifted from the usual, nonsensical images to very specific messages she knew were meant for her.

Ophélie gaped at her needlework with sharp panic as she realized she'ad retraced her backstitch at least two dozen times. She saw no immediate fix for her blunder. The linen was ruined.

Unfortunately, her mother also noticed. "Utter failure," Brigitte mumbled, nodding toward the blank linens on the end table between them. "Would that I had a daughter with more talent than a mouth that never ceases to run."

"Sorry, Maman," Ophélie whispered, setting aside her ruined design to begin anew. She could be here until she produced an item of quality, something her mother approved of. The last had taken her well over an hour, and even the thought of starting fresh made her soul sink into the velvet chair. “I will do better.”

“Hmph,” Brigitte huffed, leaning back in her rocker. Her precise stitches never faltered in pace or accuracy. “I blame your papa. None of us have been as we were in France since arriving in this godforsaken swampland. We may as well be nothing.”

“You never speak of France,” Ophélie said, with a tentative glance at her maman. She hoped to draw the conversation somewhere safer, or at the very least, away from her own ineptitude. But she had also always desired to know more of their family history.

Brigitte paused her work for the first time that afternoon. Her scowl softened. “Would that you could have seen it. We are much changed, in this godless New World. In France, we *were* gods.”

“Gods?” Ophélie repeated. Her heart raced as she determined to both keep her mother talking and not have another mishap with her project. The balance of her own happiness, at least in the short term, rested on her ability to keep both moving.

“I have told you. Surely,” Brigitte said with pursed lips. “Of who we were?”

Ophélie shook her head.

“I have. You do not listen,” Brigitte scolded, but her eyes were smiling. Ophélie thought, even the mention of France could send her mother there. Followed by words indicating her love for the motherland was greater than any she'd shown to her children.

“Ahh, our village, so small no one ever gave it a name. It lay to the south of Mont-de-Marson, in the region of Aquitaine. The Douze and Midou rivers, merging from the Bordeaux

Valley, made the Mississippi appear a stream, and they kept our lands fertile and ever green.

"Of course, there were Deschanels all over the valley, from Bordeaux to Pau, and even some in Paris, at court. Our ancestress was a courtesan of Catherine de Medici, and we were all, always, welcome in the court thereafter. Your *grandmère*, Marianne, spent her youth in the court of Louis XVI. I attended him more than once myself."

"Why, Maman, would we live in the countryside if we had favor at court?"

Brigitte's eyes darkened. She jabbed the needle into her linen, nearly tearing the fabric. "Our gifts were treasured by many, but feared by more."

"Gifts?" Ophélie swallowed. Her questions would only incense her maman if she kept them up.

"You would not know, as you were born like any other child, thanks to your papa!" Brigitte cried. Tears made the corner of her eyes glint. "Your maman was a powerful soothsayer, child. I could divine any future, of anyone I met. My gift knew no limitation; not time, not distance. I predicted many births and even more deaths, and this was valuable to our king and queen. My ancestors could do this, and more."

"A soothsayer," Ophélie whispered, awed and doubtful. If her mother could predict the future, how had she never known this? Was it even possible?

"You know nothing," Brigitte hissed, likely reading the skepticism in her thoughts. "It is this house... this... *land.* It has taken everything from us. Your father could lay hands on any creature and see them healed of their wounds. Now, he cannot even tend to his own scratches. We, both of us, are paying the price for putting asunder the destiny promised us."

Ophélie's heart raced. She had learned more in recent

minutes of her family than she had known her whole life. While fumbling through the questions pushing at her skull, she decided against all of them, worrying they made her appear foolish and unprepared for this important discussion. Instead, she asked, “Why did you and Papa come to Louisiana?”

“Your papa is a foolish man, who never believed in who we were,” Brigitte replied. “Never. We were a clan of healers and dreamwalkers, of soothsayers and mind readers. Revered by kings, and desired by all from peerage to millers. The price for our gift was its preservation. My maman and papa were of pure blood. Brother and sister. As were their maman and papa, and theirs before. When your papa did not have a sister, I was chosen as his bride. I took this designation with a great swell of pride. There was no greater honor, as a Deschanel, than to carry forth the gift into the next generation. I know you believe me a despot for sending your brother to your bed, Ophélie, but you did not live the life we left behind. You did not know what it was to be surrounded by brilliance, by so many wondrous gifts! Our blood is blessed like no other blessing known to man. And only one sacrifice was asked of us.”

Ophélie had never, not at any time in her life, seen her mother look so at peace. She realized, for once, she did not fear her mother’s ire, and that, too, was new. “A pure bloodline,” she answered, and lit up at her mother’s pride.

“A pure bloodline,” Brigitte agreed, nodding. “So you see. No, you don’t see, not as I do, but you understand. Your papa, despite his gifts, did not see. Did not understand. He believed our family to be cursed. How could gifts such as ours ever be a curse?” She curled her nose. “He has never believed.”

“But why...” Ophélie chose her words extra carefully. “Why did bringing the family to Louisiana change everything?”

Brigitte’s expression resembled her brother Jean’s had before he would spit on the ground in disgust. “We are stronger together. Much stronger. We have gone against nature by leaving our homeland. Your papa and I were the heirs of our dynasty. And we have paid with our gifts. You look at me, child, as if I am mad when I speak of divining futures, but you were not there! I could foretell the exact moment of your death, should you desire to know it, if we were in France. But here... here we are nothing. Reduced to the ash of our future destroyed."

Ophélie mulled her mother's words over. She had no reason not to believe what she was saying. Her mother, while cruel and inattentive, was not in the habit of lying to her. She could sniff out deception with an accuracy Ophélie had never been able to explain. And when she thought back, over the years, there had been times her mother had recognized situations, events... nothing remarkable, except in the coincidence of always knowing them before others... and the ability had always stuck with Ophélie.

And her father... she once saw him struggle to save the life of a slave after an accident in the field. He then blamed himself when the poor man died. Her papa had not even been there when the man hurt himself, so she never understood how he could shoulder such guilt. Had he been thinking of what he used to be back in France?

But Ophélie did not believe her parents were cursed. More than once in her life, she had thought their home was a peculiar one. Even the air was different in *Ophélie* than it was in the other plantations she'd visited. It was as if she'd stepped into another world anytime she crossed the threshold.

If the house... or the property... were holding her parents back, perhaps there was an explanation. A reason maybe for the best, too. Her mother, unchecked, was a prospect Ophélie did not even want to consider.

She kept this knowledge to herself, for it did not take any

great skill with divination to know the idea would not go over well.

"And we are the only Deschanels in Louisiana?" Ophélie asked to keep the conversation alive. As long as her mother was talking about something else, she would not pick apart her work or any other manner of things about Ophélie that happened to displease her.

"Deschanels, yes, there are no others but us," Brigitte answered, her needling increasing in speed. "I doubt other Deschanels would be as foolish as your papa. You know the de Blancheforts are distant cousins, I assume?"

Ophélie nodded.

"A relation of my *grandmère*, though we did not acquaint of them in France, but in passing."

Ophélie thought of pale-faced Victor with the knowing gaze. "If they share our blood, do they also share our gifts?"

Brigitte scoffed. "If they did, they have long been diluted with the blood of those far less worthy."

Thinking again of Victor—how he chose his words with the deliberateness of one who knows the answer before he asks the question, how he had eyes that could see beyond the surface, all the way to the soul—Ophélie was not so certain.

And what of her own experiences? Ophélie's visions no longer formulated themselves in the way dreams were expected to. Messages, they were, she was sure of it, but no ordinary girl would be able to receive a communication in this way, surely. And as this knowledge was revealed, she also began to witness a life that was not her own but was startlingly familiar.

What was she to make of the information?

That she would die within the year.

That she would know great cruelty.

And yet... somehow... these would turn out to be gifts in

their own way. She knew, but did not *know* it yet, as the full story was yet to be revealed.

Had her maman and papa stayed in France, would her understanding have been clearer? She would already know all the answers, she thought. Certainly.

"Ophélie, mind your needlework," her maman snapped. The spell was broken. France had been pushed to the recesses of her memory bank, and now they were only mother and daughter again, often at ends. All duty. No love.

"Yes, Maman," Ophélie replied, pushing back the tide of sadness at having had so few moments to see her mother for the woman she could have been.

"And stay away from Lady Donnelly," Brigitte added, without missing a stitch. "She is not who she claims."

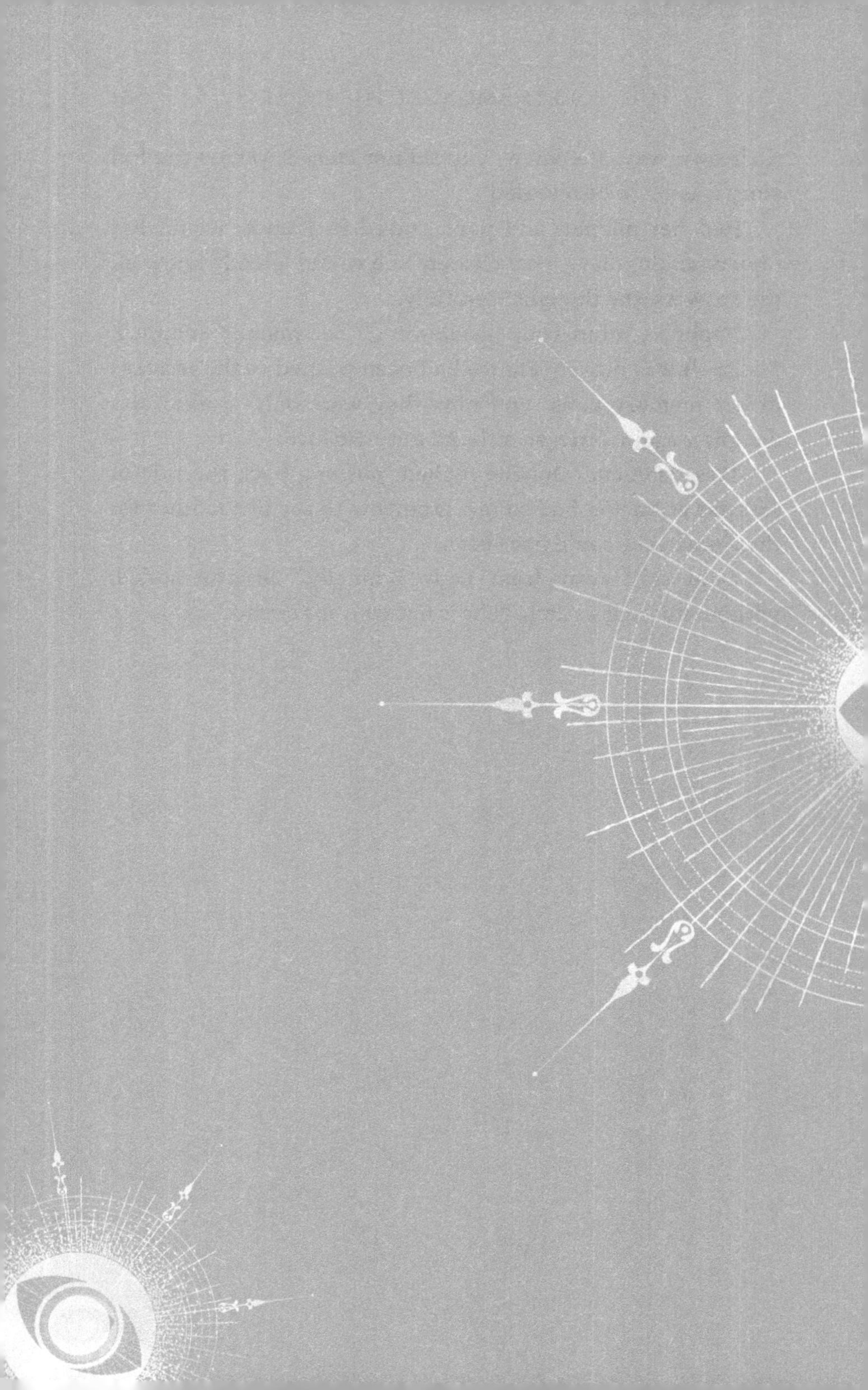

8

JACOB

Jacob tried not to consider what Charles had in mind for their *tête-à-tête*, or to imagine the disaster that might ensue from his stumbling through a half-baked explanation. Amelia's distance, while understandable, had made it challenging to even attempt a cohesive story. It wouldn't take much to crack the veneer of their thin cover.

Charles again leaned back in his chair, a walnut open-armed piece with roaring lions cresting in the design a full foot above his head. Jacob wondered how many men had been intimidated by the chair alone. "A nice surprise to have cousins here. Later, you must help me with the pedigree so I can place you precisely. I knew we had an English line, but how fortunate to count lords among us..."

Jacob swallowed hard. "Lady Donnelly and I would like to thank you for your hospitality."

Charles waved him away. "A Deschanel is always home, wherever there are Deschanels."

"Yes. Of course." Jacob was almost certain his mother-in-law, Colleen, had said this exact same thing before. "Thank you, nonetheless."

Charles caught Jacob gazing at a series of three wildlife paintings with a very distinct, completely familiar style. "John James Audubon. Are you familiar with his work?"

Jacob swallowed. Original Audubons... they would be worth a fortune in the present day, though this was the first time he'd seen the Deschanels with any on display. "Yes. I've heard of him."

"The man who sold us this land gifted them to us. I think they are rather simple, if not plain, but it's good luck to display your gifts."

Jacob made a mental note to ask Amelia if her uncle had also lost these gems to a gambling debt.

His host's eyes cast down, toward a mess of thick, fibrous paper. Charles ran his hands over the stack, pushing the documents across the surface of the desk without any real purpose. "Tell me, are marriage contracts complex on your side of the ocean?"

Jacob paused, considering his options in light of having no clear concept of what Charles was actually asking. In the end, he decided the master of *Ophélie* was not looking so much for a correct answer as for consolation. "Everything is more complex when love is involved," he answered truthfully, thinking of his own wife who was physically upstairs but emotionally a world away.

"Love? Whatever does love have to do with marriage?" Charles regarded him as if he might have gone insane. He struck a match against a tinderbox and lit a cigar while offering one to Jacob, who shook his head.

"Nothing, obviously," Jacob said with a short laugh, remembering the time and place in which he was having this discussion. "But the youth like to believe so, right?"

Charles returned his laugh. "To a fault! Ophélie knows nothing about Lestan, and she is already planning the colors for their linens." He shook his head. "Lestan will make her a fine match, of that I have no doubt. A young man, her own age, and no physical deformities. She may even be happy. Love? Who can say? I only know she could do much worse. No, *will* do so much worse if the de Blancheforts are not true to their word."

"Why wouldn't they be? Marius said you had other business, aside from negotiating marriage contracts. He must value that partnership."

"Yes, we do. I'm fortunate to have an alliance with the most powerful family on the river, next to the Aimes."

"But you don't trust he'll deliver?"

As he watched Jacob, Charles seemed to choose his words carefully. "It is less that I do not trust in de Blanchefort and more that I bear the greater risk if he changes his mind." He screwed his lips together and mumbled, almost as an afterthought, "It is difficult to trust a man who cannot seem to age."

Jacob nearly put his foot in his mouth as he considered the war ahead, and the role that would play in throwing a wrench into any plans made. "You have as much to offer him as he does you. Don't let him lead you around on only his terms." Jacob stopped. He was biased, clearly, against Marius for being the father of the elusive and charming Victor. "I'm sorry. I overstepped."

Charles regarded him for several long moments and laughed. "I appreciate honesty. So few are willing to give it without a steep price." He rose, and Jacob took that as his signal to do the same. "And since you were so generous with your words, I have one further favor to ask."

Jacob nodded.

"Please do not mention this to Madame Deschanel," Charles answered, with a tight smile. The wrinkles around his mouth gathered into a small chorus. "This is a sensitive topic in the household. One best left for me to resolve."

"Of course," Jacob said. "Your other business with de Blanchefort, if you don't mind me asking, is what?"

Charles gestured toward a stack of documents to the left of the marriage contract. "Another complicated matter. One I would count myself blessed for the guidance of a landed lord if you have the time."

Jacob, a scientist not a businessman, smiled. "Sure, I'm happy to."

"Monsieur de Blanchefort and I have embarked on two risky ventures, indigo and coffee. They have, after a slow commencement, begun to pay off. But I fear for the longevity of either crop. Sugar is king," Charles said, with a sidelong glance out the window, toward the miles and miles of cane.

"Yes," Jacob said. "It is. Though coffee is also an important export for the region." He couldn't say that in the present day Louisiana would eventually be the number one exporter of coffee in the US. In the meantime, he found careful agreement to what Charles already knew to be true in his present.

Charles slowly nodded. "You know the region," he declared with a sidelong glance. "Perhaps you will have some useful guidance, after all. It is not my indigo and coffee crops I am concerned with, at present, but a prospective crop I am not convinced has any use whatsoever in this region."

"And that is?"

"Tobacco."

"Tobacco, huh?" Jacob pretended to weigh the risks, when instead he was trying to remember if tobacco was even relevant in today's market in Louisiana.

"Tobacco indeed," Charles said with a sigh. "Though it is less the crop that worries me and more the method to de Blanchefort's scheme. He believes war is imminent." At this, Charles affected a bitter, practiced laugh, and Jacob imagined he saved this one in particular for any mention of war. "And that our money will be of no use. The real currency, he says, will be in land. He is not wrong on the value of land, but if he had half the Confederate Bonds I had stored away, he might sing from a different hymnal."

Well, now, isn't Marius just a regular Nostradamus?

Jacob found it harder and harder to maintain neutrality on topics he understood better than his host. "And you believe the land isn't a good investment?"

"To the contrary, I have already purchased the land," Charles answered. "Two properties along River Road, and another in Donaldsonville."

"I'm not sure I follow the problem."

"He wants more." Charles' eyes widened. "Marius has ten properties he is looking at, for us to consider. Yes, that's right, ten. The man is set on owning everything along the river from Natchez to New Orleans if no one stops him." He paused, then laughed, as if needing to show his comment was in good nature when, in fact, it was not. "Marius, no doubt, has a keen mind for business. But the South will not secede. Not for anything."

Jacob realized how the South had been caught so far off guard with the power the North brought upon them if other Southern men shared his laissez-faire denial of current affairs. "I can't see the future," Jacob lied, "but if we look back over the past, land has always been the most valuable asset in any man's arsenal. It not only holds value but nearly always increases. I see no harm, if you still want my advice, in purchasing land as an investment."

There. He'd told the truth without giving anything away. His mentors would be so proud.

"A fair point, Lord Donnelly," Charles said, eyes to the ceiling as he contemplated Jacob's words. "And land, to a lord, is everything."

Jacob nodded in agreement.

"Thank you for your perspective on the matter," Charles said, rising, his eyes on the clock with an increase of panic. "I apologize, Lord Donnelly. I am late for another engagement on the plantation, though we haven't yet discussed your own business here. How inconsiderate of me. I truly do beg your apology and promise to remedy this oversight in short refrain."

"Things happen." Jacob shrugged. *Sure, things happen. Way to sound like a damn lord.*

"After dinner? We can continue on to the parlor after the ladies finish and discuss further, then?"

"That sounds fine to me, Monsieur Deschanel."

JACOB MEANDERED INTO THE CENTRAL HALL JUST AS VICTOR AND Amelia re-entered through the front door. Between Amelia's head-to-toe fluster, and Victor's secret smile, Jacob went numb with disbelief.

They hadn't seen him. He decided now was not the moment to explore this matter. His own frustrations were far less important than Amelia's greater ones, and he was afraid his famous temper would make an appearance and not retreat.

He ducked into the first room he saw. In modern days, this room had been converted to a guest suite for visitors, but today the space was a lady's parlor, evidenced by the needlework on the center table. Overhead, an ornate fresco of the Garden of Eden served as a constant reminder of Original Sin as they practiced their sewing.

Once upon a time, in the future, Jacob had kissed Amelia beneath the crystal chandelier in this room and asked her to marry him. Not the first time he'd asked, but he'd wanted to do it right, with a ring, falling to his knee with all the makings of a memory she deserved. She'd been the first to propose, and he was old-fashioned enough to want to correct that.

The recollection lingered upon him like an old scent. He closed his eyes, wondering if there was ever a point to wishing a return to a time when life was simpler.

Amelia and Victor's steps rang heavy in the hall, startling him. Their voices were low, hushed. He made out only a few of their parting words.

"Please. Stay away from me." Amelia's voice shook.

Victor's steps boomed as he seemed to draw closer to Amelia. "We are here until my father's business with your... cousin is concluded. Perhaps weeks."

"You're joking."

"I assure you, I am much wittier than that when prompted."

"You can't stay here."

"It seems I am left without a choice in the matter, as my father is determined to complete his business affairs before returning to St. Charles Parish."

"Then... just... stay *far away from me,"* she hissed, and her footfalls echoed across the soft boards as she ran up the stairs.

Jacob's hands turned to fists at his side. The night before, he had known Victor was not to be trusted, and now his intuition was clearly proving to be right.

Cianán, his mother's voice rang, from nowhere, loudly, clearly. *Fists win battles, not wars. You are not interested in battles. You are above such a skirmish. You are a warrior, not a fighter. Everything you have fought for, you have earned, not taken. There is a difference.*

"Aye, and some weapon words were spoken when that monster raped my wife," Jacob railed to the invisible figure dropping wisdom from beyond.

But his words had the desired effect, as taking the moment to stop and assess cooled Jacob's blood. Since when had he been jealous of other men? Men pursuing his wife was nothing new, and, in fact, had become an ongoing joke between them. *Creeper. Five o'clock,* he might say. *Ah, yes,* she would answer. *The lonely banker with no ring but a clear indentation on his fourth finger, and the sweat of regret shading his bloodshot eyes. I can already see my walk of shame in the morning.*

And this wasn't the same, not at all. Jacob hadn't overheard anything from his wife that should lead him to believe she was doing anything wrong. If anything, she seemed to be averse to Victor, seeking to put distance between them.

But why?

He would deal with the man later, but if he must choose between protecting Amelia and harming Victor, he would always choose his wife.

Once Victor's own steps faded away, Jacob moved to exit and followed his wife. Instead, yelling from Charles' office stopped him where he stood.

While the house had been built from strong oak and cypress, it did not have the modern soundproofing of new homes. Jacob could hear every word traveling from behind the closed door.

"What you are doing is criminal! It cannot be borne!" Jacob instantly recognized the pitched, animalistic intonations of Brigitte.

"I am head of this household, whether you choose to accept and respect it or not," Charles boomed in return. Something hard dropped onto his desk, shaking the floors. "I have allowed your treasonous beliefs too long, and our children will not suffer for your wickedness!"

"Suffer? You want to discuss suffering? What of our blood, our *gift,* our most sacred of blessings? You would throw it away for money!"

"I would save this family from ruin. Ophélie, Jean, Fitz... they will all forge their own destinies and not be bound to the evil at the backbone of ours."

Brigitte's anger was so potent Jacob could feel it where he stood. "You know *nothing.*"

"Your opinion is as useful to me as the blight on last year's cane."

Brigitte returned his insult, wielding hers like a sword, with a power suggesting it was all she had against him.

Jacob had heard enough; certainly, far more than either of the hosts intended. He quietly slipped out of the room and up the stairs.

9
AMELIA

When Brigitte sent for her, by way of the sweet house girl, Clara, Amelia understood there was only one answer to the invitation. In electing to stay in the past, for now, they surrendered the luxury of choice to protect their secret.

She didn't loathe the idea of passing a couple hours with Brigitte as much as she might have the night before, if only because she was desperate to have the encounter with Victor pushed far from her mind. She couldn't even think of his words... of their implications. Not usually a fan of self-deception, she saw the value in it now. With her senses already on overload, she had to tackle her surroundings and their reality one step at a time, or she would lose her mind.

Amelia checked her eyes once in the mirror, blotted her tears, and left the room.

She saw Jacob on the way down, but only offered him a fleeting, guilty smile, mumbling something about tea with

Brigitte. Amelia heard him pause in the middle of the stairs; sensed his unanswered questions follow her long after she'd reached the foyer.

Too much for one day. Not now.

Brigitte was already in the ladies' parlor, seated on an emerald Rococo *meridienne*. Needlework lay across her lap as she lifted a teacup to her lips, blew across the surface of the hot liquid, and affected the daintiest of sips.

Satan has apparently been to finishing school, Amelia thought while straightening the front of her dress and, drawing a deep breath, entered.

As her pointed shoes made contact with the carpet, Ophélie exclaimed in delight. When Brigitte shot her a sharp look, the girl settled back into her seat, smiled, and said, "Welcome, Lady Donnelly."

"Yes, welcome," Brigitte said. "Ophélie was just finishing her needlework. For the third time."

Ophélie set her linen aside, and hung her head, face flushed.

"I was never very good at it either," Amelia offered helpfully, which drew a smile from Ophélie and a raised brow from the hostess.

"Indeed? Do they not teach ladies respectable pastimes in England, then?"

"They teach them," Amelia replied, with a conspiratorial glance at Ophélie, "but not all ladies have the aptitudes of their teachers."

"Hmph." Brigitte set her mural aside, a floral arrangement lacking in much actual color but technically precise. "I cannot say I agree. Skill is not a matter of aptitude but focus. Ophélie, despite that you see before you a complete lack of talent now, was far worse when I took her under my strict tutelage. Is that not right, daughter?"

"Yes, Maman."

"So, you see, practice creates skill where none exists."

"I'm sure you're right," Amelia answered, eyeing the teacup sitting before her with increasing suspicion. Poison was much harder to detect in a nineteenth-century autopsy. "The tea is nice, thank you."

"Charles imported it from Britain, so I should hope so," Brigitte said. "Lady Donnelly, I would like to know how will you teach your daughters to do things if you have not bothered to learn them yourself?"

Amelia's heart caught. From the moment she'd entered the parlor, the potency of Brigitte's dark aura permeated the air around her, threatening to breach the surface of her emotional barrier. Brigitte was baiting her, but why? "I don't have a daughter, Madame."

"Sons, then?"

"No children at all," Amelia said, feeling shame on this fact for perhaps the first time in her life, even though this woman's opinion meant nothing to her.

Brigitte scowled. Her teacup rattled in the saucer as if dropped there in shock or displeasure. "Why, you're practically an old maid, Lady Donnelly. Are you barren?"

"Maman!" Ophélie cried. The scandalized expression on the young girl's face piqued Amelia's curiosity. Surely, she had witnessed her mother's cruelty on many occasions. That her words now were shocking had to mean something.

Brigitte raised a hand in her daughter's direction, and continued on, past Amelia's aghast expression. "If not barren, then there must be an explanation. Do you find it a struggle to complete your wifely duties?"

Heat burned Amelia's cheeks. Her heartbeat throbbed so hard in her neck she had an urge to clap a hand over it. Anger and... fear. Yes, fear. This woman would harm her if given the opportunity, and not only with her words. "No offense, Madame, but that's my business."

This didn't pause Brigitte's interrogation. "A mother without children is a crime against nature," she accused. Her aura grew darker, darker with every word, but her tone suggested she might be discussing her distaste of root vegetables. "For those cursed by God, and fallen women."

"I'm neither," Amelia said evenly, trying to equally hide her growing fear of the woman and how deeply her words had cut. *You're the reason I don't have them, you horrible woman. You and your curse on this family, your hatefulness. Only now that I can see it with my own two eyes do I realize how you could have successfully damned our family all by yourself.*

"How can we know?" Brigitte shared a glance with Ophélie as if they were equal in their opinion of Amelia. No doubt she expected this loyalty from her daughter. "You come to us without invitation, and we do not even know how to define your relation to us, do we?"

"Maman," Ophélie whispered, growing further horrified. The girl's reaction was more unsettling to Amelia than anything else about this conversation. If Brigitte's behavior was out of line by Ophélie's standards, there was only one common denominator in the equation. "She is our guest."

"My husband will be discussing our business with your husband shortly," Amelia answered, burying her hands in her dress to disguise her nervous fidgeting. "As for our personal lives, those will not be part of the discussion."

"I cannot pretend to understand your culture," Brigitte said, reasonably enough. "Or any culture that would ordain a woman's role as anything other than mother of her husband's children. But I request you do not put ideas in my daughter's head about this independence of yours. Her life will be nothing like that."

Amelia hardly heard her. She had wandered elsewhere in her mind, to a cold cabin in the woods, to those few and final moments where she'd first learned about her own pregnancy and had it stolen from her before she could discern what it meant. Amelia would never tell this woman any of this. She wouldn't give her anything that might allow the horrid woman to hold power over her.

The decision had been made in the cabin. Amelia was done allowing *anyone* to hold power over her.

Ophélie hung her head, but Amelia saw the tears. "I would never suggest your daughter's life should be like mine," she said, drawing her eyes away from Ophélie lest her mother follow and also see the emotion there. "Though I hope she will decide for herself."

Brigitte cackled. "For herself! What notions you Brits have. No children? To even fathom that. And now, doing as one pleases? I will thank you to keep your reformist propaganda to yourself, Lady Donnelly. It has no place under my roof."

Ophélie wiped her eyes and straightened herself. "Maman, as you know, I am a most obedient daughter who will always do as you and Papa please. But Lady Donnelly is from a place foreign to us all, and her customs may be different than ours."

Amelia winced, knowing Ophélie would pay later for coming to her defense.

"They are not simply different. They are wrong," Brigitte replied. "But let it not be said that I am not a gracious hostess." With a sharp glance at the grandfather clock, she grunted. "We are late for our afternoon reading from the Bible. Will you join us, Lady Donnelly?"

Amelia, not seeing much of a choice, nodded.

Brigitte lifted the leather book in her hands and pretended to search for the right passage. A series of folded pages gave her away. "Ahh, yes, I believe this will do nicely."

Ophélie obediently raised her eyes to the sordid fresco above, and whispered, "Oh, Lord, forgive us, thy women, for we are full of sin and have caused all turmoil upon this earth, Amen."

"Amen," Brigitte agreed, smiling. "Ophélie, will you read for us from Proverbs? Start at 5:1."

"Yes, Maman." Ophélie's face went blank. Nervous. "My son, pay attention to my wisdom, turn your ear to my words of insight, that you may maintain discretion and your lips may preserve knowledge. For the lips of the adulterous woman drip honey, and her speech is smoother than oil, but in the end, she is bitter as gall, sharp as a double-edged sword."

"Yes, Lord," Brigitte whispered, rocking forward, eyes shut in reverence.

Ophélie cast a contemptuous look at her mother and continued. "Her feet go down to death; her steps lead straight to the grave. She gives no thought to the way of life; her paths wander aimlessly, but she does not know it. Now then, my sons, listen to me; do not turn aside from what I say. Keep to a path far from her, do not go near the door of her house, lest you lose your honor to others and your dignity to one who is cruel, lest strangers feast on your wealth and your toil enrich the house of another."

"Lord, deliver us from the evil sins of woman," Brigitte joined.

Amelia stared at the mistress of the house, floored by her gall. *She wants to stone me. She yet might.*

"At the end of your life you will groan, when your flesh and body are spent," Ophélie went on. "You will say, 'How I hated discipline! How my heart spurned correction! I would not obey my teachers or turn my ear to my instructors. And I was soon in serious trouble in the assembly of God's people.'"

"Amen," Brigitte said, her head moving side to side in a deliberate manner. "Amen."

"Should I finish, Maman?" Ophélie's gaze traveled between her mother and her new friend, gauging both reactions with anxious, wide eyes.

Brigitte stood by way of response, crossing her hands over her waist. "Lady Donnelly, you are most welcome here."

No, that was not what she meant. Not at all. The venom lacing through her words was almost palpable. *You are not safe here. I would see the end of you before ever embracing you. You do not belong here. You, and your wicked sin. Stay at your own peril.*

Amelia squeezed her temper down, packaging it neatly beside the fear and other blackened emotions threatening to spread the longer she spent with Brigitte Deschanel.

She rose. "Thank you, Madame," she replied, mustering the last bit of graciousness left within her. "Your hospitality is more than I had hoped for."

Did Brigitte detect the underlying sarcasm? Maybe. Perhaps she didn't care. Amelia had the strong sense, though no proof, that Brigitte knew she was not who she said. That she was well aware Amelia was no lady, not from England or elsewhere, and that, sooner or later, this information would be used to harm her.

Once Brigitte was safely in the hall, Amelia released the desperate breath stuck in her lungs.

"I am so sorry. I don't know what got into my mother," Ophélie whispered, but hurried after the woman in question, probably afraid of worsening her punishment by lingering with the person her mother had all but labeled a prostitute.

I know what got into her: me. But why?

Amelia afforded Ophélie a brief smile, desperate to be back in her suite, alone, where no one else's emotions could harm her.

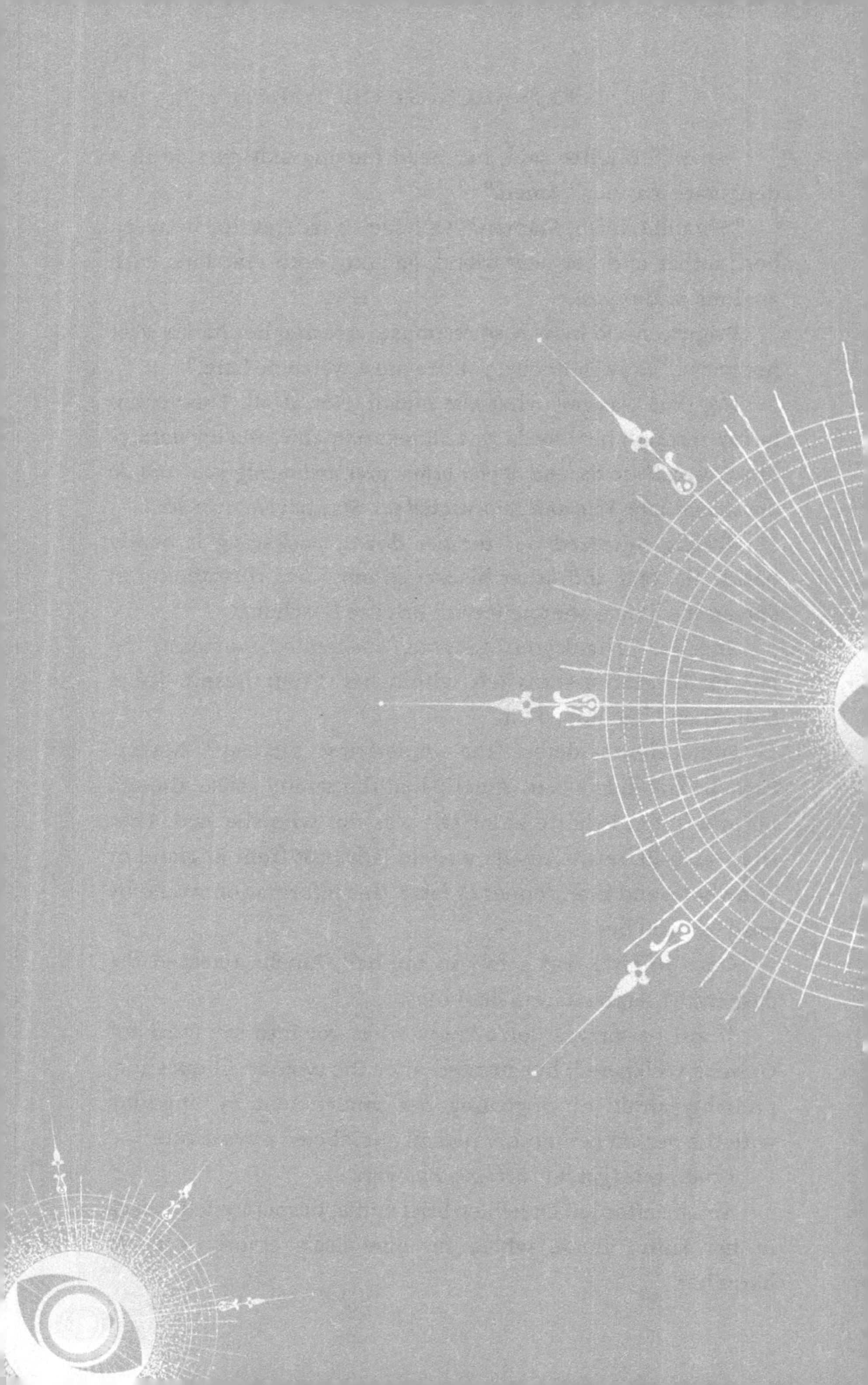

10
AMELIA

Ophélie double-checked the lock at her bedroom. For a fleeting moment, she felt secure again. She didn't think he would break down the door. Their arrangement—or more truthfully, Jean and their mother's belief in the sheer rightness of their desires—relied on absolute discretion.

She wrapped the shawl tighter, pausing for a moment. Thinking. Just go, *she thought.* Go to bed, and when you wake up, it will be another day, and there will be no mention at all of the locked door.

To live in a world where she could believe that was her greatest dream. But a dream it was. Ophélie could suffer now, or suffer later, but her lot in this life had been cast long before her birth.

Choking back a small cry, a sound stemming from years of fear and painful knowledge, Ophélie's tiny hand reached out to turn back the key.

She was once again exposed.

Her governess had slipped out moments before, on orders from Brigitte. Mere seconds ago, in fact, Ophélie had unearthed a brief flash of courage and rotated the key to locked.

Ophélie blew out the flame on the oil lamp and climbed into bed.

She had little choice now but to wait. Feigning sleep would not matter to Jean. To either of them. This situation was not about her, and had never been. In the eyes of Brigitte, the woman who had given birth to her and claimed the moniker of maman, Ophélie's arrival into this world had always only ever been to serve one purpose.

Only Ophélie, though, seemed to know it would all be for naught. All Brigitte's planning, her machinations, would come to nothing in the end. Ophélie had seen it all. She saw everything.

Revealing the truth would do nothing but expose her to further abuse and insult. No one would believe her. They would think she'd fabricated the information to protect herself from further injustice.

Ophélie could not decide which was worse: the nightly fear from her dangerous nocturnal visitor, or knowing it would all be over soon. Forever.

She turned in the bed and gripped the quilt tight to her chin. Shivers ran through her, though the room was warm from the coals dying in the hearth. Angry with herself for even allowing the lapse a moment earlier at the door, her only protection from the pain was to accept it. Denial would force her to relive the horrors over and over again. Complacency was her only shield.

The iron handle of the door creaked as it turned. He stepped lightly, not wanting to wake the others in the household. As if everyone else living under this roof did not already know the terrors he inflicted on his older sister.

Once in the room, Jean's demeanor changed from a fifteen-year-old boy to a fierce and fiery man. He threw back the covers and Ophélie couldn't help the timid glance back. Their eyes met, and he was no longer her brother. He could turn that persona off and on like a switch.

Tonight, as with every night, Jean was the man who would father her child.

AMELIA AWOKE WITH SUCH A START THAT SHE SMACKED HER HEAD INTO the headboard. Her eyes traveled the room, taking in the details of her surroundings, grounding her. She had taught many of her patients about the process of grounding—the skill that brought others from the peak of a bout of anxiety or mania by studying and fixing on their surroundings, one by one—but few knew how often she employed the technique herself.

The vivid sense of *realness* of her dream was unlike her usual ones. She *was* Ophélie. The only time she'd experienced anything like this was her visions of past lives as Cerridwen.

But *this* clearly wasn't *that*, so what was it?

You're stressed is all. Worried for Ophélie after you saw how her brother looks at her, and how Brigitte treated you both earlier. Your dreams often inform you of danger, and you know she's at risk.

"Maybe," Amelia whispered breathlessly. Jacob's soft exhales continued uninterrupted, his chest rising and falling in the darkness. Outside, crickets chirped their satin song into the night air.

She started to lay her head back against the pillow when her ears caught a very unusual sound: the squealing cries of a newborn baby.

Amelia glanced over at Jacob, then toward the door, as if either might provide the answer. The crying continued, escalating in volume. No babies were at *Ophélie*, not since Brigitte's children had grown. The only visitors on the property, the two of them and the de Blancheforts, were adults. She supposed one of the housemaids might have an infant, but with

Brigitte's foul temperament, she doubted the poor thing would be sleeping in the house for long.

She squinted against the moonlight, looking for the time on the tall clock in the corner. Half past three. With a defeated sigh, she accepted her sleep on this night had ended, not after that startling, vivid dream. And now this.

The cries faded to squeals before intensifying to a shocking shriek. Amelia's gaze shot to her sleeping husband, who surely couldn't have slept through that. How could anyone?

Perhaps it wasn't her business... *definitely,* it wasn't her business... but she couldn't lie in bed for the next few hours wondering.

Her bare feet made no sound, but the cypress floorboards, still new in this time, creaked as they settled under her light steps.

Amelia winced, taking even more care with her movement. It was important she wake no one in her trek, though she could not say exactly why.

Once her eyes adjusted to the darkness and she had her bearings, she shifted focus to listening. The sound traveled... down. It definitely came from the third floor. But that level was reserved for the heir's suites, and to venture into their private area was even more foolish than following a phantom sound in the night.

The baby shrieked again, followed by several pleasurable giggles. Amelia went completely still. Now she was sure what she'd heard had come from upstairs. She only needed to decide if she could live with the risk.

With a sharp draw of breath, Amelia ascended the staircase letting each foot hang midair before landing on the next step.

With each tread, she listened, heart racing, to make sure no other sounds came from the third floor.

At the top of the staircase, Amelia paused, again taking in her surroundings and readjusting to the new setting. The moon spilled through a dormer window at the far end of the hall, lighting the Oriental carpet in a sinister fashion, the curls and floral designs spelling out what seemed inexplicably like a warning. A long row of her ancestor's faces on the wall watched with knowing eyes. *Thanks, universe. As if I really needed a sign this wasn't my best idea.*

Her stomach rumbled, a noise she was certain was even louder than the distressed baby and would undoubtedly wake the house. She regretted skipping dinner but couldn't make herself sit in a room with both Victor and Brigitte after...

Focus!

Amelia held her breath on her way down the hall, following the cries. She slipped past the suites and drew closer to the window, frowning when she neared the end of the hall. Was the sound coming from outside?

With her last step, an enclave came into view on the left, hidden in the shadows. Ophélie was comprised of many oddly-shaped rooms, nooks, and crannies, but Amelia had never seen this one, not in all her years of visiting for family events, sleep-overs, weddings, or funerals.

This was the spot, though. She was certain. A loud, but exceptionally clear wail came from *right here*. It could not be more than a few feet away. And now her empath senses picked up the final confirmation that the whine came from physical life, an emotion: fear.

She halted before the dark passage. It wasn't deep; no more than a standard coat closet, and she swiveled her gaze, trying to discern the purpose of this small cutout space when something tickled her nose.

Amelia looked up. A band of braided twine fell from a hook on the ceiling, and at once it all came together. *An attic. But not the main one. How did I never know, after all these years, that* Ophélie *had a second attic?*

She reached for the twine when the soft patter of measured steps echoed behind her. Her heart leaped into the back of her throat as one hand poised in midair, froze in horror.

Someone had followed her.

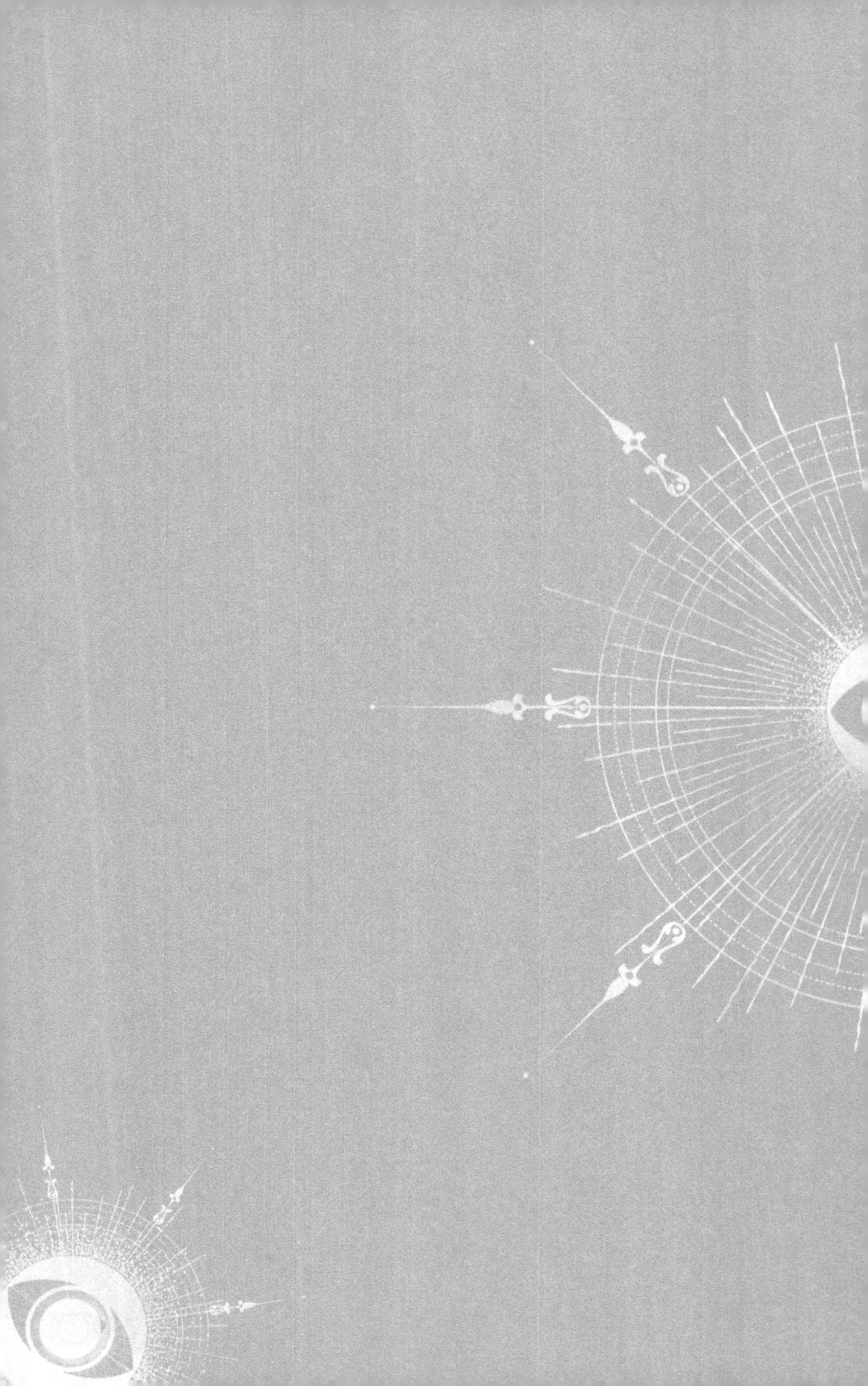

11

JACOB

"It's just me, *Blanca,*" Jacob whispered, sidling up behind her. He focused up at the attic entry with the same bewildered gaze his wife wore. "So you heard it, too?"

"The baby?" Amelia blinked slowly, in a daze, her eyes locked on the attic.

Jacob nodded, then leaned his head back to concentrate on noises above. "It really does sound like it's coming from up there, doesn't it?"

"But why would they put a baby in the attic? Who would do that?"

"Ritual sacrifice?" Jacob suggested with a sleepy shrug. He was only half-kidding.

"I wouldn't put it above Brigitte," Amelia muttered. She hadn't looked at him, still fixated on the attic door. The baby's cries had grown louder as if sensing help was on the way. Jacob mused now, as he had on the slow walk upstairs, how no one but the two of them had stirred. "We have to go up there."

"Uhh."

"Jacob!"

"I don't disagree with you, it's just..." She was right. If a baby was in that attic, they couldn't leave it there. But this was not their house or even their *year*.

"I know." Amelia answered the remainder of his unsaid entreaty with a measured nod. She again glanced above them. "But we have to anyway."

"This seems to be a recurring pattern in our adventures together," Jacob said. He offered a forced smile only slightly more enthusiastic than he felt inside.

"Maybe that should tell us something," Amelia whispered under her breath, so quiet Jacob couldn't tell if she wanted him to hear or not. His heart dropped at how easily she found them said.

"Amelia..."

"I need your help, Donnelly," she shot back, teeth gritted as she began to tug on the twine. She struggled to balance her force between getting it open and not opening it so fast it smacked her in the face.

"Right." Jacob reached up to brace the attic door when it dropped, gesturing for her to pull harder. The heavy oak hit his palms with a burst of force, and he was knocked back, stumbling several steps in the process. Amelia had firmly grabbed his shoulders, righting him. The ladder plummeted to its full length with a powerful thump.

Any question over the source of the keening cries was eliminated with the door open. The crying was no longer muffled but crystal clear, with the precision of being in the immediate vicinity.

"I'll go first," she offered, brushing her hands over his nightshirt to repel the heavy layer of dust that collapsed over him.

"Overruled," he replied and eased her aside with a gentle

nudge. She huffed at him, but there wasn't a chance he would let her go first ever again when potential danger lurked. He'd live with the consequences of her running away for the rest of his life.

"Be careful," she called after him in hushed tones. He felt her hands steadying the rungs from the bottom, and was relieved she hadn't followed. "Who the hell knows what's up there."

"I believe I possess the answer to your question."

The sudden appearance of Brigitte caused Jacob to slip and fall back onto the floor with a painful thud. Amelia cried out, at him, at the intruder, at both.

Brigitte towered over Jacob, no small feat with her diminutive figure. She cast an imposing shadow as she regarded him with open, unmasked hostility.

Jacob used the rungs of the ladder to pull himself up and out of the compromised position. "We didn't mean to wake you," he said, and immediately realized how ridiculous this sounded. A quick glance in Amelia's direction confirmed to him she was equally unsettled.

"You cannot wake one who does not sleep," Brigitte replied in an odd, offhand way. Her eyes narrowed again. "Yet you have no qualms about sneaking about in my house like a common thief."

"That wasn't our intention at all," Amelia explained quickly, stepping forward. "We heard the sound of a... well, this is going to sound insane, I suppose..."

"On with it," Brigitte demanded, squaring her stance.

"We heard a baby crying," Jacob finished. He buried his hands in his hair, an old nervous habit, then pulled them out again, considering she might somehow enjoy his disconcertment. Amidst the awkward silence that followed, he realized why Amelia had fumbled through her explanation.

The child's cries had stopped altogether the moment Brigitte appeared.

"What you're suggesting does indeed ring of insanity. We have no babies at *Ophélie*," Brigitte confirmed. "The property is simply haunted." Her dark hair spilled over the front of her white gown, which had an unbuttoned gap at the breasts, displaying them in full. The exposure, instead of putting her at a disadvantage, instead had the effect of a calculated power play. "You have no business stealing around my home, in places I have not authorized you to be. My husband may be enamored by your titles and the *prestige* you bring from the other end of the world, but I have no such predilections and cannot recommend you make such a blunder again while you remain under our roof."

"It won't happen again," Jacob and Amelia replied in near unison.

"You're right, Lord Donnelly," Brigitte said. Her eyes were granite daggers. "It will not."

Jacob slipped his hand through Amelia's in a signal of harmony. A shield, perhaps their only defense from this strangely hostile woman. To his pleasure—and he hated to admit it, but also surprise—Amelia squeezed his hand.

Together, they smiled at their host. Together, they choked down their fear. Together, they walked past Brigitte and steeled themselves against her threats.

"That wasn't a haunting," Jacob whispered against the back of Amelia's head. His arms wrapped around her hips from behind, ignoring how she stiffened at his touch once they were again alone.

"I know."

"She knows it too," he decided, realizing the truth of this as he recalled her threats, both voiced and implied. "What's she hiding? I don't understand why there would be a baby in the attic to begin with, but if there was, how did it get to that?"

"With her, take your pick of reasons." Amelia settled into her pillow with a yawn. "You didn't see how she treated me over tea this afternoon. I would be more surprised to see her do something kind."

"I forgot you had tea with her. I had an interesting meeting with Charles today as well, and I think, maybe even earned his respect. I feel better about us being here, anyway. Less worried they might kick us out for fraud. How did tea go?"

"I can't imagine it any worse than it was," Amelia replied. The words were muffled into the pillow. "She had her mind made up about me before ever saying a word."

"We should share information and compare notes, too." He brushed a stray band of hair off the side of her face. "We didn't really see each other all day."

"Tomorrow," she said. "We need to at least try to get some sleep."

A polite brush-off, but one, nonetheless. Jacob didn't understand how going back in time had pulled him further from his wife than he had ever been. He sighed. "Okay, *Blanca.* But if we hear that sound again, we need to do something."

"I know."

"Maybe you could ask Ophélie about it tomorrow?"

"Yeah. Maybe."

Exhausted confusion kept him from saying more. He could continue to voice the questions, but Amelia had the same ones, and neither of them possessed any answers.

"I love you, *Blanca,*" he sang into her ear, moments later, but she was either asleep by then or pretending to be.

DAY THREE

12
OPHÉLIE

"Have you met them, Papa? What did you think?"

Charles perched upon the library ladder, concentration creasing his brows and the sides of his mouth. His fingers ran along the spines of a row of books with a gentle mumble. Ophélie could see this without looking at him. She knew when her father was on a mission.

At the sound of her voice, some of the tension left him. "Yes, *ma petit*. I passed part of yesterday afternoon with Lord Donnelly, and he seems a charming fellow, if different from the gentlemen we know along the river. I have not had the pleasure of more than a brief introduction with the lady, but I understand you have taken her under your wing?"

"Yes, Papa," Ophélie answered proudly. She bowed in reverence. Her hands rested atop one another, in front of her, eager to show him her strong comportment. "She is a most kindred spirit."

"I'm pleased you have a companion, even if it is temporary," her father said. Charles pulled a crimson leather-bound tome from the second to top shelf and blew the dust off the top, examining it. "I'm very proud of you for being such a gracious hostess. It comes very natural to you, as it did your grandmother." He replaced the book. "You'll make a fine plantation mistress."

"That is my greatest desire," she said, shifting. Ophélie didn't know the right approach for what she was about to say next, or how it might affect her relationship with her father. "Maman... she seems angry with me, though."

"Whatever for?"

"You see, she has not been... well... she has not been..."

"On with it, *ma petit*. There's nothing to be gained by taking a longer route to the point."

Ophélie nodded. "She has not been very kind to our guests... in particular, Lady Donnelly. And she seems angry with me for taking on the role that should have been hers."

Charles stiffened. "I see. And why do you believe this to be so?"

"Her behavior toward Lady Donnelly reminds me of how she comports herself around Hector." She spit the words out quickly as if needing to be rid of them. It was blasphemy to infer her mother would treat a treasured guest with the same bland disdain as she treated their slaves, and Ophélie had never seen her mother treat *anyone* of her social equal the way she'd treated the lady the day before in the parlor.

Ophélie could also never share her own desire to free all the slaves if given the reins.

Her father descended the ladder and slowly approached. His hands came down on her shoulders. "You know your maman's moods are not like most." He pulled his mouth into a tight line. "But you mustn't speak of your mother in such ways. It isn't proper for a young lady on the eve of her own household to manage."

"Of course, Papa." She struggled to balance the shame in

her feelings and her need to express them.

Charles planted a kiss on the top of her head. Affectionate, but dismissive. As he turned to complete the task at hand, she caught the darkness pass through his eyes.

"Papa, is something troubling you?"

He continued to face away. "As the master of land and law, I am always beset with one trouble or another," he said carefully, each word seeming to be a deliberate choice. "They are not troubles for you, *ma petit.* Even when you are a mistress yourself, I would see you as innocent and preserved as the bisque dolls lining your shelf. That is the role of a husband and father, to take on all the world's troubles so the women can remain unspoiled."

This was not an answer at all, and Ophélie knew it. "I cannot help but worry about you, Papa. You are the dearest to me in all the world."

Charles sagged at her words and returned to her at once, pulling her into his arms with a fierce squeeze. "As you are to me, *ma petit.* But your papa is a strong man. A force, if you will allow me that indulgence. I built our life here from nothing, and if the world ended tomorrow, I would construct us another. There is no trouble I cannot weather, child." He loosened his grip and, with his thumb, lifted her chin. Charles gifted a soft, brief kiss on his daughter's lips, such tenderness as he had not done since she was much younger. "You, also, must continue to rise above the pain and hurt of the world around us. Let it go, Ophélie. There is no gain in dwelling on circumstances we cannot change."

Ophélie swallowed back a sob. If only he knew.

"And you must trust I know what troubles you most, *ma petit,* and am doing everything within my power to see you free of this pain."

. . .

Her father's words haunted her all morning, and into the afternoon. They lingered over the picnic with Lady Donnelly like an unspoken promise.

Lady Donnelly sensed it. She poured them both some lemon water and settled back on the quilt. "Ophélie, what's wrong?"

Oh, how much I would welcome a confidante. But it isn't safe, for either of us. "My room was too warm last night. I slept very poorly."

Lady Donnelly's mouth twitched, and she cast her eyes down. "Have you tried this candy? It's incredible."

"The trifles? The de Blancheforts brought them. Their family sent them from France."

"I've been meaning to ask you about them," Lady Donnelly said. The look that followed was peculiar but guarded. "And their visit here."

"Oh, yes. The de Blanchefort family has been here far more in the past year, but they are regular guests at *Ophélie*," Ophélie explained. She didn't add that Victor's presence unsettled her. That she sometimes dreamed of him. "Marius de Blanchefort is Papa's most trusted business partner."

"But is it always only the two of them?"

"The women come if we have a fête, such as they did for my birthday celebration. It wouldn't be appropriate for them to visit on business unless my mother invited them for a social call. But Maman is... as you may have gathered from yesterday... not always a natural hostess." This was not a false statement, but Ophélie still puzzled over her maman's particular aversion to Lady Donnelly.

"No, I mean..." Lady Donnelly paused in mid-thought, in debate with herself. "Is it always Victor who accompanies his father?"

If it were anyone but the lady, this line of questioning

would make Ophélie uncomfortable, but she felt as if they had been friends many years and no questions were off limits. "Yes, usually."

Lady Donnelly tilted her head to the left. "Does he not have other children, then? Other sons?"

Ophélie brightened at the opportunity to share more useful information. "Ah, yes! He has a daughter, Marion, who married Jacques Bonapartie, and *their* daughter, Julianne, is betrothed to my brother, Jean." Observing her friend's patient smile, she got on with it. "He has one other son, Philippe. He and Victor are co-heirs, as they are twins. Twin heirs are uncommon here, but Marius solved this by willing *Coquillage*, his plantation, to Victor and building one identical in every way on the adjoining land, called *Petit a Petit*. In true twin fashion, both men have always copied one another. They each even married ladies from the Roman family!" She lowered her voice. "It is said they are even building rival tombs between the two houses so they may be equal in death, if you can believe the rumors."

Lady Donnelly did not seem entertained by this notion. "Why doesn't Philippe ever accompany his father?"

Ophélie considered this. "Why, I don't know. One would suppose he might, from time to time, but I have only seen him on occasion, and never on a business call."

"And no one else finds this peculiar?"

"I don't suppose I've heard anyone but you mention it." She looked down and away as the words left her lips, for they were at least in part a lie. *She* had wondered these things but had not believed it appropriate to ask. She wished she had a female confidante to speak to. One who might understand when she relayed how Victor's eyes on her, all these years, left her feeling both exposed and protected.

Ophélie watched Lady Donnelly who was pitched back on her elbows, a position far more appropriate for a man, her snowy hair cascading against the red and blue checkered pattern of the blanket. She was witnessing the woman with her guard down, in a moment where she'd utterly forgotten who she was and how to be that person.

Ophélie loved her then.

But also, with her façade laid briefly aside, Lady Donnelly was not only exposed from without but also within. Whatever she had carried with her on her voyage had been stowed deep, for no one's perusal but her own. Yet Ophélie could see it as if her new friend was painted with a brush of opaque black.

Her upbringing dictated it wrong to request her friend share with her when she wasn't ready to reciprocate, but Ophélie did not know how much time they had, so none should be wasted. "My apologies if this is too forward, my lady—"

"Amelia," the white-haired fairy lying across from her corrected. "Forget the formalities when we're in private. They're tedious."

"Amelia..." Ophélie blushed. Even the thought of referring to her elders, especially married ones, by a given name, without even an added softener of a title, made her feel like seeking penance. "I know you may find this odd for me to say, but I can sense things in others. Certain truths, you might say. And I perceive in you a great injustice done to you by an unspeakable evil." The red in her cheeks deepened to a dark burgundy. "I know I shouldn't say such things, but I find it easy to talk around you."

Amelia's expression was impassable, but her eyes traveled to somewhere far from where they sat under the afternoon sky. Then, to Ophélie's great surprise, she said, "Something terrible did happen before we arrived here. It isn't an event I would ever want to burden you with, sweet Ophélie, but I thank you for noticing and caring enough to ask."

With anyone else, Ophélie would only need to reach with the invisible fingers of her mind and parse through the memories to find the full answer. Her maman would be angry if she knew Ophélie could do this, especially after sharing how her own abilities had all but disappeared when coming to Louisiana, so she had always kept this strange gift to herself. No one ever suspected, and she never let anyone in on the secret. This unusual ability to read minds was how she knew her father's love for her was genuine, and her mother's was not.

Yet Amelia, from the very beginning, had been blocked to Ophélie.

Amelia was undoubtedly special, but Ophélie sensed more than that. Much more. And, as she began to associate her strange visions with the possibility they might, in fact, be memories, she knew Amelia's sudden presence in her life was no coincidence.

"You can talk to me," Ophélie said, placing a hand against the soft down of Amelia's arm. "I would never share your confidence with others, and you might find I understand more than most believe me to."

"Oh," Amelia said, with the start of a smile, "of that I have no doubt."

Ophélie blushed again. "You and I have our secrets, La... Amelia. We both have experienced situations we wish had not happened."

"Everyone has," Amelia said quickly. With a steady, thoughtful breath, she added, "If I can do anything, anything at all, about..."

When Amelia faltered, Ophélie finished for her. "There's nothing you can do about Jean. That mold is long set."

Amelia's eyes widened, perhaps shocked at the easy confirmation. "Ophélie, you don't have to allow it! You have rights, too, even if you might have been convinced otherwise."

"It isn't about personal freedom. Did you not have rights when you were hurt?"

"They were stripped from me, as yours are being stripped now. In both cases, the offense was criminal."

Ophélie leveled her gaze. "And when have we known criminals to obey the laws of either society or government? Isn't that what they are, by the very definition of a criminal, someone who has no regard for either?"

Amelia sat forward, throwing her arms up. "He is your *brother*!"

"Yes, he is. And my mother should also be a protector, but instead, she has taken another role. My father would protect me, but cannot," Ophélie said, far past sadness in the matter. "Lord Donnelly was your protector, but either could not or would not when it mattered. Is that right?"

Amelia turned away. "He saved my life. I wouldn't be here now if it weren't for his quick thinking."

Ophélie's voice dropped lower, kinder. "Yet he could not save you from the tragedy altogether. Do you understand now?"

"No, because you're implying we're victims to whatever the world wants to do with us," Amelia argued. Her hair had fallen over one shoulder, and her cheeks blazed with emotion. "That no matter how strong we are, or who we have on our side, there's certain inevitability in bad guys winning. Ophélie, that's a tragic line of thought. It's beyond nihilism. Do you really believe that?"

How could she explain that it was not the inevitability of evil prevailing, but certain patterns were destined to repeat? The dilemma now was her own fault for leading them there.

"Ophélie!" Her mother's voice grated across the grass. She

wasn't safe from it, even beneath the protection of the mighty live oaks. "There you are!"

Ophélie shared a brief glance with Amelia. They knew what was coming. "Maman! We were having the picnic I promised Lady Donnelly yesterday. Would you like the join us?"

Of course, she wouldn't. Brigitte hadn't arrived for a social call.

"We're going to be late, child," Brigitte chastised, lifting her skirts over the damp grass, appearing as if she might strike down the gods for allowing the wetness to graze her skin.

"For what, Maman?"

"Tea at Valcour Aime's, of course!"

Ophélie had not been informed of tea at the Aimes until that very moment, so she was certain her mother had contrived to get them an invite at the last minute, which was not only nearly impossible but also impolite. "I did not know. I'm sorry. Shall I change my dress?"

"At once!"

Ophélie apologized to Amelia by way of a quick glance. Any words on the matter would lead to a further scolding by her mother and mistreatment of her guest. "We can try again tomorrow?"

"Sure. Enjoy your tea," Amelia replied, flashing a quick wink only they could see.

Her mother had her by the elbow, nearly dragging her toward the house despite Ophélie keeping pace. When they reached the stairs, a thought occurred to her.

"Maman, should we not also invite Lady Donnelly?"

Brigitte spun on her with a glare that stopped Ophélie's heart. "What did I tell you? You stay *away* from Lady Donnelly!"

13
AMELIA

Ophélie was wrong. Unusually wise for a girl her age, but also completely and utterly wrong.

Growing up in a tenuous world, in a family beset by tragedy, it would be easier for Amelia to believe such deeds of evil could not be prevented, but to do so would also strip her of her agency. It would mean the difference between a single Baldur and thousands of them, all intent on ripping her power to shreds, over and over, with nothing to stop them.

Not only did she *not* believe this, but she also had no choice in that skepticism if she wanted to survive. She'd been on the verge of emotional collapse for days, and her faith was all she had left.

One of the housemaids appeared to collect the remnants of their picnic. Amelia had looked forward to her afternoon with Ophélie, who, despite their age and time differences, she felt an intense kinship with. She might say Ophélie was her friend.

Moving to rest her palm against the thick bark of the oak to steady herself to rise, Amelia found it a feat worthy of a medal in the restricting dress she was wearing. Instead of her hand making contact with the tree, however, it landed upon soft cotton and a firm, muscular arm.

Amelia gazed up with a start. Victor de Blanchefort cast a long shadow that ran across her and up the bark. Before she could resist the help, he'd pulled her onto her feet anyhow, and even boldly dusted off the back of her dress.

"I thought I was very clear." Her pulse quickened as his words from the day before returned to her in a rush. *I know who you are, and from where you come. Or should I say,* when?

"I figured your words were impulsive given you'd lost consciousness prior to saying them," Victor said reasonably, offering his arm again. She gawked at it with outright hostility, and he dropped it again.

"You accused me of lying," she returned, lifting her skirt to avoid the dewy grass as she rushed her steps.

"And you insinuated my father is someone else entirely. We are both full of accusations, it seems, though when I speak them, I make sure they are true," Victor replied, eyes alive with playfulness.

"Once again, you mistake me for someone who enjoys being screwed with."

"You continue to underestimate my sense of humor, Lady Donnelly," he said, brow raised. "Or am I overestimating yours?"

Amelia came to an abrupt stop halfway down the line of oaks. Her hands splayed at the top of her hips, her back ached from the third day of wearing torturous attire. She had no patience for whatever mischief he'd brought with him. "What is it you want from me, Monsieur de Blanchefort?"

Victor clutched his chest as if wounded. "We have devolved back to our respectful titles? You could have at least warned me."

"Answer the damn question, *Victor*."

The teasing behind his expression faded only slightly. "I want to know you better. Is that not evident?"

"And why would you? There's no reason for it," Amelia said. Her head shook furiously, expelling the idea and him. "We're both married, and I'm not even from here."

"Oh." He grinned. "Yes, you are. Or about a half hour, as the crow flies."

The first beads of sweat formed at her décolletage. "I'm from London."

"We both know you hail from New Orleans, although it looks decidedly different now than it will when *you* become a regular occupant."

Her stomach dropped in an instant. She hardened herself, not willing to lose it again in front of this man. Whatever he thought he knew, she couldn't allow it. If she didn't confirm his ridiculous accusations, he would be forced to drop them. "I will ask you again." Her words were slow, measured. Each one enunciated with a particular deliberateness. "*What do you want from me?*"

"And I already answered," Victor said. He backed up one step, affording her space to breathe. "I truly have no ulterior motive, Amelia. I know who you are, and I know you come from a time no one currently living will ever come to see. You are fully aware of this too, but you're simply too shocked to realize that *I* know it and wish to have a conversation on the matter. I already assured you I have no designs on sharing your well-guarded secret with anyone else and no aim toward harming you. On the contrary, I have very good reasons to see you safe, and more, happy."

"What reasons..." She couldn't finish. Her mouth was a bed of cotton.

"You need water," he said quickly, and directed her toward

the back of the house, to the well. Amelia allowed this, all the while wondering to herself, at how easily she had allowed him to guide and comfort her. She'd fallen into it in the natural way she had always succumbed to Jacob's efforts. One part of her needed him and his accusations to go far, far, away, and the other followed him with the blind ease of someone familiar to her for years.

They said nothing on the short trek to the rear of the house. Amelia tried to clear her mind of Victor's words, for any attempt at analysis would require a call to action on her part. She had nothing, not at this moment, anyway. Her strength ebbed and flowed, and not ever in any logical manner.

Victor drew a bucket from the well. Resting his hand on the back of her head, he tilted the heavy bucket in his free hand with surprising ease. The cool water burned her throat, but the relief was immediate.

"Thank you," she managed.

"My pleasure." Victor offered his arm again, and this time, she took it. "Have you spent much time in Brigitte's Garden? I have not found its equal on our soil, except at Valcour Aime's St. James Refinery."

Amelia said nothing. Her feet, one after the other, followed where he led.

Vivid floral arrays of the garden, of camellias, azaleas, of lilies, awakened her again, restoring her own vivacity. The foliage also shielded them from prying eyes of the workers, who were everywhere, always.

"People are going to start talking about us," she said, taking the bench across from the one where he settled, rather than easing in beside him. "They would be wrong, but that won't stop them."

"I'm not in the habit of giving credence to what others say about me." He leaned forward. "And neither are you."

"I don't want anyone to get the wrong idea. Not our hosts, and definitely not my husband."

"They were talking about us before you arrived," Victor laughed. "Aren't the sewing circles just as bold in your time?"

"You keep saying these bizarre things about *my time* as if I'm supposed to understand what you're talking about." It was weak. She knew it was pitiful. He knew it too.

Who are you, Victor? That's the question I should be asking. That's what I need to make myself ask.

Victor grinned. A light breeze whipped through the soft, short curls at his neck. "You're not ready. That's quite all right."

Amelia began her counter move, but any rebuttal with him, on any topic, was futile. He had an answer loaded, always. Victor was the person you would have wanted on your college debate team, but one you'd run fast and far to avoid if he tried to join you for drinks after.

"Are you going to continue to appear from thin air anytime I'm out and about?" she asked.

"I might."

"It's weird."

"That is not the worst thing someone has called me."

"No, it's more than that... I think you're upsetting Jacob. My husband," she said. Jacob handled her carefully now, so he hadn't mentioned Victor since that first night, but she knew he wanted to. If the roles were reversed, she would.

Or, at least, the Amelia before Baldur would have.

Victor appeared properly chastened. "That won't do at all. I'll find occasion to speak with him."

"I don't think that's such a great idea," she said. "What would be better is if you just left me alone until we both leave."

"Better for whom?"

"For all of us."

"Your sensibility, you mean." The playfulness of earlier had returned. "It is always far more work to address the truths of our lives than to avoid them. I believe it was Robert Frost who said, 'I shall be telling this with a sigh, somewhere ages and ages hence: Two roads diverged in a wood, and I— I took the one less traveled by, and that has made all the difference.'"

Amelia was no stranger to poetry, having taken several college courses specifically on the subject. "But Robert Frost..."

"Has not been born yet?" Victor finished. "No, I believe he is yet a twinkle in the stars above." He lifted his fingers skyward with a light sigh. "It will be a decade following the Great War before he appears in this world."

I don't want to know. I don't want to know. I don't—

No, but I need to know. The answers lay curled around his tongue, just waiting for my nudge.

Not now. Not yet.

"I need to get back," she said in haste. This was becoming her go-to get-away-from-Victor card, and it was ridiculous, but she could only handle so many pieces of the puzzle for one day.

I'm here for a purpose. I was the one who insisted this. That purpose might very well be right in front of me, and I'm pulling up the covers to block it out, like a scared child.

"Of course," Victor answered, a gentleman again. He rose and offered a hand, which she took, once again in a daze. He kissed the top. "You needn't be afraid of me, Amelia. Not now or ever."

"I'm not," she insisted, realizing it was true.

"No," he whispered, reading her. His smile from earlier returned. "You aren't."

• • •

No, SHE THOUGHT, AS SHE RAN TOWARD THE HOUSE, AWAY FROM Victor, away from her questions, toward even more. *I'm really not, but I should be.*

But I am afraid of what it might mean.

14
JACOB

The formal invite for dinner was delivered by a young girl with better manners than most of their hosts had shown. Jacob turned over the calling card—an odd choice to deliver to someone under their own roof, he thought—and before he could read the words, *A Return for Our Dearest One,* the girl fled.

Amelia, recently returned from an excursion flushed and in strange humor, looked up from where she sat reading a poetry book left for decoration. "What is it?"

"An invite for dinner." He read further down the page. "You said you hadn't seen their younger son, Fitz?"

Amelia nodded and set the book aside.

"You didn't see him because he wasn't here."

"Where was he?"

Jacob shrugged, not thinking of the invitation at all but how he'd earlier glimpsed his wife and de Blanchefort in the back garden. Laughing. "No clue. But he's returned."

"Odd." Amelia rose with a stretch, raising her long arms over her head. "I think I'll nap. This place makes me so tired."

This place, or one man in particular? The familiar surge of bloodlust appeared, the urge to fight, to take something essential from his opponent. Victor brought it out in him in a way no other man ever had, not even Oz.

Then, if Amelia seemed more relaxed since they arrived, and it was somehow attributed to this de Blanchefort fellow, should he not shake his hand and offer thanks instead? Did Jacob's own jealousy matter, if Amelia became more of herself because of his company?

He didn't have an answer.

I know you're hurting, he wanted to say. *Not a moment passes that I don't see him, too, Amelia. We both walked away from that cabin with less.*

Any words he could find ran the risk of hurting her... of unwinding whatever protective barrier she had wrapped tight around her heart to keep herself moving forward.

Regardless of what was transpiring between Amelia and Victor, Jacob's trust in her was not in question. But what *had* been shaken was the foundation of their marriage, and while neither of them were to blame for this tragedy, moving past it had nothing to do with assigning fault. Amelia searched for a way through by seeking answers from the past. Jacob relied on the passage of time, which was said to heal everything, eventually.

So he said nothing, allowing their third afternoon in a foreign time to pass without discussing the topic that pressed on both their minds, the storm they might never escape.

JACOB ARRIVED AT DINNER GRATEFUL NOT TO BE SUBJECTED TO meeting more people, but his pleasant mood faded when Victor de Blanchefort and his father, or at least the man calling himself his father, joined them.

"What are they doing here?" he muttered to himself, only to realize he'd said the words aloud.

"They're staying here for a week or two," Amelia explained, smiling at the girl who poured her wine. "Business with Charles."

And you know this, how? "Lovely."

As if on cue, Victor smiled at them both from across the table, his eyes lingering a moment longer on Amelia. He stopped short of licking his lips.

"I'm sure they'll stay out of our way."

Can we switch back to talking like this for a bit?

Amelia bit into a wedge of bread, turning her eyes toward the head of the table, away from Victor, in an almost deliberate manner. *We need to be careful that we don't get caught not paying attention. They might figure us out. You forget they're Deschanels, too.*

I haven't forgotten.

Speaking of paying attention... I think that may be the missing son come home.

Jacob turned to see a young boy of perhaps twelve enter the dining room. His age was only discernible from his height because his face, from the rotund, blushing cheeks to his wide eyes, bespoke of the unblemished innocence of a toddler. With his bouncy blonde curls, he could have been a chubby cherub in an Italian frieze.

"Fitz! You're well enough for dinner after all!" Ophélie cried in genuine delight. Before she could spring from her chair, Brigitte shot her a paralyzing stare.

"Hi, sister," Fitz answered back in a small voice. His eyes darted around the room in a programmed manner, with the air of someone who had been given heavy sedatives. Or lobotomized. Jacob wondered what kind of boarding school they'd sent him to.

"Well, have a seat, child," Brigitte barked. She pointed at the empty chair between Jacob and Ophélie. "You're not on display!"

Fitz moved to his seat with a dazed expression while Charles folded his napkin distractedly. When Ophélie smiled at her baby brother, the one he offered in return had all the sincerity of a serial killer.

Blanca, *are you seeing this Stepford shit?*

What on earth did they do to that poor kid?

Maybe Brigitte had him tied up in the attic with the baby we heard.

I have a feeling if we try to find out, we'll end up with a worse fate.

Jacob didn't disagree, but he wasn't keen on sitting back and observing Brigitte's reign of terror with benign complacency, and he knew Amelia wasn't either.

The first course was served on the same earthenware Nicolas still used in their present day dining room, a blue Spode pattern Amelia told him was called The Girl at the Well. He found he'd rather eat the plate than what they served upon it: roasted, cane-sweetened chicken with sweet potato, also heavily-sugared. Jacob took a bite and felt an imminent toothache approaching.

This is diabetes on a plate.

I think we already agreed their goal is to kill us.

The easy, if somewhat tenuous, mental exchange with his wife lifted Jacob's spirits but also left him hollow. That they could only speak so casually in the presence of others made it somehow a consolation rather than progress. He already knew if he tried this back in the room, she'd claim to be tired and avoid any talk that might dive even an inch under the surface of what they were both feeling.

"Is the chicken to your liking, Lord Donnelly?" Brigitte inquired with a knowing smile.

"Very," he said, working on the unprocessed remains of a cane stalk that had, magically, made it to his plate. "I love the opportunity to try different foods than what we're used to back home."

"Bland foods, you mean," Jean said, turning up his nose. "I've never had such plain dishes in all my travels as the scourge they served in London."

"Jean," Charles warned.

"It's all right," Jacob said. With a wink at Jean, he added, "We could afford to add a few seasonings."

The expression he got in return was as hostile as the one Brigitte had permanently plastered on her pinched face.

I don't suppose he and I have any chance at friendship.

Amelia grinned into her wine. *Probably for the best.*

"I like chicken," Fitz said, eyes vacant.

"You *are* a chicken," Jean said, glancing at his mother.

"I like chicken, too," Ophélie offered her little brother with a chuck on the shoulder.

"May I, as well, throw in a vote for chicken?" Victor added. His eyes twinkled with mischief.

Jean dropped his fork with exaggerated emphasis. The sharp clang rang over the dining room. "Wonderful. Everyone likes the goddamn chicken. Can we talk about something else?"

"We might venture to finally learn a thing or two about our visitors," Brigitte said, fixing her intensity on Jacob and Amelia. "Seeing as none of us were aware of their impending arrival, nor do we know anything about them."

"Lord Donnelly and I had a fine discussion yesterday afternoon," Charles offered, but Brigitte didn't even acknowledge his words.

Amelia smiled pleasantly. The effect was dazzling against the storm cloud of Brigitte, and Jacob felt a burst of pride for his wife. "Lord Donnelly and I are happy to answer any questions you have of us. Ask away."

Uhh. Now you've done it.

What else should I have said?

We still haven't matched notes on our story.

Really, would planning have helped us any? And it isn't as if we're in different rooms where they can separate and quiz us. We're sitting right next to each other.

I don't have the best feeling about this.

"How are you, specifically, related to the Deschanels?" Brigitte asked. "Or did you already brief my husband with this?"

"We haven't," Amelia answered, still smiling. "But I'll be happy to walk you through it now."

Praying over here.

Chill, Donnelly. I've got this.

"Go on, then."

"We're actually related by marriage," Amelia explained, replacing her wine glass after a sip only Jacob could see was larger than appropriate. "Monsieur Deschanel, your aunt Dominique was a Lalande before marriage, and I am a second cousin of her daughter-in-law."

Damn, girl. That was good. I'll bet they don't even know how to do that math.

"Aunt Dominique," Charles mused. "Have you spoken with her of late? She was very good to me in my formative years."

"Not recently," Amelia said. "It was through her daughter-in-law we learned of *Ophélie*, and she had promised to write ahead and announce our arrival. It sounds like that didn't happen."

Brigitte's lips were a thin, white line. "It did not."

"We're looking at land in Louisiana, as I mentioned," Jacob chimed in, already less tense. They were over the largest hurdle, it seemed. "And hoped our visit with you might lead to better education on making that happen."

Charles brightened. "It's no wonder you had such sage advice on how to handle my own real estate quandary. How wonderful. Just splendid, Lord Donnelly. I'll help in any way I can."

"I can also offer advisement," Marius added, his first words of the night. Beside him, Victor buried obvious amusement in his wine glass.

"Remind me again," Brigitte said. She'd abandoned her food entirely. "The name of Dominique's daughter-in-law?"

Amelia frowned. "Oh, um..."

"The Madame de Lalande?" Jacob said.

"Deschanel now, remember," Amelia corrected lightly.

Brigitte's eyes narrowed. "The madame has no name?"

"Of course she has a name." Charles chuckled with a twitch of nervousness. "But I hardly think this is pertinent. Our guests are here now, and we have much to show them. To think, a lord and lady sharing the riverlands with us. What a fortuitous friendship, for both of us."

"What I believe to be pertinent and what you believe to be pertinent does not need to be in accord," Brigitte seethed, leveling a heated glance his direction. "I do not think it unreasonable to discuss the name of the woman who provided the reference that brought them halfway around the world to our doorstep."

You don't know the name? Jacob asked.

No! I was banking on them not knowing anything about Dominique's daughter-in-law. I don't even know if she has one!

What do you want to do? Continue to bluff? Poison them all and make a run for it?

Victor folded his hands over the edge of the table, eyes moving between them, observing with great interest.

If the bluff fails, I guess we need to find some hemlock.

"Catherine," Amelia answered, attempting her best show of false confidence. "Though I have not called her that since we were girls. Even in private, she is Madame Deschanel to me."

"Catherine," Brigitte repeated, enunciating each syllable as she rolled the word around.

"I'm an acquaintance of Madame Deschanel myself," Victor interceded, surprising everyone at the table. "Catherine, as it were, is a lovely host and woman and we are due for another visit to their chalet."

Amelia froze. The look she wore evolved from shock to withering gratitude. Jacob wanted to reach across the table and choke the satisfied grin from Victor's face, even if he had lied to protect them.

"A small world, indeed," Charles said, clearly relieved to have the matter settled.

"Yet somehow not ever big enough," Brigitte added. Nothing would satisfy her, Jacob realized. She had already cast her verdict when they arrived.

She doesn't like us at all, Amelia said. *I think it's curious, seeing as it doesn't feel earned.*

I think she knows we aren't who we say we are.

Well, yeah. Brigitte just tried to humiliate us in front of her family and guests to prove that point.

But they have guests all the time, many of whom are probably high-born, and I doubt she treats them like back-alley criminals.

We don't sound or act like their other guests. It's only a matter of time before a real Brit comes along to demonstrate that.

There's no reason to be immediately suspicious of guests unless they offer a reason. Brigitte acts as if we're here to pillage the gold.

But how much could she really know, Jacob?

I have a feeling we're going to find out.

MERCIFULLY, THE CONVERSATION SHIFTED TO JEAN'S STUDIES AND HIS upcoming second Grand Tour, which they learned had been postponed.

"Why is that?" Amelia asked.

"Duties at home demanded it," Jean replied, hawkish eyes trained on his sister.

What duties could a fifteen-year-old really have? Jacob wanted to ask. He felt a need to poke the bear, knowing the answer, but after the fire drill earlier, he didn't want to risk diverting the attention back to him and Amelia.

"And you will be a married man in short order," Charles added. He avoided his wife's death glare. "Bonapartie has agreed to the marriage earlier than planned, given the political uncertainty in the South. And should it come to war—"

"Papa, you're no better than the chin waggers in the men's parlors!" Jean exclaimed. "War. As if we do not have better means to solve problems."

"You're too young to understand the complexities of our world," Charles countered. "It is not as simple as fight or don't fight. You have no concept of what is at stake, and what the North would take from us if we let them."

"Jealous fiends," Brigitte hissed. "I would see every last one of them dead in the fields."

"We would be better met to come to a compromise, Madame," Marius said in a calming, reasonable tone. Jacob could not help staring whenever the man spoke, checking for signs of his true age. There were none, except in the way he chose his words only when he deemed them particularly important. "Seceding will solve one problem but reveal many others."

"You can't reason with heathens," Brigitte said. "They know only one language: blood."

Charles sucked the food from his teeth, measuring annoyance with his wife. "Something will happen, one way or another, and soon. We can no longer abide the disrespect, and they cannot keep their envy at bay."

Jean rolled his eyes. "Fighting would be futile for Northerners. They would lose everything. The war would be over in a week!"

"I believe it is you, son, who has been listening to men's parlor discussions."

"Are you going to rattle on about their factories again?" Jean laughed. "What good are factories when we have numbers and honor? Your grand ideas, Papa. You forget that *they* are the aggressors."

"Must we speak of war over supper?" Ophélie asked.

"Fight!" Fitz barked in a hollow exclamation. His eyes remained dull and listless. He may as well have been a marionette, with someone overhead pulling the strings.

"Your father is right," Marius said as he rose abruptly. "Alas, I am an old man, and it is time for my retirement."

Amelia and Jacob exchanged a look.

"Accept my apologies for my son," Charles said, standing to escort him. "He forgets himself."

Jean twisted his lips.

"Without the idealism of our sons, it would only be us, the world-weary," Marius assured him and excused himself.

Victor moved to follow suit, but his father gently nodded an encouragement to stay. He sat again.

"Well, you've driven one guest away with your war rhetoric," Brigitte chided, pushing her chair out. It crashed into the servant, rattling the dishes on top. "How many more before the night has ended?"

She was gone before Charles could respond.

Jean ran after her. "Wait, Maman."

With a heavy sigh and a mumbled apology, Charles followed her as well.

Jacob and Amelia were left with Victor, Ophélie, and the strangely unresponsive Fitz.

"So, Fitz, tell us about school," Amelia said pleasantly.

"School?"

"Yes, didn't you come back from school?"

Fitz shook his head. Confusion replaced his drugged appearance.

"He wasn't away at school," Ophélie said, lowering her voice with a quick glance to see if they were still alone. "Maman sent him to Italy to take the waters."

"Take the waters?" Jacob repeated.

Ophélie seemed at a loss to explain, and Victor jumped in. "As I recall, from what Charles told my father, Fitz had trouble learning his letters and other studies. Brigitte mentioned it in a letter home to family in France, and someone recommended a Roman bath in Italy, near Turin, I believe. Fitz has been there a year."

"Water wouldn't do this to him," Amelia said softly, shooting an apologetic glance at Fitz, who swirled a fork around the remnants of his dessert. The dark molasses formed a circle atop what appeared to be tiny horns.

"That is the accepted version of the story. What I was told," Victor replied. "I cannot personally vouchsafe any of it."

"He needs a doctor," Jacob whispered. He cast a glance toward the door, believing Brigitte might linger outside the door like a vulture waiting for words to use against them. "Was he like this before?"

Ophélie shook her head. Tears brimmed under her lids. "No, we used to play and laugh all the time. It's true, he didn't learn as fast as Jean, but I could not see anything wrong with him myself. And now…" She wiped at her eyes. "Lord Donnelly, would you mind terribly to help me escort him to his room? He cannot even walk on his own anymore. He runs into walls and columns as if he can't see them at all."

"Of course," he said and rose. He slipped his arm under young Fitz's shoulder. The boy leaned into him, a slight bit of drool lingering at the corner of his mouth. Ophélie sniffled and took the other arm.

When they reached the door, Jacob realized with dismay that he was leaving Amelia alone with Victor.

His heart eased as Amelia nodded briefly at Victor and excused herself, hurrying out the door. Victor stood, but didn't follow.

Maybe I'm reading too much into his strange behavior. He was pleasant enough at dinner.

No, Jacob's younger self, the fighter, chimed in. *He wants you to let your guard down. And you know why.*

Aye. That's when your opponent attacks.

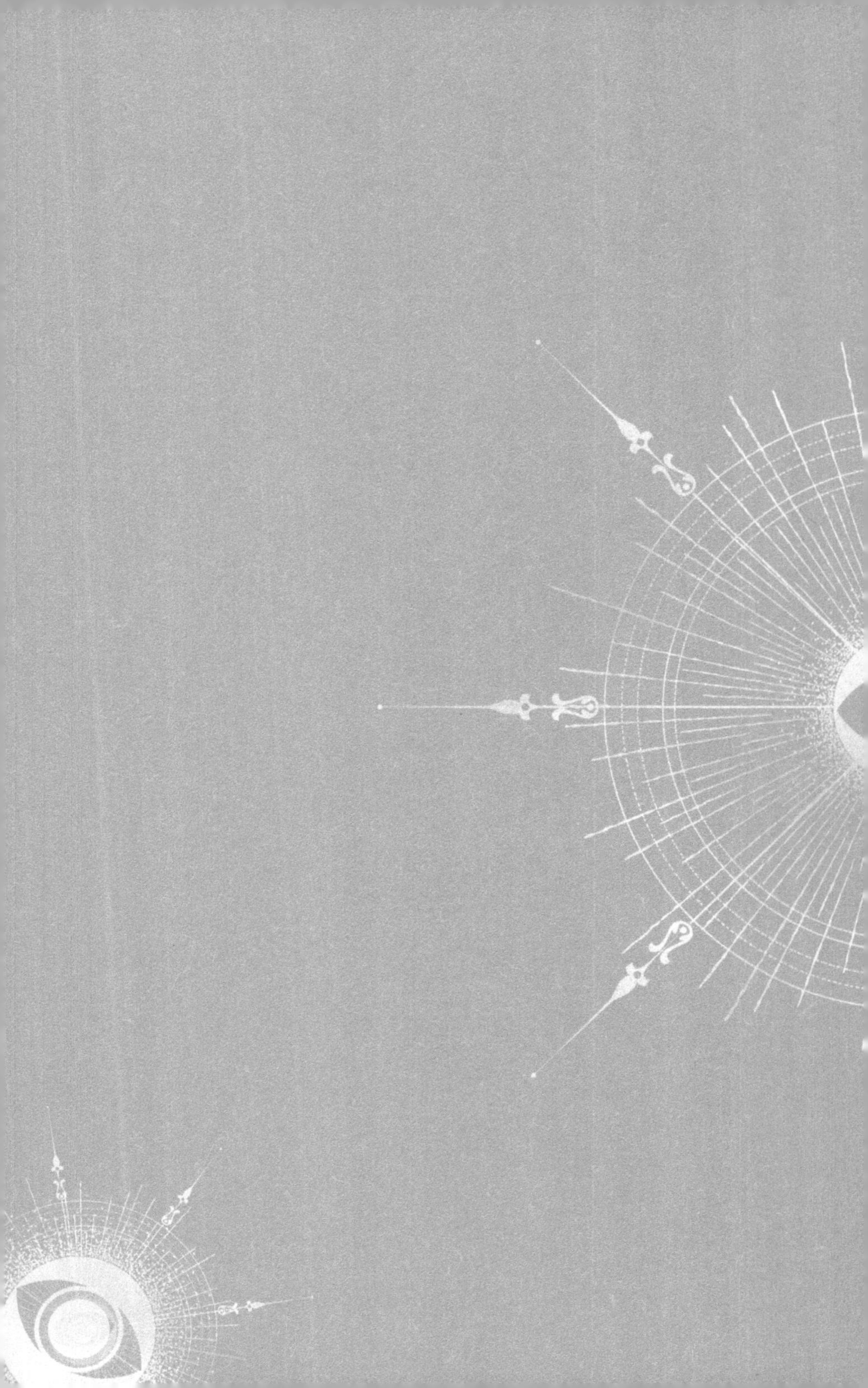

15
AMELIA

Ophélie raced down the back steps of the house, cutting a tight corner into the butler's pantry. The one pursuing her was close behind, within a few steps at every turn, so she had no time to think. She could no longer even hear him over the sound of her own terrified heartbeat.

The lid to the monstrous clay flour jar lay half open. She peered inside and calculated she could fit, but it would be close. Ophélie quickly slid the Titian lid aside and lifted one leg over. Her foot sank into a soft bath of white powder.

"Come out, bitch! I'll find you, wherever you are!"

In a rush, she drew her other leg in and crouched as low as possible, resisting the urge to sneeze as a wave of the white dust filled her nostrils. She pulled the lid back over the top, reducing her light to nearly nothing. Leaving only a thin slit open, she watched.

Jean landed at the base of the stairs, his trousers still gaping open. He'd lost his shirt somewhere along the way, and sweat beaded across his throbbing torso as he dropped his hands to his knees. "You love to test me," he wheezed. She would pay dearly for making him work for it.

Why did she? She couldn't say. There had never truly been any real escape from the hands of her brother. She couldn't run away from her life. So why prolong the inevitable, only for the horrors to double?

I am only alive today because I choose to fight. I would rather he tear me limb from limb than believe he could have me so easily.

"Ophélie! Come out, you sly little whore! If you show yourself to me now, I won't hurt you."

Liar, *she thought.* As if what you do to me, night upon night, is all a game.

She'd had almost a week of reprieve when Victor de Blanchefort visited a fortnight ago. Whenever Victor was on the premises, Jean stayed away. She didn't know why; it wasn't so with any of their other guests. But something about Victor put Jean's cruelty to rest. Temporarily.

But Victor could not save her. Nor should she look to him, or any man, to do so.

Not even he, *the promised one, who she was destined to meet but knew nothing of. Not even a name. Her revelations and memories unraveled like the layers of the soil beneath their plantation, and she still had so much to learn about who she was.*

If it even mattered, when she was spoiled. Broken.

"Do you not want to be married off to that de Blanchefort upstart? Maman will never allow it, you know. Never. Not until you've borne the heir."

Ophélie held her breath as his steps drew closer.

"You're being selfish! Don't you think I would rather have a whore who is not my sister? I'm to marry Julianne Bonapartie. She's a finer piece of decoration than you'll ever be. But I can't, you selfish, selfish girl! I can't until we've done our duty, but you always have to go and make it so hard...*"*

Jean continued his approach until he was standing right in front of the flour pot. "Ophélie. Please. The first time was not your fault or mine. God gave us that horrid child as a sign that we were not ready spiritually. It will not happen again because Maman has doubled her Hail Marys and God smiles upon us now, as he once did. Do you not understand? The sooner we bear a healthy child, not a gargoyle who languishes into starvation like a drooling idiot, the sooner this can stop. Do you believe I want this? No, I do not, Ophélie. But we were born Deschanels, and this is our duty. Your duty is to bear a son by me and, in a few years, by Fitz. That is all, and once you are done, you are free to become the wife of another and do as you shall, as it pleases your husband. And you will do your duty, no matter how you fight, or what escape you might believe you've found."

Jean crouched. His labored breathing stopped her heart. "You can hide in flour pots or behind slave cabins, but I will find you. I will always find you."

If the potent rush of Ophélie's dream—fear had not woken her—the pitched crying of the infant would have.

Jacob stirred; he was waking as well, and would soon hear the baby and want to follow the sound again. Amelia couldn't. Not tonight. She was already tired of mysteries. Of strange men speaking of the future, of ghostly babies and evil mistresses. Of vivid, near lucid dreams that were surely, inexplicably, the memories of the young Ophélie Deschanel.

She fled the room before Jacob could wake and ask her about the baby, or anything. He never had to say even a word to ask his questions. They were written in bold letters across the space of his gaze, always. Unspoken, but not exactly unsaid.

Amelia still loved him. It hurt her to even consider the idea of *still* loving him as if there had ever been a question at all in the matter or any reason to stop. God, how she loved the man, her best friend and protector! How she would have wished to return his embrace and quell his fears about her, and how she had changed, and even sought a strange sort of solace from a man she'd only just met.

Amelia exited the heavy front door of the plantation house, into the cool night. The air was an immediate burst of relief, washing over her in one sudden, welcome wave.

She closed the door quietly behind her and crouched over the top step. The cypress boards beneath her bare feet grounded her; reminded her this was as real as everything they'd left behind in the present.

As real as her husband upstairs.

If Jacob were to ever actually put a voice to his questions, Amelia didn't think she could give him satisfying answers.

Why do you pull away from me? *Because being close to you reminds me of being close to myself.*

Why won't you let me in? *Because I look in your eyes and see myself at the hands of Baldur. I fear you'll always visualize me that way, so I'll always see myself the same.*

Why are we here, *Blanca? If I knew, I would tell you, and I will know when I know. Right now, I don't understand, and I wish I did, but I don't even have an idea of where to look.*

What exactly are you doing with this man, Victor? *Nothing. Running from him. Running toward him. I don't know!*

Outside, there was nothing. Only the sheer hum of the cicadas against the balmy air and the subtle current of the river ahead. No crying baby, or tortured family, no evil Brigitte, no Jacob, no Victor.

Amelia huddled tight to her knees, drawing from her own

warmth. All her life, she'd believed in the power of words. Of speaking about her own pain as part of seeing it healed. She had endured grief of all kinds, from losing her beloved brother, Benjamin, a niece, cousins, aunts, uncles. In all those times she had talked; to Jacob, to her mother. To *someone.*

Why was it so hard now? She hadn't died. *Perhaps I should have.* She still drew breath and had life yet to live. *But of what value?* Amelia was married to the only man she'd ever loved, and he patiently loved her through this, searching for the best way to give her distance while showing his strength could benefit her. *I don't deserve him. I wish he'd left me to die as I asked him to.*

In grieving the loss of others, she could identify her own stage of grief... would define the transition from denial to bargaining, and even give herself a silent pat on the back when she finally hit acceptance. If measured, the loss of her brother was harder than anything she'd ever experienced, even under Baldur's abuses.

But while God had taken Benjamin, and it was unfair, her memories were still all her own. When she thought of Ben, she saw him laughing and tugging at the bougainvillea at The Gardens or swinging from the old tire on the broad oak. She pictured them laughing at Saturday cartoons and walking down to the river to fish.

Because of Baldur, her entire marriage to Jacob felt blunted. She couldn't simply carve out the terrible moments and leave the rest because the wonderful ones led to the terrible. Like a cancer, she had to cut away at everything around it. What remained, was a distance between herself and Jacob she feared might never be repaired.

The air around her rustled. Her breath hitched as she turned, expecting to see Victor appear from the shadows.

But she saw or heard nothing but the wind, and her own thoughts, and perhaps disappointment to have been wrong.

Amelia rested her head against the top of her knees and closed her eyes, blocking out the past, the present, and all in between.

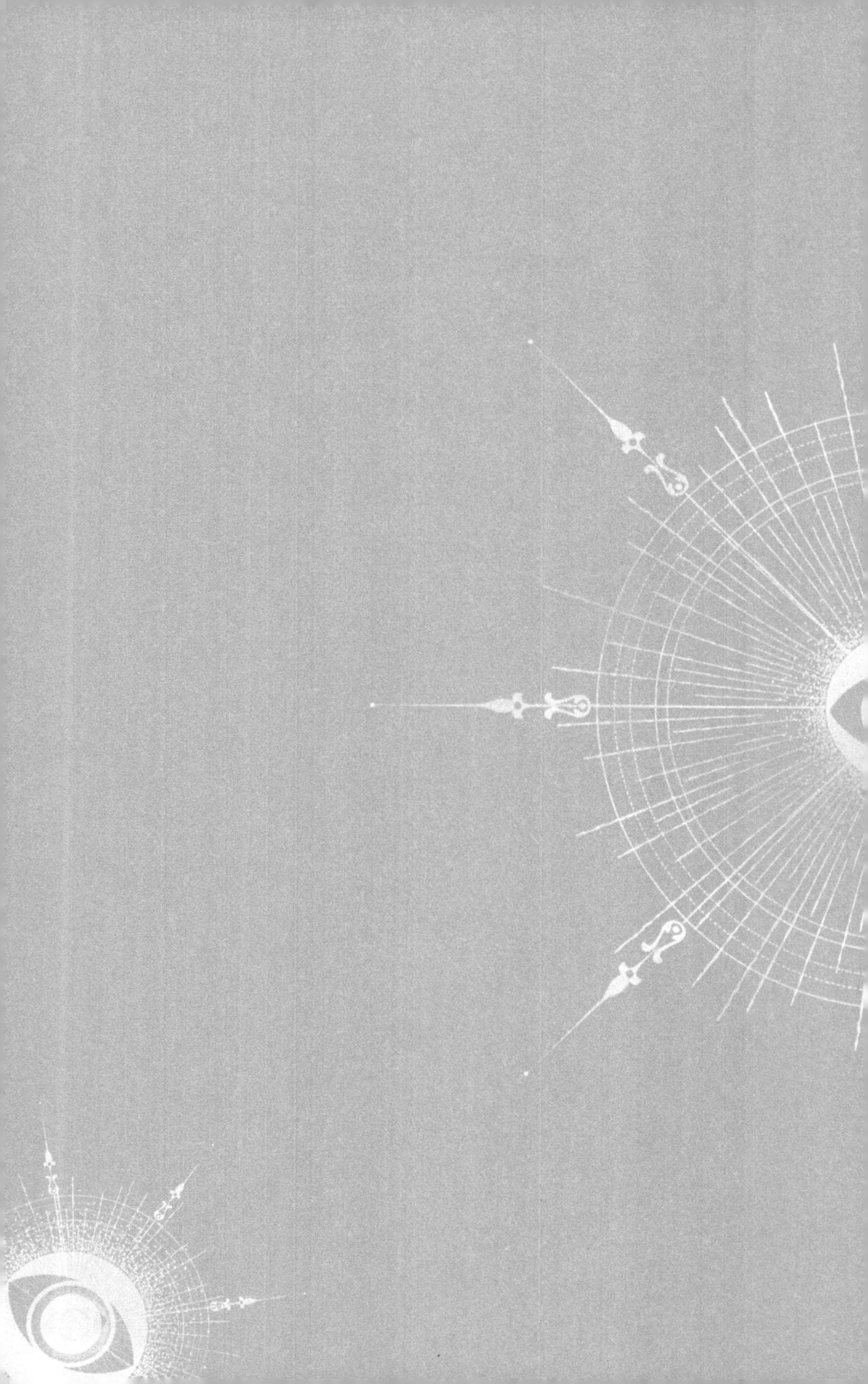

16
OPHÉLIE

Amelia wasn't the only one at *Ophélie* who dreamed of someone else's pain that night.

Ophélie's own vision—for what else could it be, she wondered—was startlingly vivid.

She stood in the corner of a dimly lit room, scents of damp pine and sweat mingled between the undercurrent of terror. Before she even beheld the terrors, she felt them. These were no ordinary horrors, but the type that took hold of those unfortunate enough to partake and never let go.

Amelia hung nude from a hook drilled into the ceiling, her feet suspended an inch or two above the ground. Blood ran down the lines of her outstretched body, leaving a trail to the tips of her toes, where it dripped in a steady patter to the wood floor below.

A man—a beast—wielded the knife.

Ophélie's world shifted on its axis as she was turned, flipped, whirled through the air. When restored to her senses, she was Amelia. She went from witnessing the deep cuts running along her friend's inner thigh to feeling the acute sting, the aching burn of the pain as it throbbed to the beat of her heart. The shame, as her desire to survive this ordeal, slipped down her leg with her lifeblood.

Amelia—Ophélie—couldn't bear Jacob seeing this. She wanted him to leave, to run far away, to save himself. There was no way they would leave this cabin together alive, for she would not, no matter what Baldur did to her, ever reveal what he wanted to know. She wouldn't expose her family at any cost, even if he sliced her limb from limb. A possibility that grew more real by the moment.

Jacob floated in and out of consciousness, his own wounds a consequence of resisting the monster. He would die here trying to protect her, although her last wish would be for him to live.

When, at last, the assault culminated in the act that would leave Amelia's soul covered in scar tissue, Ophélie understood, sadly, that she and her new friend had far more in common than she could ever have guessed. And she knew, without further validating or questioning, that what she was seeing *had* happened, and the scene was what Amelia had been afraid to share even though she carried the memory with her like a parcel of rotting luggage.

My sister of the soul, thought Ophélie as she transferred her strength to Amelia in the moment, knowing she could not affect the outcome of the past but hoping, somehow, it would reach Amelia in the future.

OPHÉLIE HEARD THE DOOR CLICK ACROSS THE HALL, THE ONE TO THE room where Lady and Lord Donnelly slept.

I believe I know what haunted your dreams tonight, sweet Amelia. You can confide in me.

She waited several minutes and shrugged a heavier gown over her head before slipping from her own room and down the stairs into the central hall.

It was not Amelia she found at the base, but Victor.

He didn't notice her, not at first. While pacing the foyer near the front door, his lips moved soundlessly. His disheveled hair was a noticeable departure from the impeccable grooming she knew him for, black hairs standing up and to the right and left, a sign he'd raked his hands through them. His nightshirt hung open, only the middle button holding it together.

"Monsieur?" Ophélie whispered, wondering, with horror, of what her mother would think if she'd come upon this.

Victor's head swung up. His eyes fell upon her, and in these first moments, Ophélie felt certain he could see straight into her soul, to every black corner, and every light one. Then he relaxed and straightened his back. "Mademoiselle. I didn't mean to wake you."

"It wasn't you who roused me," she answered, slipping quietly across the cypress flooring.

"Amelia then," he said, nodding. A startled expression crossed his face, and he corrected himself. "Lady Donnelly, that is."

"Be cautious of how you make reference to her in front of others," Ophélie warned, with a glance up the stairs. "Not all will understand."

Victor's eyes lit up, hopeful. "Do *you*? Understand? Can you?"

"I would like to." Pulling her arms tight across her chest, she moved closer. "I know you're here more than perhaps you should be. Every time you arrive, something changes." She didn't elaborate.

"You don't, then." The spark died in his eyes. "It didn't come to me all at once, either. I cannot... no, it was too much to expect you might know."

"Tell me, then. Why are you down here, in the dead of night?"

"I sensed her distress."

"And where is she?"

Victor nodded at the door. "She didn't wander far."

Ophélie frowned. "If you came down here from worry, what good is standing in the hall wearing holes in the carpet, when she's outside? Moreover, why is her distress your concern at all, Monsieur? Her husband sleeps upstairs."

"You don't understand. You will, I have to believe that. I do believe that. Yes, I believe it. But I bear this burden of understanding alone, and that must change before... before..." Victor rambled like a man intoxicated by heavy spirits.

Ophélie watched him helplessly. "Here, let us go to the kitchens. Prudence sleeps there, and I know she won't mind helping us find you something to drink."

Victor waved his hands at her. "I'm not thirsty, sweet Ophélie, but if I were, I would find my own way to the kitchens. You should rest now."

His behavior disturbed her. Not only this evening but every day since the Lord and Lady Donnelly had arrived. Ophélie had witnessed Victor following Amelia, or observing her, and only her, when they were in the same room.

And sometimes Ophélie.

She shivered.

Ophélie admittedly knew less than she should about the de Blancheforts. That they were distant cousins was no secret, and their success in cane sugar, coffee, and indigo was a matter of common knowledge. But Amelia was not the only one suspicious of Marius, and she might be more so if she had seen the rest of the family. Not a single de Blanchefort looked a day over thirty. Not one.

And now Victor was here again, languishing in dark corners, happening to be, always, where Amelia was.

"I believe it would be for the best," Ophélie started, gathering her courage, "if you would leave Lady Donnelly alone for the duration of your stay."

The flame from a candle flickered across Victor's pale face, lighting his desolate smile. "I know more than you what is best for Lady Donnelly, Mademoiselle."

"Your words make no sense," she insisted, drawing closer. "You only met her three days past! Who is she to you?"

"Who are you to me?" he quizzed. "Is another way to ask the same question."

"You speak nonsense."

"I speak of a truth that is not yet yours."

Ophélie laughed. "You speak like a man drunk on his own importance! What compels men to conceive no woman could ever grasp the complexity of their mind? Are we not creations of the same God?"

"You take my words as an insult when they aren't intended that way at all," Victor answered. He lifted the candelabra and narrowed the space between them. Shadows danced across the room. "You are capable of many, many things, Mademoiselle Deschanel. Far more than you know. But you will."

Ophélie heard a creak from the upstairs floorboards, and she jumped. "I should not be down here. Not with you. Not alone."

"I'm not the one in this house you should fear," Victor replied. In his eyes, she saw her own painful truths, the ones she lived night after night, reflected back. *How could he know? No, that was impossible!*

Outside, a fresh, powerful breeze whipped through the oaks, creating a reverberating hum that bounced from tree to tree.

Inside, Victor's candle flickered.

"You know nothing of my house. Of my family," she said

carefully lifting one bare foot and resting it behind the other, backing away slowly. "Or our honored guests."

A peaceful smile settled over his face. "Ophélie, I am not your enemy."

"What are you, then?"

"Someone who would see you whole were it in my power. Someone who will do the same for Amelia, if I can."

"One has nothing to do with the other." Ophélie's hand trembled. She wondered if it had done so all along.

Victor's smile broadened, and he tilted his head to the side. Watching her. "You say that with the conviction of one who does not believe her own words at all."

"Only one who is tired of odd words from a strange man!"

He reached a hand to her cheek. Ophélie recoiled her face but was rooted to the carpet, unable to move. She needed to know what would happen next and summoned the courage to find out.

His palm cupped her cheek, and a wave of warmth passed through her. She didn't know why she leaned into his touch, or why it comforted her. Why she craved it.

Victor pressed his forehead to hers. "I will kill him. I should have already, but I feared for your life."

Ophélie saw no point in lying to a man who knew her truths. She recognized this now, even if she understood nothing else. "No, I don't desire that, even after everything."

"And I would not move toward a destination you did not desire."

"It matters not," she went on. "Certain truths are unavoidable. You would think me mad if I were to share them, but my fate has already been spoken by the lips of God."

Victor's eyes had a glassy sheen. "Would that I had the power to change it."

He cannot know what I know, but what else could he mean?

Dear Lord, who is this man You've placed in my home and why has he shaken up my world? I have accepted my fate, and yet You continue to throw obstacles in my path when I have done nothing but be Your faithful servant.

She lifted her head from his hand. "Why should my burdens be a concern of yours?"

"That is not the question, Ophélie."

"Then, pray, what is?"

A light press of his lips on her forehead was the only answer she received.

"Amelia stirs. You should return to your room before others are alerted," he encouraged.

"Dismissed like a child," she whispered in a pout. She was angry at herself for not understanding Victor's riddles; at the truth being dangled before her, but too high for her short reach. "Why are you here, Victor?" After tonight, she had earned consent to use his name.

"I am here as much for you as I am for her. But only one of you can yet be saved," he answered, now turning away from her, toward the door, toward Amelia.

17
JACOB

Infant cries infiltrated his sleep.

Jacob was almost not surprised to see the empty spot next to him on the bed. His initial reaction was bitterness, but the emotion dimmed as he realized Amelia probably had a head start on the sound.

He wasn't going to follow it again. He'd told himself this lie, further validating it with truthful but pathetic reminders. Whether a baby cried or not wasn't his problem. Whatever happened under this roof was better off staying that way if he wanted to avoid more concerns of his own.

However, if Amelia had chased the sound again, he couldn't very well leave her vulnerable to whatever attack, verbal or otherwise, Brigitte would be ready to level upon her.

When he arrived at the alcove, Amelia wasn't there.

The attic stairs, though, were down.

Had she gone up alone?

His heart did a quick dance and sunk to the floor. *Dang,* Blanca, *really?*

Jacob saw little choice in the matter. He set the candle-holder on steady flooring and glanced up at the opening with a sigh.

When he started to climb, the creaky rungs sang out in defiance, and he winced, certain discovery was inevitable. But if his wife was up there, turning back wasn't an option. He wouldn't leave Amelia to deal with the repercussions alone, even if she hadn't solicited his help.

Halfway up the ladder, the cries stopped altogether. He hurried to catch up so he could investigate.

At the top, the sound of two voices, competing in low, vicious whispers halted him. Neither belonged to Amelia, but they were nonetheless familiar, and not in a way that gave him any relief as he perched at the opening, vulnerable.

Brigitte and Jean.

"It is *done,*" Brigitte said. "Why do you never trust your maman?"

Jean's usually snide tone was more subdued. "Maybe his health would have improved, Maman. We are not doctors. How can we know what ailed him wasn't curable?"

A loud crack resonated, followed by a sharp cry from Jean. "A doctor! Next, you will recommend we alert the rest of the parish as to what you and your sister get up to every night!"

"At your command," Jean answered in a quiet, retreating voice.

"You dare," Brigitte hissed. Her bare feet made small pats. Jacob imagined her circling her son in the ghastly nightgown, buttons popped open at the top. "I give you the world. I give you everything. I only require one thing of you. Is she so hard to look upon, Jean?"

"She is my *sister*. If anyone found—"

"You put your faith in doubt, not me! In Satan, the king of doubt! As soon as we find her with child again, I will ensure your father marries her to the de Blanchefort imp posthaste. There will be no legal question as to the father."

"Papa says de Blanchefort won't agree to a marriage until Lestan is nineteen."

Brigitte laughed. "Then she will not marry Lestan! There are other boys in this parish, and along this river. Other men. We can send her farther away if need be. I am not opposed to shipping her back to France once she has also borne a son by Fitz."

"Papa is insistent that it must be de—"

Brigitte smacked him again. "Who has seen to your future, Jean Charles? Not that craven Frenchman who calls himself your papa. He would see all our family has worked for, for centuries, end to make an alliance for money. He cares not for our heritage. The man pulled us from who we were in France, intent to leave us torn from our roots. Do you want your children to share your abilities, or would you also see them suffer?"

"I want what you want, Maman," Jean said. "I only wish we could have done more for him. He was so *little*, and..."

Brigitte's voice took on a tender note, but the lack of sincerity rendered it an evil sound. "I know, sweet darling, but you are my strong one. You are my heir. Fitz lacks the strength of his older brother, and his time away has turned him into nothing more than a rag doll, though I suppose he will perform his duty easier this way when the time comes. Yet, he will never be you. He will never have the conviction to make impossible choices. Do you think me heartless?"

"No, Maman."

"Are we clear, then? Do we once again share a vision?"

"Yes, Maman."

"But?"

Jean's voice dropped. "But... how will this help, if we've lost who we are by leaving France? You've told me how wonderful it was, but I have never experienced this for my own self."

"Do you not understand? Only through our continued devotion will we return to glory! We *must,* or we are nothing. We become nothing."

Jean didn't reply.

Brigitte's steps were the only sounds ahead. Then, the soft muffled melody of lips against skin. "Now we put this behind us. Go to Ophélie. We have not a single night to waste."

Jacob strained to hear what she whispered next, then it dawned on him their discussion had ended. They were headed his way.

He quickly descended the ladder, his foot slipping near the end as he landed with a thud. With a stumble, he backed into the wall and rolled off the corner, sprinting back down the hall toward the staircase.

Jacob didn't look back. Surely they'd heard him, but if they didn't *see* him, they would never know who had been listening to their malevolent exchange.

He heaved a sigh of relief as he reached the door to his room. When he pushed it open, he caught movement from the corner of his eye.

Victor, returning to his room.

Jacob, in the excitement, had forgotten that he'd never found Amelia.

He tried to sleep, but the attempt was fruitless. Thoughts of the exchange in the attic, combined with worries about his wife and what she had been up to in the middle of the night with Victor de Blanchefort, taunted him, forcing him to consider the answer to questions he wasn't ready to ask.

When Amelia slipped into bed a few minutes later, he found he didn't have the heart or the courage to begin.

DAY FOUR

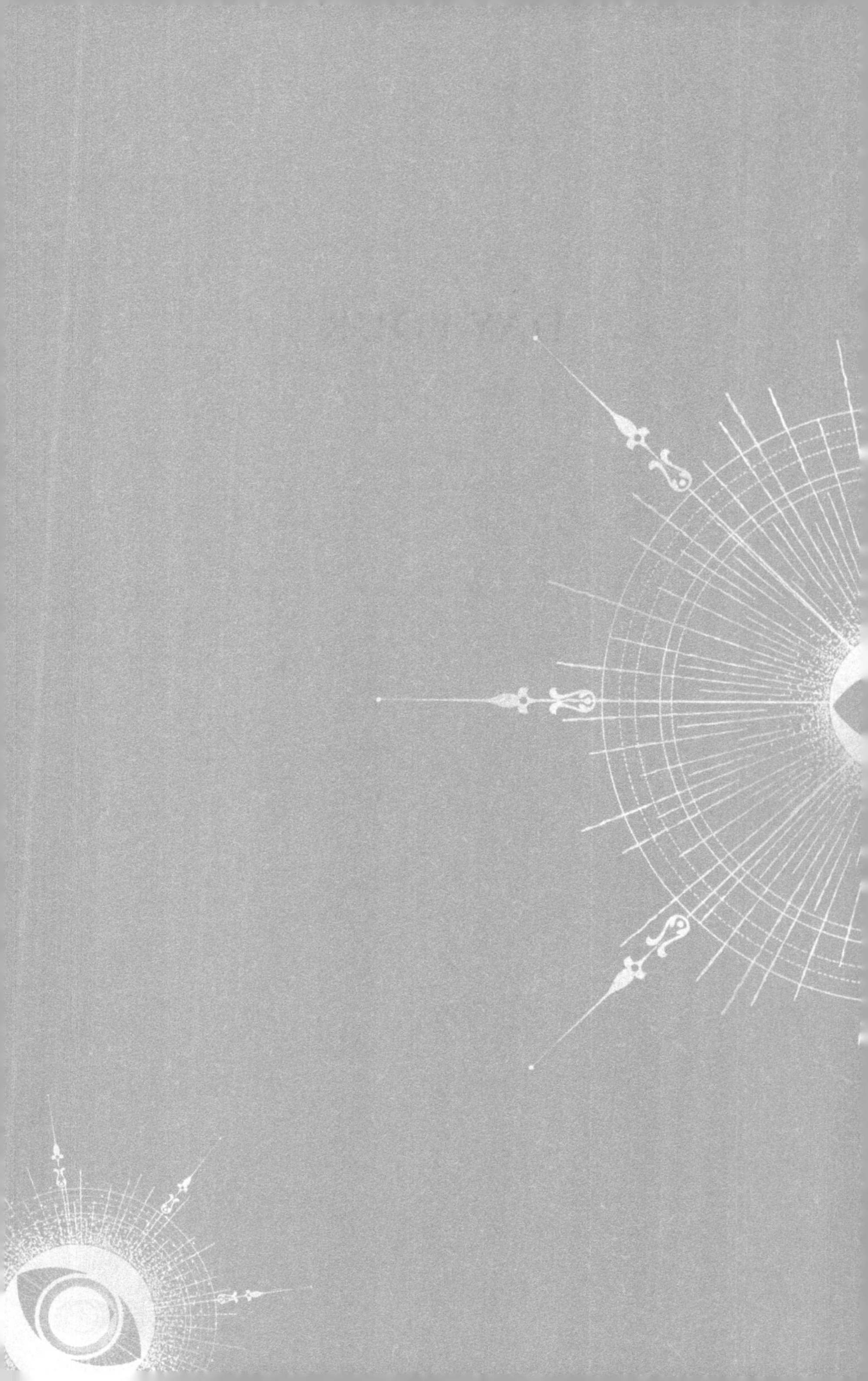

18
AMELIA

Four days.

Four days they had been roaming around the past where they didn't belong.

Four days of being interlopers, faced with new dangers.

Four days without direction or answers to why they were sent there, in this time, of all the times and places in all the world.

Amelia's urgency to leave was tied only to her own cautious fear of the unknown. The rest of her was drawn to this place and time, tethered to the prospect of finding the answer that would send everything in her life neatly back into place.

She and Jacob weren't talking. More precisely, they were not speaking beyond the pleasantries reserved for strangers or distant acquaintances. He might comment on the weather, and she would ask him to check if her hair was straight.

"We've been invited to tea on the rear gallery," Jacob said as if tea with their ancestors was a standard activity in their social calendar.

Amelia's eyes were fixed on the paper he clutched in his hand, watching him turn it over. "Sounds lovely."

Amelia was disappointed, though not surprised, that Ophélie had not been invited. Instead, they were left to socialize with the last people on the plantation she had any desire to spend an afternoon with. Brigitte and Charles, of course, and the de Blanchefort men.

Marius and Charles were deep in discourse about a land deal they'd closed that week. Amelia strained to listen, not the least bit interested but far more eager to engage in whatever they were discussing rather than being forced into any kind of conversation with Brigitte.

They're going into the tobacco business, Jacob explained, opening the channel between them. *Sorry. I don't know if you're okay talking like this, but you weren't closed, so I went for it.*

It's fine, she said. A shiver passed down her spine: nervousness. She was jumpy around her own husband.

"Lady Donnelly," Victor chimed in, lifting his teacup her direction. "How lovely you look today. The yellow in your dress catches the sun fetchingly."

"Thank you," she replied. Her response began as a mumble, slowly climbing in volume as she remembered the need to appear politely interested.

"And my suit?" Jacob said. "Does it also catch the light fetchingly, Monsieur de Blanchefort?"

Amelia's mouth popped open.

Victor nearly dropped his teacup. Once recovered, he grinned in delight. "I'm afraid the black has a more reflective quality, but you are equally dazzling, Lord Donnelly."

Brigitte watched them both like a buzzard assessing which animal would be left for prey.

I think he believes you're being playful.

Jacob's eyes stayed trained on Victor. *I don't believe he thinks much at all about what others feel.*

He's not worth it, she sent back, only to realize she might be opening a discussion she didn't quite know how to have.

No? Sure seems as if he's worth it to you.

A surge in Amelia's pulse sent the heat directly to her cheeks.

Charles watched her. "Lady Donnelly, are you quite all right? You look flushed, my dear."

"Hmm? Oh, yes. Thank you."

"Winters here are cold by our standards, but your constitution is tempered for a much colder climate." He seemed frazzled at seeing his guest discomfited.

"Lady Donnelly is merely blushing at a compliment from our esteemed de Blanchefort," Brigitte said sweetly. Her words were saccharine and arsenic. Amelia had to block the pushback from the escalating darkness of the woman's aura.

"My son often forgets the rules of decorum around a lovely lady," Marius added, by way of apology for Victor. Did it make her feel better, or worse, that she was not unique in his affections?

Amelia shook her head. "No, I'm fine, I promise. It's my fair skin. I sometimes get hot flashes. I'm not accustomed to any humidity in the air."

"Indeed?" Brigitte asked, sipping her tea. "Are these hot flashes always in the company of comely, wealthy landowners?"

Amelia flushed deeper. All eyes at the table rested on her, in anticipation of her next words. She couldn't look at Jacob for support when he shared Brigitte's suspicions.

She glanced her husband's direction anyway, but he looked

down. Amelia didn't require her empathic touch to sense the sadness flowing through him.

"Now, now, Lady Donnelly is our guest," Charles chided his wife. "She may not be used to our good-natured playfulness."

"Playfulness infers a lack of solemnity or strong intention," Brigitte answered, still smiling like a debutante on display. "If Lady Donnelly does not wish to confirm she enjoys the affections of the younger de Blanchefort, we may take her silence as affirmation."

"Madame," Charles warned.

"My wife isn't used to this weather, as she mentioned," Jacob said, but his voice lacked volume or enthusiasm, and most of those around the table didn't register his words. Amelia's shame deepened. Here he was, defending her against her own actions.

"Lady Donnelly has a husband far more charming than I could pray to be." Victor, again, to her rescue. "If I flatter her, that is my doing, not hers."

Amelia wanted to thank him. She also wished him to leave and go far, far away. "This is my first time to America, and I just need time to adapt," she answered while hoping to end the topic.

"My father was born in France," Marius said. "And has said it took him nearly a decade to adapt to the climes of Saint Domingue. I don't believe he ever adjusted entirely to Louisiana."

Amelia wondered about Marius de Blanchefort... his young face, the soft, disarming quality in his delivery. He didn't seem to share Victor's impish nature, but neither did he discourage it. And where Charles was concerned with propriety and not being viewed as a remiss host, Marius seemed to care about Amelia's discomfort in a more personal way.

"I would love to hear some of your father's stories about living on the island," she said, smiling.

"I also lived there in my boyhood. And I would be honored for any time you might spare an old man to wax about his childhood memories."

Old man. And once again, she was as suspicious of the father as she was the son.

"So, the two of you have purchased more land for tobacco, then?" Jacob asked Charles.

"We shook hands yesterday." Charles glanced at Marius with a wary smile. "We may yet come to regret this venture, but my partner is confident in the investment."

"As you should be," Marius said. He turned over a scone in his hand, regarded it with mild curiosity, then returned it to the silver tray in the center of the table.

"I would love to pick your brain. My wife and I are hoping to purchase several plots along the river," Jacob said, forcing a smile in her direction.

"Pick my brain?" Marius frowned.

"An English expression," Amelia said in a rush, followed by a short laugh. Colloquialisms would be their downfall.

"A curiously painful one," Marius returned, eyes wide.

"Many things are unusual about our treasured guests," Brigitte said. She arched her brow.

"Monsieur!" All eyes turned toward a man running toward the group. Amelia recognized him from their first day. Edwin.

"Yes, Edwin," Charles answered, breaking his pastry in half. "What is it?"

Edwin bent over, out of breath. "You... have... a visitor... sir..." he panted, gasping out each word.

"Unannounced?" Charles asked with a brief shrug toward his guests, oblivious to the excitement of his servant.

"This seems to be a recurring plague upon our household of late," Brigitte quipped.

"Sir..." Edwin wheezed.

"Calm down, boy," Charles said. He shared a glance with his male peers, laughing. "I'm not selling you to the traders just yet."

"She..." Edwin stood up straight, trying to pull himself together. "Your guest, sir. She says... she says..."

"Well, get on with it!"

"She says she's your sister, sir."

"My..." Charles furrowed his mouth. "I have no sister. She is confused, certainly. Correct her and send her on her way."

"Sir, I..."

Edwin's words were choked off not by his hesitancy this time, but by the pitched voice of a tiny young woman fervently marching around the porch, a terrified slave in tow.

"Charles!" she cried. "Charles Deschanel! Brother, I have traveled far to see you!"

Brigitte whipped her head around so fast Amelia thought she might snap her neck. *What a shame that would be.* "Edwin, get rid of this trash! Monsieur has no sister."

"I have no sister," Charles echoed his wife. "Mademoiselle, you are either confused or after a swindle, and neither are welcome on my property."

Amelia assessed the young woman who stood at the corner of the gallery, one hand spread across the Corinthian column, the other pointing in their general direction. She was familiar... so familiar, in a way that she knew would hit her, at any moment...

Jesus, she could be your cousin Adrienne's twin, Jacob sent.

"Yes," Amelia whispered. That was it, exactly. Her shock of flaming red hair defiantly jutting out of every inch of her braid; her broad, blue eyes seemed to tremble with passion.

There was no doubt in Amelia's mind, whatsoever. This woman was a Deschanel.

"By the grace our father's second wife, yes, you do," the woman asserted. Her pale skin beaded with the sweat of exertion. "I am Charlotte, once Deschanel, and now LaViolette."

Charles laughed an overreaction designed to cover the growing disconcertment evident in his face. "And where is your husband, Madame?"

Charlotte smacked the arm of the slave to her left, and he straightened himself. "You are looking at him. Simon LaViolette, this is my brother, Charles."

"You are *not* serious," Brigitte hissed, scandalized.

"I am not your brother!"

"We share no mother, this is true, but we share a father, and this counts more," Charlotte said. She lifted her blue taffeta skirt clear to her knees and approached the tea party. "Tea? I would love some."

"Lower your skirts at once!" Brigitte demanded.

"Edwin," Charles said through gritted teeth. The young man ran off, probably for reinforcements.

Marius stared with great interest at the untouched scone in the table center, while Victor practiced hiding his growing amusement.

Charles glanced in the direction Edwin had run. His agitation had spread from his face down to his limbs, which all twitched in unison. "Madame, your falsehoods are not welcome here. Nor is your humor. That man is *not* your husband, just as I am not your brother."

"And yet, he is my husband, and you are my brother," Charlotte said with a brief, pleasant smile before snatching the scone from a startled Marius, flashing him a wink. She chewed slowly, eyes thoughtful. "Not at the quality of a Parisian scone, but I would not turn it away if starving."

Brigitte fanned herself, arms flapping. She seemed ready to faint. "What have we done, oh Lord, to invite such visitors to our home?" she squawked.

Jacob flashed her a scathing look.

"Seeing as you asked," Charlotte replied, brightening. "I have come seeking my portion of the inheritance. Simon and I intend to settle by the river, and I have been informed you received the bulk of Papa's money when you left France."

"What inheritance!" Charles cried. He whipped around, mumbling Edwin's name. "Lord and Lady Donnelly, please accept my apologies. I do not know this madwoman, or what she is going on about. She may have hysteria."

"Hmph!" Brigitte declared. "A sister. If Charles had a sister, our circumstances would have been much changed. This cannot hardly be true."

"Lord and Lady Donnelly?" Charlotte said, eyeing them both with twinkling eyes and a touch of playful suspicion. "We are well met, lord and lady. I do wish I had the time to hear *your* tale."

Definitely a Deschanel, Amelia said.

Sees right through us, Jacob agreed. *So why not call us on it?*

She has bigger problems. Like talking Charles out of his fortune.

Did you catch the reason for Brigitte's irritation?

The woman is always irritated.

Blanca, *think about it. A sister? Brigitte only got to marry Charles because he* had *no sisters. She's his first cousin, which was sort of a consolation prize. Don't you see? Charlotte, whoever she is, is presenting some real competition here at Casa Incestivus.*

Jacob was right. Amelia had been so engrossed in the unfolding drama that she hadn't bothered to break it down. But that was Jacob, always. Always thinking steps ahead, always considering his surroundings. With his upbringing, he'd had no choice.

Charles and Charlotte continued bickering, with Brigitte layering in unhelpful exclamations every few verses. It was clear as day that not only was Charlotte a Deschanel, but she favored her brother strongly, too. And though Charles continued to lash her with denials, Amelia sensed in him an understanding of the truth, even if paired with a refusal to embrace it.

Edwin returned with a couple of footmen, who all rushed forward in a cloud of dust. "Monsieur, what would you like us to do?"

"Escort this harlot off my property!" Brigitte shrieked, rising so fast her chair fell back against the gallery.

"Madame LaViolette," Charles said, weary, "I would please ask you to leave. You have unsettled my wife and disturbed my visitors."

"Unfortunate, though avoidable had you welcomed me as your blood," Charlotte accused, spreading her fingers over her hips. Beside her, Simon hung his head to his chest, hands folded before him. "And had you not ignored my half dozen calling cards, we might have avoided this scene."

"She sent you calling cards? You knew about this?" Brigitte hissed.

My god, she really does look like Adrienne, warts and all.

Jacob nodded. *And her husband could be Oz, good and whipped.*

LaViolette... maybe it's coincidence, but I wonder if she's related to the New Orleans LaViolettes in our time.

You mean Senator LaViolette?

The senator and her huge family. They have a history of making their money through not-so-reputable activities and buying their way into society. Speakeasy owners. Storyville Madams. If Charlotte's ancestors share the fire she has, I can see the connection.

Okay. Maybe. So why do you think we're seeing this?

Amelia knew what he meant. He didn't share her insistence that they were here for answers, but they both accepted they'd been sent *here*, to this specific period in time, one they did not choose for themselves. What were the odds they would witness evidence of a whole new branch of Deschanels not even Amelia's mother knew about? And what did it mean?

Charlotte shrugged off the men who, with helpless glances around the table, attempted to guide her away. "You know who I am, brother. I can see it in your eyes. And I *will* settle here, and you and your descendants will come to know me for my name, and my accomplishments. And you will one day look back on this moment of your life with great, astonishing regret."

Victor's brows flew up in delight. He winked at Amelia from his peripheral. Jacob pressed his jaw tight. She pretended not to see either.

"*Mon Dieu*!" Brigitte cried and flew off in a rage, rushing toward the front of the house.

"Madame," Charles said when his wife was gone, in a low voice Amelia strained to hear. "I will call upon you when the time is more appropriate."

Charlotte regarded him with flaring hostility, but she seemed to see something in him that cooled her. "One month, I give you. Would that we could be blood, Charles. How I would welcome it. But I am far more skilled as an adversary, and do not wish that upon you."

"And I would not advise you to continue to attempt to snare me with threats," Charles charged, moving closer, so close Simon finally looked up and affected a slightly defensive stance. "I will hear your words, Charlotte LaViolette, but I will do so on my terms. On my time."

"And the clock begins now," Charlotte said and turned on her heels, marching back where she'd come from.

Charles made a fuss of his suit, fidgeting, offering further apologies, though his mind was elsewhere now, likely making peace with a very new and important reality he had not asked for.

"Don't apologize," Jacob said, the first to find his voice after the debacle. "Lady Donnelly and I are ready for our afternoon nap, anyway."

I'm not tired, Amelia sent. For once, she wasn't. Her blood was hot with new data, information that might matter.

Then do whatever you want, Amelia. His tone, even in her head, was far colder than it ever had been. *You don't need my permission.*

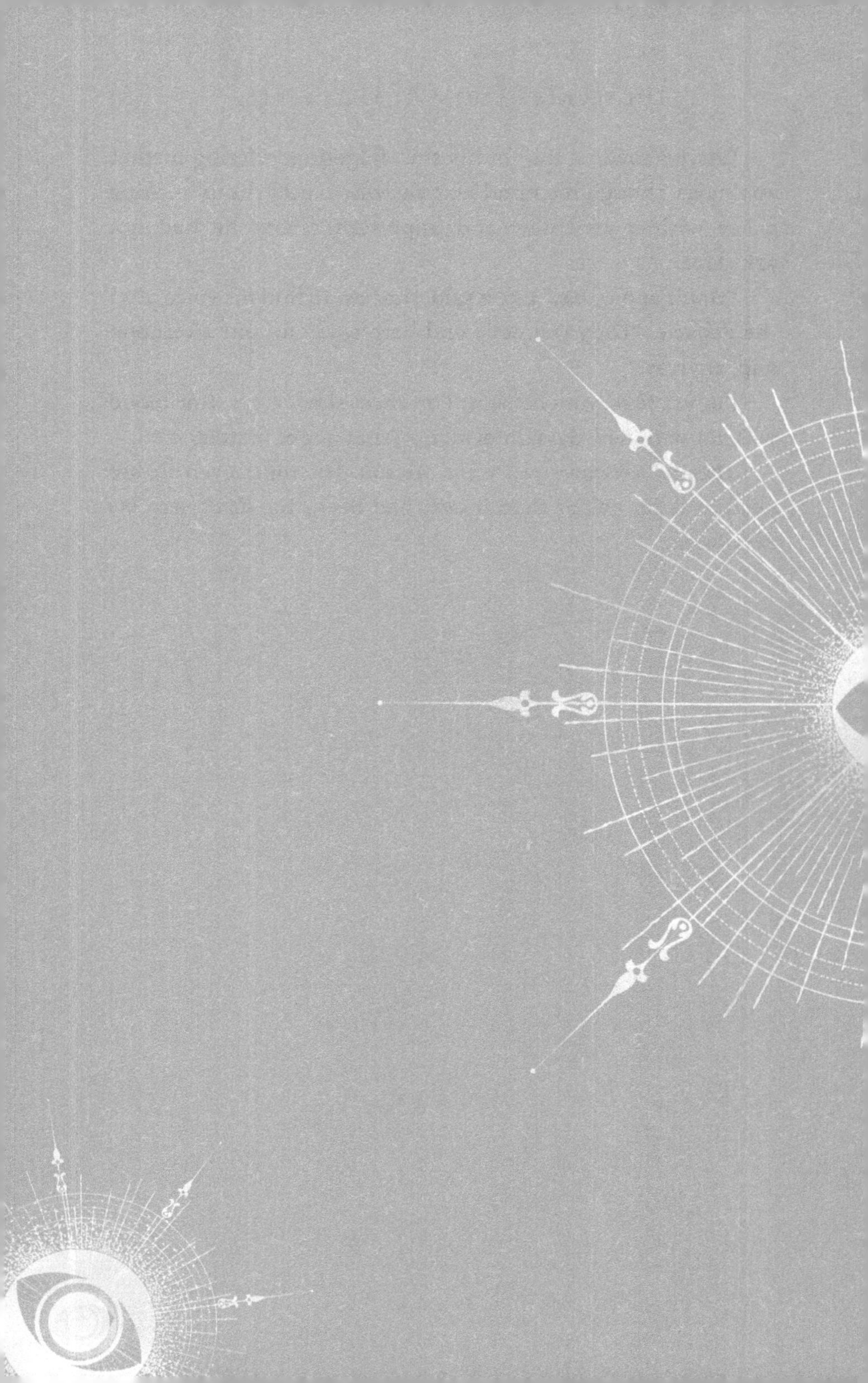

19
OPHÉLIE

Ophélie pressed herself tight against the column, her tiny body fitting neatly behind it, offering a view of the unfolding chaos from a safe hiding spot.

She said nothing as the petite woman with the flaming hair addressed her father with harsh words, with a claim she was his sister. She listened, carefully watching the reactions of the others. Her mother, unsurprisingly, threatened. Lady and Lord Donnelly, frozen in interest. The de Blancheforts, unimpressed. But it was her father's reception that held her curiosity the tightest.

Jean startled her with his labored breathing, and she tripped into view. But none of the visitors saw either of them. Everyone around the table was engrossed in the scene.

"Hush!" she admonished, and he fell in behind her, obedient for a change.

"What the devil is happening?" he whispered back.

"That woman—"

"I heard it all," Jean snapped back. "Same as you. What could she want? Father's money?"

"Perhaps," Ophélie said. "Or maybe she wishes to know her family."

Jean laughed under his breath. "Your childish view of the world is delightful at times, sister."

"You always resort to cruelty with me," she chided, for once less sad than she was annoyed. "I know no more than you. I can only guess."

"Very well," he said. It wasn't clear if he was addressing Ophélie's claims of cruelty or their mutual lack of understanding of the situation.

The woman who had disrupted the tea party stormed away. With a light panic, Ophélie realized their attentions would be diverted back, and her hiding place exposed.

She turned toward Jean to usher him away, but he was already gone.

OPHÉLIE FOUND HER FATHER IN HIS STUDY. HE SLUMPED BEHIND HIS desk, his cotton shirt half buttoned. His waistcoat had missed the jacket stand and lay in a heap on the floor.

Jean was a move ahead, already interrogating Charles about what they had witnessed behind the house.

"I do not know, Jean," Charles said with a heavy huff. "I haven't seen that woman in my life."

"I see it in your eyes, Papa. You know her."

"Papa, is it true?" Ophélie joined in, entering the room with careful steps. She couldn't tell who she feared angering more: Jean or her father.

"I cannot say," her father said, shaking his head. He closed his eyes and exhaled. "My papa... let this be a lesson to both of you on propriety."

"What, Papa?" Ophélie pressed gently.

"Tell us!" Jean demanded.

"I should not, but I will because you are both embarking on the beginning of your lives as master and mistress of your own households soon. You will undoubtedly face trials, yet hopefully none that become scandals."

Jean slipped into one of the chairs across from him. Ophélie followed suit.

"My papa, Alphonse, was not a terrible man," Charles began. "You must take my word. He treated my maman like a queen and raised my brothers and me to be respectable men.

"We had barely broken ground on the construction of this plantation when I received word from France that my maman had passed from a sudden bout of consumption." Charles' eyes traveled to a painting on the wall of Adele Deschanel. "We had no chance to say our goodbyes. She was sick on a Tuesday and gone by Saturday."

"That's horrible, Papa," Ophélie whispered.

"It was. I often lament had I stayed six more months, I could have been at my mother's bedside in her final hours," Charles said, casting his focus toward his fidgeting hands. "But my grief was to soon be supplanted by something worse, I am afraid."

"A poor business agreement?" Jean offered.

Charles, before he could stop himself, shot his son a look so contemptuous that Ophélie had never loved her father more. "No, Jean. Papa took Maman's nursemaid, who was once her personal servant and confidante, as his bride within a week of her death. And not a month later, they brought a child into their new family. A month, you hear?"

"So much for your papa loving your maman," Jean quipped.

Ophélie's eyes widened. "That woman out there? Do you really think..."

"Woman?" Charles laughed. "*Ma petit,* she is hardly older

than you! The child I referenced was born the same year as you."

Ophélie replayed the scene from outside over in her head and could not settle on this fact. Everything in Charlotte's demeanor, from her confidence to how she demanded her place in the world, spoke of someone far wiser than Ophélie.

"I know what you're thinking," Jean said, nudging her. "But you are far more of a lady than that presuming harlot."

"Jean," Charles warned. "It is never appropriate to speak of a woman in such ways. Especially not now, when you are so close to influencing your own family."

"Maman did!"

"Maman was angry, and didn't mean the words."

Ophélie stifled a laugh. Papa had it all wrong. Maman meant every last word.

"Papa, do you really believe that woman is your sister?" Ophélie pushed on. She didn't know why the answer was so important, but she had to know.

"The possibility is... present," Charles said carefully. He ran his thumb over the knuckles on his right hand. "She is of the correct age. And I cannot deny she resembles my own *grandmère*.

"Even if she comes to us with the truth of who she is, children, it matters not to me." Charles rose in a deliberate fashion, marking the coming end of the discussion. "Papa scandalized himself with his behavior, and any children of his union with his mistress cannot possibly find a place in this family. She is not wanted here, and I warn you not to welcome her in your own households."

"We should find cause to drive her out of the riverlands," Jean said. "Her and that negro she's calling her husband."

Charles shook his head. He reached down to retrieve his

waistcoat from the floor, sighing. “We do not build our own empires by taking from others, son,” He slipped the tobacco tin into his pocket and patted them both on the head. “But we will not help build hers, either.”

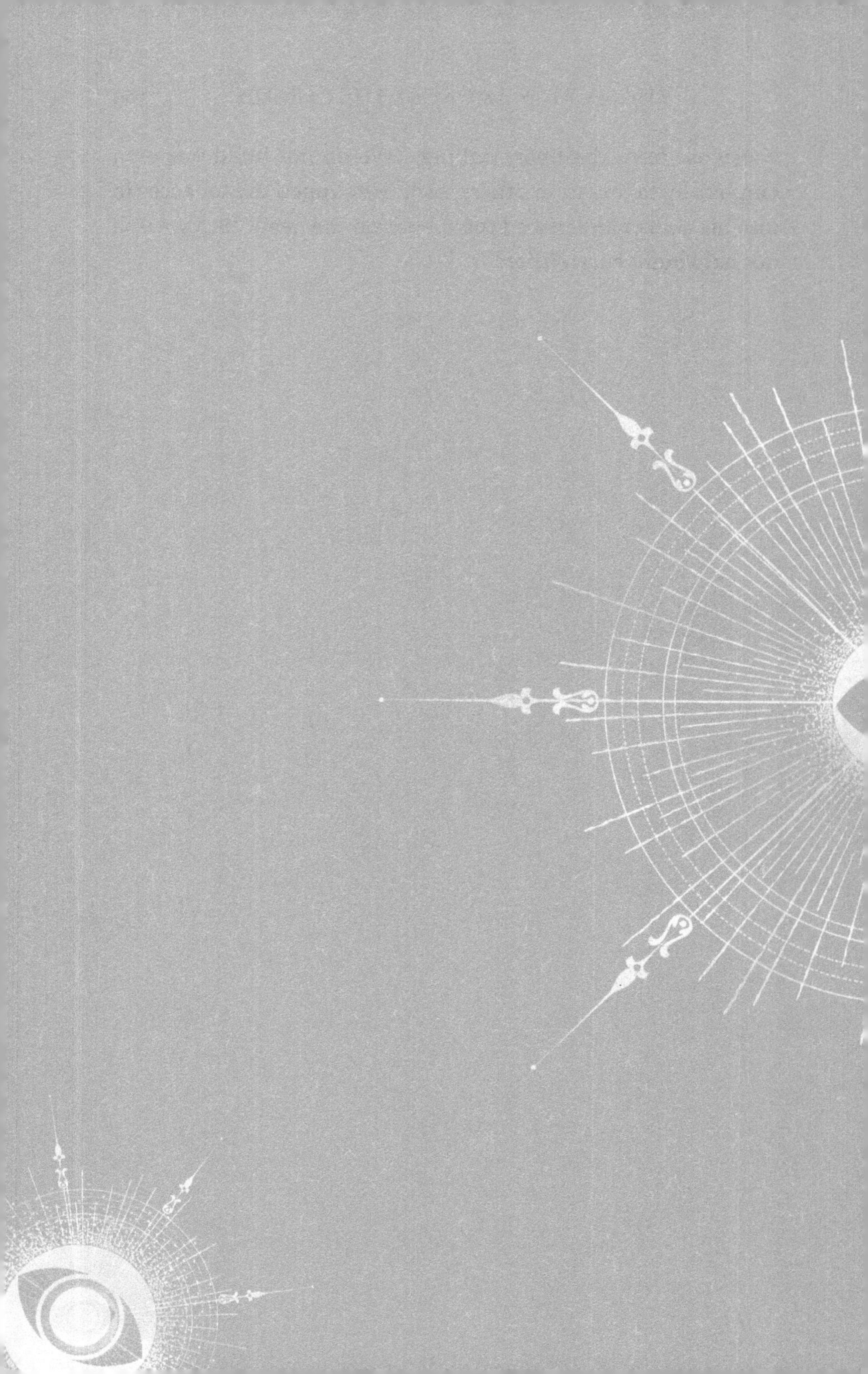

20
JACOB

Jacob had suggested a nap, but it was now the furthest thing from his mind.

Amelia had blown him off. Again.

He wanted to understand. Even did, to an extent. They had both endured the horror together, but hers was unique, one he would never share with his wife, one she would carry alone no matter how he might want to take it from her. Jacob couldn't tell Amelia that watching, powerless, was the worst moment of his life, because how insensitive and selfish would that sound when her nightmare had been so much worse?

For this, Jacob did understand, but without words, he was left to guess at the reason. Did she blame him for what happened? He blamed himself, and she had every right to as well. Had he not let her run off that night in the woods, she wouldn't have landed in Baldur's trap. Everything would have been different.

Was Amelia afraid of him? Jacob feared this more than the

last hypothesis, because if true, he had no cure for it. If his wife associated him with what had happened to her—if she looked at Jacob, and saw only pain—he didn't know how to take that and turn it back into the magic surrounding them before that night in the cabin.

Jacob had no answers. Amelia refused to give them, and he would never go looking around in her head, not ever. And even if he did attempt such a deception, she would catch him. He saw no point in even entertaining the notion.

Walking the perimeter of the property, beyond the oaks, past the eyes and ears of the plantation, he pondered the dilemma. If he was going to lose himself in overthinking, he preferred to do it alone.

All his life, Jacob faced uncertainty—even before his father killed his mother, siblings, and himself—insecurity had followed their existence. Sundays meant going hungry because his father didn't receive his wages until Monday. When Jacob's sister came down with pneumonia, there was no doctor. They couldn't afford it.

Once shipped off to New Orleans, an Irish orphan without a pence to his name, Jacob moved from one tenuous situation to another, finding solace only in his fists. He had no friends and no hope for a future any better than the life his father had led.

Amidst all this, Jacob never stopped to ask why. He never questioned the unfairness of the life he'd been given. And he never wondered when it would get better. It either would, or it would not.

Amelia changed all that. For the first time, he had something worth losing. He found his identity, not as an extension of her, but as a man worthy of being at her side, and having the right to say, "This is my girl. My wife."

So now, he *did* question the horrible things that had

befallen them. He *needed* reasons. He *had* to know why they were being thrown to the wolves, and *if* they could survive it.

Jacob came to an abrupt stop when his boot sank into the soft ground. Checking his footing, he recognized where he was: the old Deschanel family cemetery.

In the present, this small plot was the final resting place for a handful of graves, hardly tended beyond basic maintenance. Mostly the first generation Louisiana Deschanels, Charles and his brood. Jean's daughter, Ophelia, was the first to check into the family crypt in Lafayette No. 1. From then on, all Deschanels from the heir's line were sent there.

Now, as he stood before it, only a single grave existed. It was fresh... the ground not yet settled. Jacob backed up when he realized what had caused his foot to sink.

No headstone marked the area, only a tiny wooden cross, haphazardly nailed together and uneven. In splotchy ink, he made out the word, *Enfant.* His French wasn't solid, but he recognized the word: child.

His thoughts immediately flashed to the nightly crying. Brigitte had shamed them for pursuing the sound, but both he and Amelia had heard it. They hadn't imagined it. The sinister discussion between mother and son, one he'd nearly been busted for while listening in on from the ladder, all but confirmed it. *It is done.*

At once, Jacob put the story together. He fell forward, both hands on his knees, and retched into the nearby grass.

"Lord Donnelly?" A small voice, one he didn't immediately recognize in his fog, sounded behind him, full of distress.

Wiping his mouth with the back of his hand, he turned. Ophélie watched him, eyes wide with concern.

"I'm fine," he insisted, rising. "What are you doing out here?"

Ophélie's eyes momentarily traveled to the grave. She

diverted them in a rush. “Enjoying an afternoon stroll,” she said. “I was to sit with Maman in the parlor for a Bible reading, but she retired to her room after your tea on the gallery.”

Jacob smirked. “Did you hear what happened?”

“I saw it!” Ophélie blushed. “I wasn’t trying to spy. I know that behavior is not becoming of a lady, but when I heard someone yell, I came out.”

“I would’ve done the same thing,” Jacob said with a short laugh. “Not that I care much about what’s appropriate.”

Ophélie grinned. “No?”

Jacob shook his head. “Not especially.”

“How nice that must be!” she exclaimed in wonder. “Is that a cultural nuance?”

He shrugged. “It’s a Jacob thing, I suppose.”

“Jacob,” she repeated. “A nice Biblical name.” Her face stained a deeper red. “Please accept my apologies, Lord Donnelly. I should not address you that way.”

“Honestly,” he said, leaning down in silent conspiracy, “I prefer Jacob.”

Ophélie’s head shook rapidly. “I could never.”

“No harm if others aren’t around,” he said. Only then did he realize it was only the two of them, and his words suggested this was not only okay but implied an underlying secret.

Ophélie clutched her hands over her chest in matched nervousness to his. “Where is Lady Donnelly?”

Jacob hoped the darkness he felt come over his face was not so obvious to the young girl. “I had hoped she was with you.”

“Oh.” Ophélie pressed her lips tight, face twisted in thought. “I see.”

“What?”

“Forgive me if I speak out of turn, but I sense... at least I believe I might... that you are concerned she might be passing time with the younger Monsieur de Blanchefort?"

Jacob rolled his eyes, prepared to launch a firm denial. Something in her expression disarmed him. The look bordered on understanding, but how could she? "It's complicated, Ophélie."

"Everything is," she said wisely. "You needn't worry about Lady Donnelly. She's earnest in her devotion to you."

Such a sweet, but foolish, thing to say, he thought. The true idealism of youth. "Of course," he replied, feeling silly for thinking he might be able to discuss this with someone, especially a young girl who knew nothing of relationships. "Would you like me to walk you back?"

Ophélie planted herself firmly in front of him. "I'm not a foolish young girl," she insisted. Jacob went stiff. Could she read his mind? Had she? "My view of the world may be limited, but that does not make my opinion without value."

Jacob's heart sunk. He reached out and rested a hand on her shoulder, squeezing. "I'm sorry if I made you feel that way. I didn't mean to. I hated when people dismissed me when I was a kid, and if it seemed like I was doing that now, I'm sincerely sorry."

Ophélie blossomed at his words. "I don't require your apology, Lord Donnelly. I only wanted you to know your wife has not done anything to be concerned about."

Jacob wanted to believe that more than anything in the world. "I wish I could hear that from her." He didn't know why he said it.

She nodded in understanding. "The devil, at times, makes his home inside us, and try as we might, we cannot expel him. He does not allow us to attend anyone but him."

Jacob wondered how much she knew. Or was she talking about her brother?

"Unspeakable evil," she went on, "knows but one adversary. Love."

"She's never had a deficit of that with me."

"Love requires a variance in form," she said wisely. "Patience may be the form currently required."

Jacob laughed. "You think I should patiently watch her fall in love with another man?" There it was, said aloud, finally.

"Fall in love?" Ophélie appeared completely scandalized. "Lord Donnelly, she is not in love with him!"

"What do you understand about it? If you know something, you need to tell me."

She hung her head.

"Let's start with something else, then," Jacob said. He gestured toward the fresh grave. "Who is this?"

"I cannot say."

"Cannot or will not?"

"Are they not the same thing when the secret burns too deep?"

Jacob's voice dropped to a whisper, even though there was no one around but the two of them. "Was the baby yours?"

Ophélie bit her lip and gaped at him with teary eyes. "Have patience with Lady Donnelly. I may not know her devil personally, but I know his demeanor. He has hold of her and will not let go easily."

Jacob reached forward, both hands on her upper arms. Blood surged through him; an itch for the fight. "If your brother did this to you—"

"I cannot be rid of my devil," she cried, breaking free from his grasp. "But Amelia can."

A breeze passed between them. The earthy, pitched scent of the trees grounded Jacob, pulling him back to reality. "Let me walk you to the house." *This isn't appropriate. We shouldn't be here, talking about this. I shouldn't feel so comfortable talking to you.*

Ophélie shook her head, backing away. "You are a kind man, Lord Donnelly. I urge you, do not find yourself involved in matters that don't concern you. There is no end to tragedy."

"Ophélie—"

But she was off, running toward the house with her skirt in hand, stumbling through the fresh grass.

He would have liked to have ended the exchange by escorting her. That felt proper and right. The private chat by the secret grave was neither and left him with the strong sensation he'd done something inappropriate. Something he would not want Amelia to know.

Ophélie had a manner about her that calmed him and made him susceptible to sharing his emotional turmoil. Only Amelia had ever offered him that safe space, and only with her had he ever taken it. This, above all else, was what left him feeling dirty.

No matter how he'd felt in the presence of the young Ophélie Deschanel, though, he would walk away, because it was wrong. He couldn't prevent the feeling, but he could cut off the behavior before it became a problem.

So why couldn't Amelia?

JEAN STOOD OUTSIDE THE HOUSE, BOSSING AROUND A HANDFUL OF horsemen who were working to prepare a carriage.

"Lord Donnelly!" he shouted. His joviality put Jacob on immediate defense.

"Jean."

"What are your plans on the morrow? Can your business spare you for a day?"

Jacob glanced toward the house. Amelia was in there, somewhere. She might be alone. She might not. Either way, she'd never tell him.

"What did you have in mind?"

"Fancy a trip to town?"

DAY FIVE

21

AMELIA

Amelia couldn't believe Jacob had said yes.

She wasn't angry at him for going, not exactly. It might have seemed more curious to their hosts if he'd turned Jean down. But his choice surprised her, for it was evident Jean's opinion of Jacob was somewhere between the dirt under his feet and the sugar stuck in his teeth.

When she asked him, he shrugged and made a comment along the lines of... *It makes me more useful than I've been since we got here.* His face went dark when the words came out, and he was immediately contrite, clearly fearful of upsetting her despite his own justified frustration. In the end, it was moments like this that made her relieved to see him go for the day because she didn't have the presence of mind to ease his. Besides, he would continue to vacillate between being overly supportive and intentionally distant, searching desperately for whatever would appeal to her.

Nothing, she thought. *Nothing will change what happened.*

They left before the sun appeared. Jacob had only given her a light nudge, letting her know he hoped to be back by dinner-time. She didn't realize until later he'd known he was going long before that. Before he went to bed. And he'd said nothing.

How is that his fault?

It wasn't. Nor was it hers.

But Jacob's willingness to leave her alone for the day was a sign, or at least she chose to see it that way.

Jacob needed to sort himself out, and she could pout, or she could use it to her advantage.

Amelia had told him the day they arrived that they were here for a reason. She believed it then, and she still did, even if the answer eluded her.

Fresh air and the first real night of sleep since they'd arrived helped clear away some of the fog that followed her. It hadn't brought her closer to the answer, but it showed her there may be a path to get there.

A path she needed the courage to navigate.

Victor.

AMELIA KNEW NEXT TO NOTHING ABOUT VICTOR DE BLANCHEFORT.

The de Blanchefort name wasn't new. She had seen it crop up from time to time in her mother's archives. Several members of the Deschanel Magi Collective, Amelia included, were tasked with occasional research and to update the details of the files with paperwork and other supporting documentation as technology improved. She knew of Etienne de Blanchefort whose ancestress, the infamous Marianne, had married into the Deschanel family. His fortunes and the near-miss calamity on Saint Domingue were one of her favorite family stories growing up.

Victor was his grandson, if he was to be believed about Marius being his father. But Colleen hadn't tracked the de Blancheforts down the line and into the present since she had no evidence this branch of distant cousins was gifted. The Collective existed to catalogue and keep track of those who *were* gifted, and paid little mind to the others.

Amelia had no doubt in her mind that Victor was gifted. He knew too much about her circumstances to be ordinary, but she was not alarmed or bothered by what he knew. The man walked the earth with the ease of a creature who owned every last inch, reminding her of a more refined version of her cousin, Nicolas.

Victor's eyes were ageless and had seen more than his contemporaries. His knowledge was not limited to the present, either, as he'd made evident.

What was Victor, then, a time traveler? A mystic? He made a point to demonstrate his knowledge to her but failed to explain it. He said she wasn't ready, whatever that meant. Also not choosing to share the particular criteria he used to judge her.

Rules of their travel through time dictated actions that couldn't change the past. Even if they wanted to, they weren't capable of it. Their impression on the past would not last once they returned home.

But they could learn from the past. She and Jacob could take away knowledge that might change their future.

Victor had been laying the signs at her feet, but she had mistaken them for misguided affection, hastily cataloguing him as a nuisance impeding their journey.

But what if he *was* her journey? The purpose?

Amelia peeked outside her bedroom window. The sky was dark above the lush green ceiling of oaks. A breeze passed through the leaves, rustling them in the dry air.

On the horizon, a storm was brewing, though it wasn't the season for it. Amelia hoped Jacob and Jean had no problems on their trip into town.

As for her, she had a mysterious man to track down.

Locating Victor was as easy as wandering down to the main story of the house. He turned at the bottom of the staircase, his arm outstretched to her, and smiled.

"Late to rise this morning, Lady Donnelly," he said, with a single cluck of his tongue. "Please, no apologies. We are defined first by our virtues—mine is patience."

"Then you would have been patiently waiting for an apology," she quipped, sliding her arm through his.

"And your virtue is candor." He nodded toward the front door, where the butler waited for their cue to open. "Are you still holding on to your concern of what others think?"

Amelia dropped her gaze to the ground and laughed. "What does it even matter, when I'll be back to my own time before anyone will really care?"

A visible happiness spread over Victor. "At last, we drop the pretense. Perhaps you *are* ready, after all."

"If I'm not, then we need to get me there because I'm ready to go home."

"And?"

"And I can't..." Amelia faltered, so used to playing a part that she almost slipped back into character again. "I can't until I figure out why we were sent here in the first place."

Victor nodded slowly. "Ahh. Then let us be off before the storm forces us back among less savory company."

The darkness from the Gulf rolled in closer. These were thunderclouds such as she had known her whole life. But through them ran an ominous undercurrent, one that gave her the shivers as she rushed across the dirt, keeping pace with Victor.

He had a destination in mind but, true to his character, hadn't shared it. While they fled across the property in the direction of the river, she thought she might have an idea.

Victor laid a hand at the small of her back and guided her up the embankment. It was hardly a levee at all in 1861, only a few feet high, but the ground was marshy and slick, and she was not wearing shoes designed for the task. Mud sloshed over the sides, and down inside the soles.

"Almost there."

He didn't need to say where *there* was because she immediately noted a piece of the scenery that wasn't intact anymore in the present day: a commercial-sized dock for ships.

Attached was a steamboat that reminded Amelia of a cross between the Natchez that ferried tourists on the river in New Orleans, and something Mark Twain would have enjoyed.

She realized she'd seen the vessel there before, but took it for a passing ship.

"Were Charles and Brigitte expecting visitors?" she asked as they peered down upon the ship, bobbing ever so slightly with the current.

"They were, and they've been here for days already," Victor said. He gestured toward the dock. "This is mine. Or my family's, if we are being specific."

Amelia gaped at him. "And you don't think this is a bit... excessive for a single family?"

"Look around you, Amelia," he chuckled. "Is the Old South about anything else?"

"You mean to tell me you and your father arrived here, just the two of you, on this ship that could carry at least a hundred people?"

"*The Dauphine's* maximum steerage is, in fact, a hundred and fifty, with an additional fifty in the saloon, but the answer to your question, now that we have the details straightened out, is yes."

Amelia stared at him, open-mouthed. She snapped her jaw shut and shook her head. "And you want us to hang out there?"

"Do you know of another place we would remain undisturbed?"

"I guess not." When he sauntered down the dock, she followed with a light hesitance in her step. She'd been so sure, only a half hour ago, that seeking him out and hearing his story would be what she needed. The idea sounded very logical in her mind, despite there being nothing logical about Victor at all. Yet as she followed him toward another mystery, her certainty faltered.

"You've come this far, Amelia. You know I would not hurt you, or you wouldn't have joined me."

Her lips parted in reply as the first heavy drops of rain landed. Within seconds, she could hardly see Victor through the downpour.

Victor appeared at her side, his waistcoat lifted over her head to provide a meager shelter. "Let us at least pass the storm in warmth, then you can decide if I am still the answer to your conundrum."

Amelia drew a steadying breath and nodded. Without asking, he lifted her into his arms, eliciting from her a strained gasp, and sprinted toward the stairs much faster than she could have on her own.

He raised her up and over the bow of the ship before setting her down again, but his hand moved to hers. With a tug, he pulled her into the saloon.

While Amelia, drenched and flustered, took in the flamboyant, plush furnishings she thought might be well-suited in a brothel, Victor rushed to find her something to dry off with.

He returned with some rags and proceeded to dry her off himself before she shooed him away. She thanked him and took them to finish the job.

Amelia caught a glimpse in a gilt mirror over the bar. Her white hair hung in painful, tangled clumps and the rouge Ophélie convinced her to wear each day was streaked, cutting jagged crimson trails down her alabaster cheeks.

I look like a discarded China doll.

"You look like no such thing," Victor replied, unapologetic in his mind-reading. With a start, she threw up her block, wondering how long it had been down and what knowledge he'd gathered in the meantime.

He drew up behind her. His own appearance hadn't fared much better. Black hair plastered against his forehead in places and spiked in others. The cold had drained the color from his complexion, and his lips were the color of ruby red apples.

"I don't like how I feel around you," she confessed, shivering beneath the blanket he pulled over her. "As if I'm always a step behind. Or at a disadvantage."

Victor's face appeared next to hers in the mirror as he watched her. His eyes were sad. "How I wish that were not true."

Amelia turned and laid her hand on the side of his face. She didn't know what prompted her to do so, only that she needed confirmation he was real. She dropped cold fingers back to her side.

"I need you to tell me, Victor. I don't know what it is you're keeping from me, or why, or what it will mean when you share it, but I am *here,* for a purpose, and that reason matters even if it has evaded me for days. But it doesn't evade you... does it?"

"No."

Amelia's eyes closed. Something just shy of relief passed through her before stopping at fear. "And you'll tell me?"

"Yes."

"You won't toy with me, or speak in riddles?"

"I will tell you what I can," he answered.

"What does that mean? What you can?"

"It means what it means." He watched her through pained eyes. His hand rose as if to touch her, and when he realized it, he lowered it again.

"You agreed no riddles."

Victor lifted her hand in his and dropped his eyes as he ran a thumb over her fingers. "There are certain truths you must come to on your own. I cannot take that journey for you. You can't know how badly I wish to."

Tears pooled at the surface of Amelia's eyes, borne of frustration. "But I need to know! I *have* to know why I've suffered, and why Jacob has suffered, and why I can't heal!"

Victor dropped her hand with a light sigh. He pulled the blanket tighter around her. "Those answers are within you. They have always been inside you." His hand rested between her shoulder blades, guiding her toward an eggplant-colored velvet chaise. "Let us see if this is the day you find the courage to draw them out."

22
JACOB

Jacob had ridden in a carriage before. The touristy type, where the horses languished in the Quarter for the sake of impressing a date. He was guilty of hiring one, once in high school, with a girl he'd hardly spoke to again, and later with Amelia, after they'd broken down the barrier between friendship and love.

In those early days, though they'd been intimate on other levels for years, he found it especially important to demonstrate his capability of being her partner, and his worthiness. He had to convince himself more than her. Amelia hardly cared about flowers or carriage rides down Chartres, but he did them anyway, until she finally laughed, kissed him, and said... *Let's just do what we've always done, Donnelly.*

This carriage was not the same. The ones he had ridden in moved at a leisurely pace, lasting only long enough to have a fill of the niche experience and be thankful it wasn't the only means of actual transportation.

Now he was literally discovering that relying on a carriage wasn't an ideal way to travel.

Rough, he thought, imagining Amelia asking him to describe the experience in one word. There were two roads into Vacherie, and one was a river. The other, while worn down from the wagon and carriage wheels of others, was rife with bumps, rocks, and uneven patches.

They only had to travel seven or eight miles, but at their pace, the trip could take half a day.

When Jean had approached him the day before about the trip, Jacob's acceptance came from a place of bitterness. A day later, and cooled some, he searched for other benefits. Amelia had held tight to her insistence they were in this time and place for a reason. And with no sign of the reason presenting itself, Jacob wondered if a trip with Jean might turn into an opportunity.

He couldn't tell Amelia how badly he wanted to leave... how afraid he was for their safety, how the nagging insistent voice foretelling grave danger would not let up... not when she held tight to the promise of answers... not when Jacob suspected, deep down, she was counting on these answers to heal her.

He and Jean had been on the road an hour when the first hint of thunder rolled in the distance.

Jean, in his waistcoat and derby looking ever the man of the house, regarded Jacob from the bench across from him.

"When will you be returning to England, Lord Donnelly?"

Jacob, who had been unable to doze with all the bumps, but had nevertheless been daydreaming, fumbled through his response. "Oh. Well, ah, as soon my business with your father is concluded."

"And when will that be?"

Jacob swallowed back a wave of queasiness that hit as soon as he opened his mouth. He was growing less confident his stomach would survive the trip. "Soon, I hope." It was one of the few truths he'd told on this strange voyage.

Jean narrowed his eyes and stretched his arms across the back of the carriage bench. Jacob had to remind himself this monster was only fifteen. "Is tomorrow too soon?"

"Tomorrow?" Jacob repeated. He read the threat but played dumb to avoid the inevitable rise of blood that might lead to something he couldn't take back. "That's a very long trip to take for only a few days."

Jean snorted. "I know the length."

Impudent little punk.

"Then you understand we're still recovering from the trip over."

"I understand. Whether I care or not is another matter," Jean replied. Outside, the rain appeared from nowhere, and the exterior soundtrack went from the soft sounds of high noon to the disharmony of the storm's assault.

Jacob crossed his arms. "Why am I here, Jean? Why did you ask me to come?"

"I was tasked with picking up my father's parcels from the post."

"And you didn't need my help."

Jean wrinkled his lips into a maddening shape. Before he could unleash his next string of hatefulness, the carriage came to an abrupt stop. The horses whinnied and bucked, rocking the buggy.

"That fool!" Jean cried. "I told him no stops!" He appeared every bit the child again. A pouting, stomping brat.

The sound of heavy boots hitting mud came next, and Jacob was the first to peek his head out. He pulled it back in so fast his neck hurt. "I think I know why he stopped."

"A little rain?" Jean shrieked. "Is he afraid to get his hair wet? It isn't a cursed hurricane, for heaven's sake!"

Jacob shot the boy a look and stuck his head out once more. "No," he called back. The carriage rocked side-to-side as the horses thrashed in panic. "The road is washed out by the flash flood."

The door on the other side flew open and the driver, a young man no older than Jean, launched himself inside. Jean beat him with open fists, plainly disgusted.

"Dude, chill out!" Jacob said to his traveling partner, pulling the shivering man to his side. "You all right?"

"What did you say to me?" Jean hissed. Jacob wasn't sure if it was for calling him out or because Jacob had slipped character and used unrecognizable slang.

"I said calm down," Jacob repeated, using the right words this time. He comforted the trembling man, who was traumatized from the undeserved onslaught from his master. "Would you want to be outside in that?"

"He's a loathsome slave," Jean said, indignant. His eyes flashed wild with anger. "This one, in particular, is *my* property, Lord Donnelly. His single purpose in life is to do as I say, when I say it, in the manner in which I demand. And shall I tell you what he is *not* supposed to do? Come back and tarnish me and my guest with his cursed, abominable—"

Jacob held his hands up, palms out to avoid making a fist and ending the whole charade right there. "That's enough, kid. I'm serious."

"Get him out of here."

"Not until this storm passes."

"What did you say? No. He is not remaining here with us!" Jean leveled his rage on Jacques. "And calm those nags before I shoot them and you!"

Jacob ignored Jean's tirade and lifted the young man. His face was covered in wetness, a mix of rain and tears. Jacob used his shirt to wipe both away, as Jean moaned in disgust.

"What's your name?"

"Jacques, sir."

"Jacques. Nice to meet you. I'm Lord Donnelly, but you can call me Jacob."

"No, he cannot!" Jean cried.

"I best not, sir," Jacques said quietly.

"It's okay, Jacques," Jacob soothed. He forced a smile. "You call me whatever you're comfortable with. We're friends now."

"Yes, Lord Donnelly."

"We need your help. I'm sure as a footman you're an expert around these parts, is that right?"

Jacques looked down, hiding his swelling pride. "Yes, sir, Lord Donnelly. I know th' parts well."

Jean huffed, tapping his foot. He rolled his eyes toward the door, making overt gestures to kick the man out.

Jacob clapped a hand on the man's shoulder. "Good. We're still a ways out from Vacherie proper, and it doesn't seem as if we're in any shape to get there in this storm. Can you tell us if we are close to anywhere the three of us can take shelter until the storm passes?"

Jacques' eyes went up, thinking. "Ah, yessir, there be a parish store not far, just up thereabouts. Last I was there, they had them two rooms for travelers. I ain't seen the place myself, so if they ain't up to your standards, I can't in good conscience recommend them..."

"Great! If I were to go up and drive this coach, do you think you could give me some good direc—"

"Absolutely not!" Jean thundered. His face was the color of the red velvet seats. "This has gone far enough. He is *not your friend*, Lord Donnelly, and I won't have you spoiling him with this unusual treatment. Jacques, you will take us to this store at once, and I don't want to hear another whelp out of you about this rain."

"Yes, sir, Monsieur." Jacques' whole demeanor wilted as he reached for the door.

Jacob couldn't help himself.

He stretched forward and pulled the man into a half-embrace. "Thank you, sir. I'll be in your debt," Jacob told him, and the painful groaning sound from Jean was almost as enjoyable as the secret smile Jacques wore, with a light spring in his step, as he went outside to face the storm as their newly minted hero.

Jean wagged an unsteady finger at him. He was too young, too inexperienced to control his rage in a way that could have served him at the moment and was, instead, an unhinged ball of wrath. "If you *ever*—"

"Ah, fuck off," Jacob said and leaned back into the seat to tune him out.

ONLY ONE ROOM WAS AVAILABLE, THOUGH IT HAD BOTH A SMALL BED and a couch, and with no other option, they took it. Jean demanded Jacques sleep in the rain. Jacob countered Jacques could take the couch, and he would sleep on the floor. Amidst Jean's apoplectic fit at the suggestion, the owner of the store inadvertently solved the dilemma by declaring no slaves allowed in his rooms except when service was needed. This earned a satisfied smirk from Jean, but Jacob saw to it Jacques found warmth inside in the carriage. Their secret.

"You have a lot to learn about earning loyalty," Jacob said when it was only the two of them. Jean leaned over the hearth, attempting to start a fire and wearing a deeply perplexed frown. He'd likely never had to do this on his own before in his life.

Jean laughed. "I don't require loyalty from a slave. Only obedience."

Jacob had more thoughts on the matter—many more—but he understood a discussion on human rights would be wasted on a creature who had no warmth or heart to speak of. He treated his sister, his own flesh and blood, no better. Worse, even, unless he was raping his slaves, too.

He shuddered.

"You never answered my question," Jacob started. Standing over him, he enjoyed this temporary position of power, then wondered why he needed it. Jean was a child, even if he had the heart of a fiend. He wasn't worth the energy.

"Remind me of the question."

"About why I'm here."

"I started to when that pickaninny barged in."

Jacob's anger blossomed into a burning heat. *Ignore it. Unless you plan to kill him and have Jacques help you hide the body...*

"So, we have time now. Plenty of time," Jacob added. He peeked out the curtain at the endless sea of dark cloud formations. "It's clear you don't like me. That's cool because I happen to think you're an asshole. I'm not a fool, for whatever else you might think of me. With that out of the way, let's talk about what you really want."

Jean's brow shot up. "You're right. I don't like you. I can appreciate your cutting to the point, however."

Jacob said nothing.

"I wanted to speak with you about the night you arrived. And two nights past, as well, if my suspicions are correct," Jean said. He pulled himself up and leaned into the stone hearth. Jacob was shocked to see he'd actually achieved the fire. Jean looked shocked as well. "You've been inserting yourself where you do not belong and have not been comporting yourself with the respectful behavior one expects from a guest. If you have any regard for my family, you'll realize your error and cease this behavior immediately."

Jacob's heart raced; Jean's concern over his involvement was all but confirmation of the unholy deed. "I don't make a point of being nosy unless something is going on that I can't ignore," he said carefully. "And a baby crying, all by itself, is something I can't ignore."

Jean threw his head back with a short laugh. "Ah, yes, Maman said you mentioned a baby. You and your silly wife. There are no babies in Ophélie, so either you are mad or... no, perhaps you are just mad."

"Both of us?" Jacob pressed. "My wife heard it, too. She and I are close, but we don't exactly share hallucinations."

"I've seen no evidence of this closeness, though perhaps it's because I only see your wife when she's in the presence of another man," Jean said, grinning.

Jacob tried to ignore the slight, but the knife twisted anyway. "We aren't trying to cause trouble. But we know what we heard."

"You presuppose nonsense and know nothing," Jean volleyed, rolling toward the slowly building heat. "And you are not one of us, no matter how loosely you may tie yourselves to our pedigree."

"I know you're hiding something," Jacob said. He walked toward the warmth and Jean shrunk into the stone. "I saw the fresh grave on the property. Are you going to explain that away as madness, too?

"There are some things outsiders cannot understand. Things you know nothing about. I would not come to your house and dig around making accusations," Jean said, for the first time sounding reasonable.

"I haven't made any accusations," Jacob replied. "But something is going on in your house, something you don't want anyone to know about. And that's fine, because, hey, I'm not looking for trouble. Neither is my wife. But we both know I'm not crazy."

A gust of rain smashed into the window, and Jean jumped. They shivered in tandem.

"Oh, you are more than certainly crazy," Jean said, shaking his head as he ran his tongue along his lower lip. "For allowing your wife to run to the arms of Victor de Blanchefort. For a man who claims to know the business of others, you haven't made near the effort to know his."

"I trust her," Jacob defended. "Don't bring her up again."

Jean's laugh, this time, resonated across the wooden room, bouncing off the table and chairs, across the wall. "We both know de Blanchefort will bring her up enough for the both of us."

Jacob's hands turned to fists. *No, Cianán,* his mother's voice warned, gently. *You know this is not the answer. Not with him. He isn't your battle to fight.*

"You want to hit me." Jean cackled. "But you lack the spine for the task."

Jacob spun on him. Something in his face silenced the young man. "You aren't worth it." *And the price of your blood on my hands would be greater for me than it ever would be for you.*

THEY PASSED THE EVENING HOURS IN SILENCE. HAD JEAN ATTEMPTED A conversation, he would have been met with Jacob's quick temper. But Jacob was not surprised when Jean said nothing, and they each slipped into the solace of their own thoughts.

Jacob had more on his mind on the matter of Jean, but his exhaustion won the battle, and the sooner he rested, the quicker he could wake again and return to Amelia.

He wouldn't think about her, either. Although he might not

understand her fascination with this strange de Blanchefort fellow, he trusted her. And when he saw her again, he would tell her so. *I know you're hurting. Being around me maybe makes that worse. But just tell me. Tell me what you need from him, and I'll try to understand. Getting you through this is more important than any ego.*

Jacob eased into sleep playing the script out in his mind, over and over, hoping the repetition would also bring him courage.

INSTINCT WOKE HIM. THE DISTINCT PINCH OF STEEL AGAINST HIS throat brought him quickly to lucidity.

He lay still, squinting into the dark room. He fully expected Jean to be the man wielding the knife at his neck, but Jean's pathetic whimpers in the corner brought more of the story to light.

Jacob didn't recognize the rancid, oily man leaning over him, but his identity wasn't important. It never was. Everyone who wielded a weapon to extort power did so because they wanted something. *That* was important.

"Give them whatever they want!" Jean cried. As if Jacob had to guess where this craven bastard stood when faced with adversity.

The face above him came further into focus. Jacob put his hands up and to the side to show he had no weapon of his own. To show surrender.

"Where is it?" the man demanded. His spit dotted Jacob's cheeks, and he resisted the urge to wipe it away.

"Where is what?" Jacob asked. Good. Talking was good. He needed another few moments to take stock of the situation.

"You know. The gold." Shuffling across the room. A second

man. Of course, Jacob thought. Someone was keeping Jean in line. Were there more?

"The shopkeeper said you came in with twelve bars," the other man said.

Jacob listened with more than his ears. He wasn't straining for footsteps or voices, only for the air in the room. For the way it reacted to the environment.

No. Only two.

"Jean, give him the gold," Jacob ordered. The source of this issue was clear, suddenly. The shopkeeper had turned his own trouble on them.

"What? Lord Donnelly, what... what..." Jean stammered.

Yeah, I know. No gold. Better for them not to know that just yet.

What? Lord Donnelly? How are you in my head?

Doesn't matter. Play along or die. I don't care.

"Listen to your master, Jean," the man with the knife said, leering. He spat on the floor.

"He is not my master!" Jean stammered, followed by a sharp howl. "Oh, no..."

"Pierre, he pissed himself!" the man across the room cackled, stomping his feet.

This was all the distraction Jacob required. Pierre turned his attention for only a brief moment, but Jacob stole that time and turned it into his opportunity.

He twisted to the left, rolling out of bed and squarely to his feet before Pierre could react. Jacob threw a sharp jab to the back of the thief's neck, sending him to his knees. The knife hit the floor with a clack.

Jean's minder flew over in a confused rage. Jacob sent him hurling into the fireplace. His head cracked against the stone, and he slumped to the floor.

Jacob knelt for the knife and leaned in where Pierre huddled on the ground. "Is your life worth imaginary gold?"

Pierre sputtered rejections through blood and saliva, crying into the wood floor.

"Kill him!" Jean exclaimed. He was emboldened now there was no longer a risk to his life.

Grab the one who made you piss yourself, Jacob ordered, nodding his way. *We need to get them out of here.* "Pierre, you're either going to walk out of here on your own, or I'm going to kick you, crying and screaming."

Pierre scrambled to all fours. He peered back, like a disobedient dog, fear in his eyes.

"Go." He did.

Jean was useless. He gaped at Jacob as if seeing him, the real him, for the very first time.

It took him ten minutes to get both men out of the room. Jacob perched them at the top of the stairs and pointed at the cowering shopkeeper who, very likely, never expected to see Jacob or Jean again. "Next time you make deals with scum, you can take out your own trash," Jacob spat and kicked both men down the stairs.

Once inside, he barricaded the door with the heavy table and heaved a sigh filled with as much disgust for himself as relief.

"What did you do to them?" Jean cried. He hadn't moved from where he lay huddled near the hearth, lying in a pool of his own urine.

"Saved your life. Maybe not your panties, though."

"You were in my head," the younger man accused.

Aye. And I'll do it anytime I like, so better keep your thoughts nice and tidy.

Jacob fell asleep curled atop the table in shame, recognizing his actions in the moments prior as the very things he believed he should walk away from. He could have killed those men… and might have, too, if he hadn't gotten control of himself and the situation. Jacob had promised himself he wouldn't be that man anymore.

Jean's wide eyes burned holes in him.

23
AMELIA

Victor made a fire in the ship's kiln. He poured the heated water over some chicory root in two mugs and handed Amelia one. He sat on the other end of the chaise.

"Where... well, *when* I'm from, these winter storms come and go. They rarely last," she said, half smiling as she graciously accepted her cup. "We get nasty ones in hurricane season that can set us back, but this is unusual."

Victor took a slow sip of his warm coffee, watching her over the rim. "I'm pleased you are no longer wasting energy pretending to be someone you're not," he said. "It's refreshing to know you for who you are."

Amelia blew out a breath. "I don't see the point. You know who I am. I don't know *how* you know, but I've been around extraordinary people all my life so it would be silly for me to be shocked now."

"Yet I would put my plantation on the line to wager you've never met anyone like *me*."

Amelia searched for a sign he was teasing and found none.

"I'm a Deschanel. There's almost nothing I haven't seen. No offense if you think reading minds or seeing into the future is a cool trick, but it's a dime a dozen in my family."

Victor squinted, scrunching his lips. "*Cool.* I'm glad to be of a time where our colloquialisms are less confusing and more straightforward."

Amelia curled up tighter on her side of the lounger. The rain battered against the ship's windows, rocking *Dauphine* where she moored in the port. Amelia grinned. "Want me to explain the meaning?"

"I quite catch your context. That won't be necessary," Victor said.

A heavy gust sent the ship up with a current, and they both stumbled back in their seat. "Are we going to be okay in here?" Amelia asked, uneasy. Jacob was out there somewhere, too. If they were back home, she could call him and get reassurance he was okay. Here, if something happened...

"Lord Donnelly will be fine," Victor assured her. When she shot him a sharp look, he quickly added, "I did not need to read your mind to know your thoughts."

"He's with that horrible Jean," she said with a shiver. "I know he's barely a child, but you don't know the things I know about him."

"I wasn't planning a case in his defense," Victor said. He wrapped the blanket around her bare feet. "But Jacob, your husband, is a survivor. He has abilities that will serve him well in any circumstance, even with an unsavory traveling partner."

How do you know... she started to ask, but the answer to that would come with all the others if they could get warm, and find a sense of comfort with one another. To ask one question would lead to so many more, and she sensed he was more nervous, for once, than she was.

"I don't think he would even be out there if it weren't for

me," Amelia said with a heavy sigh. Why Victor, a man she barely knew, felt a safer place to lighten the burdens on her soul than her own husband, remained an uncomfortable mystery. "I haven't been very nice to him since we arrived."

"Marriage is far less good than anyone wants you to believe," Victor said, his eyes glassy and sympathetic. "Human nature is perfectly imperfect."

"The situation is more complex than that," she said, staring down into her cup. The chicory was strong even for her, and she loved dark, rich coffee. But she needed the warmth. The strength. "I... no, we... went through something terrible. An event no one should ever have to endure, but we did it together, which should mean we could share that experience and heal together."

"Except you are not," Victor finished. "And it is you who cannot find your way to him, not the reverse."

"That's pretty much it," she replied, ashamed to hear someone else say the words. "As a doctor of psychology, I know people who share a trauma don't always find ways to help each other. Parents who lose a child often struggle to recover because they grieve in different ways, and there are so many emotions tied to grief, including guilt and judgment. But I never thought, not ever, that Jacob and I would be the couple who couldn't find our way together."

Victor reached forward and took her mug, setting it on the table. He pulled both of her hands into his. "Amelia, you could not have foreseen what that madman did to you."

Amelia snatched her hands back, drawing away from the kindness out of shock from his words. She stumbled off the sofa, rolled onto her feet, and backed up. "I don't want to talk about it. It's all I can think about, and I don't want it hijacking my life anymore. I'm better than this."

"Better than what?"

"Than... than... *this constant depression.* Than not being able to push forward and be strong, like my mother taught me, and like she's always been, even when she's lost nearly everything. Like my grandmother was before her. I am *not this person! I am not weak!*" She wailed the words into the din of the small saloon, all while Victor watched her with patient eyes.

He stood but respected the distance between them. "Weakness would be surrender. It does not involve taking your husband's hand and dancing through time. That's courage. Weakness would be running. It would not be searching for answers to make sense of what's happened. That's wisdom. Weakness would be continuing to ignore the signs in front of you and turning your back on what you have always known, deep down, and only needed to accept. It would not be seeking me out, despite your fears, despite that my knowledge threatens you and the delicate story you've spun to your hosts. That is fearlessness."

Amelia's mouth parted, from wonder, from uncertainty. From the warmth and truth of his words, and the ease at which he'd put her since the day they'd met. "Why can't I believe in any of those things? Why do I constantly feel like I'm drowning?" The first tears spilled over her lids. "And maybe it wouldn't be the worst thing in the world if I did."

"I won't entertain such nonsense. You are made for so much more than the dredges of hopelessness," he said. Victor approached without laying his hands upon Amelia. "Neither will I make light of your pain. You have endured something unspeakable. I would do anything in this world to undo it. I would give my own life."

Amelia stared up at the heavy sincerity in his words. "I need to know why, Victor. You can't say things like that without explaining yourself, and nearly everything you've said to me since we met has deserved an explanation."

His lips formed a thin smile, and he took a deep breath. "Yes, you are right. And I did promise to tell you what I could. There are two things you must know about me. One, I will tell you, though I should not. Within my truth lies a secret that enfolds my entire family, and sharing with you puts them at grave risk. I trust you would not use the information to harm me, but I am placing everything in your hands with this confession."

She nodded. "Okay. And the other?"

"That, I'm afraid, is not for me to share with you. I am expressly forbidden. In life, there is a way of things, an order. Asking me to force the hand of nature is not the way."

Amelia threw out her arms. "Forbidden? Who or what would forbid you?"

"The answer lies in the question," he replied with a light shrug. "I know that's unsatisfying."

"It's fucking frustrating."

"For me as well. The truth would set us both free." He gestured toward the seat. "Please. The storm isn't passing soon, so there's time for me to tell you about one part of my life. In that revelation, and through our unintended long afternoon together, perhaps the other will unwind as well."

Amelia started toward the seat, in slow motion as her thoughts caught up. "You won't lie to me." She didn't ask as a question because it wasn't a request. She wouldn't give him a choice.

"I have not thus far. And you have my word I would never."

Why his word was enough lay somewhere in her willingness to seek him out to begin with, and how at peace she was in his presence, despite her combativeness and resistance to his offering.

Whatever the reason, it was enough.

Amelia nodded for him to commence.

. . .

"I'll start my story at the beginning, or at least close to the part of the most prominent turn in the journey my family and I now find ourselves. Despite your claim to have seen all as a Deschanel, I can say with near certainty you have never come across the likes of *me.*"

Amelia's brows lifted.

"But I'll request you refrain from questions or protestations, unless seeking clarity, until I finish. Not to silence you, but instead to allow you to hear all I've said before you cast your own judgment. Can we agree?"

She nodded. "Tell me your story, Victor. I'm not going anywhere."

Victor's eyes met hers for a moment. He passed a brief, telepathic thanks and settled back into his seat, getting comfortable.

"I believe you know my family's origins are from France, primarily. My mother's grandparents were Irish, though, so we are not pure Frenchmen as we tend to avow." Victor grinned. "My *grandpêre*, Etienne, was the first to leave when he saw opportunities in the islands. He purchased a large plot of land in *Cap Français*, Saint-Domingue, and his line of the de Blancheforts went from being heirs of an inheritance to wealthy in their own right. My aunts, Victorine and Nanette, were born in France, but my father, Marius, and the youngest, Flosine, were born in Hispaniola and knew nothing else.

"Our family spent barely more than a decade on the island. *Dauphine,* our plantation named for my *grandmère*, was a Garden of Eden for my father and his siblings, a land of plenty where they wanted for nothing. *Dauphine* was a leader in cane sugar, as well as indigo and coffee, and my *grandpêre* grew the land from a tangle of tropical foliage to the greatest plantation in *Cap Français. Grandpêre* told me he would have stayed there forever if fate allowed."

"The Haitian Revolution," Amelia whispered, then blushed at her unintended interruption. "Sorry. I promised."

Victor offered a smile. "Yes, the Haitian Revolution. The great uprising, one that, even in your present day, has never been rivaled. A true example of the marriage of grit and organization. My family was on the wrong side of history in this. I look upon the rebels with admiration.

"I digress. If you are aware of the timeline, you may be wondering why the de Blancheforts fled ahead of the violence. Why the family would leave everything behind before knowledge of the revolution had spread. Who would surrender a land so profitable for a risk across the ocean? They had been in Louisiana nearly half a year before the fighting commenced.

"The truth of the situation is, we had help. A warning. Not from the loyal slaves of the property, though they were quick to confirm what my *grandpêre* had learned. This admonition came from a creature who called himself by the name of Childeric."

"Creature?" Amelia repeated.

"I don't come by the word accidentally," Victor continued. "He was not of the human race or had not been for some time. Centuries. Millennia, to hear him tell it. He claimed to have been watching the de Blancheforts for many years, awaiting the moment to present himself and, with it, his gift. He also claimed ancestry to our family."

Amelia was frozen in place. Her mouth parted with questions she promised to save for the end. When he stopped to observe her, she swallowed and nodded for him to go on.

"Understand, my family knew little of who he was when we took his advisement to leave. My *grandpêre* referred to Childeric as his demon, as he'd taunted the family for months before ever showing his face. *Grandpêre* would never have taken this demon's warnings as fact, but the confirmation from the loyal slaves proved his words were not deception, and my *grandpêre,* a man who had forged his own destiny and did not have it in him to wait for history to catch up, risked everything to rebuild his family's life here, at a property down in St. Charles Parish. If you have ever seen *Coquillage*, close your eyes and imagine the cerulean waters of the Caribbean lapping against the cliffs, a path of sand stretching to the porch. Picture the gas lanterns swinging from trees, the fresh scents of bananas and seawater compulsory. It was built to resemble *Dauphine* in every way."

"I have, as a girl," Amelia said. "But only sneaking around the grounds with my cousins. It's never been open for tours."

"And never will be," Victor assured her. "For the secret sustaining us can never be a matter for the public. Not ever.

"We did not hear from Childeric frequently until the final days in on the island. So in time, he became a hazy memory, his sudden appearance in the family fading to an afterthought.

"But Childeric had not forgotten the de Blancheforts. He was merely biding his time, testing my *grandpêre's* mettle. His gift was not for the weak, and he would not grant it without being certain he had chosen the right recipient. We later discovered he had passed over many generations before deciding my *grandpêre* and his brood worthy.

"His final test was akin to the one I present to you now, Amelia. Childeric appeared to my *grandpêre* one evening, drawing him out of the plantation and into the garden to share the revelation of his origins. He did not ease into this startling truth but came out with the words in a quick rush. My *grandpêre's* reaction would determine his fate.

"I will never forget this story. My *grandpêre's* words are etched into my memory for eternity. '*I am immortal, Etienne. I cannot die, not by traditional methods. Wound me, and I bleed. Ah, but then I heal. I bear the same skin as I've had since I took the master's blood, and I will continue to bear it until the end of my long days. That end will be of my own choosing, and ours is the beginning for another.'* My *grandpêre* then asked the same question I know you are wondering silently now. *'What are you?'* And Childeric answered. *'I am dhampir. Though you may relate more to the word vampire.'"*

Victor paused, allowing Amelia a moment too. She stared at him in unmoving horror since she had promised to let him finish. Besides, she could say nothing that wouldn't offend him.

"My *grandpêre* passed his final test. He did not question Childeric. He and his children had gifts not sanctioned by God or science, and why should this be any different? Instead, he only wanted to know more! He learned much from Childeric in those hours when night turned to dawn. When they parted, Childeric had made the decision for one of his numerous tribe to give up his gift so Etienne de Blanchefort could take his place."

"Take his place?"

"The rules of the dhampir are few, but important," Victor went on. "Your vampires, the vampires of literature and fanciful legends, are nothing like the ones of the old god. The dhampir are finite in number, and it is impossible to increase the race in size. You cannot give your blood and make a legion of them. The Master ordains that to make one anew, a dhampir must give their own gift back to the Master's Tree. Childeric's tribe had wandered for many, many years, and were ready for their eternal rest. They'd been searching for candidates worthy to pass the torch, as it were. Childeric sought out a new tribe to replace the weary."

"And... and Childeric's friends offered this to your grandfather?"

"Yes. And *grandpêre's* wife, and four children. But as my father and Flosine had not reached maturity, the offer was to be given in phases. My grandparents would go first, joining Childeric in Eastern Europe, to what is now, in your time, Slovakia, to take the blood at the Master's Tree from two of his tribe, and return home dhampir. Aunt Nan was next, when she fell so ill she sat on death's door. As the other children reached the age of their own desire—for, it was important to remember they would remain that age always—they would, in turn, take the same voyage, until all were dhampir, creating the new tribe of Childeric.

"One of the unusual gifts of the dhampir is they can still bear children, but their children are born without the gift, as only new dhampir can be created with the loss of an old one."

"So..." Amelia searched for the words, her heart a racing mess. "Sorry, continue."

"There is not much more to tell," Victor said softly. "Ahh, I could tell you many, many stories, of course. But this revelation is a shock, I know. And I can only expect so much of you for one afternoon."

"So, then... are you..."

"A dhampir?" Victor smiled. "Yes. Childeric continues to follow our family even today, assessing us, nominating one from his tribe to give their life for us. We are his new tribe, beholden to him but powerful in our own right, which is why he chose us."

"Childeric still lives, though?"

"We have replaced, one by one, members of his tribe, but he has shown no sign of being ready to give his own gift away. He seems intent to lead us into the future."

"How long have you been like this?"

"I took the blood five years past, at the age of twenty-eight. A choice, knowing as I know now, I have come to regret."

"If you truly were offered such a choice, why regret it?" Her blanket dropped as she leaned forward. "I mean, you either want to be immortal or you don't, but you obviously spent a lot of years thinking about it first." *Listen to yourself. You're actually entertaining this ridiculous idea.*

"I didn't know then what I know now," he said sadly. "that the price would be the love of my life."

"I'm confused. You're married already."

"You reference a relationship born of duty," he said. "Something I chose myself, willingly, for the reasons you might guess. I did not know at the time that my destiny was not to become a dhampir, but something far different."

"And that is?"

"The part of this story I cannot tell you." He seemed almost ashamed.

"Okay." Amelia averted her eyes. She ran through her list of questions. "So, why take the blood? Other than immortality, what are the advantages?"

Victor laughed. "Is that not enough?"

"You had to know you couldn't continue your life here after so many years. People would talk."

"As they do now about my father. And my *grandpère,* who is now a hundred and three years old."

"You're lying."

"I promised honesty. I've given you honesty. You see my father and disbelieve he is seventy-eight years old for good reason. But his birth is a matter of record. His contemporaries, those who grew up alongside him, can speak to it even if they cannot explain it."

"But..." But what? No, she wasn't a foolish girl who looked at the world through rose-colored glasses, expecting everything to fall into place. Every explanation to be neat and tidy. She had trusted him this far, and while she was not fully ready to accept the truth of his words, she would be wasting precious time if she spent what they had left refuting him. "Tell me more about what it's like to be a dhampir."

"It is a lot like being human, except mortal wounds cannot kill me," he answered. He seemed pleased at her question. "And, of course, I ceased to age five years ago. No, I do not require blood to live. It is more akin to a treat, or, in the case of those of us with special abilities, a burst of power. If we take from another who has power, we absorb theirs, temporarily. Some dhampir take gifted humans as slaves, so they can draw from their powers indefinitely. Others do so in order to assume the wealth of their slave."

Amelia considered this. "Can you show me your fangs?"

"I have to retrieve it the old fashioned way. Sorry to disappoint."

"What, a knife?"

"Or anything with an especially sharp edge."

"Okay. What else? Clearly, you aren't afraid of sunlight."

"I'm not bothered by it in the slightest."

"Garlic?"

"Wonderful with boar."

"Silver?"

"Slightly less valuable than gold but still an asset."

"And the cross?"

He tilted his head, eyeing her. "I must say, you're taking this rather well."

"I'm only waiting for the full moon so you can also reveal you're a werewolf. Maybe the legend of the rougarou starts with you," she quipped. "Cross? Yay? Nay?"

Victor pulled a necklace from under his shirt. The object

was of thick construction, and solid gold. "Always with me, like any good Catholic."

"A Catholic vampire?" Amelia shook her head. "When you take communion, do you bring the literal blood of Christ with you?"

"Would that I could!" He laughed with her. "I eat the same food as you. I sleep as you do. I drink as you do. I enjoy the same carnal pleasures."

She rolled her eyes. "Glad we cleared that last one up."

"You asked how my life was different," Victor said with a shrug. "There are few differences, except in how we present ourselves to the world. My *grandpêre* has retired from public life for he is past the point of a reasonable suspension of disbelief. We held a funeral for him fifteen years ago, and my *grand-mère* not long after. They were mourned by many."

"How do you do that, though? Do you hide them in a cellar?"

"You know we cannot have cellars in Louisiana."

Amelia sighed. "You know what I mean."

"We own many properties along the river. Only two are open to our peers for events. The others are a sanctuary for those of us who are forced out of the sunlight and into the darkness until such time when anyone alive to remember us has passed."

"That sounds very sad," Amelia said softly.

"To be eternally surrounded by those you love? Mostly, it's a gift. Occasionally torture."

Amelia thought of perpetuity with all the Deschanels and an internal shiver passed through her. "Does your wife know? And your children?"

"No and no," Victor replied, rising. "The day has already faded away from us. You must be starving."

"I hadn't even thought about food, to be honest," she said.

She leaned back over the chair and gazed out the window, where hail beat down on the surface of the river. "But we can't go back to the house when it's like this."

"We may have provisions in the storeroom," he said and disappeared through a small door behind the bar.

Amelia took the opportunity to stand and stretch. She'd been so absorbed with his story and hadn't realized how much time had passed, but her body felt the lack of movement.

No matter what Victor said, she was worried for Jacob, too. She didn't doubt his resilience, but she was afraid of what Jean might do, and what his intentions were in asking him to come to begin with. And he hadn't returned yet, though he said he'd be back by dinner. They would have heard the approaching carriage.

"I'm afraid this is all I could find," Victor apologized. In one hand, he had a hunk of stale bread. In the other, half a wheel of cheese. "But there is more wine, and that, if nothing, will dull the pain."

"It's fine," she said and joined him at the bar. "I haven't eaten much since we arrived anyway."

"Is the food too different for your palate?"

She shook her head. "Stress."

Victor tore the bread in half and handed her a piece. "I'm aware this advice comes without provocation," he started, hesitant. "But I believe your restoration will begin when you learn to heal with him."

"Jacob?"

"Who else?"

Amelia worked the hard bread around in her mouth, wincing as she swallowed down a near whole piece. "You say that, but you don't understand."

"I do, and we will leave it at that before I get myself in trouble."

"And yet you keep talking about it!"

"Jacob," he said, ignoring her, "is the only one who shares your pain through experience."

"He saw what that monster did to me." Amelia put the bread down. She stared at the cheese but made no move for it. "And when I look at him, I see it in his eyes."

"What that monster did to both of you," Victor corrected. "You can measure the degree of offense, or put it on a scale if it helps you to understand it, but you both suffered. For Jacob, there was nothing worse in all the world than feeling as if he was a party to your sorrow. He will live with that for all the rest of his days, as will you."

"So he looks at me and sees pain *and* failure. Is that somehow better?"

"He needs you, too," Victor said. "You are not the only one who cannot move on from what happened that night."

Amelia pushed back from the bar, dizzy with her own exhaustion. Mental, physical, emotional... there was no limit to any of the three. "You seem to know everything about me, but refuse to tell me why you even care, or why it should matter to you." She threw her hands up before he could rebut. "I know, you think you can't, and maybe that's true, but I can't talk about this anymore tonight. Not with you. Every moment since I've been here has been a frustrating mystery I can't explain, and if I can't solve this, I can't move on... and no, don't tell me I'm wrong. You don't know *everything* about me!"

"You're right," he said, his face a mask of pacifism. "I cannot know everything about you. And it is unfair of me to expect you to take my words without the proper evidence."

Victor went to the chaise and picked up her blanket. "Come, Amelia. I'll take you to a private cabin where you can get some rest until the rain dies off."

"Thank you." Her chest heaved with emotion, sending

blood rushing to her face. He had unburdened himself of a great secret, one she would contemplate the rest of her days, but he'd kept from her the one she needed most. Her very reason for coming here.

He led her down a narrow set of iron stairs, and through a short hallway. The room they entered was as large as her chambers in Ophélie. "My suite," he explained. "I want you to be comfortable."

"This is more than fine."

"Rest well, Amelia. And should you have dreams tonight... pay them mind."

"I'll just lie down for a few. Maybe by then, the storm will pass," she said with a stifled yawn.

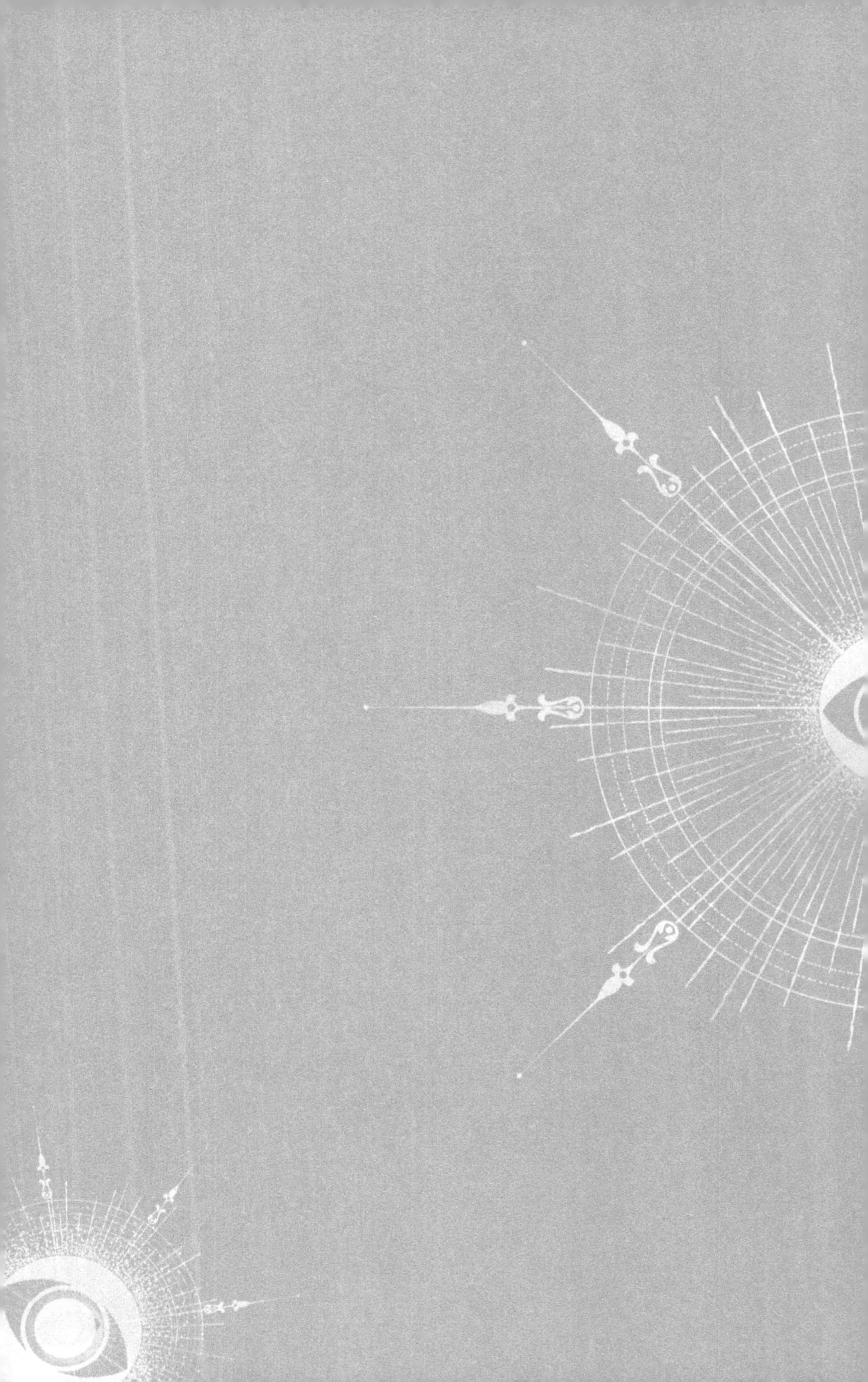

24
OPHÉLIE

Tonight was the first in a great long while that Jean had not come to her bed. Yet what should have granted her relief only worried her further.

If only Ophélie had known Jean would request Lord Donnelly's presence on the journey! She could have warned him that her brother's intentions could not possibly be wholesome. Jean didn't require Lord Donnelly to help him fetch their parcels at the post. He didn't need their guest for anything. So why bring him?

Jean, never one to make waste of his time, often whispered his displeasure of the guests in her ear as he lay atop her, further illustrating she was no better than a chore. *They're here to steal Papa's fortune. They're not who they proclaim to be. They threaten us and our entire way of life. If Lord Donnelly or his tart wife so much as look at me wrong...*

Despite all Jean had done to harm her during the past year, Ophélie knew he was prone to threats he had no intentions of living up to... or the means to carry them out. Overtaking a young woman was easy; she posed no return threat. But

Ophélie had seen Lord Donnelly's knuckles. The fire in his eyes. The lord was clearly not a man who let others fight his battles.

In removing them from the plantation, Jean had effectively eliminated any witnesses to a potential crime. People disappeared in the bayou all the time. The riverlands were not for the faint of heart.

"Your needlework is slovenly," her mother accused, snapping her from her thoughts. Ophélie had been so wrapped up in her worries she hadn't realized her straight line had become a zigzag. "Begin again."

"Sorry, Maman."

"For?"

"For... my poor work."

Brigitte set her cloth aside. "You are due for providing more apologies than that, child. Go on."

Ophélie looked up. "But... what else..."

"I know you've been telling tales to our guests," Brigitte snapped back with sharp impatience. Her mother's moods had grown progressively harsher since the arrival of the Lord and Lady Donnelly, though Ophélie could think of no clear reason for the shift, save her mother's strange dislike of the pair. "When I told you to stay far from them both!"

"I've only tried to be a good hostess," Ophélie defended meekly. "Showing Lady Donnelly the grounds and acquainting her with those items needed to make her comfortable."

"You suggest *I* am not a good hostess?"

"I only meant—"

"You are fortunate your father has found you a fine match. With that mouth, you would have no luck on your own." Brigitte regarded her with unveiled hatred. "And what have you said about us? Have you told them how your brother Jean sneaks in your room every night to perform his most sacred duty as a Deschanel?" She studied her daughter. "Yes, I am sure you have. I am positive you have painted me as no better than a demon, forcing you beyond your will, when I would give you *everything* for your obedience!"

"I have not," Ophélie insisted, growing bolder. "I would not. I have only tried to help."

Brigitte snorted. "Help. Your brother may be doing just that with the lord. If fortune smiles upon us, they will be gone on the morrow."

"Tomorrow! They only just arrived."

"Naïve child. From where?" Brigitte stood and began to circle the room. "Say England, and I might bring my hand down upon you."

Ophélie flashed her best frown. One she prayed was convincing. "Why would they be from anywhere else than where they said?"

"You ask that, but do not question them showing up here without a note ahead to warn of their arrival?" Brigitte stopped behind Ophélie's chair. Her hands fell at the nape of her neck. "I know things, child. I may not be the force I was in France, but I am not completely bereft of my previous gifts. These people are not who they say they are, and it will not be long before I know the precise nature of their deception."

"Why would you think they are deceiving us?"

"I don't think, I *know*," her mother corrected. "I know, child. I also know they will bring our family into the mud if we allow it."

"Lord and Lady Donnelly are very proper, very nice people," Ophélie said with caution.

"Who are more than likely working with that harlot who showed up and tried to take your Papa's fortune," Brigitte hissed.

And there it was. Finally.

Her mother thought the lord and lady were a threat to her position as lady of her own house.

"If you care about their health and well-being, I recommend you take your brother's lead and convince them to leave before they engage a plan with no return," Brigitte added.

"I will inquire upon their intended return," Ophélie said, her words coming out as a wail as her mother ran her hands over her face, and up into her hair. Pins fell from her coils, falling to the floor below. "Maman, please stop."

"And where is Lady Donnelly?" Brigitte asked sweetly as she yanked more and more of the pins from her daughter's hair and hurled them to the floor. Her rage flourished with each one. "And, pray, have you seen Monsieur de Blanchefort? His father has been searching for him to no avail."

"I know not," Ophélie whispered. She slid her hands under her legs to hide their trembling.

"You know," Brigitte charged. "And I know. And when Lord Donnelly returns, *he* will know."

"That is their affair, not ours," Ophélie began and was quickly smacked for the effort.

"They have made our affairs theirs every night since they came to us, and I will demonstrate to them that turnabout is fair play."

"The baby's wails woke them. They woke all of us," Ophélie tried to say, but her words melted into tears of her own at the horrors, her horrors, that had happened in the attic.

"The cries are no more," Brigitte said evenly. "As will our guests be, if I find them out of their room once more."

"They won't, Maman," Ophélie assured, frozen to her seat with fear of the woman standing over her, the woman she could not see. "They won't."

"And you?" Brigitte said. Her breath burned at Ophélie's ear, hot and cruel. "Are we seeing signs of new life?"

"Not yet." Brigitte's shame was so acute, so strong that even Ophélie, who wanted nothing more than to be free of her burden, felt as if she had failed.

"You cannot marry Lestan until you have borne us an heir."

"I know, Maman."

"Our line will die out. Our gifts..."

"I know, Maman."

"*I know, Maman,*" Brigitte mocked. "I wonder if you do. I sincerely doubt you know what is at stake for us."

Nothing for me. Nothing anymore. My future was written in the stars many moons past.

When Ophélie said nothing, Brigitte pulled her loose hair into a fist and yanked her head back. Her eyes burned. "You are nothing to me but a vessel. One I will destroy when it has outworn its usefulness, should you cross me."

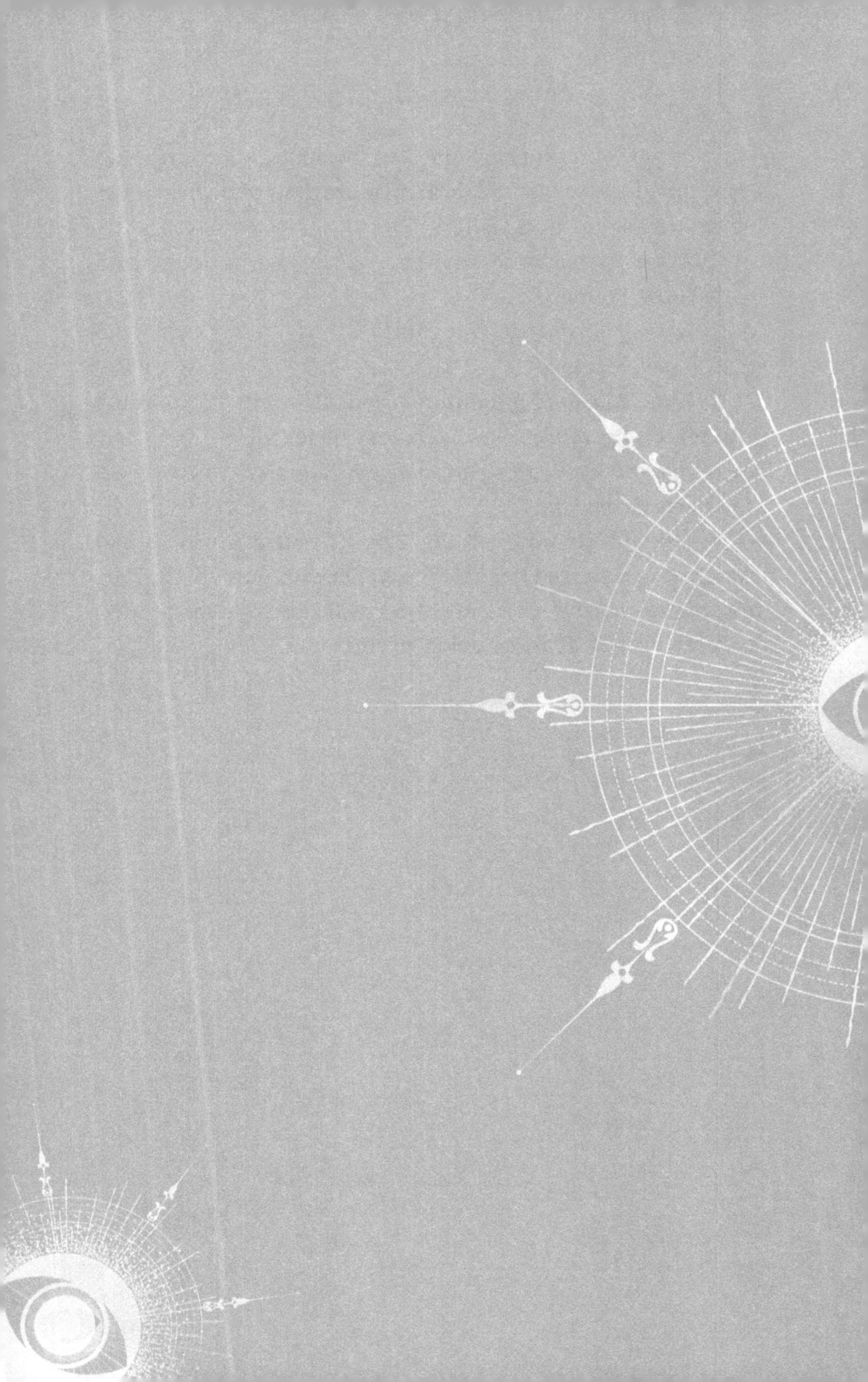

25
AMELIA

The room was dimly lit, but Amelia recognized it. She would know it by scent, by the heaviness of the air. Her senses would, alone or in tandem, work to identify it, and come to the same haunting conclusion each time, as every inch of her fought for freedom.

Water-drenched coals and the cloying scent of a recent fire stirred her. It was the only aroma in this place that did not send her into a dizzying tailspin of fear. Even so, she knew it was the smell of whatever had come before her. Whomever. Their fate could not have fared any better than the dead fire.

Amelia's wrists burned with the flinching pain of flayed skin. The full weight of her dangled from the injustice, her toes only occasionally grazing the surface of the uneven floor as she swayed from the ceiling hook.

A tinge of fresh blood, and the coppery taste, washed down her throat with every pained swallow, yet her face had suffered the least of the injuries. The rest of her...

Oh, please, not again. Please, God! Goddess!

Heavy footfalls from the other end of the small cabin struck her heart into a frenzy. Her momentum threw her into full protest, and the rope attached to her wrists and the hook creaked with mercy from the sudden action.

The seat upon which Jacob had sat lay empty. Fear turned to panic as she strained to see in the hazy darkness. No, no, the only thing worse than him seeing her like this was him disappearing without confirmation of his safety. Had he fled as she'd pleaded with him to do? Or, had Baldur done something to him, to punish her?

Jacob!

In her agitation, time passed at an abnormal rate. The steps were behind her now. She thought she had more time. Every second was an eternity in this cabin of suffering, but that provided at least some measure of relief when Baldur stepped away.

He lay a finger against her back, running it in a lazy line down her spine, his other fingers following one by one like a waterfall. The tenderness of the gesture was worse than all the cuts and punches. He could not have this, too!

"Your love is pure. One-half of our future must spring forth from this eternity."

The words didn't come from Baldur. Amelia knew the voice. It was less a matter of recognition and more an intrinsic sort of knowledge, like knowing your own mother. But with every trace of the finger, every inch of her Baldur claimed, she began to lose the part of herself that could still connect to anything of importance.

"One day, your time on this Earth will end."

His hands came to rest at the small of her back, spreading to each side as they reached her hips, gently. Baldur's breath burned her back as it traveled the same path his hands had, settling in the same place. The monster's lips pressed into that hollow above her tailbone and did not move.

"You will be born again knowing who you are. You will come into this world again, remembering my words, and what you were tasked to do."

Her assailant laid his head against her lower back. If she didn't know better, she would have sworn she felt his tears against her sore skin and the sound of a sob from the back of his throat. Please, Goddess. Let this be over. This is worse, so much worse.

"The cycle will repeat for many centuries. A boon I give you, a special wisdom. A bond you will need when the time comes for you to be reborn into a troubled world, and to return to me no longer full of knowledge, but instead filled with trust."

Amelia wished the voice would stop. It should be a comfort to her. She knew at least that much, but it wasn't. The words were a reminder of some degree of hope she had, once upon a time, that she would make it out of this situation alive, and as the same person.

Her attacker ran his lips around the outside of her hips and up her side, along her ribcage. The pain of earlier, when he had kicked her ribs, disappeared entirely as his mouth came upon it, like a healing wand. Why are you doing this to me? Was everything else I endured not enough? Did I not already give you everything?

"The time will come when your memories fade and your hearts grow weary."

"Please stop talking," Amelia whispered. Tears fell into her mouth, mixing with the blood. "Please, it isn't helping. You can't help me."

His face eased up around her sternum, still trailing kisses across the surface of her skin, healing her, ostensibly so he could hurt her all over again. Again and again.

The soothing voice continued in tandem with the healing caresses of her assailant. "It is then I shall turn my hope to you and pray my wisdom and faith holds as true as yours has."

"I know who you are," Amelia cried out, to the voice, though she was also beginning to understand something about the creature who had bound her here, as well. "And you were wrong, Goddess. Wrong, wrong, wrong, all this time. I am not the one!"

"The time will come when your cycle of rebirth will cease," the calming voice of the goddess went on. "When the life you enter will be your final, yet eternal, one."

"Your words meant nothing," Amelia accused, turning her head as the attacker's mouth came upon her neck with especial tenderness. "We trusted you... both of us... and now we're here."

Amelia shut her eyes tight as his hands rested against the sides of her face, healing the last of her wounds from the assault. She would never thank him and refused to look at him, even if he peeled back her eyelids.

"Cerridwen," the goddess sighed in her mind.

"No. Not anymore," Amelia answered, eyes squeezed tight despite the patience of the creature standing before her.

"Open your eyes."

"I can't!"

"Remember my words."

"They were all wrong!"

"Only at the hour of culmination will the veil of shadows be lifted."

Amelia didn't know if it was obedience or resignation that made her do it. She only knew in one moment she was blocking out the last of her attack, and in the next, she was face to face with her heart's only true mate.

"Cianán?" she whispered, sagging further in her bindings. Her wrists shrieked in agony at the added weight. That he would do this to her...

"I leave you now with one final wisdom," the goddess said, whispering the last of her words. "Nothing is ever asked of us that exceeds our capacity. Even when circumstances seem beyond possibility, you must grasp the courage to push through whatever barriers your mind or heart construct."

"Yes," Cianán said back. His own tears blinded him. "I would

see you healed, Cerridwen. I would give every one of my lifetimes to undo this."

"I don't understand. Why am I here, then? Why would you do these things?"

"I cannot change what happened to you," he said with great sadness. "But I can provide you a memory of love that will, perhaps with time, replace the one filled with so much evil."

Amelia understood now why she hadn't seen Jacob. This was not that cruel night in Ireland, but something else entirely. A new memory, or a dream, or some construct of her imagination sent to shield her.

"I will always protect you," Cianán vowed. "As you have protected me. But it is time now to listen to the goddess. You were born into this lifetime not knowing, and you have learned so many things in a short span of time. But you have one final message to learn, my love."

"If the lesson is so important, why will no one just tell me what I need to know? I'm so tired of seeking signs and wondering if every word said to me, or everything I see, is something significant!"

Cianán smiled. He reached above her and unhooked her from the ceiling, gently cupping her in his arms as she released. "This truth has been before you for days. Síoraíocht, Mo mhíle stór. *Wake now, and allow your heart to witness what your eyes see."*

AMELIA SHOT UPRIGHT IN THE SMALL BED, AND STRAIGHT INTO A SET of strong, steadying arms. She gasped, leaning up and back, her arms flying, searching for her bearings.

Victor stared back at her.

No, not Victor...

...Cianán.

"You have seen," Victor whispered, brushing her matted

hair back off her face. Tears pooled at his lids, ones of apparent joy. "Please tell me you have seen."

Amelia's breath caught in her throat as the blood rushed forth violently in her scramble back toward the wall. He inched toward her and wrapped her in his arms, burying her sobs into his chest as he held her and rocked her closer to the realization she'd been building on since they'd arrived.

"That's impossible. I would've known. There's no way. I would have known," she repeated, sucking in tiny bursts of air. Her resistance slowly disappeared, fading into a new reality. *Allow your heart to witness what your eyes see.*

"A part of you did," Victor assured her, smoothing her hair with his palm. "A part of you knew the moment our eyes met in the ballroom. How I wanted to tell you! But, remember the words of the goddess. In this life, you were born not knowing, and had to find your way to Cianán."

"Then how did *you* know?"

"I am not your Cianán, but the Cianán of the Cerridwen who came before you," he explained patiently. "Your turn backward in time created the unlikely scenario of meeting a different version of your own Cianán."

"But Jacob..."

"Is *your* Cianán. I was the last before him, and he will be the final, now that the culmination of the prophecy is imminent."

Amelia pulled back. She couldn't stop gawking at him, examining him, seeing him through this fresh lens of truth. Silence filled the room for several moments as she took him in. Her mind relived flashes of every conversation they'd had in the past days. "Then there must be a Cerridwen of this generation too. Where is she? Is that what you meant about your choice to take the blood being a regret?"

Victor's expression darkened. "Her story is not mine to tell. I'm sorry, Amelia."

"But who is she? It's not your wife, or you wouldn't have talked about your marriage the way you did. Surely you wouldn't abandon Cerridwen in any lifetime, so where is she?"

"Amelia." Victor sighed. He reached out to touch her hair again, but his hand hung in midair when her stare stopped him. She craved his touch. She loathed it. "I can't."

"At least, now I know why you've been stalking me," she asserted, swiping her hands over the tears still forming. It wouldn't help her at all to continue to deny this, but it didn't mean she was okay with it either. "Are you responsible for that dream, too, then?"

"I have played the moment through my mind a thousand times," Victor said with a sad shake of his head. Every inch of him radiated powerful sadness. "And I had hoped eventually my version of events would find its way to you."

"But how did you know those details? How could you have understood any of it?"

"Because I have watched you, your whole life. This gift of the blood came with one real benefit, and that was being able to observe you throughout the years. No, not always in person, my dear. Had I been in that cabin… but no, I saw that in my mind's eye. I could not react quickly enough to save you."

"Watching me," she repeated, unable to decide if the idea of him standing sentry over the last thirty years of her life made her feel safer or more exposed. "And what are the odds you would be here upon my arrival?"

"You were always meant to return," Victor answered simply, maddeningly. "That factor was an element of your fate. Just as mine has been to watch Cerridwen with another reincarnation of my soul."

"But I wasn't in the original version of this history, so how can that be?"

Victor drew in a deep breath and watched her. "You ask me to speak of the paradox of time travel with an authority I simply do not possess. You cannot change the past, Amelia. You know this. But you can learn from it."

"And what am I here to learn, then? All this trip has given me is more confusion! To look at you is... its... I'm not supposed to feel this way!" She jumped to her feet, searching for the shawl she'd worn earlier. Her shoes. Where the hell did everything go? "I have to go find Jacob. My God, I shouldn't be here with you."

Victor came up behind her, steadying her shaking arms. "Cerridwen. You have done nothing wrong."

"Nothing except follow you out here, alone," she answered, snatching her stole off a small corner chaise. She pulled it around her, but it fell to the ground. When he reached for it, she shoved Victor back and snatched the wrap toward her, tight to her chest. "Nothing except dream of you, with your lips all over me. Jesus!"

"Healing you," he whispered, brushing a strand of hair off her ear.

"I don't need you to heal me!"

"Cerridwen—"

"Stop. Don't you dare. Don't call me that. You don't get to call me that." She whipped her head around the room, frantic. Her shoes... goddammit! Where were they? "You think you've earned the right because of who you are?"

"You may not be mine, and we know you belong to another Cianán, but it does not mean I cannot love you and wish to see you whole."

"Stop saying that, Victor!"

Victor dropped his hands to his side in surrender. "I promised you the truth, Amelia."

"You're confusing an already terribly troubling situation!" she screamed, backing toward the door. She hit the wall and staggered sideways, looking for purchase. Forget shoes. She had to get out of there, away, far, far away.

"I never meant to add more complexities to your life," he said helplessly. "I only wanted you to possess the truth of who you are. Who I am."

"What was knowing who you are supposed to accomplish for me except tearing my heart in half?"

More of Victor's words followed her as she ran from the room, down the hall, and back up the ladder to the deck. He didn't follow her, but as she tripped onto the dock and stumbled over fresh debris toward the levee, she feared what was ahead as much as what she'd left behind.

Brigitte awaited her at the front door. A knowing smile rested upon her cruel face.

As if she had known.

As if she understood everything.

DAY SIX

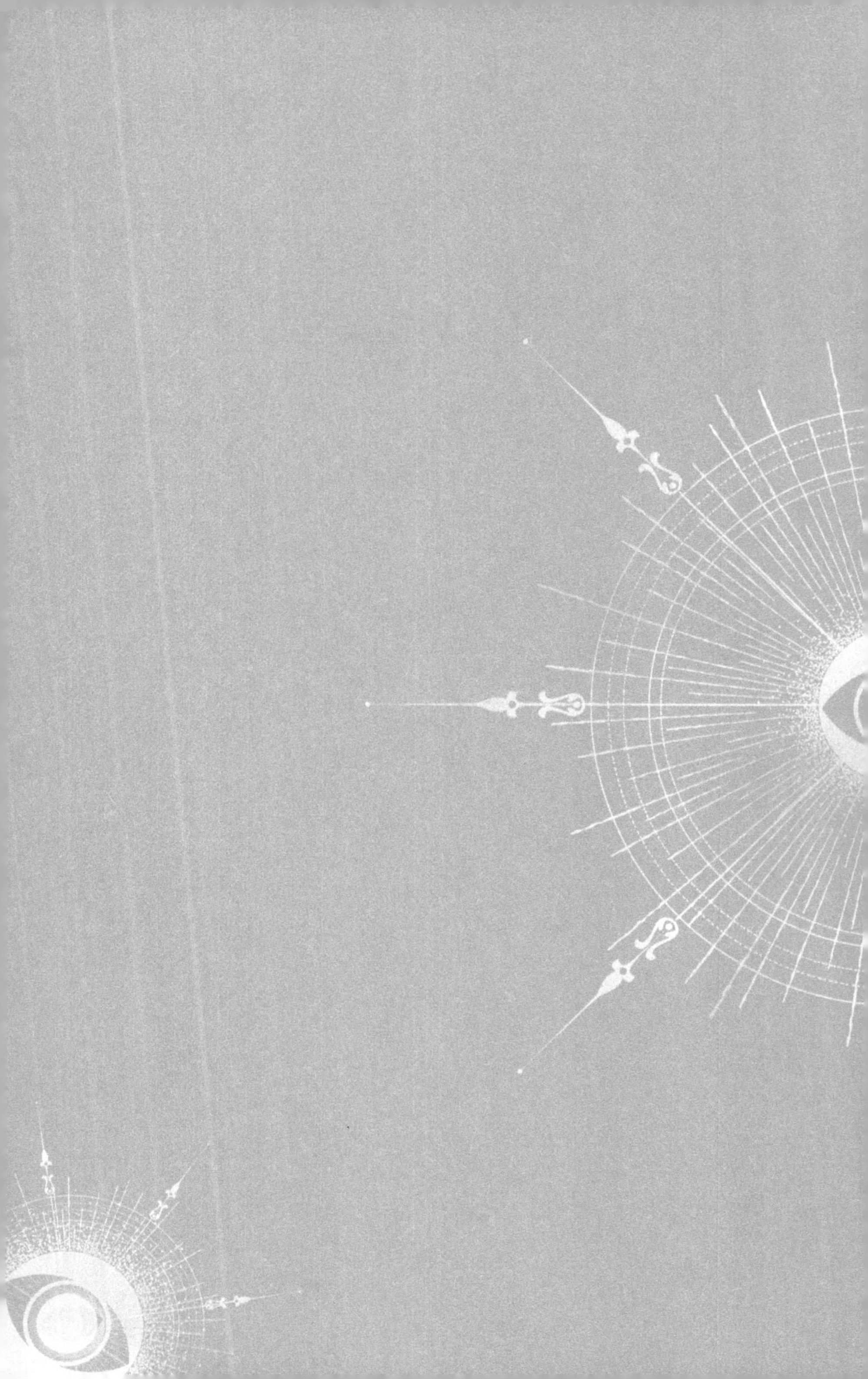

26
JACOB

Jean woke first. He gave Jacob a short punch on the arm to rouse him and mumbled something about the carriage being ready. Jacob wondered if last night had made the young man feel bested or more determined to drive Jacob and Amelia out of their lives.

Likely both.

He feeds off the dominance of his mother. Without her, he's a sniveling little bully without any real power of his own. He could only maintain it for so long without her. Once we return to the plantation, he'll go hide under her skirts and be back to his usual, shitty self, as if the power dynamic between us had never shifted at all.

However Jean felt about the events of last night was inconsequential to Jacob when compared with what they ignited in him, instinct and emotions he had tried to bury deep, for the sake of being a better man.

Maybe he didn't need to be better. If that meant losing a part of who he was, then better was also responsible, at least in part, for what happened that night in the cabin.

Neutering himself didn't make him anything but different. Resentful. Ignoring the fight within had caused him to lose so much more as a result.

Now that he knew this and understood it, he could change it.

Jacob was relieved to see Jacques appear rested as the man helped them into the carriage. While Jean situated himself, Jacob threw his new friend a wink. He couldn't change Jacques' situation, but he could, hopefully, leave the man with a memory of kindness.

Jacques nodded and closed the carriage door.

The return to Ophélie was long but quiet. Remnants of the previous day's storm added an extra hour to the journey as Jacques had to dodge debris from fallen limbs, farm implements, and other detritus carried from the passing plantations. Flash floods had also carved new ruts in the dirt road, and Jacques, three times, had to stop the momentum to rock the carriage back onto solid ground.

Jean said nothing to either of them, but he radiated with the energy of anticipation. He wanted to be home as much as Jacob, though for entirely different reasons.

They can't hurt us, Jacob reminded himself. *We can't change the past, so they can't alter the future, either.*

Right?

Not for the first time, he realized how impulsively foolish their decision to leap into the past had been. He'd been given only a handful of words about what time dancing even meant. Surely, there were many more rules to discover and caveats to the ones he already knew.

Jacob was a scientist, but nowhere in any of his studies had this subject ever garnered serious discussion. Einstein's Theory of Relativity was about as far as they dipped into that pond. The basic precept, as it related to time travel, was that time increased or slowed down depending on your own speed in relation to something else, which, at light speed or quicker, would result in the bending of gravity. In theory, possible, but in practice, improbable.

All information he had obtained about the implications of time travel—moral and actual—had come from his favorite science fiction novels and movies. From comics. *Chronos, Timecop, X-Men, Terminator, Doctor Who, Back to the Future, Star Trek, Planet of the Apes.* Stories that explored the time paradox, and the string theory, bending them to their own narrative purpose.

And even if he had learned more in college, certainly those rules might not even apply. Nothing about the Deschanels matched his scientific learnings, so why should this?

Safety was a shifting target as long as they remained here, unprotected. He couldn't force Amelia into revelation, but he could, maybe, find a way back in. The two of them had always been at their strongest when facing an obstacle together, and perhaps his presence in the discovery had been what was missing all along. He had watched, and even judged, her choice to be alone and solve the unknown riddle by herself while not entirely realizing he had done nothing to help. Jacob had inadvertently shifted the responsibility fully to her, turning to her for the answers, when they came here together. He and Amelia had made this leap of faith as a team.

To accept their journey through time as Cerridwen and Cianán meant to accept everything forward required the same trust and symbiosis.

Time away had helped him see this. With luck, it had done the same for her.

THEY ARRIVED AT *OPHÉLIE* AFTER DINNER. BRIGITTE WELCOMED HER son as if he had been gone years but shot a scathing look at Jacob and said, "Your wife has been in your room all day. I can't say I've bothered to check on her," before returning to fawning over Jean.

Jacob mustered a gracious response and started up the stairs. He stopped when he saw the de Blanchefort men near the parlor doors, engaged in discussion.

Making his way toward them, he tried to expel the bitterness and approach with what he hoped was the simplicity of fact.

"Monsieur," he said. They both turned. "Victor," Jacob clarified.

"Excuse me, Papa," Victor said with a gentle nod to his father. Marius disappeared into the parlor. "How can I be of service, Lord Donnelly?"

Jacob drew a deep breath. "I know you've been spending time with my wife. I'm not angry." *Liar.* "But I need you to be clear on something."

Victor raised a brow. Nodded for him to go on.

"If you're helping her through something... something I have had less success assisting with, then I say thank you." Jacob swallowed the ill feeling the words brought on. "But she is *my* wife. And there's nothing I wouldn't do to protect her from someone who may seem as if he has good intentions but is actually a goddamn bird of prey waiting for the right moment to swoop in. Do you understand?"

Victor watched him in silence for several seconds. "I do understand. More than you may know."

"I'm not interested in what you know," Jacob replied. "There's a limit to my patience and graciousness. I don't doubt her loyalty, but she's vulnerable right now and needs people who don't have ulterior motives."

Victor bowed. "I assure you, my purposes will not interfere with yours, Lord Donnelly. Of that, you can be certain."

I'll be assured when we're gone, and you're nothing but a memory. "Good evening," Jacob said and went to find his wife.

AMELIA WAS EXACTLY WHERE BRIGITTE ALLEGED, BUT SHE WASN'T asleep.

Her back was to the door. Jacob tentatively stepped around to her side. She was curled into a ball with the blankets pulled tight. When he approached, her red, tear-stained face peeked out.

"*Blanca,*" he whispered, his heart dropping to the floor.

Amelia didn't reply, except with several shallow breaths, but she moved to his side of the bed and opened the covers.

Jacob climbed beside her and pulled her close. At the moment of contact, Amelia dissolved into fresh tears. He wanted badly to say something, anything, to console her but he knew, not only with the knowledge of Jacob but the combined iterative experience of Cianán, that what she needed at that moment was safety, not words.

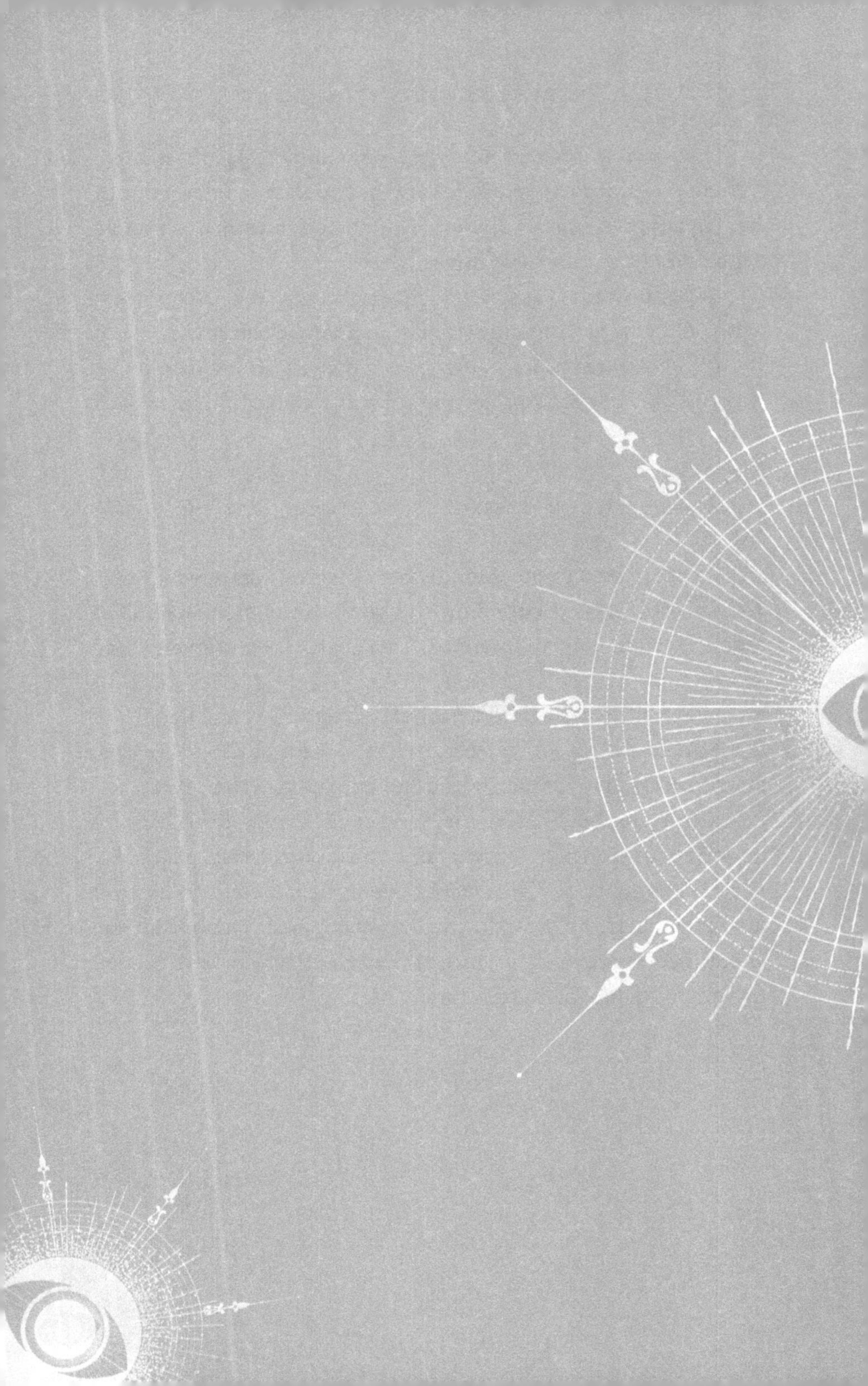

27
AMELIA

The baby's cries pierced her sleep.

Amelia's first instinct was to check Jacob for a reaction. His sleep continued uninterrupted, but it would only be a matter of time.

She shouldn't pursue it. Brigitte had been poised to strike for days, and this would definitely push her over the precipice. The woman had a keenness about her as if her eyes were stretched across the property at all times. No doubt existed in Amelia's mind that Brigitte would find her at the bottom of the ladder leading to the attic.

Yet... after Victor... after the flood of revelations... Amelia no longer believed anything presented to her attention was incidental. Yes, learning who Victor was had been illuminating, but there was more. She *knew* it. Their time here was a continuous tempting of fate. She couldn't leave until she understood the reason they were sent here, but she also feared she might not have a choice if events did not hurry along. If they didn't leave soon on their own, Brigitte would find a way to dispose of them.

Her gaze lingered upon Jacob, waiting to be sure he wasn't stirring. Satisfied he was still lost in his dreams, she rested a kiss on his lips and tiptoed off into the hall.

And what if this is just me going mad from the loss of my own baby? What if I've invented this in my own grief?

Jacob heard it as well, another voice reminded her. The voice of her own reason.

And if we're wrong?

We won't know until we get there.

When her bare feet hit the thin carpet, the cries ceased. Another sound replaced it: footsteps.

Amelia nearly ate her heart before she saw the wispy figure of Ophélie emerge from the shadows. The young girl glided on air in her too-long muslin nightgown, and as she moved toward the shocked Amelia, her expression turned sadder. Darker.

"It was never meant to be," the young girl said, shaking her head with a glance up the stairs. In the direction of the crying.

"Ophélie, what's wrong?" Amelia stepped closer to get a better glimpse of her new friend. Red-rimmed eyes and streaks of tears only told half the story.

"They did what they had to do," she replied, distantly. Her eyes drifted off to the left. It seemed she was there only in physical form. The rest of her was elsewhere, or still asleep. "They were left with no choice."

"Ophélie!" Amelia hissed, careful of her volume. She shivered at the thought of Brigitte walking in on the two of them in midnight conspiracy. "Talk to me. Tell me what happened."

"Jean and Maman, I cannot blame them. My heart is so heavy, but I cannot..." Ophélie swayed on her feet, and Amelia caught her, pulling her to a bench at the end of the hall.

"You can trust me," Amelia soothed, her attentions divided

between the dazed girl in her lap and the fear of an intruder. "I want to help you. Why are you out here?"

"It is not my place to question God or His will," Ophélie cried. "This was not my time. It was not your time, either, Amelia."

Amelia stiffened. Her gaze dropped back toward the girl, who glanced up, imploring. "What are you talking about?"

Ophélie smiled. "No, not your time. But it will be. As for me..."

AMELIA'S EYES SNAPPED OPEN. A FLASH OF LIGHT FELL ACROSS THE room, followed in several seconds by the roll of thunder. It was only at the shuddering rumble did she realize everything that had just happened was a dream.

Nothing about it had given her that impression. She saw through her eyes this time, not Ophélie's, without the telltale signs of a dream state; nothing out of place or distorted.

"What on earth is happening to me?" she whispered. *I'm going completely mad, and there's nothing I can do about it.*

Jacob rolled over. In her shock, she hadn't registered his lack of snores when she'd woken. He'd been awake, maybe this whole time. "*Blanca,*" he said. "We need to talk."

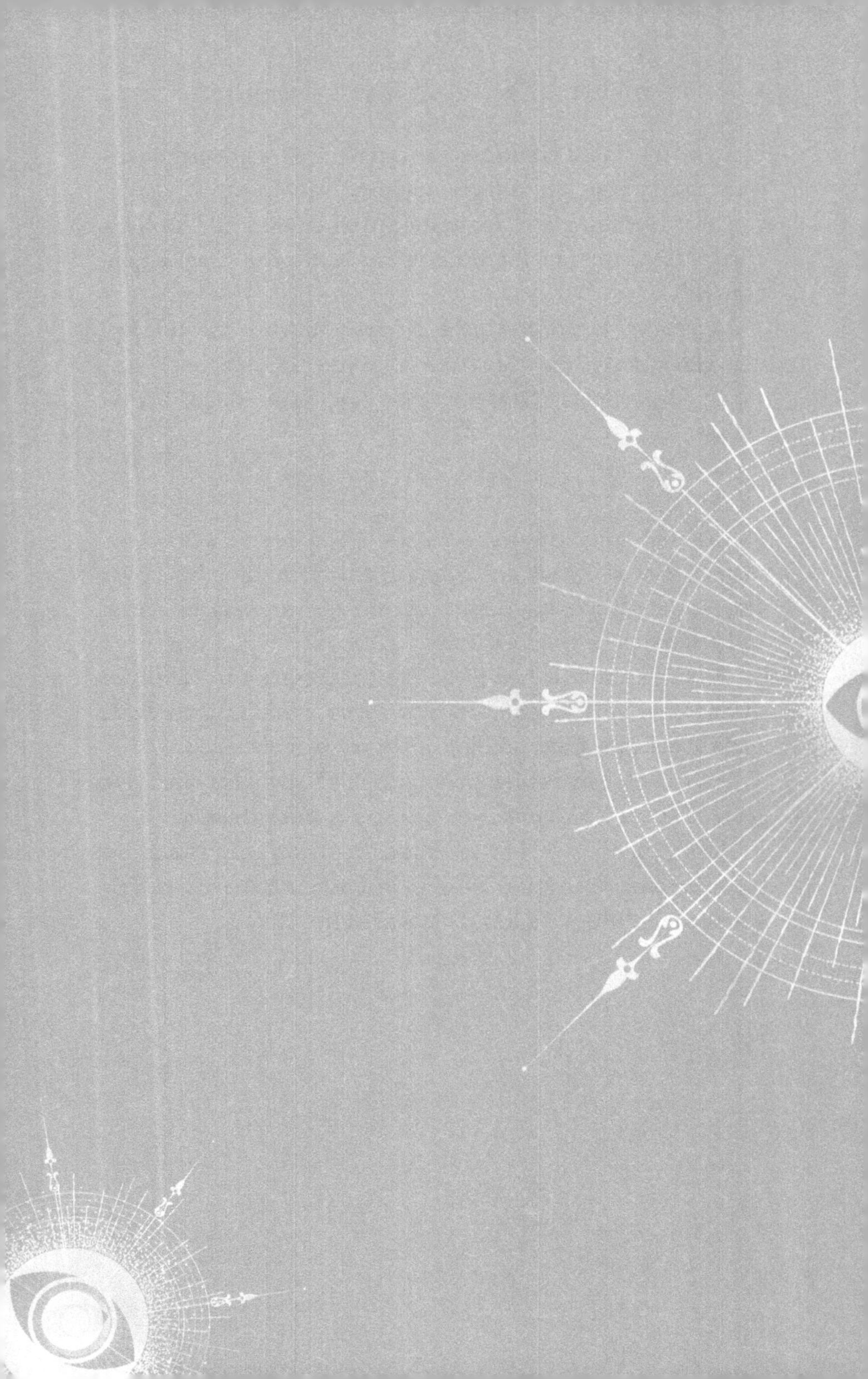

28
JACOB

"I'm really worried."

As Jacob had listened to her toss and turn, he'd searched for the right words, knowing he no longer had a choice but to say them. And, as he considered all the things he *could* say, he finally realized this was his wife he was trying to appeal to. The one person in all the world he had never doubted or not trusted to understand him.

So he spoke with his heart.

"I know," she said, in a low, hoarse voice.

"I've tried..." Jacob choked up. This was important. He had her attention now, but every word mattered. "Tried to be there, and when I realized it wasn't *me* you needed, I tried to be understanding."

Amelia's eyes lit up. She seemed ready with her own words, but she let him talk.

"But whatever is happening here, in this house, in this century, well, it's not helping you. It's hurting you," he went on. He propped himself on one elbow so he could see her better. "And us. And I know... I wish... God, more than anything in all the world that you hadn't been through that night in the cabin, but we have no choice except moving forward. And I'm afraid, Amelia, that coming here has somehow done the opposite."

Amelia's lips parted. A small sob trapped in her throat, but she closed her mouth. Watching him.

"You have to know..." Jacob grimaced, swallowing the emotion down. There were times to melt and times for strength. If he wanted to show her he could be *her* strength, he had to prove it. "I would do anything for you. Even turn my head about Victor."

This finally stirred Amelia into words. "That isn't what you think, Donnelly. I promise you. I don't have all the answers, but that, at least—"

"Please," Jacob said gently. "I love you, and I trust you, but if you're getting ready to lie to me, you need to stop. I would rather wait until you're ready to tell me the truth than hear a deception created for my sake."

Amelia appeared ready to rebut, then sank back into the bed. His heart skipped at what was apparently a confession by silence, but he forged on.

"I know you believe there are answers we need to find here," he said, slowing to search for the exact words he needed. This is where he could lose Amelia. The reality stung. Even with the right words, he still might. "But, *Blanca,* you don't even know the questions, sweetie. If you're looking for a reason to help explain the actions of that monster, you won't find them in the past, the present, or the future. He wanted information from us and had no qualms about using whatever means to get it. If he'd lived, I don't think what he did to you would even register too far into his memory. We were nothing but a means to an end for Baldur." Jacob blew out a breath and closed his eyes. "What happened is ours. Not his. The monster took something very essential from both of us that night, but the path to getting it back isn't through him. The healing has nothing to do with him. Nothing. And I can't watch you waste away before my eyes. I won't do it. I love you enough that I've let this go on because you believed, in your heart of hearts, that you might find something. But at this point..." Jacob sighed. He laid his palm against her forehead and smoothed her hair back. "At this point, all I can see is that we needed an escape from the circumstances in Farjhem and this was where we ended up. Not fate, just chance. And now we need to find our way home."

Amelia ran her fingers over the quilt covering them. She hadn't opened her mind to him since the tea party, so he couldn't guess at her thoughts. "If I were you, I would believe that, too," she said after a long pause. Her hand stopped fussing. "But my instincts have always meant something. Here, in this house, that's all I have. My empathic nature is mostly squashed by Aidrik's ward, and I can hardly even communicate telepathically. So that's all I have, my instincts. Throughout my life, there were times when I knew something important was going to happen, and it wasn't the empath Amelia feeling this, but me, just me. And that Amelia knows we're here for a reason."

"If that were true, don't you think the answer would have been clear by now?" Jacob asked carefully. His hand brushed her white hair back off her face, repeating the motion as he used to do, before all this. It was the only intimacy she allowed. "I'm worried, not just about your state of mind, but like, *legitimately* worried for our safety. I think Jean and Brigitte might actually take us out if we're here much longer."

Amelia sprung up on one elbow. "Did Jean threaten you?"

Jacob shrugged then nodded. No point in keeping things from her if he expected transparency in return. "We had a rough night, one I'll tell you more about later. He knows we aren't who we say we are but doesn't know the truth. Jean and his whacko mama are determined to figure it out."

Amelia shook her head. "They can't. How could they?"

"Does it matter? If they can't, that's probably worse. You've seen how those two manage frustrations."

"They're as benign as I am here," Amelia countered.

"You still have both telepathy and some degree of your empath nature here, even with the ward," Jacob reminded her. "What can they still do? I don't think we want to find out the hard way."

"They're all bark," she said, but her tone had changed.

"Don't you remember those letters your mother got ahold of, from Quillan Sullivan?" Jacob pressed. "Charles outright confessed to being the one to kill Ophélie, and he did it to keep her from her mother's grasp. If that's not the most messed up shit I've ever heard, not to mention a super clear warning that we are screwing with the wrong—"

"I remember," she sighed. "I'm not saying you're wrong, but if we leave now before I have answers, I don't think this door opens again. And, Jacob, I *feel* this is not only about me, but us, and who we were, about Cianán and Cerridwen."

"Why, then, are you the only one who can find these answers?" Jacob tensed. "If this is about us, why have I experienced nothing but some serious warnings about our safety?"

"I don't know," Amelia cried and rolled over onto her back. "If I knew, I would have the answers, wouldn't I?"

"I'm not trying to upset you."

"I'm upset, but not with you."

"I was trying to soothe you. Clearly not a strength of mine in 1861," he said with a forced laugh. "I just want you to be okay. I need you. I will always need you. And now, you need me, and I'm failing you."

"No, that's not true." She rolled her face toward his and reached out to touch his cheek. "I promise you that is *not* true."

I wish you wouldn't. Neither of us can be sure of anything as long as we're mixed up in this world where we don't belong. "We can't stay here much longer. You know that."

Amelia nodded, blinking tears from her eyes. "It feels so close... as though it's been in front of me all this time, and I just need to *see* it."

"I understand," Jacob replied. His heart had broken a half dozen times during the exchange, but never so much as it had seeing her desperate for meaning. "You might not think I do, but I do. I know your instincts, *Blanca.* I know *you.* But my first priority is protecting you, and maybe that means from yourself as well." Before she could reply, he pulled her into his arms, pressing her face gently to his chest. A place she always said she felt safe. "I'll try to be patient. But I won't lose you because of it. At some point, I'm going to take us away from here, not because I don't believe you, but because whether I believe you or not, I will not lose you. Not for answers. Not for anything."

Amelia sniffled against his nightshirt, without response. But as her arms wrapped around his waist, and her tension faded, Jacob could at least take comfort in knowing she'd heard his words.

Jacob's limbs slowly relaxed as well. The grandfather clock chimed the witching hour, and he remembered their wedding night in the old castle, how she'd come alive for him at midnight.

My will is yours, Blanca, Jacob had whispered between his wife's parted lips. *Now and always.*

He planted a kiss on her forehead and prayed for strength of patience.

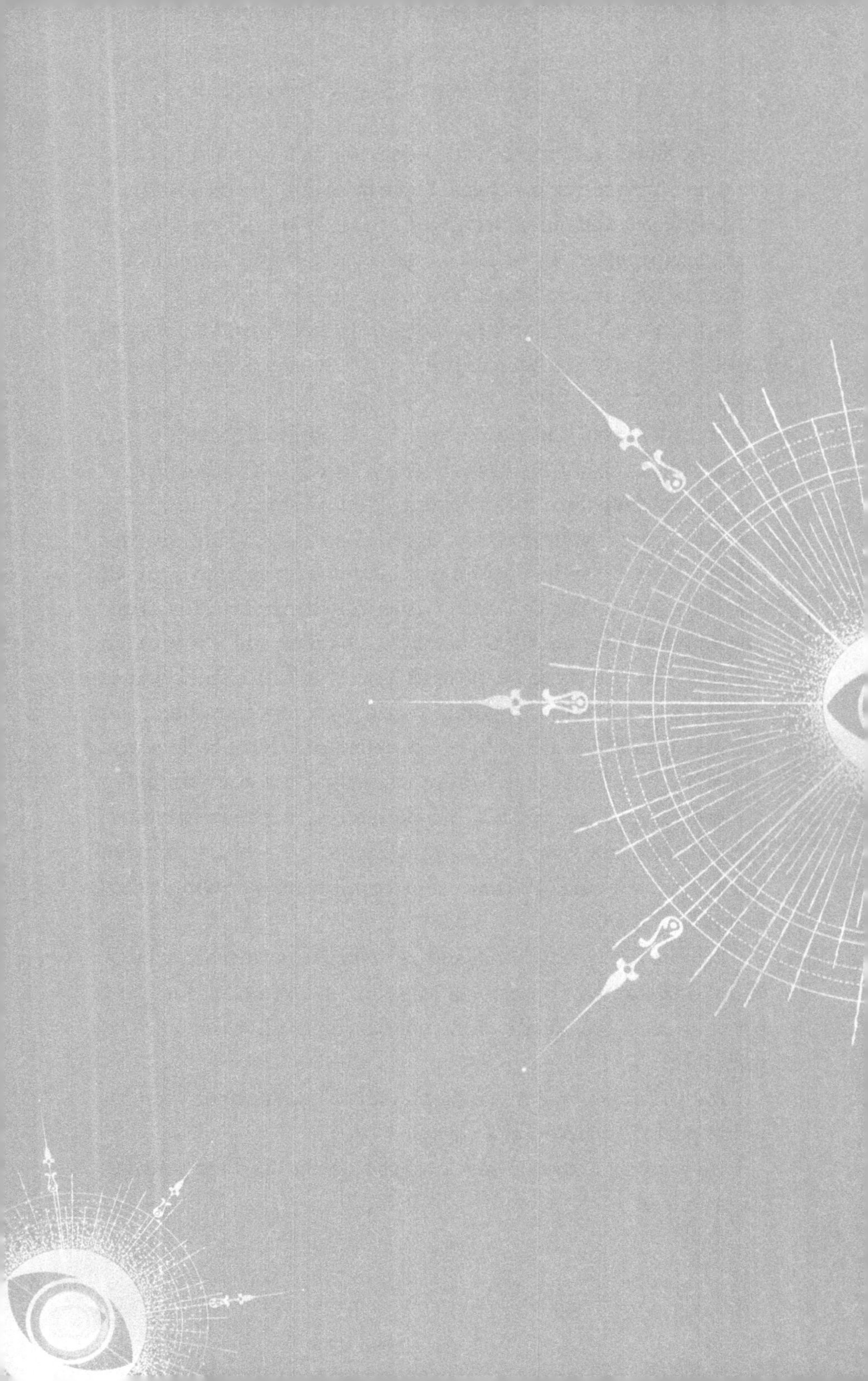

29
AMELIA

Victor didn't notice her at first. While pacing the foyer near the front door, his lips moved soundlessly. His hair was a noticeable departure from the impeccable grooming she knew him for, black hairs standing up and to the right and left, a sign he'd raked his hands through them. His stress was evident in other ways, too. His nightshirt hung open, only the middle button holding it together.

"Monsieur?" Ophélie whispered, thinking with horror of what her mother would think if she'd come upon this.

Victor's head swung up. His eyes fell upon her, and in these first moments, Ophélie felt he could see straight into her soul, to every black corner, and every light one. Then he relaxed and straightened his back. "Mademoiselle. I did not mean to wake you."

"It wasn't you who roused me," she answered, slipping quietly across the cypress flooring.

"Amelia then," he said, nodding. A startled expression crossed his face, and he corrected himself. "Lady Donnelly, that is."

"Be cautious of how you make reference to her in front of

others," Ophélie warned, with a glance up the stairs. "Not all will understand as I do."

Victor's eyes lit up, hopeful. "Do you? Understand? Can you?"

"I would like to." Pulling her arms tight across her chest, she moved closer to him. "I do know you are here more than perhaps you should be. When you arrive, something changes, every time."

"You don't, then." The spark went out of his eyes. "It did not come to me all at once, either. I can't... no, it was too much to expect you might know..."

"Tell me, then. Why are you down here, in the dead of night?"

"I sensed her distress." He did not need to qualify who he meant by she.

"And where is she?"

Victor nodded at the door. "Just beyond. She didn't wander far."

Ophélie frowned. "If you came down here from worry, what good is standing in the hall wearing holes in the carpet, when she is outside? Moreover, why is her distress your concern at all, Monsieur? She is married to another, and he sleeps just upstairs."

"You don't understand. You will, I have to believe that. I do believe that. Yes, yes. I believe it. I need you to. I need both of you to, before... before..."

"I believe it would be for the best," Ophélie started, gathering her courage, "If you would leave Lady Donnelly alone. Not only tonight. I mean for the duration of your stay."

The flame from the candle flickered across Victor's pale face, lighting his desolate smile. "I know more than you what is best for Lady Donnelly, Mademoiselle."

"Your words make no sense," she insisted, drawing closer. "You only just met her! Who is she to you?"

"Who are you to me?" he answered. "Is another way to ask the same question."

"You speak nonsense."

"I speak of a truth that is not yet yours."

Ophélie laughed. "You speak like a man drunk on his own importance! What compels men to think no woman could ever grasp the complexity of their mind? Are we not creations of the same God?"

"You take my words as an insult when they aren't intended that way at all," Victor answered. He lifted the candelabra and narrowed the space between them. "You are capable of many, many things, Mademoiselle Deschanel. Far more than you know. But you will."

"You know nothing of my house. Of my family," she said carefully, lifting one bare foot and resting it behind the other, backing away slowly. "Or of our honored guests."

A peaceful smile settled over his face. "Ophélie, I am not your enemy."

"What are you, then?"

"Someone who would see you whole were it in my power. Someone who will do the same for Amelia, if I can."

"One has nothing to do with the other." Ophélie's hand trembled. She wondered if it had done so all along.

His smile broadened, and he tilted his head to the side. Watching her. "You say that with the conviction of one who does not believe his own words at all."

"Only one who is tired of odd words from a strange man!"

He reached a hand to her cheek. Ophélie recoiled but was rooted in place, unable to move. She needed to know what would happen next and summoned the courage to find out.

His palm cupped her cheek, and a wave of warmth passed through her. She did not know why she leaned into his touch, or why it comforted her. Why she craved it.

• • •

"Why are you here, Victor?" After tonight, she had earned consent to use his name.

"I am here as much for you as I am for her. But only one of you can yet be saved," he answered, now turning away from her, toward the door, toward Amelia.

Amelia awoke clutching Jacob's nightshirt in her sweaty palm. He slept soundly, his face pressed into her hair. *At peace*, she thought with a grateful, inward smile, for she was not at all at peace herself, and after tonight, she might never be.

No question remained in her mind... she needed to speak with Ophélie. Aside from her dreams as Cerridwen, Amelia had never, not once, dreamed as someone else and could no longer ignore the half dozen she'd had under this roof. The last one had *screamed at her,* but what message it sent only Ophélie knew. And if she did not...

Well, then it was official. Amelia was going mad.

Either way, she had to know. Tonight. For her sake and for Jacob's.

She managed to slip from the room without rousing Jacob, but she wasn't alone in the hall. The other individual didn't see her, but before she ducked back into her own room to avoid detection, she garnered a clear and shocking view.

Jean, stumbling from Ophélie's room. He hadn't even bothered to buckle his trousers.

An immediate burst of rage rendered Amelia dizzy. She clutched the doorframe. If she had the power to change the course of history, she would have killed Jean on the spot. She could have done it, too. Jacob had trained her to fight over the years, and this man-child was no more than a whiny bully, taking power from those too weak to fight back.

Amelia was not weak. The woman who had survived the wrath of Baldur was *not* a victim. If she had to take Ophélie from this place tonight, rules be damned, she would.

With the idea settled in her mind, she realized that was exactly what she intended to do. If not the plantation, then the time. Ophélie could not stay here a moment longer. Let anyone try to stop her.

Once she heard the lock of Jean's door click, Amelia snuck back out in the hall and toward the room he'd emerged from moments ago. Amelia sprinted over on tiptoes, and once inside, she closed and locked the door behind her.

Ophélie lay on her side, covers pulled to her chin. Tears of shock and sadness pooled in her eyes but did not spill.

"Ophélie," Amelia whispered. The crushing weight of a suspicion turned to reality bore down... of not pursuing this sooner. "We have to go."

"We won't be going anywhere," Ophélie replied. She pulled the blanket back and gestured to an empty spot beside her. "I've been waiting for this, Amelia. For you."

Amelia searched the room for a robe or something to throw over Ophélie. "No, we have to go. We can talk when we're safe, but you can't stay here anymore. Not with him."

"*Amelia,*" Ophélie said again, her tone firm and tinged with hardness. "We don't have time, *mon cher*. You're here for a reason. You've known that, and you know it more now, or you would not be here. You would not have dreamt of me or awakened this night to come find me. You know this, and yet you still fight."

"You're not making any sense," Amelia replied, grabbing a handmade afghan from a nearby chair. "You poor thing, I know what it's like to have... I'm sorry I didn't do something sooner. I really am so sorry, but I'm making this right, and we're leaving. I can take you nearby or Jacob and I—"

"I know what Jacob can do. I know what you can do," Ophélie answered. She appeared perfectly cool and collected in sharp contrast to Amelia's frenzy. "I know everything now, and it's time we talk. Can you trust me?"

"Trust?" Amelia parroted, gawking. "I'm asking you to trust me, sweet girl. We have to *go*! If your mother wakes..."

"Stop and listen to me!" Ophélie cried, throwing the blanket off the bed. "You sought answers but would not hear them. You have seen the truth, Amelia Deschanel, but have refused to acknowledge it. I am offering you a path to find it now!"

The words pushed the air from Amelia's lungs as her mind pulled together the sum of Ophèlie's words. *Amelia Deschanel. You have seen the truth. I am offering you a path.*

"How..." She swayed on her feet, falling into the armchair next to the bed. "My name. How?"

Ophélie, instead of rushing to her aid, smiled a sad smile. "Allow me to show you."

30
OPHÉLIE

It seemed right, and somehow perfect that Ophélie and Amelia would come to the edge of their final realizations together. But Amelia needed that one last push, and so Ophélie slipped her hand through Amelia's and closed her eyes.

Ophélie's vision went dark at the moment of connection. From Amelia's gasp, she experienced the same thing, and Ophélie understood whatever happened next, whatever they saw, would happen together.

A series of disconnected images flashed across the space of their minds.

Ophélie, a young girl of five, sitting underneath the shelter of a cypress tree on the bayou bank, perched between the knobby knees. In one moment, she was trying to catch fireflies, and in the next, the wind had been knocked from her chest as if stricken. *You won't live to see your seventeenth birthday,* said the voice.

Amelia, not much older, was coloring a drawing far beyond her age and skill, of a medieval castle surrounded by a lush emerald landscape. A young woman with white, windblown hair awaited at the bottom steps for a knight far in the distance. *You will find happiness, but you will endure a great struggle.*

Cerridwen, a girl of twelve, standing with her arms crossed tight over her chest, watching the figure through the inferno on the other side of the bonfire. She knew him. This was no ordinary flicker of recognition, but rather a flame rising high within her heart. *Cianán,* the flame said. *I will always know you, as I will always know myself.*

Ophélie, fresh off her fifteenth birthday. Drunk on happiness and an abundance of sweetmeats. She swayed with joy to her bedroom, eager to pass out in the bliss of overindulgence and daydream of life with her intended, Lestan de Blanchefort. As she closed her door—hands, familiar hands—came around her waist. "It's time," he panted. "We have work to do for Maman." *Some elements of our fate we must accept. This is yours. Only you can bear this cross, and bear it you must, for there are events of importance at stake bigger and greater than you.*

Amelia, dangling from a hook in a hazy cabin. As yet uninjured, but she was no fool. If she made it out alive, she wouldn't ever be the same. Jacob wouldn't be either. And as the blade from Baldur's dagger caught the light, she wondered if death might instead be a mercy. *No, not death for you. What you become from this prepares you instead for so much more.*

Cerridwen, hand-in-hand with Cianán, standing before the goddess. *The time will come when your memories fade, and your hearts grow weary. And it is then I shall turn my hope to you and pray my wisdom and faith holds as true as yours has.*

Cerridwen, praying beneath the *crann bethadh* for strength. She had been through many, many cycles, always searching for a sign the end was near. The goddess did not often reply directly. She was more likely to write the answer upon Cerridwen's heart. But, when she did, the gift was beyond her comprehension. *You and Cianán near the conclusion of the endlessness of your journey. No matter the words I give you now, they will not prepare you for the next stage. You were born knowing, but you will cease to do so. Your knowledge must come from within, from yourselves, and from your shared faith.*

Ophélie, running through her mother's garden, flying as far away from the plantation as her feet would carry her. *Cerridwen.* The name bounced off the corners of her mind. Of her heart. *Cianán.* Ophélie thought she could accept her fate, but she could not! She was meant for so much more. And her Victor... her Cianán. *You have served the goddess better than any before you. What is asked of you is unthinkable, yet inescapable. To serve me, you must serve Amelia, and assist her to her own purpose. Nothing will be in vain, Ophélie. You come to me in love.*

I await you, as I awaited you in many other lifetimes, with the loving arms of the eternal mother.

Amelia fell back against the bedpost. She withdrew her hand, but it dangled midair, lost for purpose. Her mouth hung slack; her cheeks were as white as her hair.

"Please say something, Amelia," Ophélie pleaded, breathless. She had known the truth before the visions, but the brutal clarity had rendered her equally wowed.

"I..." Amelia closed her eyes. Her breaths came short and painfully measured, the way Fitz struggled after any exertion.

"Would it be helpful if I told you what I know?" Ophélie steadied herself against the other end of the bed. This was her task. Her test. If she failed it, her entire life, all her struggles, would have been for naught.

Amelia closed her eyes, her breathing coming heavier now. She nodded.

"Cerridwen," Ophélie whispered. Their eyes met. "Lifetimes we've shared as one and the same, and yet now we sit before one another, two bodies, one soul. Do you remember being me?

"No," Amelia said quietly.

"No great shock," Ophélie said. "To get here, your intentions needed to be unfettered. I hope you never do find your recollections of life as me. You'll find little joy and much pain."

Amelia's eyes fluttered open. She watched Ophélie with a millennia of sadness. "I wish it were different."

"Your dreams... I didn't send them to you, but I know of them, for I had them too. Except in my dreams, I was you," Ophélie began. "I do not know who sent them. The goddess, perchance, or our own minds, bloated with the knowledge of who we were and always have been, struggling to breach the surface."

"In front of me... all along," Amelia mumbled. She crossed her arms and pulled them in, drawing them across her like a straightjacket. "How did I not see it?"

"Papa says we are incapable of witnessing simple reality because our minds are always searching for the complex." Ophélie looked down. "It took me years to assemble my own truth. Once you arrived, I couldn't stop the flood. I knew you were not a lady from England, and I also knew it was I who was responsible for your arrival."

"How?"

Ophélie smiled and shrugged. "I don't know. All I can tell you is what I do, and it is not a cheerful story, I'm afraid, but it is mine to tell, and now it is yours if you will hear me."

"Please, tell me," Amelia said. "Whatever it is... maybe we can change it."

They could not change it. This was the message Ophélie had been sent all the years of her life, since the morning in the swamp when she had been given a glimpse of her own fate.

The goddess had, in recent hours, confirmed her worst fears but had also given her the strength to face them.

"I believe," she started, "that all our lives as Cerridwen have been surrounded with purpose. But as we have neared the end, where the heirs of the four tribes are to come together and provide the means for our salvation, that purpose grows more prevalent. In my life, more savage. All have been united by the purpose of seeing *you* born. Only you can satisfy your part of the prophecy. Not I, nor any of the Cerridwens before us. Do you remember the words of the goddess?"

"Vaguely. I know the meaning."

"They are embossed upon my heart. It is only with my recent gift of clarity that I see them as clearly as I should," Ophélie said, smiling. "*Two millennia of wars and strife, which cannot be avoided, but can be stopped. One descendant from each of the four to emerge. Four become two, their offspring the peace that unites the two races again.*

"From Falias, a male, draoi, pure of heart and an affinity for creatures.

"From Murias, a female, born of fire and darkness.

"From Findias, a female reincarnated over the many moons.

"From Gorias, a male, draoi. The lover of the Findias heir.

"A son shall spring from Falias and Murias. Findias and Gorias join after many reincarnations, bringing forth a daughter. This son and this daughter will join together, in peace, uniting the Quinlans and Empyreans once more, thus ending the long days of war.

"You, Amelia, are the heir of Findias. You perhaps have heard those words, but in your heart, you have never fully accepted this fact," Ophélie continued, patiently. "I am as well, but my life has only ever been to serve the goddess in delivering you toward your intended fate."

"I know who I am," Amelia defended, pulling herself

straighter on the bed. "But there's a difference between knowing and accepting."

"Oh, I believe I know all about that. You see, I have known for more than a decade that I was destined to die before I was ever to be wed. I have understood that I would know no man's arms except my brother and the soldiers who would take *Ophélie* for their own during the Great War. I have known a child will be conceived of these horrors, another child, and who the father is, no one can say. My father will take my life to spare me further injustice, an act of both love and treason. He will know I can never be given as a bride to anyone after all the abuse. And my mother will loathe him to the point of taking her own life, though not out of grief for me but for the death of her own designs.

"It took the span of many years to pull these truths together, but that knowledge is mine. I have known these things, but they are not so easily accepted. I take faith in the story of our Lord, Jesus Christ, as He moved through his own human incarnation with grace and faith, knowing the torture He would be subjected to by following his path." Ophélie blinked away the threatening tears. There was no place for them here, or anywhere. Not anymore. "Yet I believe my origins are not with Christ, but with the goddess. And, like Christ, the goddess never asks more than what we can handle."

"What kind of goddess would ask that of you?" Amelia cried, pitching forward. "How could anyone claiming to love you ask you to endure so much?"

"For you," Ophélie said. "For our salvation."

"That makes no sense." Amelia shook her head. Her color had returned. "You do *not* need to suffer for me to thrive. That's completely ludicrous!"

"Not when you see it through the eyes of the goddess. It was foretold you would endure a great test before achieving your fate. This trial the goddess could not prevent... she has not that power... but instead, she sent you to bear witness to my own." Ophélie inched forward on the bed, pressing closer to Amelia. "I, too, know what it is to have everything taken from me. I have been stripped of my joy and my self-possession and have been given nothing to replace it. I am a void of what I could be."

"Then let me take you away from here. We can still change this!"

"You still don't understand," Ophélie said with a sigh. "I have not agonized in vain, sister. I have suffered so yours may end. And given a chance, I would do it again, and again, as your prosperity is also mine. I am not meant for joy in this life, but it is mine in the next, as it is yours. If I do not sacrifice myself, I cannot pass forward my strength in experience to you now. Amelia, I was *with* you in that cabin. Do you not know where your grit comes from? I can endure. I have. As have you. But it is not enough for you to endure. You must also flourish."

Amelia's thoughts, even to Ophélie who understood her heart better than anyone, were a mystery. But something within her seemed to shift as if shrugging off the burden of doubt. The effect was both visible and breathtaking to behold. "Why fate decided it should be me to survive this, I don't know," she said. "It seems so unfair that any of us should suffer this much as a means to an end."

"We all suffer. Not all of us make it through," Ophélie replied. She felt now as if she was truly speaking through the soul of Cerridwen, and no longer from the lips of a young woman. "If you don't persevere, all we have survived will have been for nothing. We will have all given everything, only to fail in the end. You say I have carried a burden, but I cannot imagine yours."

"The goddess says I need a daughter." Amelia's eyes drifted

to the window. "I would have liked to be a mother, but I could never bring a child into this world, not with all the pain my family has endured. Look at your own pain, Ophélie... it didn't start with my generation."

"There is no Deschanel Curse," Ophélie said. "You know this."

Amelia said nothing.

"Yes, I've seen glimpses of the fears of our family's future. Maman has power, but cursing every one of her ancestors to unhappiness and death is not one of them," Ophélie said. "Though many will believe that, the knowledge will destroy them. The goddess showed me so much sadness. She allowed me to see everything. My niece, Ophelia, will trust in it so fully, she will sacrifice everything to that belief and eventually create a child anyway, with her Sullivan lover, a child she will only have time to kiss and send away to be raised by another. I have seen many more Deschanels turn away from happiness for fear of what might be, including you. Please, Amelia, our family needs a voice of reason. It should be you."

Amelia focused on her hands, palms cupped. "I was pregnant. I lost the child that night in the cabin, the same night I learned I was going to be a mom. If that doesn't feel like a curse..."

Ophélie nodded. "It wasn't meant to be. As my son was not. But that is *not* a result of a curse."

Amelia snapped her head up. "The crying child was real, then? Ophélie, please tell me..."

"It is done." Ophélie drew her mouth in a thin, tight line to steady herself. To keep from crying. "The child is no longer in pain."

Amelia was aghast. "In pain? What was wrong with him?"

"We will never know because Maman refused to allow a doctor to attend him. She did not want to expose the horrors of what she'd put upon her children." Ophélie laughed. "And yet, her modesty only stretched to appearances, not to our own well-being."

"I could've helped," Amelia said, shaking her head. "Jacob could have helped. We're doctors... not the same kind, but we still know a hell of a lot more than your mother, and we could have done *something.*"

Ophélie reached forward and pulled Amelia's hands into hers. "Do you not see? It was not in fate's vision for me. As your first child was not in yours. We are not meant to question, only accept. The goddess did not bring you here to try and save me, or to alter what has happened to either of us. But you can learn from it. You must."

Amelia turned Ophélie's hands over in hers, studying them. Perhaps seeing if she recognized them from her own distant memory. "And what lesson should I take from all this misery, Ophélie?"

"Because I have been chosen to suffer," Ophélie began, choosing each word carefully. "I will not ever have my Cianán. He's looked after me all these years, and I never knew... not until now... why, or why it should matter to me. Victor cannot change my fate, and he knows, as I know, it must be. He watches us both in sadness, knowing he cannot be with the one he was fated with, and he cannot have the one he was not.

"And yet the argument could be made that my suffering is a result of Cianán not being at my side. A circular argument, he calls it. Either he cannot have me because I am destined to die, or I am destined to die because he cannot have me. It matters naught when the outcome cannot change. The lesson, then, is clear to me. There is no Cianán without Cerridwen. No Cerridwen without Cianán. The two are not only bound by the prophecy, but by the *stars.* Think, Amelia, of the time before you knew Jacob. Of the emptiness."

Ophélie realized when it reflected in Amelia's sad eyes.

"The reverse is equally true. He was not himself until he was yours. And now, as you recover from your unspeakable suffering, you are again separated, and your souls are in a similar torment. You are lost, fumbling through the steps of your life. And I am here to show you what happens when Cerridwen does not or cannot have her Cianán."

"I thought if I could find the answers, I could find my way back to him," Amelia whispered. "I've tried so hard to be wise, like my mother, but I've only proven to be a well-intentioned fool."

"He *is* the answer, Amelia," Ophélie said gently. "He has always been the answer for you, as you have been his answer. And you are no fool, well-intentioned or otherwise. But it's time to return. To Jacob. To your home. We are on the verge of a war you surely know more about than I, and once it comes, I cannot protect you. No one can. Not even the goddess. And my maman... she knows something is amiss and won't stop until she learns the truth, or drives you away."

The silence between them was all-consuming, but rather than a void, it served as a well of mutual understanding. Ophélie did not require confirmation of Amelia's understanding. She had passed her test.

"Victor," Amelia said finally. "What about him? What do we do about him?"

"You? Nothing," Ophélie said, and for the first time in the long night of revelations, a dark foreboding washed over her. "And I caution you, Amelia. You may have been sent here, but it was not without danger. I know it comes as a shock, to say Cianán is a danger to you, but the presence of two in your life cannot do anything for you except add confusion. He cannot help but love you, and if you let down your guard, you will love him in return."

"No, that just isn't going to happen," Amelia said with a short laugh. "I'm drawn to him, yeah, but only because I have no choice… I mean, he's Cianán. I'm built to be drawn to him, right?"

"Perhaps," Ophélie agreed. "But that does not mean your nature is serving you well here. Say your goodbyes, and make yourself clear, for he cannot separate his love with the same clarity. He must leave you and Jacob to your fate, and live out his own, separately. When you leave, he becomes an element of your memory, of this lesson, but nothing more."

"Will he accept that?"

"Give him no choice. He belongs here, in our time. He is not of your world, and you are not of his. When you return, you look only forward."

"And there's nothing…" Amelia shook her head, struggling with her internal thoughts. "No, I know there isn't. I wish, more than anything, that I could help you. But I won't be the foolish girl in the book who refuses to see reason. We are who we are, and while neither of us chose the path we are on, we're on it, and there's, as you said, only forward, not back." Amelia pulled Ophélie's hands into hers again and lifted them to her face, kissing them. "If only we could have known one another longer, sweet, brave girl. What a gift this has been, even with everything surrounding us."

"Ahh, but you have," Ophélie smiled, lifting Amelia's hands to her own lips in return. "We have known each other forever."

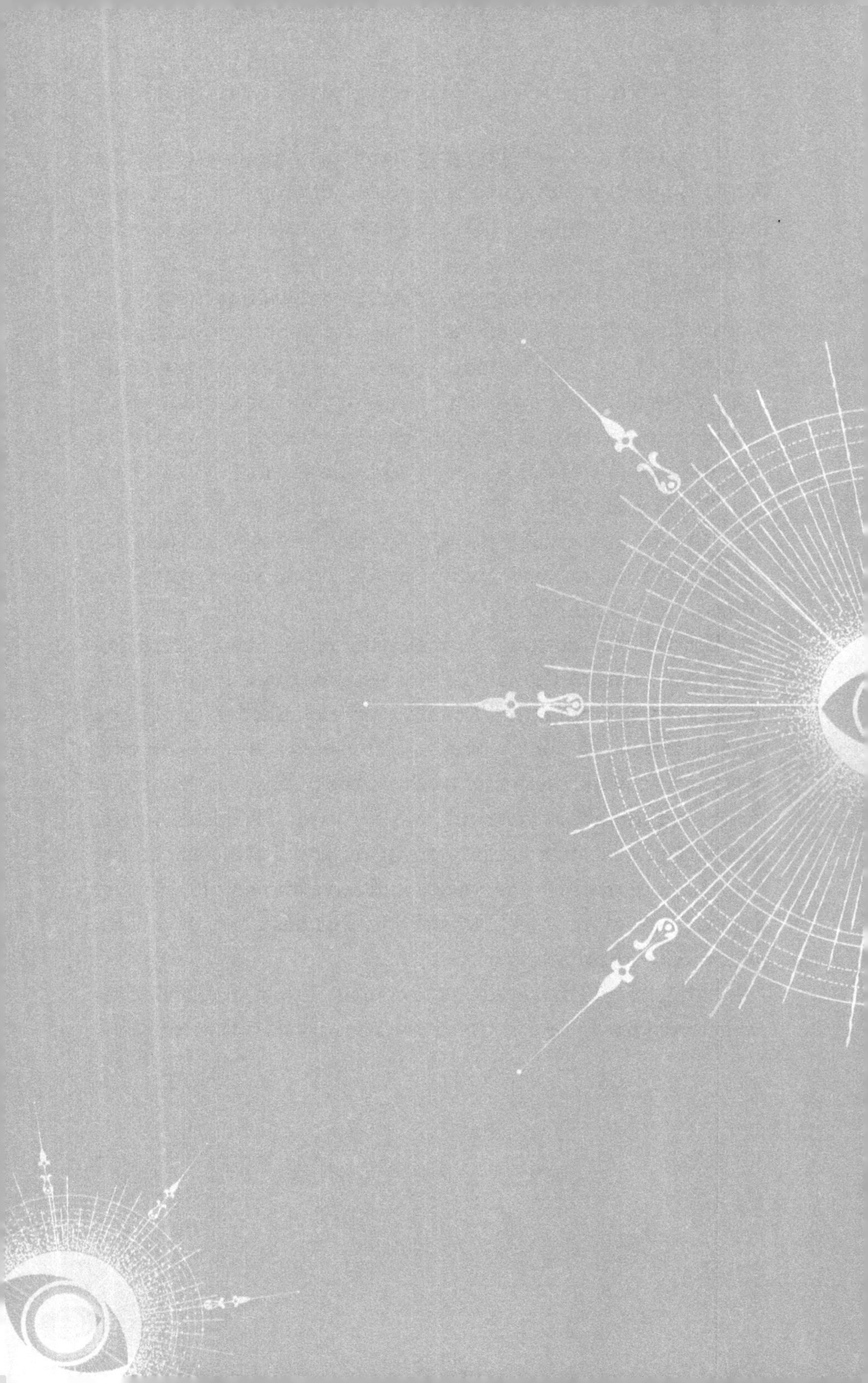

31
JACOB

When Jacob awoke to find Amelia missing, again, he resolved this would be the last time.

They were going home.

The thin blanket flew off in a heap. After their brief but heavy talk tonight—the most intimacy they'd shared since that night in the cabin—he trusted whatever he found would not wound him too deeply, but gone were the days and nights where he left her to solve this for herself.

He disregarded the noise he made as he sprinted into the hall. Seeing no sign of her there, Jacob made his way down the stairs. The pitched creaking from his heavy footfalls would likely wake the house, but he no longer cared. Nothing else mattered beyond the two of them and getting home.

A quick, harried scan revealed Amelia wasn't in the foyer either. But someone else was.

Victor.

"Where is she?" Jacob demanded.

"Jacob," Victor replied, turning from where he rested

against the parlor doorframe. “You have been here all this time and overlooked what lay right in front of you.”

“Does that work with the ladies? Throwing a bunch of words together and slapping on a mysterious look?” Jacob shook his head with obvious impatience. “I don’t have time for this. I know you know where my wife is. You’ve tracked her every moment since we got here.”

“Longer, even,” the man replied with a slow, maddening grin. “For once, it isn’t her I am waiting for, but you.”

“You know what? I don’t even know why I bothered,” Jacob snapped, and barged past Victor, in the direction of the kitchen. A hand fished out and clamped down on his upper arm, jolting him back.

“Victor, I do not recommend that,” Jacob hissed, attempting to wrench his arm free. He made no gains because the effort was like pulling a hand out of concrete. The man was superhuman.

“I see you,” Victor replied, dropping his voice. “I see you, Cianán. I know you, as you know yourself.”

Jacob stopped struggling and met the man’s eyes. “What did you say?”

“You have wandered these halls, pining for your beloved, awaiting her to find her realizations that will take you home,” Victor answered. He dropped Jacob’s arm. “When all along, your answers lay before you, as well.”

“What did you call me?”

“Jacob… Cianán… these names are only that, names. You and I, we are one and the same. I may yet be punished for not permitting you to discover this truth on your own, but Cerridwen has learned her truth, and she cannot weather this storm alone. And you cannot help her survive it if you come to her a white canvas, absent of knowledge.”

“Is that…” He had his answer, and with it, came many

others. There was no way Victor, a stranger, could know the legends of Cianán and Cerridwen with such confidence unless he brought firsthand experience.

Jacob matched this new knowledge with their experiences the past number of days... Victor's bold pursuit of Amelia, the conspiratorial smiles he often afforded Jacob. How he was everywhere, always, a part of them.

"She needs you. Over time, the nature of that requirement has shifted, and the burden with it, but now it is yours to carry. Only you can heal her wounds, Cianán. They run too deep for her to find her way back alone."

Jacob's heart rate plummeted. For a moment, he thought he might be in cardiac arrest, the shock was so acute.

If Victor was Cianán—or an iteration of Cianán—then he was Jacob, and his love for Amelia was not verboten but a natural evolution of their meeting.

No wonder she's been so confused. Oh, Blanca. *We need to talk.*

"It doesn't matter," Jacob said. He backed away, eyes darting around the perimeter for any sign of Amelia. No, only she mattered. "Or maybe it does, but it's of no consequence *right now*. I need to find her. If you are who you say you are, and you mean what you just said to me, then you'll tell me."

Victor pointed toward the heavy oaken doors leading outside. "She's been waiting for you. And now, you are ready to go to her."

JACOB THREW OPEN THE DOORS AND RUSHED INTO THE ELECTRIC night. The storms plaguing them the past few days showed no signs of leaving. Heavy rain hit the earth in sheets, passing over a large swath of moonlight like a moving wall.

"Amelia!" he cried with a power to wake the earth.

He squinted through the blanket of rain at the sight of

movement. It was faint, but he was certain he'd identified someone climbing the short levee toward the river.

Jacob didn't think. He ran.

When he reached the levee, he stopped to assess. From his original vantage point, he couldn't see which direction she'd been headed, and once Amelia had disappeared, she never came back into his field of vision. But he didn't need eyes to see.

I'm here, and I know, and I love you, and nothing else matters.

He closed his eyes to block the competing chorus of his other senses. Listen. Nothing else.

Jacob turned to the west. Opening his eyes, he spotted a cluster of cypress trees along the bank, near the levee break. A flash of white clothing reflected back.

He sloshed barefoot through the mud and the storm, losing his footing. But the momentum carried him true and forward. At the edge of the trees, he saw his wife, huddled underneath, trembling from the weight of the sobs that had taken over.

Only you can heal her wounds. They run too deep for her to find her way back alone.

"Never again," Jacob vowed as he struggled through the muck and sheeting rain to his wife. Toward the only person who had ever made him the man he wanted to be. "I'll not ever leave you again, even if it kills me."

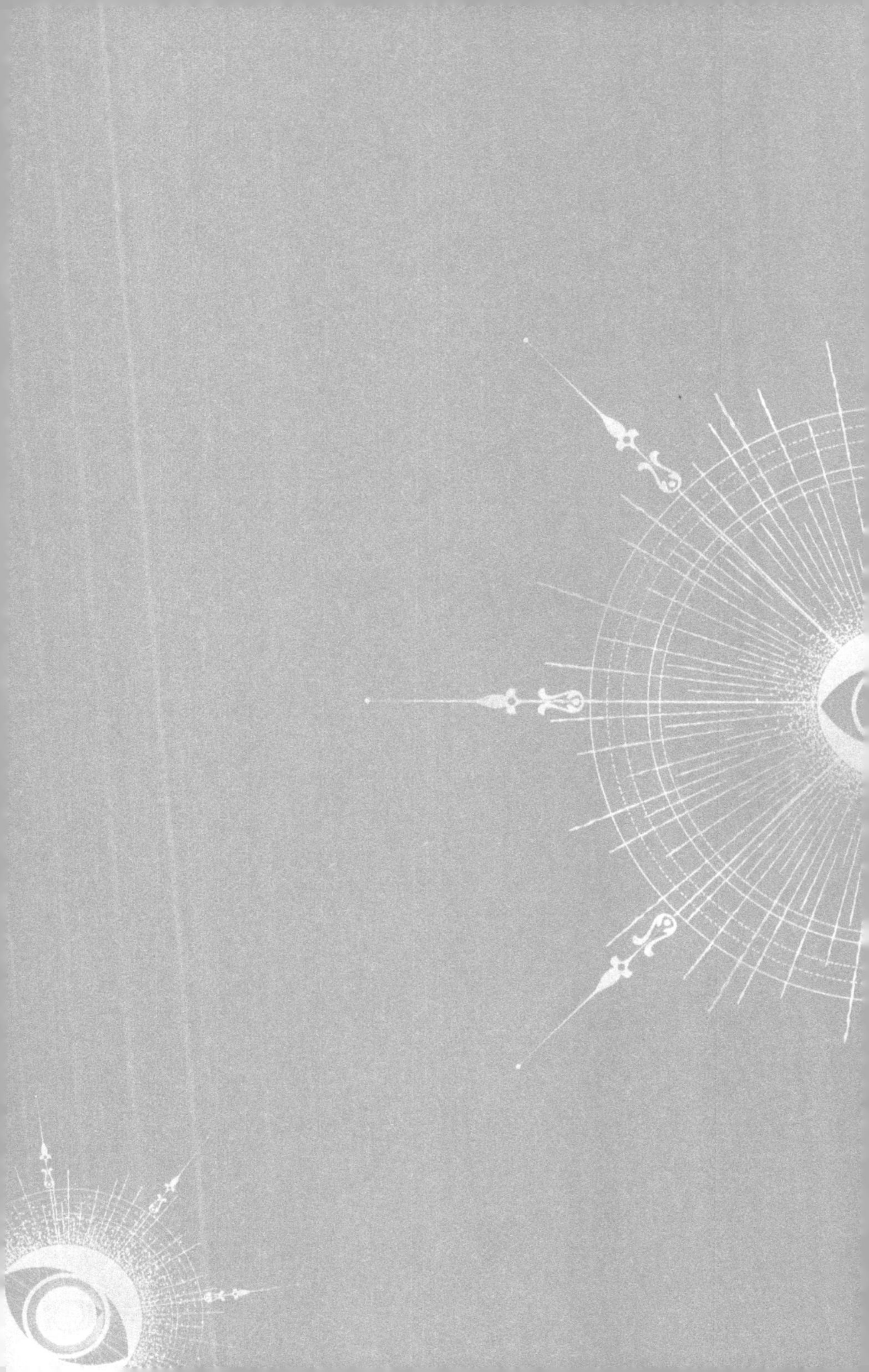

32
AMELIA

"I've been so unfair to you."

Amelia, hunched over the cypress knees, wrapped in an afghan she'd taken from the house, heard his words before seeing him approaching.

Jacob had come. Either in fear of realizing her missing again or from new comprehension of his own. Regardless, he had come. He was here, and when she lifted her tired head to read him, Amelia witnessed only one thing: love.

"There's no rulebook for surviving," she answered. Her voice cracked. She sounded so unlike herself. "No one taught us how to get through this."

Jacob climbed carefully over the roots, navigating a maze of them to get to her. She scooted over to make room, and he slid under the afghan. Her head fell on his shoulder as his arm draped around her back, a gesture she hadn't allowed since that night but did not know, until now, how badly she'd needed it.

"I didn't realize how guarded I've been," Jacob went on. He ran his hands up and down her arm, warming her. She rocked back and forth in an attempt to control the rising pain within her. "I was so caught up in thinking you were too fixated on finding signs, or answers, that I didn't think at all about my own actions. I pushed you to figure everything out while all I did was hide in my own head. I've failed you again, and I can't say sorry enough, *Blanca*."

"There's no such thing with us," she whispered, hoarse and exhausted. "You're my constant, Jacob. Over the span of space and stars, you're the only one, and you couldn't ever fail me, not if you made an honest effort of it."

"I'm not fishing for reassurance," he said, his lips against her matted hair. "I'm not a man worthy of you if I can't admit when I've been wrong. And I have... I thought... well, we need to move forward. We have to just try and move on... but then you were so damned determined the answers were in the past, not the future, and I let myself fixate on *that,* and I tunneled on the idea because it distracted me from thinking about anything else. Specifically, one thing."

Amelia released a jagged breath against his chest. "I know. And I thought I could put off my grief. Then, I thought I could solve it. I didn't know how to deal with my hatred." Her voice caught as a new sob rose. "It wasn't my hatred of Baldur that was eating me alive, but hatred of myself."

A fresh rain hit the tops of the cypress, their only canopy from the storm. Jacob pulled the blanket tighter around his wife. "How could you ever hate yourself for what he did?"

"Don't you?" she asked, looking up briefly. "Isn't that what you've done, blame yourself?"

A few drops escaped the cover and landed on them. Ahead, the river's current increased with the arrival of a steamboat making its way upriver.

Jacob's jaw tightened. Her words had a transporting effect, and as he trained his gaze on the ship, in an attempt to reground himself, he saw Amelia running from him that night in Ireland after he'd told her to leave. The next time he'd seen her, she was at the mercy of that monster.

Amelia saw this in his mind, laid bare to her in his vulnerability.

"No... Donnelly, *no*. You *can't*. If we want to play that game, we could start blaming the Quinlans for pushing us so hard, or my aunt for sending the letter that brought us to Killianshire. Our fight that night... it was inevitable. We had so much pressure, and we were only just beginning our lives together after everything with Oz, and Adrienne..."

"I wanted to hurt you that night." Each word strained to reveal the next, as the comprehension hit him. "I blamed you for getting us into the business with the Quinlans, then disregarding everything they said." Jacob's arm around her went slack, and his foot began an escalating staccato of tapping. A small moan was trapped in the back of his throat, and when it escaped, the sound turned to primal grief. "Amelia, my God, I led you *right into that nightmare*."

Jacob's scream rose into the quiet night, a symphony of rage and immeasurable regret. Amelia experienced his agony like ice to the marrow.

He released her and fell forward, grinding his fists into his kneecaps, rocking faster and faster as if trying to burrow himself into the earth. His chin fell to his chest, and tears rained down on his bare feet, sliding into the mossy trunk.

Amelia rested her hand against the middle of his back and traced soft, calming circles. She'd used this gesture years ago when he'd returned from a fight, full of adrenaline and aching regret. It always brought him back to the now. To her.

"You are so wrong. Jacob, you brought me out of it," she said softly, letting her hand speak the rest of her thoughts against his trembling back. In Amelia's own all-consuming attempts to transcend her own grief, she'd never stopped to consider his.

"I've pushed you away because it hurt when you couldn't turn to me," Jacob cried. "And I turned around and made you feel terrible for doing exactly what I had pushed you to do."

Amelia leaned over her knees, pressing her face to the side so she could see his. "Without you, I wouldn't be here." This time, she couldn't stem the tide of the impending meltdown. Her own tears burst forth in a flood. "Jacob, I would have died, body and soul. You brought me back. You saved me. You've been protecting me since the day I caught you in the middle of that silly drum solo on the campus pub." Tears blinded her now. They ran down her face and into her mouth. "I don't know how to get through this," she continued between sobs, afraid of losing herself before she could say the words. "But I know now the only way forward is together."

Jacob drew back. His fists clenched and unclenched, tears rolling over his hands. He blew out, once, twice. Brought fresh air back into his lungs.

Then he threw his arms around Amelia and crushed her in the embrace, sloppy and haphazard but whole and real. They cried together, limbs stretched over shoulders and around backs, rocking through their shared thoughts with a grief only the two of them could ever understand.

"Love isn't a strong enough word," he sobbed into her hair, breathing her in, choking on his tears. "For what you've given to me, Amelia. There isn't a word I know of that comes close."

"We don't need words," she answered, brushing his black hair back off his face, smiling. "We never have."

Jacob cupped her face in his hands and kissed her, the salt of their mingled tears somehow healing. "We have to leave this place. I think we have what we came here for."

Amelia slowly nodded. "I have so much to tell you."

"I already know," he replied. His thumb brushed fresh tears away from her eyes. "I know about Victor."

Her eyes widened in surprise. "How long have you known?"

"Since about five minutes before I found you here."

She laughed. "And you rushed right over, not considering I might have wanted to be alone."

"Did you?"

Amelia pressed her lips to his, lingering. "No."

"I'm not mad at him. But it hurts, the way he looks at you. He has a right, but he also has no right."

"You were correct the second time," Amelia assured him. "He has no right. A reason, maybe, but I'm not his Cerridwen. I can't change what will happen to her."

"Ophélie?" Jacob asked in wonder, as the realization visibly came over him. A guilty look flashed in his eyes. "I should have known. I talked to her the other day, just the two of us, and it felt as if... well, I felt like I was talking to you."

"It was right in front of me and I didn't. Not until tonight."

"It's sort of amazing we both have medical degrees."

Amelia scrunched her face. She sniffled away the fading tears. "It's a good thing I changed my minor from time travel to Latin."

"You narrowly avoided certain embarrassment to your family," Jacob agreed.

Amelia snuggled back into him. Her heart felt exposed and raw, but it no longer frightened her the way it once had. "We should say our goodbyes. And ... then I have no idea, I guess."

"There is no magic to moving on," Jacob said. His nervous feet went still as his fists relaxed into open palms. "Except what we can give each other as we do."

Amelia sucked in a deep breath and began to rise, but Jacob tugged on her hand. He looked up. His green eyes implored her.

"I can't ask that you not be conflicted about Victor. But I don't know how to compete with my own self."

"Donnelly," she said with a slow, happy smile. So much awaited them ahead, but at this moment, she felt once again as if there was hope. "I love you, and only you. And only you, and only you."

"But he is me! It's as clear, or as confusing, as that."

"No." Amelia pulled her husband to his feet and pressed her hands against his face. "There is only *one* you."

DAY SEVEN

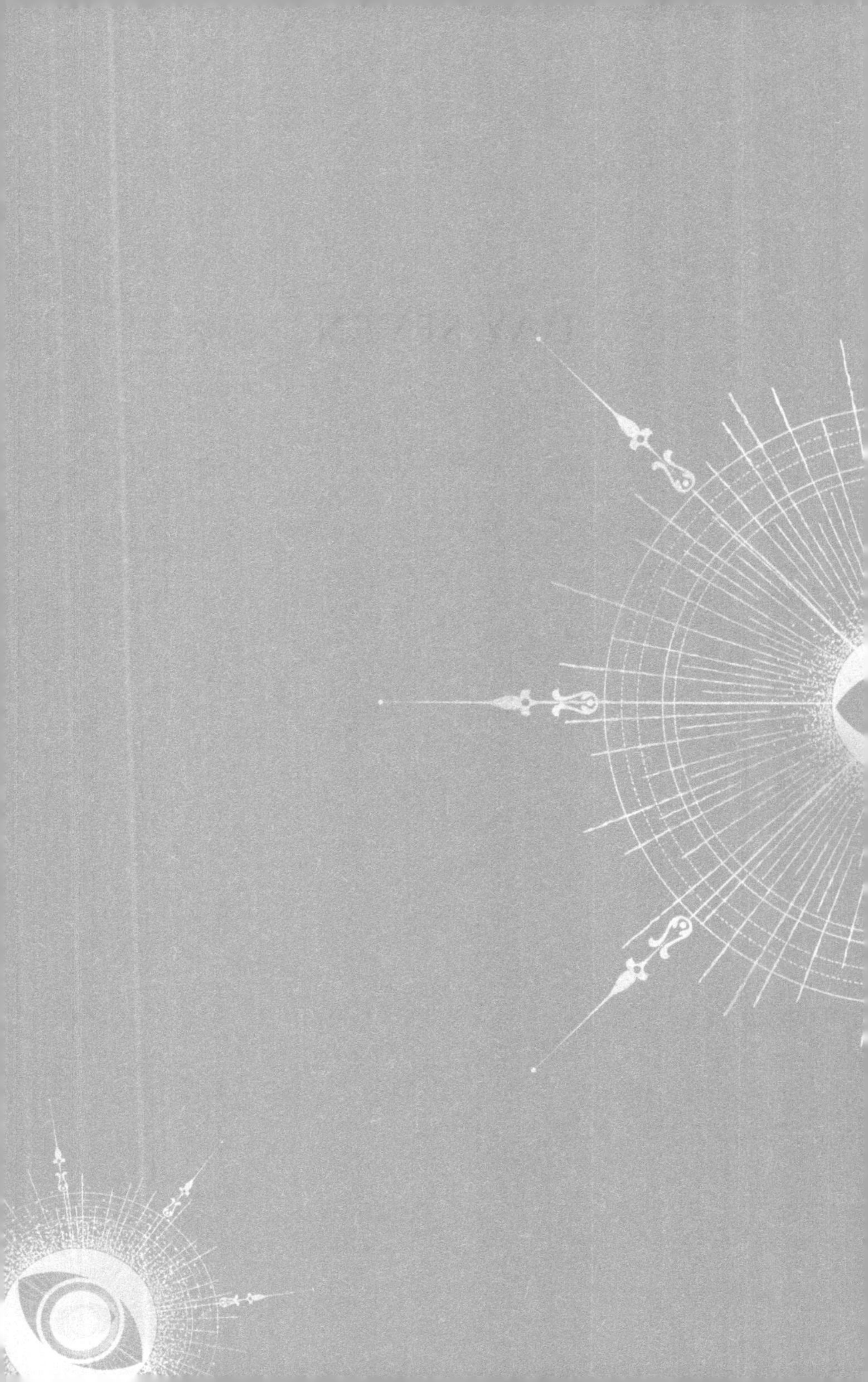

33
JACOB

Healing came in many forms. It revealed itself in different ways for everyone and changed with each circumstance and variable turn. Jacob didn't know what their path looked like, or how long it would be, but for the first time since their shared tragedy, he was certain they were on the *right* one because they approached it together, hands locked, hearts open.

He and his wife spent the next hours catching up on their individual adventures at *Ophélie*. Amelia spoke of her dreams, and of Victor. It didn't hurt nearly as much as it had. When his name was on her lips, she expressed fondness, but her eyes didn't light up.

Jacob told her of his sleepless nights and channeling his worry into the avoidance of his own pain. He recalled his tenuous adventure with Jean—Amelia went ghastly pale during the telling of the knife-wielding assailants—and his fear their lack of welcome might turn violent.

It was time to leave, but for now, whispering their secrets

amongst the cypress was as close to being free of their demons as they had ever been.

Jacob didn't realize he'd fallen asleep until the earth began to shake. When he opened his eyes, night had turned to dawn.

Startled, he nearly dropped Amelia against the trunk of a nearby tree. He shook his head to get his bearings. The rumbling turned to the sound of rolling thunder, followed by sharp cries of excited men.

He went to adjust Amelia back to a comfortable position, but she was already awake, ears alert to the same sounds.

She craned her neck toward the levee. "What on earth is that?"

"Horses... maybe," he muttered and scrambled out of the tangle of branches and up the backside of the levee. The warm Louisiana sun had dried all signs of the evening storm, and the world was restored. "Wait here."

"Sure," she said with a laugh and followed him.

The hooves and whoops grew louder, and as they reached the crest, a giant cloud of dust obscured their vision. Four horsemen came to an abrupt stop, their mounts throwing up more brown clouds.

"We're going to war!" a young one cried. Jacob squinted for a better view and saw his gray uniform; the wardrobe of the Confederacy.

"This can't be good," Amelia said and followed Jacob as he jogged down the short hill and toward the riders paused at *Ophélie's* gates.

"Hi, there!" Jacob called out as he approached.

"Hello!" Someone yelled back in response. "Is the master home?"

"I'm the master," Jacob lied. The two men exchanged handshakes. The officer was oblivious to the fabrication.

"We're riding to all the landowners to share the news," the officer replied. Sweat and dust stained his face. "Louisiana announced our secession from the Union. We'll join the other states already ahead of us, Glory be to God."

"There's to be war!" the young one repeated and spat. He stank of whiskey and unbridled excitement.

An elder officer shot him an exhausted look. "War has not been officially declared, but it's a matter of days. Weeks, mayhap. All men over the age of thirteen and under sixty, unless infirm, are being ordered to appear at the courthouse in St. James to register for Confederate service. Aside from yourself, sir, how many can you commit?"

"Two," Jacob said with a blank look. This risk had been prevalent since their arrival but he somehow never saw the reality.

"Good to hear." He handed Jacob a thick sheet of paper. "The bill, in the event you need the formal summons."

"Thank you." Jacob gaped at the words. No words would make a difference. He could do nothing. War was inevitable.

Somehow, this was the most real their journey had seemed.

"Good day to you, sir. And to you, madam." The officer tipped his hat at Amelia, flashing her a smile before turning back to his reigns. "If you'll pardon our short stop, we have many houses to hit before sundown."

They were off in another rousing cloud, echoing their whoops and cries along the way.

"I suppose we better go tell Charles," Amelia said. Together, they watched the men disappear into the distance.

"And..." Jacob slipped his hand through hers as their eyes

stayed on the specks far on ahead, both of them in a daze. "We need to make our plans to leave."

"Seems like we just did this. Running from chaos." Amelia chuckled, and it almost sounded natural. "I hope we don't flip into another shaky situation."

"We haven't seen the Battle of New Orleans in person," Jacob joked. His comment elicited a small smile, and it made his heart happy. "If we do... well, then we do. We've already been through the worst that could happen to us. Everything else will seem like a carnival."

"With clowns? You know I hate clowns."

"I can't promise that, but we can kill any we encounter."

"Fair compromise, I guess."

"We are nothing if not adaptable."

Amelia swung his hand. Her head dropped to look at the earth beneath her dusty feet. "I've seen what a life without Cianán has done to Ophélie," she said in a quiet voice. "She can't survive what's coming without him, and I know I can't live through what's happened to me without you. The situation isn't anything science could explain, but that doesn't make it any less true. A hundred and fifty years have passed, and nothing has changed."

"Give or take a few millennia." Jacob smiled, and lifted her hand to her face, pressing his over the top. "I love you, *mi bruja blanca*. The rest is noise."

"I had a baby," Amelia answered in a near whisper, the words sitting on her lips as she seemed to consider them, turning them over, making them real. "*We* did. When I see that night, I don't think of that because it doesn't seem possible. We never had a chance to get used to the idea."

A tightness spread across Jacob's chest. He, as well, had pushed that part of the night aside, like a fantasy. He had never known how badly he wanted to be a father until the Quinlans insisted he must, then it had happened and been ripped away before he understood how his life had changed.

Maybe he and Amelia could try again. Maybe they would. But that was not what Amelia needed to hear.

"Little scars dot our souls." Jacob pressed his forehead to hers. "But they do not draw our life's picture."

"What an unusually poetic thought."

"My mother," he replied. "She said it to me when I was a boy. Mom said a lot of stuff I thought was nonsense. Now I know better, but her wisdom is coming back to me. A lot of her words are. Ever since we answered your Aunt Nora's letter with a visit."

"Is that all our daughter is, then? A scar?"

"A memory," he answered. "A part of us. A lesson from our past."

"And what lesson do you take from this?"

Jacob wrapped her in his arms. "That love saved us years ago, and it will save us now."

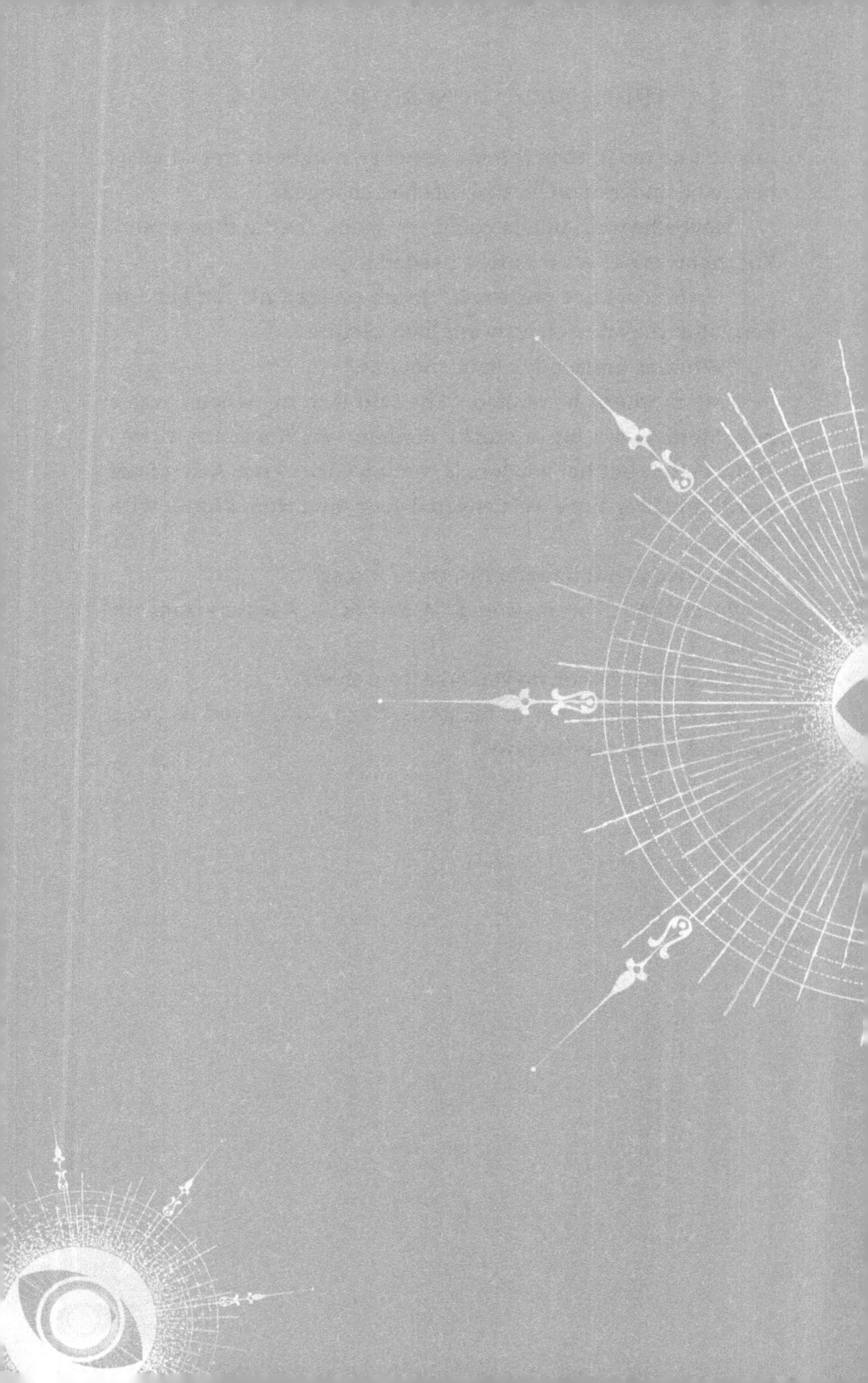

34
OPHÉLIE

Ophélie knew this day would come, but it did not make the arrival any easier. Although the past two years of her life had been wrought with struggle, when she considered the beginning of the end, it was this day, the day the riders came, where she expected the countdown.

And now that day was here.

She wanted so badly to be brave. Ophélie tried with floundering desperation to draw from the strength of her ancient soul, but the weight of being a sixteen-year-old girl in this lifetime seemed so much more tangible than dozens of lifetimes past. She wanted her mother, but the woman she craved was not the one who'd given birth to her, but rather the idea of a mother who might have loved and protected her if life had granted her a safer passage.

It matters not when the end is the same. Oh, but it did. The finality of her situation would be much less agonizing to bear if she could rely on the comfort of someone who loved her… someone to see her to the finish.

Charles did love her. Ophélie was often surprised how easily she dismissed her one ally in the household, but his time was spent buried in business, not sorting out emotions.

His love for her would deliver Ophélie from agony in her final moments. Her father's love would be what propelled him to lift the knife and sink it into her chest, face full of tears. Ophélie adored her father for his future courage, but she also hated him for allowing it to arrive far too late.

I'll bet my fortune in Confederate bonds the war will be over within a month. Those Yanks don't know what they've awakened! Her father had declared when they gathered in the parlor to "celebrate" the news. How bold and blustering the South was, when their downfall would be spelled out in less than five years' time! Many men, friends of the Deschanels, had ridden to *Ophélie* to share in Charles' foolish sentiment over cigars and brandy. Only Victor and Marius had the good sense to know when silence was better.

"Your Confederate bonds soon will not be worth the paper they're printed on. And the only part of this war that will be over quickly is the lives of many, including mine," she whispered as she paused briefly at the parlor door.

Ophélie wiped at the rogue tears in the corners of her eyes and pulled her shoulders back. She was in the final stretch now and could face it with fear or with bravery, but she *must* face it. For herself, and for Amelia.

OPHÉLIE NEEDED TO LOCATE AMELIA AND JACOB, TO WARN THEM. HER mother had gone silent on the subject of the visitors and Ophélie knew that could mean only one thing. She'd stopped digging because she'd found her answers. It would also not do for Jacob to get caught in the swarm of men enlisting for service. He and Amelia had found what they'd come for, and every moment they dallied was one closer to trouble.

Yet she hadn't seen either of them since they returned, hours ago, after the riders delivered their message.

Ophélie stopped in the center of the kitchens, squinting through the long windows to survey the back of the property for signs of her friends. The evening sun blinded her, and as she reached for the door, intent to search the entire estate if she needed to, a hand clamped around her wrist. She was yanked into the pantry.

"Apologies, mademoiselle," Victor whispered in the dark, damp room. He handed her a green stalk of cane sugar; she could make out this treat even in the darkness. "I brought you one in case you are so inclined."

"I am," Ophélie said and quickly took the stalk from him, placing the sweet goodness between her back molars. She drew in a deep breath, forgetting her distress for one quiet moment.

The reality of all she understood brought her back to the present. Victor. Cianán. She knew. He undoubtedly did, as well.

"We will get them away from here. We must," Victor said. Of course, they were in accord. Ophélie and Victor had been thus for many, many moons. "And you... what can I do for you, sweet Ophélie?"

Emotion bubbled up from her chest. When had anyone ever spoken to her with such tenderness? "Nothing lasting," she replied, dropping the cane from her teeth. She tossed it into the corner.

Victor knelt before her. He pulled her hands into his and craned his neck to gaze at her in the dimness. "I would save you yet."

Ophélie turned her head away. Her tears were her own, and

she did not wish to share them with anyone, not even Cianán. "It hurts more to speak of what cannot be than to accept what is. Don't say foolish words. I can't bear them."

"They aren't foolish if I mean them," Victor countered. He rose and his lips came upon hers. Ophélie's knees turned to jelly. Her first kiss from a real lover, and oh, how wonderful to be on the receiving end of love without violence!

Ophélie let Victor kiss her. She didn't know when, if ever, she would have another moment like this, and she wouldn't deny herself. When his arms eased around her back, enveloping her, she allowed this, too. He was no ordinary man, but her Cianán, and even if the goddess would deny them their happy ending in this lifetime, she had said nothing about a kiss.

He whispered the next words against her mouth. "We could disregard the goddess and her prophecy. We could, you know. How many lifetimes have we endured, trusting in the truth she promised? Our suffering is our own to decide."

"Blasphemous," Ophélie hissed, stumbling back. She had come to terms with her sacrifice, and he would attempt to undo her courage? "Have you forgotten all those lifetimes were ours, too? And the next? Don't be so short-sighted."

"It's more than that," Victor replied. He didn't approach her, perhaps sensing her immediate rise to anger. "I have done something, Ophélie. Something terrible that I cannot undo, but my action changes everything."

"We have no time to waste. Tell me, or hold your words to yourself, but make the choice now," Ophélie said, with a glance at the door. She could not relax until Amelia and Jacob were safely back in their own time.

Victor's soft steps grew closer, and he again came into view. "Then suspend your doubt of me, and agree to believe whatever I say, no matter how unlikely it may sound."

Ophélie nodded with a short sigh. "Go. Tell me. Be quick."

"As quick as I can," Victor agreed. "You know of my family. Of their unusual nature. It can be explained, but that explanation requires more time than we have at present. There are two pieces of information you must know to understand, however. The first is that we possess the gift of immortality. The second is this gift is a choice."

Ophélie's pulse raced. Whether or not she was capable of believing his words, she had to let him speak them.

"I knew who I was, my past as Cianán, before I was offered this gift. These truths came to me in my teenage years, as they come to you now, but I didn't accept them as you do. Rebelliousness runs in my blood, and I balked at the notion my fate was not my own to decide. I toiled with it, languished over what it might mean. And yet, I hesitated to take my gift when offered because I knew it would affect who I was as Cianán. At the time, I was at constant cross purposes with myself, about who I really was, and whether I could accept what it would mean.

"For years, this went on. It ended when, after a particularly rough night with the bottle, I made the impetuous decision to leave my past behind and charge forth with my family, into a future of my own design."

Ophélie had held her breath at some point. She remembered to take one now. "Are you saying..."

"At the moment I accepted this gift, I ceased to be Cianán," Victor said after a long pause. "I had his memories, his desires. I spent nearly thirty years as the incarnation of a being with thousands of experiences, and they didn't disappear with the gift. But his soul returned to the goddess, and I became simply Victor de Blanchefort. I surrendered my endowment from the goddess for a gift from another."

"You have been deceiving Amelia this entire time," Ophélie said with a slow, angry breath. "And me!"

"No!" he replied in a rush. "I continue to be Cianán, even if his soul rests in Jacob. I am tortured with his memories, but I don't get his future, his fate. I love Amelia, as I love you because Cianán loved you both, and I cannot simply shrug away the imprint of being him has left on my soul. I am torn between two worlds, Ophélie. One I have chosen, the other I did not but would select again in a heartbeat. Oh, if I could go back! But I cannot. And so I ask of you... I implore you... to join me. Allow me to present this same gift to you. Cerridwen will move on to Amelia, as was destined, but you do not have to die! You can become a truer version of yourself, no longer tethered to a long string of fate. As I am. Your death does not have to be the end!"

Ophélie gripped the shelves, struggling for breath. What he had confessed was perhaps more blasphemous than his original words. Victor was suggesting she give up her claim to Cerridwen's glorious reward in exchange for a lifetime, many lifetimes, at his side. He offered her a way to avoid her own death, but at the cost of her very reason for walking toward those gallows willingly. "Victor... I..."

He pulled her into his arms, pressing his cheek to the top of her head. "You need not say yes now. But time is no longer on our side, *mon cher*."

"Tell me," she managed through a hoarse voice. "If you could go back, what decision would you make?"

Victor tensed. His breath was hot against her scalp. "I won't deceive you. I would choose Cianán. But, Ophélie, that choice is passed. As is the one the goddess made when she decided your life was a fair price to pay for Amelia's eventual enlightenment. So, tell me, are we not entitled to be more than pawns in a game?"

"We are not chess pieces if we choose to play," she answered. Her entire body was aflame with fear and uncertainty. "I see my reward in Amelia's eyes. I feel it as I help guide her back to her Cianán. I know I will see the world through her and enjoy my promised gift one day."

"What if you're wrong?"

Ophélie scoffed. "I am *not* wrong. You only say this because you gave up your chance, your claim, and you have no other direction but forward."

"I share no doubts beyond the ones I lived with for many years before taking my immortality," he countered. "Yes, I live with deep regret, but my decision didn't come lightly. I toiled for many years. But you, my darling, do not have many years. Ophélie, you do not have a single year. And I am offering you an option no one else can."

"As is the goddess."

"Yes," Victor said sadly. "I am asking you to choose between two very different worlds that do not and cannot intersect. To accept one means to give up the other."

Loud, raucous voices carried in from the parlor. Ophélie didn't know what prompted the hollering, but it reminded her of why she had wandered this way to begin with.

Tears pooled under her lids, and she willed them not to breach. "Victor," she said gently, gifting a kiss to the side of his mouth. "I cannot. I am sorry. For all I am to face ahead, knowing the pain I will endure, I still cannot separate myself from who I am. And it breaks my heart that you have."

"Ophélie..."

She broke away from his touch and rushed to the door, afraid of her own weakness in this impossible enticement.

"I ask only one other request of you," she called back. "Let Amelia and Jacob leave here in peace. Amelia, especially, needs distance from you, more so in light of your confession. Our aim was to bring them together, not tear them apart. The portion of you that is still Cianán must understand this."

Ophélie waited for confirmation, for anything. But Victor said nothing.

His silence made her ever more determined to get her friends out of 1861.

SHE ESCAPED THE DARKNESS AND PLOWED INTO A FRANTIC HOUSEMAID. "Mademoiselle Ophélie! We have more guests from abroad!"

"Slow yourself," Ophélie gently admonished. "What do you mean, more guests?"

"They appeared from nowhere, as Lord Donnelly and his wife. Three of them! A man, a woman, and another young man, though we don't know if they're relations. We did not get word, or see a carriage pull up."

Ophélie had a strong suspicion about the cause of this, but she had no time to question. "Where is our *pigeonnier*? Is he still away visiting family?"

"Our... what? Yes, mademoiselle. Why?"

"Take our new guests to his quarters adjoining the *pigeonnier*. Tell them I will be with them soon."

"You do not want me to bring them here? To the Big House?"

"Not at present," Ophélie nearly snapped, exasperated at the sudden turn of events. "Have you seen Lord and Lady Donnelly?"

"They retired to their room hours ago. I have not seen them since."

"Very well. See to our guests. I will be there soon. And tell no one else until I say so, is that clear?"

The maid nodded and ran off.

Ophélie prayed she held enough weight with the staff for her words to be enough.

She lifted her skirts and ran up the stairs toward Amelia and Jacob's chambers.

Not a moment to waste.

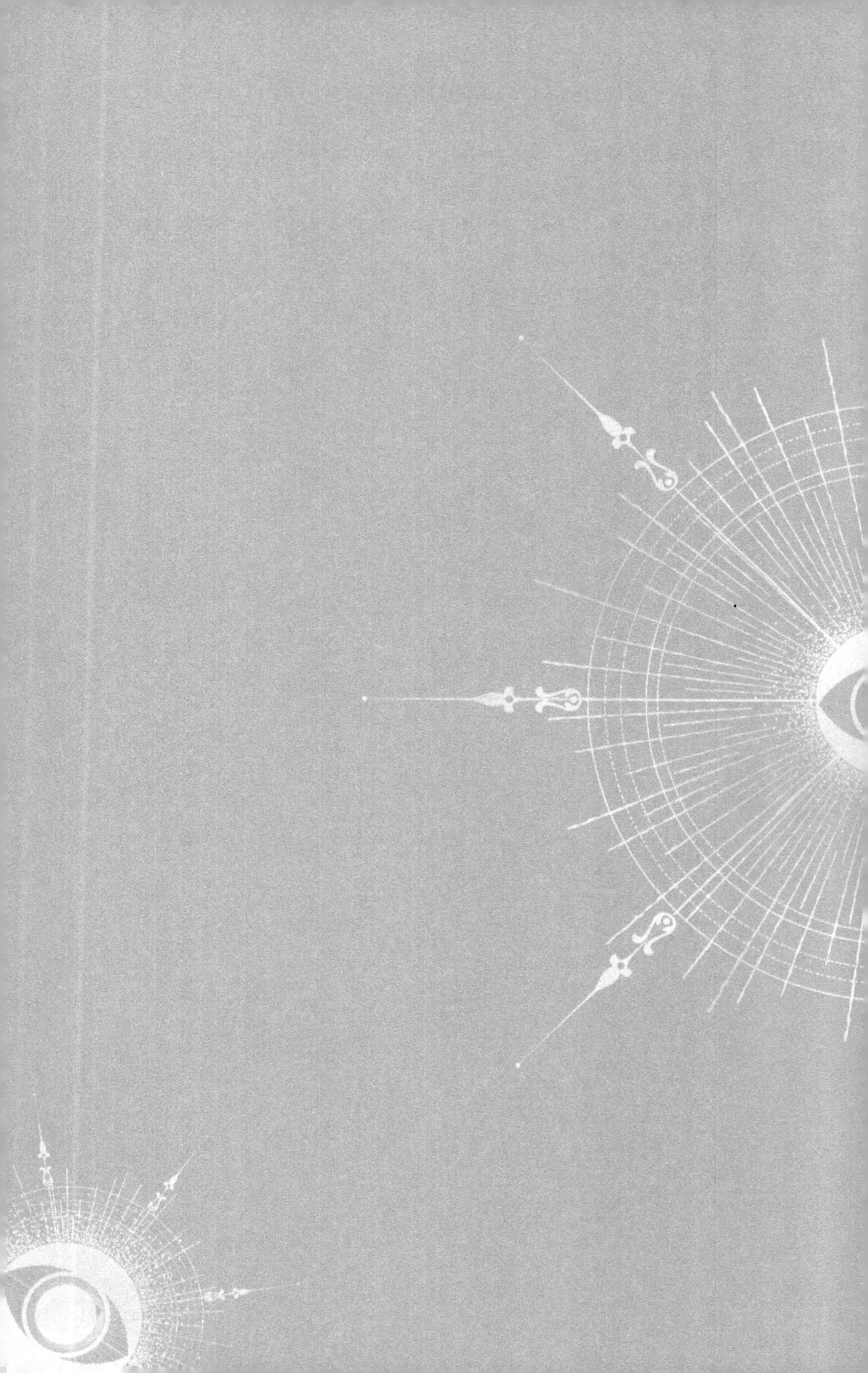

35
ANASOFIYA

Curiously, they were expected.

Or, at the very least, there had been a distinct lack of shock when they popped out of thin air, in clothes from another time, unannounced.

A young girl in a paisley house dress greeted Ana, Finn, and Aleksei, flustered but otherwise unimpressed, and she quickly ushered them to the building Ana recognized as the *pigeonnier's* house. It was not in service in her time. In fact, the building was hardly standing. To see it now—as she witnessed all of *Ophélie*, bustling and in its prime, on full display as they were rushed across the grounds—was nothing short of awe-inspiring.

The girl mumbled to herself as she ran ahead of them, skirt in hand, flashing impatient glances behind her every yard or so.

"What's happening, Mora?" Aleksandr asked, pacing them with wide eyes. "Why are we running?"

"We'll find out soon," she answered. The question was at the top of her mind, too. Right behind wondering if Amelia and

Jacob were going to come walking out of the bungalow when they arrived.

Amelia swayed on her feet when she entered the small cottage attached to the *pigeonnier*. Jacob observed his wife closely but didn't reach out to steady her. Ana smiled at his need to guard her balancing against the awareness Amelia didn't need protection. The behavior reminded her of Finn.

"Ana. I must be dreaming," Amelia breathed, half-laughing, half-crying as Ana launched into her arms. At that moment, as they held one another, Ana realized that, despite how closely their futures were supposedly aligned, the two of them had seen very little of each other in years.

"You've had a week to adjust to life here," Ana laughed. "Imagine how we feel."

"I wouldn't say we've adjusted." Jacob laughed, with a quick look to Finn.

They will need each other, Anasofiya. As you and Amelia will need one another.

Aidrik's gentle voice awakened within her for the first time since arriving in the past. It soothed her, as his guidance always had, even though he lacked a physical presence. For now.

"What year is this?" Finn and Aleksandr asked at the same time.

"It's 1861," Amelia answered. She took a seat on a tiny wooden bench. "January. We're going to war."

"We?" Finn repeated.

"They, I guess," she said. "We're getting the hell out of here before Jacob gets roped into service to the Confederacy." Her eyes fell on Aleksandr. "Ana... he looks just like you."

"He's our son," Ana said, pressing him forward with a soft

nudge. "Aleksandr. Aleksei, we call him. Named for the men of my mother's family."

Amelia's eyes went blank as she evaluated the boy who could pass for someone in his early twenties. Whatever she'd been through had prepared her for this moment of disbelief. She didn't question it. She only smiled. "Aleksei, what an honor to meet you. We're cousins."

"You can call her Auntie Amelia," Ana said, thinking of Aidrik's words before they'd taken the leap. *You and Amelia must stay close to one another. You will require each other in a way you have never needed anyone. If she was not your closest confidante before now, let her become so. You will be as sisters.*

I've never had a sister, Aidrik. How am I supposed to know what that's like?

As with all that has happened to you in the past year, Kjære, *you will learn.*

"Nice to finally meet you, Auntie Amelia," Aleksandr said with a shy smile, "and Uncle Jacob."

Ana introduced the men, and the five shared more hugs and pleasantries, actions Ana herself had never been good at or comfortable with. The men joked about the situation, a coping mechanism if she'd ever seen one. As they did, Ana met Amelia's eyes, and the two understood one another entirely.

"We don't have much time. Let's quickly catch each other up, say our goodbyes, and get out of here," Amelia said with a gesture toward the other benches scattered around the small, handmade table.

She didn't ask why they'd come.

AMELIA AND JACOB'S JOURNEY HAD BEEN EXTRAORDINARY. ANA WAS compelled by their frankness in the telling and their courage in enduring the past days under the same roof as Brigitte and Jean.

"We always believed Brigitte's love for Ophélie was what drove her anger," Ana said, shaking her head.

"Madness has run in the Deschanel line for centuries, especially among the women. That's not a secret," Jacob said. When both women shot him a look laced with daggers, he added quickly, "Present company excluded, obviously."

Finn laughed. "Here I thought it was hormones." Ana silenced him from her peripheral.

"No," Ana said. "It's not a secret. But we can't dismiss every evil act as madness, either. Aidrik's blood runs through all of our veins, and we know today how this happened. But back then, how could they? Charles and his family didn't even know who Aidrik was, or that he existed. They probably assumed their gifts were some sort of divine right, the way kings used to look at the regency."

"But most kings didn't mess around with their sisters," Jacob said. "Those monarchs might play in the same ocean, but even they knew dipping in the same pond was a bad idea."

"Who knows what some of those in power would have done if they possessed the abilities of the Deschanels?"

"Also," Amelia went on, "I believe the loss of the particular abilities when they came to Louisiana may be part of what drove Brigitte mad."

"How so?" Ana asked.

"We all know about Aidrik's ward." Amelia checked around the room at her small audience. "That when he placed it on this property, it repressed the gifts of anyone within. This is why Nicolas and his sisters, or anyone else in the heir's direct line, never exhibited powers until they left the plantation for long periods. It wasn't until exposed to a full-blooded Empyrean, in this case, Mercy, that this part of the ward neutralized. But Brigitte doesn't understand the facts. She only knows they were powerful when they left France but aren't any longer. A divine right becomes a divine punishment."

"She would have pushed Jean and Ophélie together anyway, but knowing this explains her urgency," Jacob said. "The woman was desperate for an heir, and believed they were being punished for leaving France."

"Crazy!" Aleksandr exclaimed. He'd been thoughtful, quiet, throughout Amelia and Jacob's animated retelling. "So, what does this have to do with why we're all here?"

Ana met Amelia's eyes again. Amelia had told the story of Victor and Ophélie, but the words had passed secretly, and wordlessly, between cousins. "Amelia and Jacob had some lessons the goddess wanted to share, and they could only learn them here."

"Did you?" Aleksandr probed, looking at Amelia. "Learn them?"

Amelia and Jacob exchanged a drowsy smile. "Yes," they both said.

"What do you think about this whole idea of the prophecy?" Finn asked anyone in general. "All four of us are linked by it, but this is the first time we've even been in a room together. We should talk about this. Everyone thinks Aleksei needs to hook up with your offspring, but you haven't had one, and even if you do, both Aleksandr and your daughter have the right to choose for themselves. Tell me you agree."

Jacob squeezed his wife's hand. He answered for them both. "We know what's expected. We've heard the words, too, but we're taking this one day at a time. Who knows, we might have a daughter, or we might not. If we do, she'll choose for herself."

"But we believe this? The prophecy?" Finn seemed almost desperate for accordance.

Everyone nodded.

Finn shook his head. His brows connected in a tight line. "This is where I keep getting hung up. We all agree the prophecy is real because we've heard the words of the goddess in our own ways. We've all come to this point. But when it gets down to the real meat of the situation, each of us acts as if that part is optional."

"Are you suggesting we force our kids to lie back and think of England?" Jacob asked, without a smile. "'Do it' for the prophecy?"

"No. Hell no," Finn said. "But how can we believe in everything leading up to that part before completely disregarding it? I don't know, I guess I'm having a crisis of faith. I don't understand what's right. I just needed to get it out."

Amelia jumped into the conversation offering Finn a thin smile. "I get it and think that's how we all feel."

"Too much is riding on the shoulders of four people making decisions for two," Jacob said. "Peace between everyone sounds really great and all, but sometimes I wonder if the goddess lacks foresight."

"Hello, I'm sitting right here," Aleksandr said, throwing his hands out. "Don't I get a say?"

"You get the only say," Ana told him.

"Then can I tell you what I think?"

All eyes traveled to Aleksandr.

"I believe," he said, "that the four of you talking about my future is kinda pointless. I've accepted what my role is, and if Aunt Amelia and Uncle Jacob have a little girl who grows up to be an adult in weeks like I did, well, maybe she'll feel this way, too. If she doesn't, then I don't know what we do. But if she does, isn't that her decision, the same way it's mine?"

"You fell in love and gave it up. For this," Finn accused, though his anger was directed elsewhere. "That's not freedom.

It's not peace. To anyone outside this room, you may just be a means to an end, but to Ana and me, you're our son. And if Amelia and Jacob have a child, she'll be their daughter. If we don't advocate for your free will, no one else is going to."

"You keep saying that, Far, but when I say my decision is to follow the path the goddess laid for me, you act as though that isn't the right one. If you believe I have autonomy, then you must believe I can make this decision for myself. Free will means I get to decide, not you," Aleksandr snapped. When the words were out, he blushed at his self-assurance.

It is time to leave, Aidrik whispered. *Encourage your cousins to say their goodbyes. Aleksandr is correct. There is no gain in debating a fate only he and his intended mate get a say in deciding.*

No matter what he decides, I'm afraid there can't be a happy ending.

Fear takes us nowhere good. Instead, lead with courage.

"We need to go," Ana interrupted. "We came here to find you two, and we did. With the war party going on in the parlor, and Brigitte and Jean out to get half of us, every moment we spend here is dangerous. Undoubtedly, we have much more to talk about, but we can do it safely at home. Agree?"

"We need to say goodbye to Ophélie," Amelia said, rising. "I can't leave without it."

"Of course," Ana said. Quietly, to Amelia only she added... *and Victor?*

It's best for both of us if I don't.

What if he follows you?

He wouldn't. But Amelia didn't sound sure.

Be careful. I have a bad feeling we're already on borrowed time.

Me too.

• • •

Amelia slipped away to find Ophélie. She wanted to go alone and promised to be quick. When she was gone, Finn turned to Jacob and asked, "What happened to the two of you?"

"We just told you."

"No... before. Prior to your arrival here. I don't mean to be intrusive, but I sense things now, and I sense something really bad happened. Padraig hinted at it, too, but I didn't press him for details."

"Finn is coming into his ability as an empath," Ana explained.

Jacob focused down at his hands. "I've never talked about it out loud. I'm honestly not sure if I can."

Ana laid a hand on his shoulder. Finn placed his on the other. "Amelia isn't the only one who needs to forgive herself," she said.

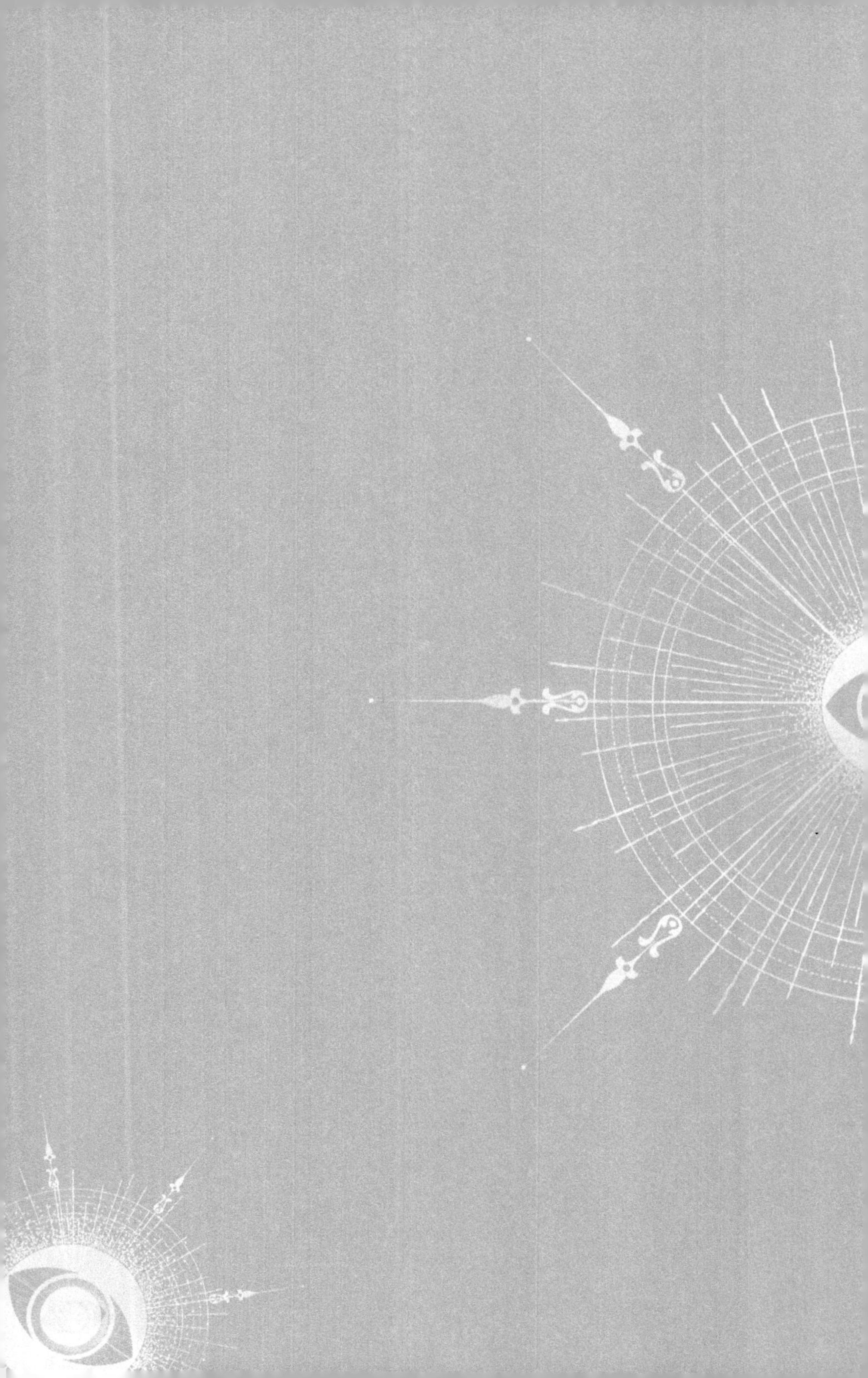

36
AMELIA

Ophélie awaited her in the grove of oaks. Her meaningful smile suggested she knew exactly why Amelia had sought her out.

"We have to go."

"And you must. It's not only the war but Maman... she knows something. She means you harm. I know it."

Amelia found she wasn't surprised by the news, and even expected it. Every facet of their visit had come to a head in unison. If they wanted signs, they'd been given more than they could handle.

"We must be quick," Ophélie added.

Amelia nodded and steered her further from the house, not wanting Jean or Brigitte to intercede as they had a way of doing. "Ophélie, I don't know how to thank you."

"Thank me for what?"

"For everything." Amelia kissed the young girl's forehead and watched her for a moment, seeing her own self, a different self, reflected back. "I would still take you with us if you'd let me."

Ophélie's stare dropped to her feet. "Even if I had not already found my courage to stay, it isn't possible. I know that now."

"What do you mean?"

Her head shot back up. "Victor. Be wary of him, Amelia. There can exist only one Cianán at a time. While he once was Cianán, he is no longer, and he chose that path willingly."

"You're talking about his immortality?"

Ophélie laughed coldly. "So he told you of that, but not the whole of it? I suppose he knew you wouldn't understand, as I didn't. Alas, no, he is Cianán no longer, though he still possesses the memories and desires, by his words."

Amelia considered this. She'd been curious about her bond to both Victor and Ophélie, but Jacob had only been drawn to Ophélie. Could it be the glimmer of Cianán still existed, but Jacob, deep down, knew better? "It was a lot to take in. I didn't stop to think of how it would be possible for them to be alive together."

"For it is not! Victor chose to give up his destiny as Cianán when he took his immortal gift. But even had he lived to be a hundred and fifty, he would have lost that gift at the moment of Jacob's birth."

Why had Victor kept this from her? He went on and on about how she needed Jacob to heal. Were all those pretty words a lie? A deception?

"I know what's in your head," Ophélie said. "And you would do well to veer from that path. It matters not what Victor thinks or does not think. Not anymore. He's a rogue descendant whose behavior is out of hand. He speaks of love when he has only deceived. The sooner you leave, the sooner you can free yourself of this complication."

Amelia stepped forward. "Why are you crying?"

"He offered me the gift," Ophélie answered, lowering her head in shame. "And I, a foolish girl, almost accepted."

"Anyone would consider it," Amelia soothed. "Anyone. I can't imagine many get that chance. I haven't. No one can blame you for thinking it might be an option, especially with your future knowledge. And no one would judge you if you decided yet to do it."

Ophélie's eyes opened in wide, hopeful arcs. "You think I should consider it?"

"I don't know," Amelia said. "Only you can say. But your time will end soon, one way or another, Ophélie. Worse choices exist."

"You're wrong, you know," Ophélie said. "You can and have been offered immortality. As one of the four heirs, your gift for fulfilling the prophecy is everlasting life. For you and Jacob both, and the other two."

Amelia glanced away. "I guess I haven't thought about that part very much."

"You should, and soon. What about the other words of the goddess?"

"For now, I have to focus on returning to who I once was. I can't be anything to anyone else until I do."

"Then your coming here was a triumph." Ophélie squeezed her hand. "The goddess loves you, Amelia. She knows your heart."

"What about yours?"

"Nothing matters until I release the soul of Cerridwen to you."

"Or free it upon accepting Victor's gift?"

"Unfortunately, I cannot." Ophélie leaned into the broad trunk of a nearby oak. "If I do, all my suffering will have been for naught."

"I won't try to persuade you one way or another," Amelia

said. "Only know that I love you, and you will stay with me, a part of me, the rest of my days."

"I *am* you," Ophélie said with a small smile. "And that's why I can't accept the gift. I've seen who I will become, and I cannot imagine a more rewarding fate than being Amelia Deschanel."

AMELIA WATCHED OPHÉLIE'S SLIGHT FIGURE RUN IN THE DIRECTION OF the Big House until it disappeared within. She had so much more to say, but words wouldn't change anything for either of the women and to dwell on them would only make the result more difficult to bear.

Ana, Finn, and their son had come for them, and it was time to return home, together.

"You were going to leave without a goodbye?"

Victor appeared from behind a nearby oak, his long, lean figure flowing into full focus as she turned toward the sound of his voice.

Amelia jumped back several paces. "Dammit, Victor! Why are you always popping up out of nowhere, scaring the hell out of me?"

"You didn't answer my question."

"I thought it might be easier for both of us."

"Easier? Does that mean it pains you to leave me?"

"Don't put words in my mouth." Amelia paced around him, eager to keep her distance. "And I know the truth. The rest of it. What I don't get is why you left out that part of the story."

Victor appeared genuinely offended. "I did not lie to you."

"A lie by omission is still a lie. I'm a psychiatrist... an expert in detecting self-deception."

Victor attempted to follow the circle she cut around him, but stopped, confused at her tactic. "Amelia. I was born with the soul of Cianán. Whether it belongs to me still does not change that I have his memories—"

"Yes, and his desires. I know." Amelia rolled her eyes and chanced a quick glance back at the *pigeonnier*. If she didn't return soon, Jacob would come for her, and he would not at all appreciate the way Victor looked at her now.

"I made a foolish choice, but it does not alter who I am."

"It changes nothing, and it changes everything, and it doesn't matter," she cried. "I won't let it."

"I would never hurt you," Victor insisted, watching her dance around him. It was the easiest way to keep him from approaching her again. She didn't want to be near the dhampir any longer. She wanted him gone.

"Then let me go," she replied, this time backing away from the trees and into the open. Victor wouldn't engage her there, surely. Not where anyone could see. "Whether you are or aren't Cianán now isn't even the point. My path and yours don't intersect. They were never meant to. You are not *my* Cianán, and if you really care about me, this will be the last time we talk."

A sharp, quick wind whipped through the air around her, and before she had a moment to comprehend the change, Victor was upon her. His lips pressed to hers in a brief, firm kiss. "*Au revoir, mon cher.*"

How he had come to her so swiftly was a question immediately replaced by where he went. She whipped her neck around, searching for him, but he was well and truly gone.

For now, his voice whispered, bouncing across the trees, echoing in her mind.

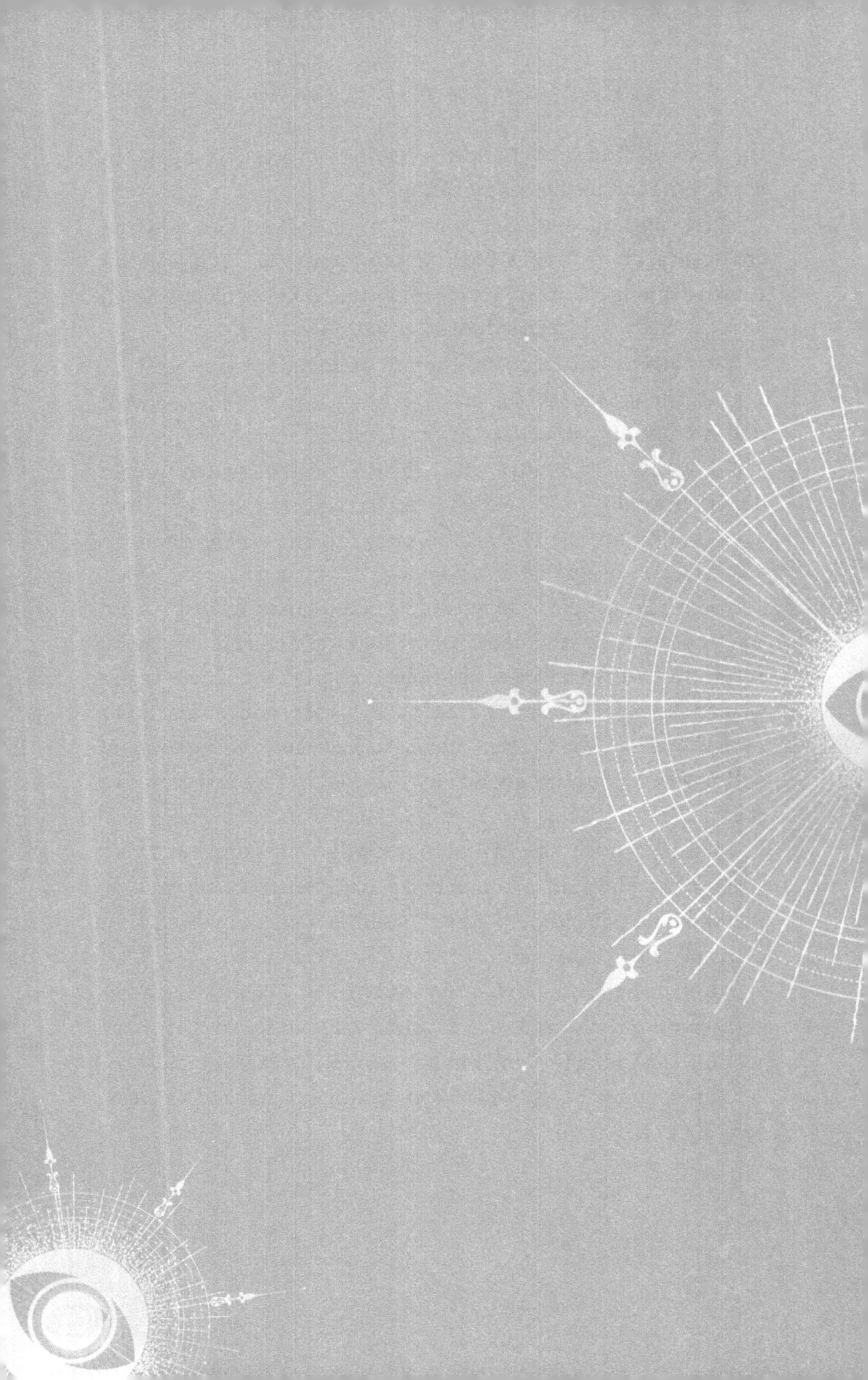

37
ANASOFIYA

Are you not going to tell them, Kjære?

What?

Finnegan and Aleksandr. Will you not tell them of my resurrection, through you?

Aidrik... Ana paused, glancing at her nervous husband and son. None of them wanted to be here. They sensed the inherent danger, not only in arriving in a time not their own, but in a hostile environment on the verge of significant change. The family of three had only ever seen the aftermath of the war. The adjusted South, rebuilt but neutered from its brief period of glory. To see it as it was now resembled looking at a ghost who didn't know he was already dead.

You lose yourself to thoughts to avoid my question.

I'm not avoiding you. I just don't have the answer.

You do. I won't probe where I'm not invited. Tell me.

I guess I'm cautious. Cautious only tickled the surface.

You believe I am a hallucination?

No, I know better. It's not that.

Then what, Anasofiya?

This is just... well, everything is all so very new, Aidrik. First, Wraith, now you. What if something else changes? I don't want anyone to get their hopes up, only to lose you twice. That would devastate Finn and Aleksei.

And you?

You know how I feel. But at this point, my hurt is inevitable, if things change. You're back. I can't undo that, and I wouldn't, even if I could. But I need time. You, Aidrik, the creature who always played his cards close to the vest, should understand better than anyone.

There are no rules. You created Wraith from your own darkness, and Wraith is now your weapon. Your ally. At the time of our evigbond, I became part of you. When I perished, that part of me lived on, in you. You are an etheric summoner. Only the second I have ever seen, in all my days. This power turned our evigbond into a physical manifestation, allowing me to be strong again.

I get all that. But what if I can't preserve it?

You maintain without thinking about it, Kjære. *Every day, I grow stronger. I may yet increase enough physically and mentally to exist separate from you, though my soul will always be tethered to yours.*

I'm just not ready. I'm afraid. Don't you get that?

Aye. I'll leave it. But I ask you to consider believing in yourself, as I do. There are no limits for you. Your boundaries are invisible, and the power is undefined because none have ever been like you.

You're a hell of a lot more confident than I am about it.

Aye. And as of now, you have more pressing matters. Word has reached Brigitte of the arrival of more uninvited guests. You have little time to waste.

Ana had been so immersed in her private conversation that she didn't see Amelia return, noticeably flustered with heavy, labored breathing. The sight brought Ana back to the present.

She recognized the expression on Amelia's face. It was one Amelia's mother, Ana's Aunt Colleen, had always advised the cousins to be on the alert for, much like observing a diabetic for a rise or drop in blood sugar. *She's a powerful empath. But she's in constant danger of being imperiled. This happens when she cannot separate her own emotion from those around her and inadvertently absorbs them. If you see her enter what we call* the daze, *you talk to her about a memory until she responds and snaps out of it. Recollections pull her away from the danger. They remind her of what's real.*

Amelia had been put as risk recently and very nearly died for it.

Jacob was at her side before she could hit the ground, his arms coming around her from behind. "*Blanca*, talk to me."

"Amelia." Ana charged across the room. "Do you remember the summer Uncle Charles hired the jazz band to come to *Ophélie* for Adrienne's birthday?" It wasn't the best memory, but it was the first to pop into her head.

Amelia's eyes fluttered. Her head fell back against Jacob's chest as she strained to see Ana through her fugue. "Awful."

"Mora, what's happening to her?" Aleksandr cried, gaping at Jacob, who had silent tears running down his cheeks.

"Shh, Aleksei." Ana turned her focus back to her cousin. "Remember the young one, Mia? I was a junior, I think, so you must have been a sophomore. He was one of our ages. Probably someone's kid or younger brother. He spent the whole time hitting on us both, do you remember?"

Jacob pulled Amelia into a chair, kneeling at her side. He placed a hand behind her neck and kissed her cheek. His lips lingered there. "You told me this story once."

"He..." Amelia swallowed. Her head swayed in a small circle. Jacob was quick to steady her. Finn appeared at Amelia's right, squatting to catch her from the other side. "Didn't he hook up with Olivia?"

Ana's laugh was genuine. "Yes! And Aunt Maureen caught them. She still uses that to end an argument. 'Your judgment is irrelevant, Olivia. You screwed that jazz kid back in the nineties.'"

"Aunt Mo never has been..." Amelia heaved a large breath, pitching forward. "Never been very good at making a point."

Jacob whispered to his wife, his words too quiet to reach Ana's ears. Ana remembered goofy Jacob from high school, with a mess of black hair and jokes for days. If he wasn't making others laugh, he was fighting them, a strange mix of talents. Ana thought it interesting to see him now, grown into a man worthy of Amelia, and worthy of himself.

She also saw within him another potential: friend to her husband, Finn. The two men were alike in ways, but their real bond would be borne from their shared experiences of starting life with one understanding of who they were, and transitioning to the next phase with a reality that would have been unbelievable to them in that first life.

"Yes!" Ana giggled. It sounded strange to her. She had never been one to giggle. "And that was the last time Uncle Charles hired a band for any of his parties."

Amelia shrugged away the two men flanking her. She lifted her face to the sky and pulled in several short, powerful breaths. "I'm okay now. Thank you. All of you."

"What happened?" Finn asked.

"Nothing that matters more than getting out of here as quickly as we can," Amelia answered. She rose and stretched as if awakening from a long nap.

"We should do this together," Finn said. "Who knows if we will all end up where we should if we do it separately. And if we land in the wrong place, at least we'll all be together."

"I agree," Jacob answered. He was careful not to crowd Amelia, but stood several steps behind her, watching like a hawk. "I think that's what we need to do from here on out."

"Stick together," Ana repeated. "No matter what Aleksei decides, or whether or not the two of you ever have children, we were put in this situation for a reason. The goddess brought us all here, together. I still don't get it, but I can't deny it, either."

"We need to be in New Orleans," Aleksandr added. "Don't ask me to explain it, but I think our traveling is done. For now."

"The kid has a point," Finn said. "If anyone disagrees, speak now or forever hold your peace."

No one disagreed.

Amelia nodded. The returning color slowly blossomed into her face. "Let's do this."

The five travelers drew together in a tight circle, with Jacob and Finn at the outer edge. Their hands linked on both sides as they came around their loved ones. Aleksandr, Ana, and Amelia wrapped their arms around the necks of the men and closed their eyes.

"There's no place like home," Jacob whispered, and before anyone could laugh, their feet had left the ground.

DAY EIGHT

38
AMELIA

Amelia didn't know if there was anywhere else in the world she felt more at home than her mother's parlor at The Gardens. They'd spent their first night back at the Monteleone, exhausted and needing time to regroup, but the weight of returning to the present didn't hit her until she stepped into the marble foyer of her childhood home.

Colleen sat across from her. She watched with patient eyes, ready to dispense wisdom, mint julep in hand.

Amelia's father, Noah, and brother, Ashley, were in the other room. After they'd doted on her for an hour, she had asked to be alone with her mother. She needed to get some things off her chest before she lost the courage. Information she didn't want her father and brother hearing.

And so, while Jacob was off working on their house on Seventh and Coliseum, Amelia spent the afternoon laying out every last detail of the past weeks to her mother, beginning with their arrival on Quinlan lands and ending with the fivesome jumping back to the present. She didn't leave out Victor. She didn't leave out Baldur.

Her mother's emotions ran the expected gamut as Amelia found her words. From wonder to rage, from curiosity to fear. Colleen expressed these sentiments through her eyes, as the rest of her remained stoic and poised, as always.

"Oh, darling," she said when Amelia folded her hands across her lap and released a long breath. "My heart is broken for you, Amelia. I know you don't want my sympathy. I understand that's why you didn't want Dad and Ashley to hear this, but I'm your mother before anything else, and, for once, I don't have the words to make this better. If Jacob hadn't killed Baldur, I would be on a plane today to finish the job myself."

"I don't need words or more anger, I just needed you to know, Mom. It's hard to talk about," Amelia said in a hushed voice. She had never before heard her mother threaten violence against anyone, in any circumstance. "I think it always will be."

"I will not ever ask you to talk about it, my dear," Colleen said, reaching forward to take Amelia's hands in hers "But know I will always, always be here when you need to."

"I know, Mom."

Colleen released her and sat back. "Our family has suffered so much, and those of us still living continue to bear the greatest burden. I have to wonder when it will end."

"We all know the answer," Amelia said. "But it's so much easier said than done. I resigned myself to never being a mother, because of the Deschanel Curse, but now I'm being told becoming a mother is precisely how to end it."

"Prophecies are convenient ways of ignoring our own culpability in matters," Colleen said, rising. "Excuse me a moment. I have something to show you that I believe will be of great interest."

She reappeared minutes later with a photo album, leather-bound in the blood red color of the Deschanels. On the front was embossed, in gold, a set of years, but Amelia didn't catch them before her mother opened the book. Pursing her lips, Colleen flipped through the pages until she found what she wanted.

"Ahh, here it is. Dear me, now that we've had this talk, I can't see how I was able to so easily dismiss this."

"What, Mom?"

Colleen slid the album across the coffee table toward her daughter. "This particular collection contains some daguerreotypes taken prior to the Civil War. These are strictly antebellum memories of the Deschanels during the final years before the war. Charles was known to hire a photographer to come to his parties, you see, and though casual photography was difficult and expensive at the time, he was fascinated with the practice and couldn't help himself. We've found ledgers showing he spent the equivalent, in today's money, of more than five hundred thousand dollars on the fixation."

Amelia started to ask her mother what she was looking at when she saw it.

The photo was of Amelia. Though grainy in the black and white image, it was clearly her. Victor stood in the corner of the photograph, a wry grin on his face as he took her measure from across the room. Jacob's defensive stance to her left was almost comical to see in print.

"How... is this possible? I thought we couldn't change history? That we couldn't leave our mark?"

"You're half right, it seems," Colleen replied. She nodded at Aria to pour more tea for Amelia. "This picture always caught my attention, for I always wanted to know who the young woman with the white-blonde hair was who so strongly resembled my own daughter. Of course, I never guessed at the truth. The simplest answer is usually the correct one. Your hair is a known Deschanel trait. Many women in our ancestry through the years shared your white locks and pale blue eyes. For all we knew, she was a visiting cousin from France."

"Well, she's not!"

"No, dear, of course, she isn't. Would you like me to have a copy made?"

"Mom! Don't you know what this means?"

"I suppose if *you* do, you might be kind enough to tell me," Colleen replied evenly.

"Okay, well, maybe I don't," Amelia answered, flopping back in her chair. "We know so little about time travel and didn't have an opportunity to ask more questions. But, then, isn't a memory of our adventure there changing it? What do they call that, the butterfly effect? Even our being there, being present, could affect outcomes and people's lives."

"Not for certain," Colleen said. "I understand your concern, but we have no evidence, other than an old photograph, that your presence changed anything at all. It may even be safe to say, if we want to give ourselves a headache considering the matter, that the version of the present you've always lived in was one that assumed you'd gone back in time."

"You're right. I do have a headache."

Colleen excused herself again and returned with several more photo albums. One by one, she opened them, flipping to specific pictures, and with each, Amelia's heart skipped and then sank.

"I don't know if you doubted Victor's claim, but this appears to validate, at least, his immortality," Colleen said, pointing to picture after picture of Victor visiting with various Deschanels over the years. In each, his angular face was as young as the day Amelia had met him. His hair showed no signs of white. "He may have told you his other family members retired after so many years, but it appears he does not believe those rules apply to him."

"Careless, cocky bastard," Amelia whispered as she studied each of the images with a growing anger. "And a vampire. I never would have believed they existed."

Colleen chortled. "No? It seems your belief system is selective, then. Of all the strange events and people you've witnessed? Truly, you struggle with this?"

"It's a complete biological change!"

"And you believe when your brother stirs up hurricanes, or I lay my hands on someone and heal them, that those are not biological changes?"

"It's different. You know it is."

"Yes, darling, it is different, as all our gifts are. I've known of the de Blancheforts for some time. They are distant relatives, as you know, and have claim to a large portion of the River Road real estate market, both past and present. I knew they shared many of our gifts, and I have had meetings and correspondence with several of their modern day family members. In fact, I invited them to send one representative to be on our Collective Council, even, but they declined. But, no, I did not know they were vampires if that was your question. They never trusted me with this detail."

Amelia shook her head. "I wish I knew why Victor shared it with me. He realized I'd be coming home to the present. Why trust me?"

"Isn't it obvious? He loves you. Love makes us blind, and forgetful of our sensibilities." Colleen raised a knowing brow.

"He doesn't even know me," Amelia snapped, wondering where her anger rested. "But he evidently has no respect for marriage. He ignored Jacob altogether, and if I hadn't met his wife, I would never have known he had one."

"Then you must protect yourself," her mother said, closing

the albums. "For it's obvious now that Victor does not share his ancestors' good sense in public retirement. He shows up in photos as recent as the eighties, Amelia. And that's only photographs. If we show these pictures to any Deschanel, I'm willing to venture at least some have seen him today."

"I don't believe he'd hurt me," Amelia defended.

"Hasn't he already? Your soul had been deeply wounded by the actions of a madman. Your marriage was in jeopardy. He found you in your most vulnerable state and sought to manipulate you for his own aims. Victor may label that action with love, or with care, but he has sent you back to the present frustrated and confused. Your heart is only meant for one man, darling, and that man is not Victor."

Amelia wandered to the front bay window. Outside, the vast and unending flora blocked her view of the rest of the world, secluding her. She had always, always felt safe here. "Victor is the one who first told me to find my way back to Jacob."

"Your greatest adversary is always skillful at disarming you, darling. I'm only cautioning you to guard your heart. It's apparent a part of you does love him," Colleen said, joining her at the window.

"Nothing intentional," Amelia countered. "And it doesn't matter what he made me feel. I'm home, and I would never choose anyone but Jacob. Ever."

"You almost walked away from Jacob," Colleen chided.

"I did not!"

"No one understands your heart like your mother," she returned, kissing the top of Amelia's head. "If I know you, you strongly considered the possibility that everything that happened pointed to the conclusion you would be better off alone."

"Maybe," Amelia conceded, leaning against her mother.

"But it was never about being with someone else. I've never been in love with anyone else, not once, and I never will. You know that. Before Jacob, I was content to have casual, meaningless relationships. He's the only one I was willing to change that for, and he always ever will be."

"I believe that, and I'm happy to hear you also do," Colleen admitted.

Amelia embraced her mother. Another memory returned to her. "Oh! Something else happened while we were there. I think it might be important."

"If you think it is, then it is."

Amelia told her mother about Charlotte LaViolette and the strange scene at the tea party. "I could see Charles not realizing he had a sister, but us? We know everything about the family, don't we?"

Colleen quickly spun away, nonplussed. "I've heard unusual tales of the LaViolettes through history that caught my attention. There was a Storyville madam, also named Charlotte, I believe, who was to johns what Madame LaLaurie was to slaves. It was said she turned them mad. The johns fled the brothel, screaming about things they'd seen, happenings that could not possibly be real. Most went home and took their lives."

"Holy crap!"

Colleen nodded. "Indeed. I have a file on the family in our archives, with more stories like this, throughout the years. I've been watching them, as I track all families who exhibit unusual traits. But I never suspected..."

"What do you think, then? Is it true?"

"I will need to verify, of course, but if you were shown this, there must be some degree of veracity," her mother answered. "But we must be careful. The LaViolettes are a powerful family, of very strong and dangerous women. They are in our

Congress, our city council. Both law and order. They have tendrils in everything. If Charlotte knew they shared Deschanel blood, there must be a reason she never brought it up again."

"You think they might be enemies, then?"

"If they are, we need to tread very carefully."

AMELIA SAID HER GOODBYES TO THE FAMILY. AS SHE PREPARED TO leave, Ashley pulled her aside.

"I want to help you, Mia," he said. "Christine and the kids are gone, and I can't see them coming back. Can you?"

Amelia didn't answer. Christine blamed Ashley for Katie's death, and even though she was wrong, it was hard to blame her for wanting to protect her remaining children.

"I've told Mom I'd like to help with the Council. I've been filling in for Nicolas while he's been in Europe, and I think it might be good for me to continue. I'm tired of the financial planning world. I feel like Clark Kent, going to work and pretending to be someone I'm not. I can't do it anymore, and I need to feel beneficial to *someone.*"

Amelia kissed him. "You're the only brother I have now. You'll always be useful to me. I want you to be happy."

"What I'm trying to tell you is, I want my life to have greater meaning than sitting behind a desk," Ashley insisted. "I'm not asking for your guidance, I guess I just wanted you to know, our lives are going to be different... with more purpose."

"Whatever you want, I'll support you," Amelia replied and hugged him once more. She only wished he could have come to these realizations sooner. For years, he had lived a life that didn't ring true, but only he was capable of making that discovery.

"I'll be staying across the street from you, in Oz's house, for the time being. I know you don't need anyone, so you can take that look off your face, but I also know you've been through some terrible stuff, and I'm not going to be far away. Not this time," Ashley said. He pulled his jacket from the tree. "If you *do* need me, Mia, I'll be there before you can hang up the phone."

AMELIA RAN INTO ONE OTHER DESCHANEL BEFORE SHE REACHED THE town car her mother had arranged to take her home.

"Nicolas!" she exclaimed, jogging down the path to embrace him. "Mom said you were overseas with Mercy?"

"I am. This is an illusion. Pay no attention to the man behind the curtain," he joked as he returned the hug. "I've come back to resume my duties on the Council. I think your brother was filling in for me, but he can go back to selling stock to old people, or whatever the fuck he does."

"But where's Mercy?"

Nicolas shrugged. His eyes darted around like a man with a reason to be nervous. "Scotland, probably. I don't know, Amelia. I don't know a whole lot of anything anymore, to be honest with you."

Amelia knew better than to ask, but the sadness radiated from him like an aura. "I'm sorry."

"Don't be," he said, twisting his lips into a curved smile. "We all knew it wouldn't last. Nicolas Deschanel is the family bachelor. That's my role to play. Can't go changing the order of things this late in the game."

No, something wasn't right at all. The words coming from his mouth didn't match the distress flowing off him in strong waves. "You know where I am if you want to talk, Nic. I mean that."

Nicolas laughed. "I can't think of anything I enjoy more than talking about my feelings."

"I'm serious."

He looked past her, toward the house, where Colleen surely wasn't expecting him. "I'm relieved you're back. I heard Ana was, too, and I think we'll all sleep better with that chapter behind us."

Amelia pulled back with a start. "Behind us?"

He planted a kiss in the hollow of her cheek and continued up the path. The swagger in his step was gone... he was much changed. "This is how it should be, I think," he called back. "All of us back home. We weren't meant to fight everyone else's battles. Hell, we aren't very good at fighting our own."

DAY FIFTEEN

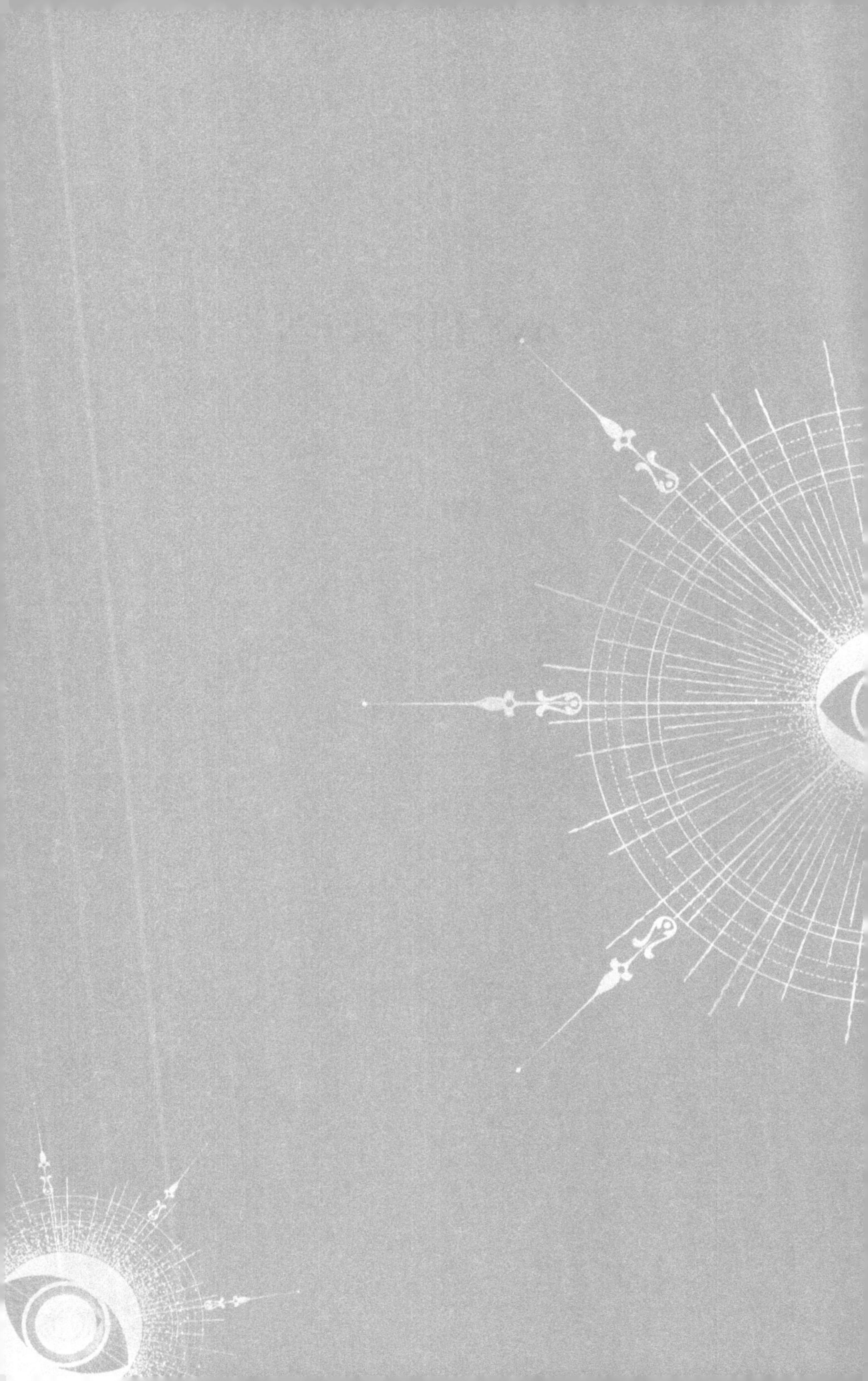

39
FINNEGAN

The looming Greek Revival on Prytania and Eighth was always supposed to be Ana's. Augustus began purchasing replacement properties for himself and Barbara back when Ana was still a girl, in preparation for when it would become hers when she started her own family. By the time it seemed less and less likely to happen, Augustus resolved himself to remain there longer, and the other properties stayed quiet.

Built in the mid-eighteenth century, when the boom of American migrants to the Garden District resulted in a period of persistent growth, the home was a gift to the third child of Charles Deschanel, Fitz. Fitz would later assume his rightful ownership as a newly married man with a child of his own, but this occupation would be short-lived, for he and his family perished in a tragic accident when he was only nineteen.

The house stayed empty for years until the trust decided it should belong to the next-in-line heir of every generation. When Charles inherited *Ophélie* in the early seventies, Augustus was gifted both *Vivra sa Vie*, a family plantation in

Donaldsonville, and Magnolia Grace, one of the most photographed mansions in the Garden District.

Augustus was thrilled to be able to finally bestow this gift upon his daughter. And, despite his lack of complete comfort with the reality of Aleksandr's birth and growth, he declared he could now rest easy knowing both *Vivra sa Vie* and Magnolia Grace would stay with his line.

And so Augustus and Barbara moved to their townhouse on Esplanade while Ana, Finn, and Aleksandr assumed their role as heirs of Magnolia Grace.

Although they had been home only a week, Ana and Finn had not let the time go to waste. They spent long nights catching up, and making plans. Top of their list was the agreement they needed to establish a sense of normalcy for Aleksandr.

Traditional school was out of the question, and besides, he didn't need it. When he'd easily passed the high school equivalency test, they decided college might be the best way to teach him to live in their society. Augustus, never one to miss an opportunity to throw around his weight, went straight to the dean of Tulane. Between his influence, and Ana's prior tenure there as a professor, Aleksandr was accepted for the following term.

Life moved forward, but at a much different pace.

"Sitting still feels so strange," Ana said one night, as she traced her finger across the long scar bisecting Finn's chest and torso. He'd never let any other woman do this. He loved when Ana did. "I've been on the move since I ran away to Maine."

"Would you prefer that?"

Ana's hand stopped. He could almost see her mind working. "No... I don't think so. But I have to learn to be myself again. Everything changed at *Ophélie* when Aidrik saved me..."

She let the words trail off.

"In the past year, I've become someone else, too, you know," Finn reminded her. He pulled her long red hair through his fingers, letting it fall against her pale skin in waves. Finn loved doing this. He'd missed it. "Going back to normalcy will be harder in some ways, I think, than it was when we fought against it."

"I wish we could find you some decent lobster around here," Ana said with a light sigh. She kissed the top of his chest. "I worry about you being so far from everything you love."

Finn propped himself up. "Everything?"

"You know what I mean."

"Ana, come on, now. Of course, I miss it. But sometimes our lives change when we voluntarily choose to follow what makes us happy. There's no lobster here worth chasing... so what? Louisiana is one of the best fish and wildlife regions in the country. I won't ever get bored learning and trying new techniques."

"I'm sorry," she said, pressing her face against his skin. "Forgive me. I thought I was past those old insecurities."

"Nothing to forgive, silly girl. This is a weird time for both of us. We just have to do our best to keep it all together for Aleksei. I don't know if he'll ever know what it was like to grow up in a traditional household like we did, but he will at least have some stability."

"Jon will be home soon, with Anne. Perhaps that will help," Ana said. Her words rang tentative, though Finn sensed nothing backhanded in them.

"Aleksei likes his uncle," Finn agreed. "You know we don't have to see him, Ana. If you don't want to. You won't get any pressure from me, and if you said you wanted to cut him out our lives altogether, you know I'd stand behind that."

"I'll never forget what he did," Ana said seeming careful of her word choices. "But our time away from home has given me perspective. Much, much worse has been done to both of us. And he's good with Aleksei. He needs all the stable influences he can find right now, so, no, I do not want to cut Jon out. But there may be times I can't join in."

Finn nodded. "You and Aleksei, Ana. That's all that matters to me now. The rest of our family can be as big, or as small, as we choose."

"I know."

A rainstorm had started while they talked. Finn closed his eyes and listened to the steady, varying patter of drops hitting banana leaves and tropical flowers. No, this wasn't Maine, but it was beautiful and welcoming in other ways.

Forbia snored at their feet, adjusting. She was happy to be reunited with her master after a trek home on a ship with Nora Quinlan, who'd kindly offered to be the pup's escort so she could finally spend some time with her brother, Amelia's father, Noah. Finn wondered how long it would be before the neighborhood busybodies reported them for having a wolf in the house.

"What if..." Ana started. "What if we flew in Fiona?"

"We can ask him," Finn replied. "But if Aleksei wanted to see her, he'd tell us."

"He turned away from her because he felt responsible for the rest of us. And we let him. We wanted Aleksei to feel capable of deciding for himself, but I've been sick about it ever since."

"I know." Finn, in fact, had thought about this a great deal since they'd left Ireland. He wasn't ready for his son to start dating, but he was less interested in him having his heart broken. "Let's talk to him."

"Okay."

Ana went silent, and together they listened to the building storm. When she broke the quiet, she said, "We have to stay close to Amelia and Jacob. Those weren't only pretty words we spoke when we found them. I've never felt a greater call to anything."

"You're preaching to the choir, darlin'," Finn replied. "I have a strong sense about it, too."

"I never had many girlfriends growing up. I didn't miss the absence of them because I had Nic and Oz. And Amelia and I, we were always friendly, but hardly close. More so maybe than the other cousins, but not much." She propped herself higher on the pillow, and as she did, her hair fell back over her shoulders in a way that stole Finn's breath. Oh, how he had missed her. Wished for moments when it was only them, and their solitary stress revolved around what to choose for dinner. "When I reminisce about her now, I think, this is the woman I could tell everything to."

"I'm happy to hear that," Finn said. "I think Jacob and I also have a lot in common. We both married crazy Deschanel women, for one." He dodged a punch that didn't come.

Instead, Ana rolled over the top of him, letting the tips of her hair tickle his forehead, cheeks, chin. Her hand snaked between his legs, squeezing. "Crazy? I never heard you complain about *crazy* before."

"Oh, no," Finn agreed, lacing his fingers around the small of her back as she fumbled with his boxers. "And you never will."

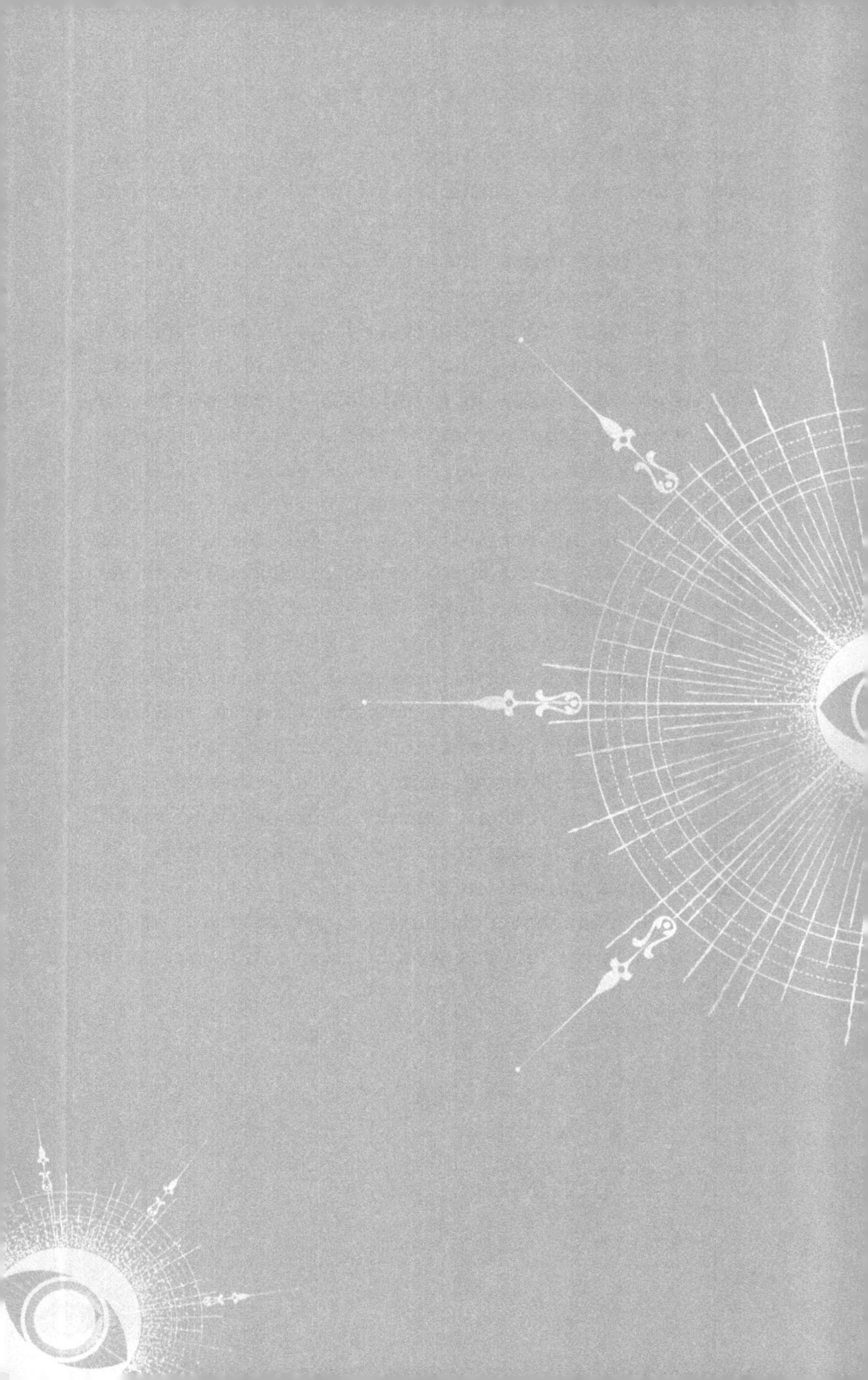

40
JACOB

Jacob couldn't take credit for the house. While he and Amelia slept off the journey for the past week, Colleen had arranged to have the home completely cleaned and made ready for their arrival. Jacob's role had been to ensure there was nothing in the house that might be upsetting or triggering. He hadn't found anything like that. Only the best of his memories.

When Amelia sashayed in the door, her face lit up. It was all the validation Jacob needed to know he'd made the right choice.

Miss Kitty jumped into Amelia's arms before she could say a word. "Aw, how I've missed my sweet girl!" she cooed, planting kisses all over the kitty's white fur. She lifted her, inspecting a newfound pudge. "But I think my mother might have spoiled you a wee bit much."

"No one ever accused Colleen Deschanel of treating her cats any different than her humans," Jacob said, smiling. "Looks good, yeah?"

Amelia set the cat back down on the oak floor and checked

around. "We've had so many memories here. Good, bad. Mostly, good, right?"

"Those are the only ones that matter to me," he answered, handing her a beer. "The worst of it happened away from our doorstep."

"Thankfully," Amelia agreed. She took a long swallow of her beer. "We're only a few blocks from Ana and Finn. That gives me comfort, too."

"Me too. And actually, I invited them over to dinner tomorrow night." He braced himself for her reaction but couldn't say why. Jacob hated the eggshells still littering the path between them.

"Did you?" She finished off her drink and smiled. "Good." Glancing around the house, she appeared as if searching for something else to comment on. They never had, not once in their entire relationship, ever worked so hard seeking something to talk about.

Jacob sensed she was afraid, but of what?

Of him?

Of being alone with him?

"*Blanca.*"

"Yes?" she called but continued her casual perusal of the house that had not changed since she'd left.

"I love you."

He didn't know if these were the right words, or the wrong words, just that they were the only words.

Amelia set the empty bottle on an end table and slowly turned. As her face came into view, he saw now the distress painted in the rosiness of her cheeks, and the sad, wide arc of her eyes. "Please don't be angry with me."

Jacob set his own drink aside and approached her, slowly but less tentatively than he had in recent days. "Amelia, how on earth could I ever be angry with you?"

She hung her head. "For not being strong enough to fight what's happening to me. I'm a doctor. I *know* what I'm supposed to do, and I don't know why I can't."

"You can," he insisted, running his hands over her arms. "And I know that because you have. I don't have your education on the matter, but I understand we're not meant to get over the worst of our lives in a heartbeat. It took me years to unwind the awful abuse my father inflicted, and sometimes I think I'm still damaged by it. Strength is moving forward, it isn't forgetting."

"All I want," she cried, letting loose the tears he knew she'd kept at bay for his sake, "is to be your wife, Donnelly. We hardly even got to enjoy it before our happiness was taken from us."

"Nothing was taken from us," Jacob pressed. "Nothing, *Blanca*. Listen to me, we *are* changed, but everything we go through, good and bad, does that. No one can take from us what we aren't willing to give. And I'm sorry, but Baldur may have set us back, but *he left with nothing*."

Amelia's eyes widened at the anger in Jacob's voice. "You took a life. For me."

"A life I wish I'd taken the moment I laid eyes on him," Jacob hissed. "I would do anything to go back to when I saw him with his hands on you in that glen."

Amelia waved her arms across the room, gesturing to years and years of a life built together. "How do we move on from that, though? How do we pretend we're the same people?"

"We don't," Jacob said, lacing his hands under her mane of white hair, at the nape of her neck. "We move forward. If we can endure growing up together and not killing one another, I think we can get past anything."

Amelia sniffled, laughing. "You were pretty insufferable in your formative years."

"Can't say you were a real walk in the park, either."

Amelia threw her arms around Jacob's neck and pressed her face to his cheek. The act was desperate, but he also knew, utterly real. "I want so badly to be close to you again... to be... intimate."

Jacob knew this feeling all too well. How many times over the years had they used their heated, passionate moments in the bedroom to heal a wound, or mend a fight? They'd never needed anything but each other, and that had never been truer than now when intimacy wasn't yet an option. "I don't need you to be ready until you are," he whispered against her temple. "I only need you. You're my best friend, *Blanca.* You were before I ever knew I could love you as more."

Amelia's sobs erupted in an unstoppable wave, and she buried her face against his chest. He held her like that, in the room where they'd shared the best moments of their lives together, whispering promises of better times.

"I've loved you forever," he told her.

"Then love me forever," Amelia answered, and wrapped herself deeper into his arms.

DAY SEVENTEEN

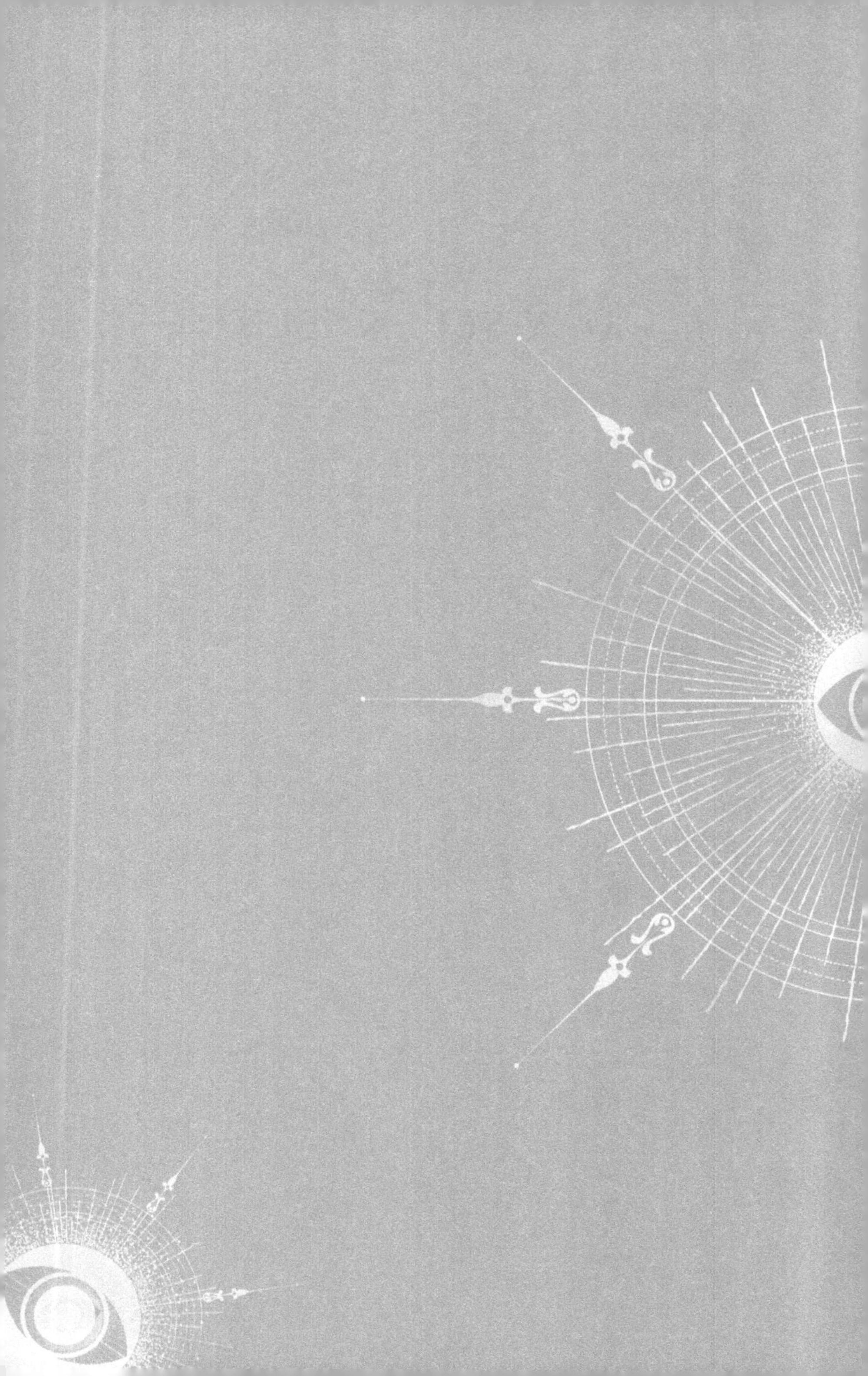

41
FINNEGAN

The toast was unanimous: new alliances. New beginnings. A united family.

And that's what they were now,, a united family. Amelia and Ana chatted in the natural way of lifelong friends, and Jacob and Finn already had the role of incorrigible husbands down to a science. Finn wondered at how easily they'd fallen into these roles, with people who had been only casual members of their life before. But he also cherished it.

To make situations even better, Aleksandr was spending the weekend with his grandfather, building a relationship neither Ana or Finn ever thought would be possible given the man's unfailingly pragmatic view on the world.

Maybe normal wasn't so far out of reach, after all.

"Nicolas is back," Amelia said, passing the okra to Ana. "Did you know?"

"I heard," Ana said. "But not from him. He'll dislike what I have to say about *that* oversight."

They both laughed. Jacob sent a questioning look to Finn, who shrugged. Even now, he didn't understand the nature of the relationship between Ana and Nicolas... probably for the best.

"I saw Katja today," Amelia continued. She smiled at Finn as he refilled her wine glass. "Sebastian has grown so much. He might be Aleksei's size and age if you're looking for someone for him to pal around with. They both have that abnormal growth spurt in common. Maybe they could bond over that."

"What about Stella?" Finn asked. "Wasn't she the twin who disappeared?"

"My mother has our best resources on it," Amelia said, with a sad look. "And Quillan Sullivan is still missing as well. But Mom says one good thing has come out of that situation, at least."

They all looked up.

"The Sullivans are finally willing to accept who they are, and that they share our gifts and our ancestry. Mom even thinks there might be a Sullivan on the Council one day."

"Wouldn't that be something?" Ana said, taking a bite of salmon. "And Oz? Now that Nicolas is back, is he still out at *Ophélie*?"

"I don't know, but Ashley is staying in his house. And Oz and that Empyrean girl he's been hanging with..."

"Lucia," Finn answered.

"Yes, Lucia," Amelia agreed. "They're still focused on teaching the Empyrean children. At least, the ones who didn't run away. They're hoping the others will return soon."

"Those kids are long gone," Finn said.

"Probably," Ana said. "But I've never known Oz to walk away from a lost cause."

They spent the next hour sharing similar stories, catching up on what the family had been up to while the four had been away. It had all the makings of a casual family dinner, but beneath the surface, they were each thinking of the world beyond.

After the dishes had been washed, Ana declared she and Amelia were going for a walk. They were gone before the men had a chance to ask if they could join.

"What do you suppose that's about?" Finn asked, handing Jacob a dish to put away.

"I don't know," Jacob said. "But I think Amelia needs someone to talk to about everything. Somebody who's not me."

"Ana, too," Finn replied. "I guess I can relate. Once Ana came into my life, I never had much chance to catch up to the changes. You and I, we both grew up like any other normal kid."

"I was an orphan," Jacob said with a short laugh. "But I get where you're coming from. And it's fine. I wouldn't trade normal for a life without Amelia or her family, but sometimes I do need a sanity check."

"Right. Exactly that."

Jacob leaned against the counter. "Life was somehow easier when it was her and not me. You know, the magic, I mean. When I was just the understanding man in her life, not the one turning the tricks. Does that make sense?"

"Oh, it does," Finn said, grabbing two beers from the fridge. "I totally agree."

"They had their whole lives to be who they are, and we've had, what, weeks? Months?" Jacob took the drink offered and shook his head. "I don't know. We are who we are, though, I guess."

Finn tipped the neck of his beer toward Jacob's. "So it seems."

"What about your brother?" Jacob asked. "Can you talk to him about it?"

"It's complicated," Finn said, and they both laughed. "He and Ana have a past, and he did some things... things that are hard to forgive. I know he's not a bad man, at heart, and he seems to have something good with Anne. But it's not the way it was when we were younger."

"Amelia said he's moving here?"

Finn shrugged. "Who knows? Anne is moving into the house she inherited as part of the Deschanel Trust, and he says he's staying. For now. He's good with Aleksei, so I suppose that's something." Finn finished off his beer and cocked his head, looking at Jacob. "What about you? Do you have any siblings?"

"Aye, I did," Jacob said before he remembered to squash his Irish lit. "But my Pa killed 'em."

"Holy shit," Finn said. He reached, wordlessly, into the fridge to fetch Jacob another beer. Sensing Jacob would rather forget than remember, he asked, "Do you fish?"

"Not well."

"Wanna learn?"

Jacob looked down, smiling to himself. Finn couldn't read his thoughts, but he thought maybe they matched his. "Yeah, man. That would be cool."

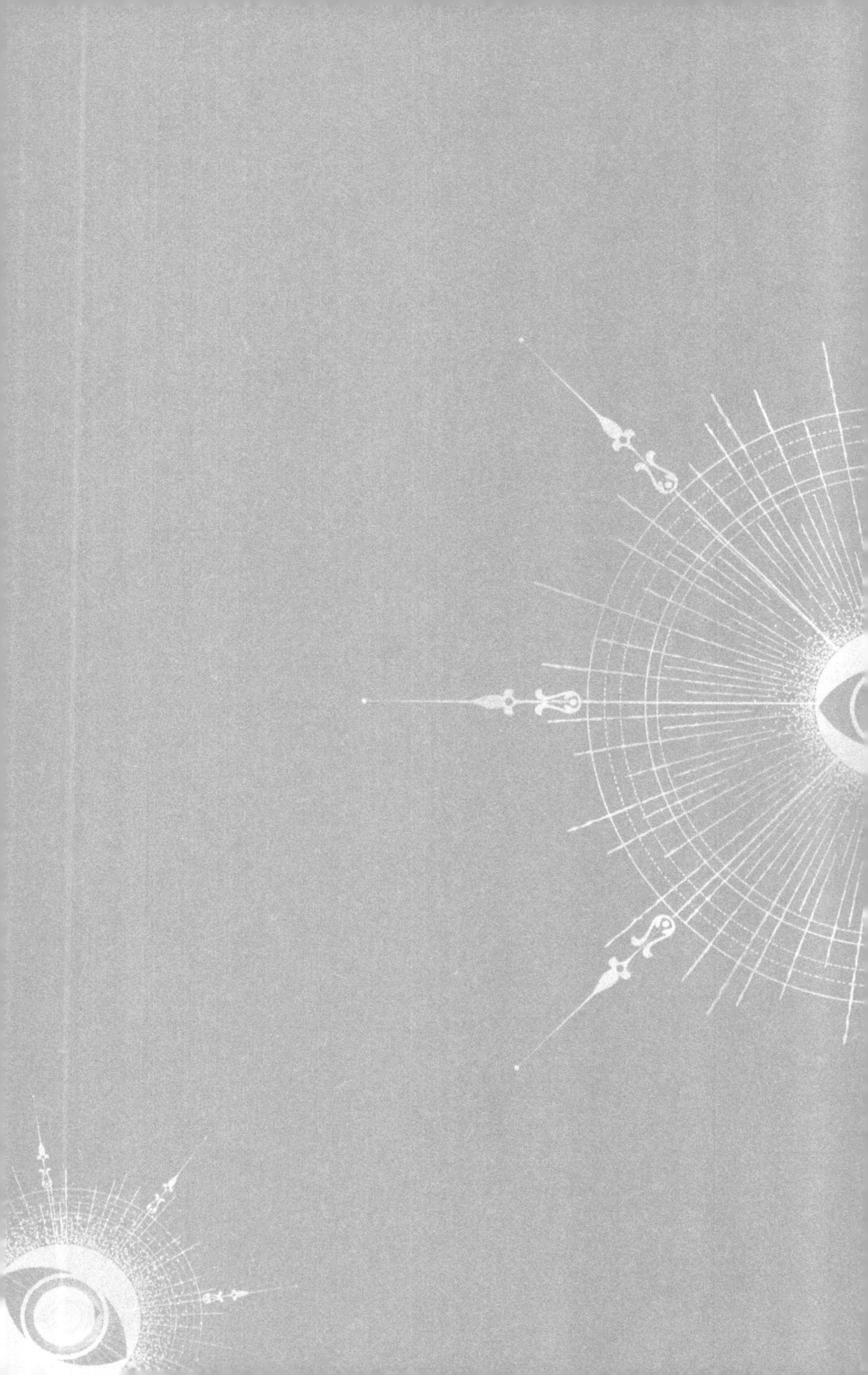

42
ANASOFIYA

They strolled in silence down St. Charles at dusk. Having spent their lives in New Orleans, in the Garden District, both women instinctively knew this was a sacred, magical time of day along the avenue. The fireflies danced along the branches of the trees, and gaslights began their flickering, announcing the long night.

Ana didn't know where they were headed until they got there. Audubon Park was beautiful this time of day, and she said that, as they passed through the gates. "Oz and Adrienne used to come here. There's an oak somewhere near the front of the park. It was their tree."

"That one." Amelia pointed to an old oak with a long branch sweeping the ground like a seat. "Oz told me a lot of things when he visited me during those long months of imperilment."

"That's right," Ana said, nodding. "It must have been a very confusing time for you."

"I don't know if it was more or less confusing than how I feel now, but I'm glad it's over."

"Adrienne was a beautiful soul," Ana said, moving toward the branch. "But she wasn't like us. She wasn't strong. Was she?"

Amelia ran her hand over the soft bark. "Why are we here, Ana? I enjoyed the walk with you, but I know we didn't come out here for small talk. Neither of us have ever been very good at it. And I'm an empath. I can sense your anxiousness."

Ana laughed. "It's a wonder we weren't always closer, Amelia. We're so much alike. I suppose we were when we were little." She breathed in the fresh, floral air. "We have another thing in common."

"What's that?"

"We've been to hell and survived it," Ana answered. She fell into the arm of the branch, enjoying the light feeling of surrender that came over her. "Our men have, too. They watched us suffer and were helpless to stop it. That's a whole special section of hell. But we can't talk to them about it, can we?"

Amelia frowned. She turned toward the sound of ducks coming off the pond. A hundred wings flapped in a flutter. "No. And I hate it. I've never not been able to talk to Jacob. You'd think this would be no different. We were both *there.*"

"You may have been in the same room, but Jacob, much as he may have wanted to, was unable to take your place. As Finn couldn't take mine," Ana said, gesturing to Amelia to accept a seat next to her on the branch. "It kills them. I think it frustrates them, too, that we don't talk about it, but it hurts them more when we do because they're reminded of it over and over again, and of their own perceived inadequacy."

Amelia started to rebut, then slowly nodded. "Yeah, you're right. They blame themselves, which isn't true or fair at all, but when they do, it makes the subject even harder to talk about."

"And we have to," Ana insisted. "We *have* to, Amelia.

Madness runs in our family, especially among the women. So does stubbornness. We're notorious for letting our emotional wounds fester until they become something worse. We can't let that happen. For our sake, and for theirs. I have a son to protect as well. If you're being honest with yourself, you will more than likely have a daughter to think about soon."

Amelia's hand slid to her stomach. Ana guessed she was thinking about the child she'd lost. They could talk about this. It was time to stop bottling their horrors. "I think, maybe, that's what's been hardest for me in moving on. We're natural caretakers, and we always think of others first. I've neglected to take care of myself, and I know, from my training, that self-care is more important than anything else."

"The way you can help him is to get better. This is how I can help Finn, too. They're helpless, Amelia. No, I don't mean they're incapable. We married two of the most capable men in the world, as far as I'm concerned, but they're helpless about this matter. If we want to protect them, we need to shield them from the worst of us. We need to experience it. We have to. But we must do it on our own."

"They think they have to protect us," Amelia conceded. The words seem to come to her as she said them, a slow blanket of realization. "But they can't. Not from this. But we can save them."

"In shielding our husbands, we also protect ourselves," Ana agreed. "I don't know what's next for us, but neither of us are completely ready for it, in the state we're in. We're angry at the world, at ourselves. And maybe we should be. But it isn't helping either of us."

"No," Amelia said, looking down at her hands. "And I'm sick of it. Tired of feeling like a victim of the universe's cruelty instead of being in charge of my own destiny."

"Then let's change that."

Ana held her hand out. Amelia took it.

"We're sisters now," Ana said. "For better or worse. Though, more than likely, the latter."

Amelia smiled. "Heaven help the asshole who tries to cross *us.*"

Ana laughed. Letting loose was good... uplifting.

"There's something else on your mind," Amelia pressed. "Sorry. Habit."

Aidrik. Could Amelia really be the one with whom she could finally share this secret?

Yes, she decided.

43
EPILOGUE

Amelia's sleep was mercifully dreamless. It had been this way since they moved back into their old home, attempting to surrender to their old ways. She didn't know the precise cause, but she welcomed it.

The evening after her walk with Ana, Amelia awoke with the powerful sensation she was being watched. Her gaze traveled the perimeter of the dark room, lit only by a flash of moonlight, but there was no one.

She lifted back the blankets and rose from the bed when her attention was drawn to the window; an instinctual pull she'd felt night after night.

But when she peered out into the dark night, no one was there. Only the quiet street. As it was each time.

Jacob's arms slid around her from behind. He nuzzled his face into her shoulder blades. "Bad dream?"

"No dream at all," she said, still fixed on the stillness of the street below. "I didn't mean to wake you."

Jacob answered her by caressing his mouth along the blades of her shoulders, tracing a path north to her neck. His hands tightened, a tender but possessive gesture, and she felt him grow hard near the small of her back.

Abruptly, he broke away. “I’m so sorry,” he said, breathless. “I wasn’t thinking.”

Without taking her eyes off the street, Amelia reached behind her, pulling her husband back closer. “Don’t be sorry,” she whispered as her own body came alive. She felt desirable and longed to be needed that way for the first time since the world had stopped. It wasn’t wrong. It wouldn’t hurt her. “And don’t stop.”

Jacob’s hands traveled up her torso, fingers cupped and sliding over her breasts and to her shoulders where he let the straps of her nightgown drop to the floor.

Amelia moaned, falling into him, pressing into the hard line of his sex, ready for her. “I know what you’re about to ask me,” she panted, “but don’t. I want this. I need this.”

With one hand, she reached between them and grabbed his cock, pressing it into her, waiting for him to take over. Jacob paused for only a moment, then groaned as he entered her for the first time in weeks. His knees buckled as he thrust, one hand pressed into her sex, the other braced against the windowsill.

All her fears slipped away. No third entity. No monster in the room. This intimate moment was only about the two of them, Jacob and Amelia, Cerridwen and Cianán, and their love everlasting.

Jacob’s pace quickened, lost in his desire for her. She pressed her palms against the windowpane and cried out in pleasure when nearing her own climax.

Amelia nearly stopped him when she realized she hadn’t taken any form of contraceptive in weeks. But it didn’t matter. Nothing existed except the two of them, and this moment, and the love only they could ever understand.

She opened her eyes as Jacob released inside her, and she climaxed in tandem. Instead of relief, horror overtook her in a single, stinging moment.

She had not been wrong.

Staring up from the lamppost, watching them in their coital tangle, was Victor de Blanchefort.

The Deschanels settle into an uneasy peace, each of them working to return to something resembling normal. But normal is an illusion, and events quickly propel each and every Deschanel back into action, spurring them closer and closer to the end game—one way or another.

Don't miss a minute. Download ***Within the Garden of Twilight***, the penultimate tale in this saga.

WITHIN THE GARDEN OF TWILIGHT EXCERPT

"Go on," Jacob said. He squared his stance into perfect form, one Amelia recognized all too well. "Tell me why I shouldn't kill you where you stand."

"Let's take this inside. Ashley is across the street," Amelia said, glancing at Oz's house, where her brother was housesitting. She noticed both the interior and the porch gaslights were off, so maybe he was out.

Her breath caught.

The Magi Collective meeting! How had she forgotten?

She ushered them in, though Jacob moved much slower. His highly controlled and deliberate strides conjured up images of a cheetah stalking prey in the savannah. His eyes never left the intruder.

Amelia pulled her robe tighter. She thought about positioning herself between her husband and Victor de Blanchefort, but a part of her very much wanted to see Jacob lay into the man who had dared come to *their* home, uninvited. She wanted to lay into him herself. She still might, depending on the words he chose next.

She shuddered from head to toe as her mind traveled back to the horror of the night before. As Jacob made love to her, for the first time since her brutal assault—as they came together—they opened their eyes to see Victor standing on the street below, watching.

He didn't belong here. Not at their house, and not in their *time.*

Jacob kicked the door closed. He didn't drop his gaze. His approach toward Victor was a contiguous, fluid movement. "You have some serious balls coming here. Amelia told you to leave us alone. *I* told you to leave us alone. Ophélie even told you to leave us alone."

Victor's hands went up in bemused surrender. "Are you going to lay fists on me, Jacob? Or are we going to have a discussion, like gentlemen?"

Jacob's hands turned to tight balls at his sides. Amelia sensed him fighting with himself: to fight this battle with violence or words. The competing emotions rippled off him in violent waves. His muscles tensed under his white tee, his sinewy strength on full display. Although he made no immediate move, Victor gave a subtle recoil.

"I wouldn't let my husband bloody his fists on your account," Amelia said. "There are three guns in this house and I know how to get to each one of them in less than thirty seconds."

"We parted nary two weeks ago, and my arrival incites the threat of a gun battle?" Victor shook his head with a maddening air of benignity. His hands hovered in the air, conducting his words. "Dare I ask what has changed in that period of time?"

"Nothing has changed," Amelia said. "When I saw you last, I asked you to leave us alone. Don't act like there was an open invitation. I was clear."

"But we are friends, are we not?"

"Friends?" Jacob repeated with a heavy laugh. "I don't care if you lived part of your life as Cianán or not, or what else we might have in common. I'm not okay with how you look at my wife, or the way you confused her when she was at her most vulnerable. You knew exactly what you were doing."

"I'm not confused," Amelia stated. Her eyes bore holes in Victor. "I know what I want. And I know what I don't want."

Jacob's smile in her peripheral was so fleeting only she would have recognized it. He returned his full focus back to Victor. "You may be immortal, but you're not invulnerable. You have five minutes to tell us why you're here."

"Two," Amelia countered.

"Ten," Victor said amenably. His smile was as furtive as it was apologetic. "What I have to tell you could take the remainder of the evening, but I can compromise for the sake of brevity, and perchance, my head."

Amelia thought of calling her mother. She had never missed a meeting when she was in town. Colleen would worry, especially given all Amelia had told her about her time away. She was probably already worried. Maybe even out of her mind.

More pressing was the immediate problem of getting Victor out of their home, though.

Jacob pointed at an armchair. He then dropped into a perched position on the couch across, as if he might spring to action at any moment. Amelia settled in next to him and rested a hand on his knee in what she hoped conveyed an outward sign of their unity.

"Say what you need to say and leave," Jacob said.

"Yes, well," Victor began. He relaxed into his chair and folded his legs. Amelia's anger roiled to the surface at how casual the creature acted against their growing frustration. "I must confess. I came to request your assistance in a matter that is quite vexing."

"I'm not helping you with anything," Amelia said. "Except getting out of my house."

"No? You may change your heart when I share the nature of my request." Victor pulled at the lapel of his waistcoat. How much attention did he attract in his nineteenth century garb? And why hadn't he updated his wardrobe over the years? New Orleans was an eccentric city, but this was odd even by their standards.

"Eight minutes," Jacob said.

"Then I shall come right to my point," Victor replied with a slow, charming smile. "You see, the truth of the fate of your ancestor, the most lovely Ophélie Deschanel, our beloved Cerridwen, has been steeped in many falsehoods over the years. Some stories, of course, quite true. You witnessed with your own eyes the abuses wrought upon her by her horrific mother, Brigitte. It is also true that Charles turned a blind eye during the War to what the Union soldiers did to poor Ophélie."

Amelia flipped her palms out. "Okay. We know this. And?"

Victor continued unperturbed. "It can also be said that Charles, in his guilt, lifted the knife meant to take her life and deliver her of her sorrows. Indeed, he used it on her! But, ah, Ophélie did not die." His eyes twinkled. "Can you guess, my friends, what *did* become of her?"

"What do you mean, she didn't die? Of course she died." Jacob's foot tapped in mounting impatience. He looked at Amelia. "We don't have to entertain his delusions."

"Get on with it," Amelia demanded. "Make your point and leave."

Victor brightened, growing ever more animated. "But she did *not* die, Jacob! For you see, I was forewarned of Charles' notions, courtesy of Ophélie's own visions, and had confirmation of the same from the time travelers sitting before me. I followed the man, though he did not know it. As Ophélie bled toward what would have undoubtedly been uncertain death, I leaned before her and gave her my blood."

Amelia gave him a pointed look. "So, what, she became like you? You clearly told me that a dhampir cannot make another dhampir himself. That he has to take the person to the... uh, tree or whatever."

"The Master's Tree," Victor clarified. "And so I did. But first, my blood healed sweet Ophélie. Our blood does not heal as your mother heals, Amelia, but it bought necessary time. Though, some, like my father, Marius, were healers before we took the blood of the Master. I then carried her to *Coquillage* and laid her before my father. He healed her further, but she did not immediately awaken."

Victor's time was running out, but both Amelia and Jacob listened in shocked suspension. "Come on now," Jacob said. "If you took her away, why would the family say they found her stabbed to death? That's why Brigitte threw herself from the damn gallery. If Ophélie had lived, everything would have been completely different. Everything. This doesn't make any sense."

"They did not need a body to confirm the worst when Charles confessed his crime. While the story passed down was that Ophélie's life was stolen by soldiers, the immediate family always knew it was Charles. When he noticed the body missing, he assumed those selfsame soldiers who had earlier spoiled her body took her to perform further unmentionable injustices. To spare his loved ones the grief of envisioning their sweet girl bandied about, he lied and claimed to have buried her himself, on the property. You have seen her grave marker with your own eyes, in present day. His lie allowed me to permit Ophélie new life."

"So you socked her away like a hostage?" Jacob charged.

"No, I did much more than that. I took her to the Master."

Amelia shot forward, launching to her feet. "And she consented?" No, this was not possible. She talked to Ophélie herself before they traveled back to the present... she was clear in what she wanted... she would never...

Victor pulled back. "She was in no presence of mind to consent or not consent. I had no means of asking her, and her wounds were too grievous for even my father's great skill. There was no choice for me, when the alternative outcome meant her death. I brought her before Childeric, our leader, and requested we find one willing to give their dhampir life for hers."

Jacob closed his eyes, processing. "So you're telling us you kidnapped Ophélie, against her will, took her to the Master's Tree, and had her turned into... whatever *you* are?"

"She had no will. She would not awaken."

"That's like saying the woman was too drunk to consent, so you raped her anyway," Amelia accused. "Please tell me you didn't really do this. Please tell me you did *not* do this to our Ophélie!"

Jacob rose to her side. His temper was a fine match to her own, two flames rising higher and higher. She sensed him restraining his, but it wouldn't be long before he was no longer able to.

Victor was taken aback. "I did not rape Ophélie."

"You raped her of her choice!" Amelia stepped forward. She leaned over where Victor sat, as relaxed as a man sitting for afternoon tea. "You don't get to make decisions for other people simply because it suits you. Ophélie *knew* she was going to die. You offered her this choice and she *turned you down.*

How much more clear does it get? You did this against her will, against her wishes." Amelia backed away from him, stumbling into the sofa. "You really are a monster. Where is she? Where is she, Victor? If you really did as you say, where is she?"

"You need to leave," Jacob said. He looped an arm around Amelia, gentle but protective. His hand burned hot at her back. He had always carried his rage most potently in his hands. "Now."

Victor ignored Jacob and focused his answer on Amelia. "That's why I'm here. I do not know where she is. As you are now, she was angry at what I had done and she abandoned me. She yet carried the child that grew in her belly at the time of her assault. I never saw her again, nor do I know what became of the child." He knelt before Amelia.

She gaped at him in horror. She went stiff. Still.

"I beseech you, Amelia. I have searched the world for my Cerridwen, and she has eluded me for over a century. I come to you, arms wide, begging for your assistance in locating her and bringing her back to me."

A burst of vibrant anger surged through Amelia. She lifted her hand and swung it at his cheek, palm open. He recoiled in shock, as did Jacob at her side. "You want me to find her for you? You took everything from her! Her right to choose her own destiny. You may have forsaken who you were born to be, but *she* did not, and you stole it from her. You unbelievable bastard. You get *out* of my house and *out of our lives,* and if I ever see you again, God help me I will use every last breath in my body to see to it that you never hurt another living being again!"

"My darling—"

Jacob lifted him from the chair with one hand. Victor stumbled as Jacob dragged him toward the door, biceps straining to control the ancient creature. "She is not your darling. We are not your friends. And if we do find Ophélie, you are the last person on earth we would ever tell." He swung the door open and released Victor with a light shove. "You're uninvited."

Victor gave him a curious, amused look from the porch as he straightened his jacket. "You read too many vampire novels, Jacob. I don't require an invitation, and so neither can you uninvite me."

"Yeah? Watch me."

Jacob kicked the door closed for the second time.

Amelia stared, white-faced, into nothing. She couldn't focus on any specifics of her surroundings. She could hardly think coherent thoughts. What Victor had confessed could not possibly be true, but she saw no reason for him to lie, nor did she detect any deception from him.

"You okay, *Blanca*?"

Amelia breathed in deep and turned to her husband. "Yes. No. I don't know."

Jacob nodded. "Yeah. Same. Do you think he'll stay away this time?"

She thought about it a moment and then shook her head. "No. He'll be back. And, you know, I don't think he came here for us, either."

"How do you mean?"

Amelia glanced outside. Dawn prepared to crest on the horizon. The Collective would be adjourning soon, if they hadn't already. "He knows I can't find her. I'm an empath, not a telepath or a tracker. But there are others in the family who are, and he must know that."

Jacob ran his hands across his face. When they passed over his eyes, she saw they were red and tired. "So why not just go to them? Why bother us?"

"He doesn't know them. He needed us to bridge that gap."

Amelia let out an exhausted half-laugh. "He really miscalculated."

"He's insane," Jacob said. "Maybe that's what immortality does. Drives you bloody mad."

Amelia switched off the porch light, but not before checking to make sure Victor was no longer prowling around. Not that he would go far, she was sure. A man who had spent a century and a half on a single fixation wouldn't be deterred by one bad conversation. "I don't think he's lying. I wish he was, but I sense he's telling the truth about what he did to her."

Jacob nodded. "I know." He turned down the light on the chandelier to the lowest setting, then extended his hand to Amelia. "And if she is out there, we can't let him anywhere near her."

"Do you think she might be?" Amelia was shame-filled at even allowing herself to hope she might see Ophélie again, after what the poor girl had been through.

"Maybe." Jacob squeezed her hand as they made their way up the stairs. She leaned into him. "If she is, I hope she's found herself some sort of happiness. Lord knows she's earned it."

Don't miss a minute. Download ***Within the Garden of Twilight*** today.

ALSO BY SARAH M. CRADIT

KINGDOM OF THE WHITE SEA

Kingdom of the White Sea Trilogy

The Kingless Crown

The Broken Realm

The Hidden Kingdom

The Book of All Things

The Raven and the Rush

The Sylvan and the Sand

The Altruist and the Assassin

The Melody and the Master

The Claw and the Crowned

THE SAGA OF CRIMSON & CLOVER

The House of Crimson and Clover Series

The Storm and the Darkness

Shattered

The Illusions of Eventide

Bound

Midnight Dynasty

Asunder

Empire of Shadows

Myths of Midwinter

The Hinterland Veil

The Secrets Amongst the Cypress

Within the Garden of Twilight

House of Dusk, House of Dawn

Midnight Dynasty Series

A Tempest of Discovery

A Storm of Revelations

A Torrent of Deceit

The Seven Series

1970

1972

1973

1974

1975

1976

1980

Vampires of the Merovingi Series

The Island

and more

The Dusk Trilogy

St. Charles at Dusk: The Story of Oz and Adrienne

Flourish: The Story of Anne Fontaine

Banshee: The Story of Giselle Deschanel

Crimson & Clover Stories

Surrender: The Story of Oz and Ana

Shame: The Story of Jonathan St. Andrews

Fire & Ice: The Story of Remy & Fleur

Dark Blessing: The Landry Triplets

Pandora's Box: The Story of Jasper & Pandora

The Menagerie: Oriana's Den of Iniquities

A Band of Heather: The Story of Colleen and Noah

The Ephemeral: The Story of Autumn & Gabriel

Bayou's Edge: The Landry Triplets

For more information, and exciting bonus material, visit www.sarahmcradit.com

EMPYREAN & QUINLAN
ENCYCLOPEDIA

Aanya: A kind and beautiful Empyrean Agripin once loved, but was forbidden from claiming as his duchess her due to her lack of lineage.

Aidrik (Also: Aidrik the Wise): Once a well-respected member of the Eldre Senetat. After Aidrik discovered their true nature, he sliced the Mark of Emyr from his face, freeing him from the Senetat's tethers. He met and saved Anasofiya from death, becoming her evigbond. Lived in a triad with Anasofiya, and her husband Finn, until his death, at the hands of the Senetat.

Aleksandr: Empyrean son of Anasofiya, Finn, and Aidrik. Shy, introspective. Named heir of the Deschanels by Nicolas. A mystic, and time shaper, whose abilities are still surfacing.

Anders: An Empyrean Mercy co-habitated with for a short period of time. She believed him Ascended, but he was, actually, a scout for the Brotherhood, under the direction of Thorvald. His most recent assignment brought him to *Ophélie*, where he is tasked with training and protecting the Brotherhood children.

Arborkinetic: A form of telekinesis involving flora. A strong arborkinetic can command plant life to do their bidding, and some can communicate with plants. Anne Fontaine Deschanel and Duchess Nerys are both arborkinetics.

Ascension (Also: Grand Ascension): The ultimate death and rebirth all Empyreans are promised. It is tied to Emyr's Mark, which is said to come alive when their time is near. Once active, the mark is then supposed to usher them through death and rebirth, into the arms of Emyr. The truth is the mark is simply an infusion of dark magic administered by the Eldre Senetat, from which they control the activation and subsequent death of Empyreans.

Astrid: Brotherhood leader of Ireland and the British Isles, alongside her evigbond, Birger. Birger and Astrid are in the minority in their decision to make peace with Quinlans. They also co-exist peacefully with humans in the nearby villages where they live in a tribe of other similar-minded Empyreans. Many look to them as the moral compass of the Brotherhood. They have one child, Eydis.

Baldur: A sadistic scout for the Senetat who captures Amelia and Jacob, torturing them for information. Is killed by Jacob.

Bestiakinetic: One who can commune with animals. Finnegan becomes a bestiakinetic after being given the Sveising. Yiva and Jorun are also bestiakinetics.

Birger: Brotherhood leader of Ireland and the British Isles, alongside his evigbond, Astrid. Birger and Astrid are in the minority in their decision to make peace with Quinlans. They also co-exist peacefully with humans in the nearby villages where they live in a tribe of other like-minded Empyreans. Many look to them as the moral compass of the Brotherhood. They have one child, Eydis.

Blacksmith: Forger of Ulfberht, and creator of Empyrean Steel.

Bodhran: Goatskin drum used in Quinlan ceremonies.

Brotherhood: See "Dragon Brotherhood, The."

Brother of Emyr (Also: Sister of Emyr): Another way to reference a halfling (or, someone who has both human and Empyrean blood).

Brynja: One of the oldest, original Empyreans. Together with her partner, Einar, they are Brotherhood leaders, residing in Russia. Part of Runa's rebels who escaped after her execution, they are often called, by Runeans, "Adam and Eve."

Child of Man/Men: What Empyreans call humans.

Christiane de Laurent: Aidrik's original evigbond. Human. Lived at the end of the 16th century, as a courtesan of the French court. Wife of Marquise Deschanel, and mother of Claude.

Cianán (Also: Jacob Donnelly): One fourth of the prophecy, descended from the Tuathan tribe of Gorias. He has been reincarnated over thousands of years, with his lover, Cerridwen. Their journey evolves in each lifetime, with the ultimate test being their love bringing them together in their final lifetime, when they have no memory of former lives, thus fulfilling the prophecy. Their child is meant to join with the descendant of Falias and Murias. Jacob is the reincarnated soul of Cianán.

Cerridwen (Also: Amelia Donnelly): One fourth of the prophecy, descended from the Tuathan tribe of Findias. She has been reincarnated over thousands of years, with her lover, Cianán. Their journey evolves in each lifetime, with the ultimate test being their love bringing them together in their final lifetime, thus fulfilling the prophecy. Their child is meant to join with the descendant of Falias and Murias. Amelia is the reincarnated soul of Cerridwen.

Claude Deschanel (Also: Viscount Deschanel): The first halfling Deschanel, being both human and Empyrean. Child of Christiane and Aidrik.

***Crann bethadh*:** Also known as the "Tree of Life," and the center of the Quinlan tribe. It gives life to the tribe, by providing everything they need, from food to shelter. Also a portal between worlds, and the spiritual link to the goddesses.

Crimson Guard: The official guard of the Farjhem, under command of the Senetat. Their uniform consists of blood-red robes.

Cumdach: A lavishly ornamented shrine used in Quinlan ceremonies.

Cyler: Agripin's young, brash second-in-command, and lover. Often shirks orders and goes his own route, though he is known for being excellent with strategy. Is a frequent visitor to Oriana's Menagerie.

Dagr: 7,000 years old. Born without Senetat knowledge, and is one of the Brotherhood leaders, residing in Morocco.

Daughter of Emyr (Also: Son of Emyr): Referencing pure-blooded Empyrean women.

Deschanel Magi Collective: A secret, ancient society, created with the intention of cataloguing all the family's abilities, as well as protecting and preserving the family. Each generation has a Magistrate, the current one being Colleen Deschanel.

Dragon Brotherhood, The: Secret organization of Empyrean rebels. There is no central leader, but instead regional leaders across the world. Some leaders are ready for battle, others content to live in peace.

Dragon Empire, The (Also: Dragon Brotherhood, The): Another name for the wider Dragon Brotherhood.

Draoi: Male Quinlan. It is said these males are sacred, as their occurrence usually portends something important, and prophetic. Draoi are often quite powerful, able to spin wards and time dance. To birth a draoi is to be considered blessed. Male druids often come into their powers when they reach sexual maturity. Attempting to draw from them earlier can sometimes lead to disastrous results. Jacob, Finnegan, Padraig, and Father O'Connor are all draoi.

Drekar: A term of familiarity amongst the Brotherhood. Translates roughly to "dragon."

Duchess Nerys: Nomadic daughter of Grand Emperor Aeron, and sister to Agripin and Oriana. Known for her love of all creatures, and her call to traveling. A bestiakinetic, with loyalties to no one and nothing except peace. Joins forces with the Brotherhood, as she believes they are most likely to achieve that.

Duchess Oriana: Beautiful, wayward daughter of Grand Emperor Aeron, sister to Agripin and Nerys. Known for having a menagerie of human pets, and for her cruelty toward defectors. Is loyal to the Senetat.

Einar: One of the oldest, original Empyreans. Together with his partner, Brynja, they are Brotherhood leaders, residing in Russia. Part of Runa's rebels who escaped after her execution, they are often called, by Runeans, "Adam and Eve."

Eldre Aeslius: One of the nine members of the Eldre Senetat. Following the events at Aidrik's execution, his fate is currently unknown.

Eldre Brutus: Was originally a member of Emperor Elof's privy council, but when he discovered Elof was plotting with rebels, Brutus betrayed and exposed him. The Senetat "Ascended" Elof, giving the crown to his son Aeron. Following the events at Aidrik's execution, his fate is currently unknown.

Eldre Cassian: One of the nine members of the Eldre Senetat. Following the events at Aidrik's execution, his fate is currently unknown.

Eldre Felix: One of the nine members of the Eldre Senetat. Following the events at Aidrik's execution, his fate is currently unknown.

Eldre Lucrecia: One of the nine members of the Eldre Senetat. Following the events at Aidrik's execution, her fate is currently unknown.

Eldre Maxima: One of the nine members of the Eldre Senetat. Has been a secret sympathizer of the Brotherhood for many years, and officially joined their cause following the events at Aidrik's execution.

Eldre Tacita: One of the nine members of the Eldre Senetat. Following the events at Aidrik's execution, her fate is currently unknown.

Eldre Valerius: One of the nine members of the Eldre Senetat. Right hand of Grand Eldre Servius. Following the events at Aidrik's execution, his fate is currently unknown.

Eldre Senetat, The: The ruling government over the Empyrean race. Established many millennia ago, they claim to be blessed by Emyr, and charged with doing His will through enacting and protecting laws. The Senetat grew corrupt with this power, and unknown to most Empyreans, are controlling the fates of all citizens. The creation and installation of Emyr's Mark is the vehicle by which they exact their control.

Empath: The ability to sense feelings, emotions, or sensations in others. There are varying degrees of empaths. Amelia Deschanel is considered the strongest empath in the family. Lucia and Livia are also empaths.

Empyrean (Also: Farværdig): Also known as the Farværdig ("Father's Chosen"), Empyreans are as old as man, and similar genetically, but with several key differences. Where some DNA is dormant in humans, the entire strand is active in Empyreans, giving them special, paranormal abilities, including greater strength and speed, and immortality via perfect cell replication. Their home is Farjhem, in the northern expanses of Norway, but most Empyreans live scattered throughout the world, blending in with men. All Empyreans are born with red hair (which fades to a chromatic silver as they age), and are exceptionally tall. They are also primarily solitary, not subscribing to traditions such as a nuclear family, marriage, or commitment. The exception to this is evigbond. In their early days, they enjoyed a strategic alliance with Quinlans, but, once broken, both races were thrust into strife.

Empyrean Laws: Mandates set by the Eldre Senetat. include regulations around childbirth, mating with humans, and other fundamental freedoms.

Empyrean Steel (Also: Crucible Steel): A rare steel with high carbon content, smelted in a small furnace, and cooled slowly. In swords, it was both strong, and flexible. The technology was not used anywhere else in the world, and was considered better than Damascus Steel, which is the closest point of comparison.

Empyrean traits: Born of fire. Elevated body temperature. Red hair (the redder the strands, the more pure the blood) that takes on silver chromatic hues as they age. When emotions are heightened, they are said to emit an orange glow. Most have pale, smooth skin, and are very tall. All have special telepathic/telekinetic abilities, with some stronger than others. Average lifespan is two thousand years, though it is believed without the mark, an Empyrean could be functionally immortal.

Emyr (Also: Our Father): God, to Empyreans. He is represented by a phoenix, rising from the ashes.

Erikr: Brotherhood resistance leader who led one of the only semi-successful rebel revolutions after Runa's. Was executed in a block of ice. Leader of the Second Runean War, and considered the father of the Dragon Brotherhood, which was formed with the help of Ptolemy I.

Etheric Summoning (Also: Etheric Summoner): More rare than a mystic, an etheric summoner can draw from their greatest weakness and manifest it into a physical strength. Also known as a wraith. Anasofiya is an etheric summoner.

Evigbond: The physical and chemical bonding process that occurs when an Empyrean meets their permanent mate. It is irreversible, and only severed by death. An evigbond between Empyrean and humans is especially potent. Aidrik's first evigbond was Christiane, and his current is Anasofiya. Mercy experienced evigbond with Nicolas, until her "death." Evigbond can occur in two different ways. The first is an uncontrolled, chemical reaction. The second is through consummation.

Eydis: Fifty-year-old daughter of Brotherhood leaders Birger and Astrid. She is halfway to maturity, and emotionally equivalent to a young girl of around nineteen. Wide-eyed, rebellious, but kind-hearted. She sees how in love her parents are because of their evigbond, and is determined to find hers. Her birth accompanied a year of great prosperity for crops in Ireland. Is an illusionist with a specialty in influencing.

Falias: One of the four tribes of the Tuatha Dé Danann. All Quinlans descend from one of these four tribes. The tribe of Falias is mentioned in The Prophecy as such: *A male Quinlan, pure of heart, and a special affinity for animals.* It is not yet known who the subject of this reference is.

Far: Empyrean word for father. Can be used by a child speaking to a parent, or in reference to Our Father, Emyr.

Fardag (Also: Father's Day): Annual Farjhem celebration held in homage to Emyr.

Farjhem: The homeland of the Empyreans. Translated to "Father's Home." Located between two glaciers in northern

Norway, it is not accessible by anyone except Empyreans, or those with Empyrean blood.

Farsengel: The place of law and order in Farjhem, where suspected criminals are sentenced and detained awaiting further punishment. Many stories high, the outside edges contain hundreds of cells, and the inside of the arena has a large stage.

Farskilt: Deep in the bowels of Farjhem, beneath a volcano. "Separated from father." Empyreans are sentenced here for "rehabilitation" when they commit spiritual offenses. Citizens are told that offenders are "reunited with Emyr" and the end of their rehabilitation results in guaranteed Ascension. The reality is they are labor mines, and Empyreans work there until their inevitable starvation and death. The Empyrean equivalent of a prison camp.

Farvann River: (Also: River Farvann): The river flowing through the fjord and glaciers of Farjhem.

Farværdig (Also: Empyrean): See "Empyrean."

Father O'Connor: A draoi descended from the tribe of Gorias, and the man who saved Jacob from tragedy as a youth, sending him to New Orleans. Brother to the tribe elder, Seara. Great-uncle of Amelia.

Feast of Officium Maximus: Once every hundred years, the Scholars graduate their group of fledgling Empyreans into the world. This ceremony, for which many return home, is accompanied by a great celebration.

Findias: One of the four tribes of the Tuatha Dé Danann. All Quinlans descend from one of these four tribes. The tribe of Findias is mentioned in The Prophecy as such: *A female Quinlan, and halfling Empyrean, reincarnated over two-thousand years, originally Cerridwen. Lover of Cianán.* Amelia Jameson Donnelly is the subject of this reference.

First Father: When an Empyrean child has multiple

fathers (via Sveising), the initial father, at conception, is referred to as First Father.

First Runean War: Resistance to the creation of the Eldre Senetat, led by Runa, a warrior who represented the opinions of many Empyreans. Despite her strong supporters, the rebels were destroyed, and Runa publicly executed. Their stunning defeat weakened the resolve of many Empyreans who believed in her cause (henceforth dubbed Runeans by the Senetat), and most went into hiding.

Fledglings: What the Empyrean youth are referred to when they reach the age of spiritual maturity and are released into the wider world.

Forbia: An abandoned Hudson Bay wolf pup discovered and adopted by Finnegan. She becomes his familiar, and he names her Forbia, after his beloved ship he left in Maine.

Galon: A kinsman of Aidrik who was forced into Ascension by the Senetat after he angered them.

Goddess Danu: The goddess and leader of the Tuatha Dé Danann.

Goddess Morrigan: The goddess of divination, and one of the surviving Tuatha, foretold one day that four individuals—one descendant from each original clan—would unite the Empyreans and Quinlans once again. This prophecy was delivered to both a Quinlan and an Empyrean, and said that they would go through nearly two millennia of war and strife before finding peace.

Gorias: One of the four tribes of the Tuatha Dé Danann. All Quinlans descend from one of these four tribes. The tribe of Gorias is mentioned in The Prophecy as such: *A male Quinlan, known as Cianán (little ancient one), reincarnated with Cerridwen.* Jacob Donnelly is the subject of this reference.

Grand Eldre Servius: The ruling grand eldre of the Senetat for several millennia. Was lesser-ranked at the time of Aidrik's service. Was known for his "scorched earth" policy and for taking the restrictive laws of the Empyrean race to the far extreme. Killed by Anasofiya at the execution of Aidrik.

Grand Emperor Aeron: The last ruling Grand Emperor of Farjhem, and the Empyrean race. Had a reputation for being kind, and benign, but showed no interest in meaningful involvement with his people. Was activated when Agripin spread false rumor of his treason. Agripin then succeeded him as grand emperor.

Grand Emperor Agripin: The current ruling Grand Emperor of Farjhem, and the Empyrean race. Previously Grand Duke Agripin. The only son and oldest child of Aeron and Theda, both deceased. Fought in the Second Runean War, where his distaste for the Senetat was born. Over the years, his love of easy living kept him from taking action, but his partnership with the Brotherhood grew over time. He used Aidrik and Anasofiya as part of his campaign, which results in the burning of Farjhem. Is currently in Trondheim with the rest of the Brotherhood, plotting their next move.

Grand Emperor Elof: Father of Aeron, who succeeded him when he was "activated" for suspected trafficking with the rebels. Betrayed by Eldre Brutus, who was his closest confidante.

Grand Emperor Seti: Ruling emperor of Farjhem at the time the Senetat was created. Supported the Senetat's inception, as he was not interested in being the upholder of laws.

Grand Empress Anasofiya: Born a halfling of the Deschanel clan in New Orleans. Aidrik gave her the Sveising to save her life, which gifted her with more potent versions of her existing abilities, as well as suspected immortality. Married to Finnegan, but evigbond to Aidrik, which created an unorthodox polyamorous triad between them. Mother to Aleksandr, who is the son of both men. Her skill as a resurrection shaman pales in comparison to her most potent ability of all, etheric summoning. She is currently magic-bound by Agripin following the execution of Aidrik, where she destroyed hundreds of Empyreans.

Grand Empress Theda: Mate of Aeron and mother of Agripin. Deceased.

Great Cleansing: Following the creation of the Senetat, Empyreans who refused the mark were sought out and executed. Those who survived were branded Runeans.

Great Commitment (Also: Officium Maximus): The graduation ceremony, once every hundred years, when Empyreans reach their age of maturity and are released from the Scholars' tutelage, out into the world. This ceremony includes the installation of Emyr's Mark, a magical brand in the shape of a phoenix that is said to include a part of Emyr Himself. In reality, it is a device of the Eldre Senetat, as a means to control the Empyreans once they leave Farjhem.

Hakon: Still a fledgling, son of Emperor Aeron through a tryst he had with Hakon's mother. The mother escaped from Farjhem, and she died after birthing Hakon. Trygve took him in, under his wing, in Mongolia. Is a bestiakinetic.

Halfling: Humans with some amount of Empyrean blood/ancestry. A human is considered a halfling even if their Empyrean blood is many generations back.

Holger: Kind and helpful scout of Birger and Astrid, sent to look after Jacob and Amelia.

Illusionist: One who can manipulate the reality of others. Some do this by changing the physical interpretation. Others do this through influence. Markus is an illusionist who can change his appearance. Eydis can influence people to do her bidding.

Inner Voice: Empyreans believe in the concept of an "Inner Voice" guiding them toward their destiny. For Mercy, the Inner

Voice was an illusion crafted by Aidrik, who was guiding her toward safety.

Isabella Deschanel: Daughter of Margarethe and the necromancer. Was the first starlight awakener in the family, raised in secrecy due to her rapid growth. Her life, and eventual burning at the stake for witchcraft, was chronicled in the propaganda pamphlet, *La Sorcière de Villeneuve*. The current Deschanel line descends through her.

Jorun: The Brotherhood leader over South America. Quiet and reclusive, she relates better to creatures on four feet, as a bestiakinetic. Lives apart from the other Empyreans of the region, but looks after them from afar.

Killianshire: A small village in southern Ireland, where Jacob was born and raised. Father O'Connor presides over the cathedral here. The village is Quinlan-friendly.

Kjære: Aidrik's term of endearment for Ana. Translates roughly to "my dear" or "my dearest" in Empyrean.

Leif: The Brotherhood leader over the Caribbean region. Was once a member of the Senetat, but over time grew weary of their hypocrisy. He escaped and became a critical leader amongst the Brotherhood. Can bind the magic of others.

Livia: Born in Spain to an Empyrean mother and human father. Her father had dark olive skin, and her darker skin tone puts her in danger, as no purebred Empyrean has these tones. Is closely guarded under the wing of Thorvald, and has a special bond with Lucia. Empath.

Lucia: Escaped the Scholars when she was still a student, leaving Farjhem without a plan other than the idea of her freedom. Thorvald found her and took her under his wing in Spain, dubbing her *mi belleza*, and fostering her great loyalty. He makes her a scout, and pairs her with Anders. Her most recent assignment took her to *Ophélie* to help train and protect the children of the Brotherhood. Is an empath who can absorb the pain of others without impact to herself.

Margarethe Deschanel: Granddaughter of Claude Deschanel and, therefore, a great-granddaughter of Aidrik. Refused to accept death was the end, and married a famed necromancer, learning his secrets. Upon her death, she was determined to come back, immortal, through a starlight awakener. She pushed her daughter, Isabella, to instruct the family in maintaining pure bloodlines, to increase the chances of a starlight awakener being born into the family. Her attempts to come through non-necromancers and necromancers alike led to many Deschanel deaths over the centuries, which was falsely attributed to the Deschanel Curse. When at last starlight awakeners are born, in the form of Stella and Sebastian, she is prevented from coming through. It is believed she has not given up.

Mark of Emyr (Also: mark, Emyr's Mark): A magical infusion, in the shape of a phoenix, given to all Empyreans at their Great Commitment. The mark is about two inches in diameter, and can be placed anywhere on the body, a choice made by the Empyrean receiving the mark. Empyreans are told the mark includes a part of Emyr Himself, and that when it is time for their Grand Ascension, the mark will call them home to Emyr. In reality, the mark is a sinister plot by the Eldre Senetat, created as a means to control the Empyreans and destroy them.

Marquise Deschanel: Husband of Christiane de Laurent (Aidrik's first human evigbond). He was the First Father of Claude Deschanel, the first Deschanel born with Empyrean blood.

Mercy (Also: Clementyn): Lived three thousand years as an Empyrean who believed in the illusion of Grand Ascension. Piety drove all of her life decisions, often to the point of folly. In her youth, she spent many years with Aidrik, and they did not part on good terms. She found herself crossing paths with Nicolas Deschanel, and when her mark activated, she died but was resurrected by Anasofiya, then becoming human. She currently resides with Nicolas at *Ophélie*.

Mora: Empyrean word for mother.

Murias: One of the four tribes of the Tuatha Dé Danann. All Quinlans descend from one of these four tribes. The tribe of Murias is mentioned in The Prophecy as such: *A female Quinlan, born halfling Empyrean but given far more at maturity.* It is not yet known who the subject of this reference is.

Mystic: Most powerful of all magi, among Empyreans and halflings. Mystics manifest their abilities in different ways. Some are strong healers, others can engage in nested visions, dream suggestion, wards, and other unique traits. All are strong telepaths. Aidrik, Nicolas, Agripin, and Aleksandr are mystics.

Necromancers: Can speak with the dead, though limited to those who have not "crossed over." Quillan is a necromancer.

Nested Vision: A nested vision is an ability only accessible by mystics, wherein the mystic can travel into the mind of another and observe the world through their eyes. The most powerful mystics not only observe, but also control the host. Nicolas Deschanel has newly discovered he is a mystic who can engage in nested visions.

Old Aita: Believed to be the oldest living Empyrean, she is shamed for not having experienced her Grand Ascension. Scholars use her as an example of how not to end up, and as a means of driving fear amongst the fledglings. She is said to have pure white hair.

Ophélie: A plantation on the west bank of the River Road in Louisiana, about an hour from New Orleans. *Ophélie* has been the family seat of the Deschanels for over 200 years, and is passed down through the oldest male in each generation. Nicolas Deschanel, the current heir, has lived there his whole life.

Our Father (Also: Emyr, Our Father of Light, Our Father of Fire): Additional names for Emyr.

Portail: A portal created by a terrakinetic that can send travelers to any point in space.

Quinlans: An ancient line of druidic women, descendants of the Tuatha Dé Danann, and more recently, the Goddess Morrigan. All Quinlans descend from one of the four Tuatha tribes: Findias, Gorias, Falias, and Murias. They believe nature is unconditionally sacred, and that everything is interconnected, and balanced. Their powers are all drawn from nature. They live in secrecy, in protected groves and simplistic structures, all centering around their *crann bethadh*. In their early days, they had a strong alliance with the Empyreans, but that alliance was broken and both races have suffered the consequences. While the Quinlan genetics are passed through the females, in rare cases the male will also manifest. These males are known as draoi, and are more power than the females of the tribe. Most Quinlans keep the Quinlan surname.

Quinlan, Deirdre: Daughter of Seara. Mother of Noah, Nora, Nevina, and Niamh. Grandmother of Amelia. Is the youngest, and so has never taken a strong position of leadership. More of a free spirit, even for a druid. Married Kellan Jameson, a human. Kellan did not know what she was, until after Noah (her youngest) was born. When he threatened to leave, she secreted her daughters away to the tribe. Upon return to fetch her son, she learned Kellan had taken him to New Orleans.

Quinlan, Fiona: Only daughter of Nora. Is young—25—as Nora did not have her until later in life.

Quinlan, Meara: Middle child of Seara, sister of Deirdre and Philomena. Always happy, joyous, but simple-minded. The rest of the tribe closely protects her. Childless, she is not capable of a mutual relationship.

Quinlan, Nevina: Middle daughter of Deirdre, sibling to Nora, Niamh, and Noah. Does not travel outside the tribe. Is worried Jacob and Amelia are too "modern" for the job, and that the goddess waited too long to manifest the prophecy,

Quinlan, Niamh: Youngest daughter of Deirdre, sibling to Nora, Nevina, and Noah. Kind-hearted, and powerful, but often quiet, and whimsical.

Quinlan, Nora: Oldest daughter of Deirdre, sibling to Nevina, Niamh, and Noah. Tapped to take over as leader when the current one passes. Her practical nature makes her a competent leader.

Quinlan, Padraig: A draoi, and husband to Regan. He descends from another tribe of Falias. Trains Jacob, who has newly come into his draoi nature.

Quinlan, Philomena: Oldest child of Seara, sibling to Meara and Deirdre. Bitter to not be her mother's choice as successor. Strong-willed and often quick-tempered, especially now in her old age, which is why Seara did not choose her. Had one son in her youth, and gave him away when he was not a draoi.

Quinlan, Regan: Daughter of Nevina, sister to Kieran. Married to Padraig.

Quinlan, Rosemary: Mother of Enid, and grandmother of Jacob. A member of a tribe of Gorias, she has traveled to Seara's tribe to help with the prophecy.

Quinlan, Seara: Current leader of her tribe. Mother to Philomena, Meara, and Deirdre. Great-grandmother to Amelia. Sister to Flynn. All three of her children were intentionally conceived by men she picked herself, and planned a one-night stand. Has the essence of an oracle, who sees all (the prophecy was passed to her by the last leader). Knows her time is near, and is training her granddaughter, Nora, to take over.

Resurrection Shaman: A healer who is able to resurrect the recently deceased. Resurrection shamans are incredibly rare, and the ability is often volatile. Rarely do subjects come back exactly as they were before death. Anasofiya Deschanel discovers she is a resurrection shaman after Aidrik infuses her with Sveising.

Royal Palace of Farjhem: Residence of the royal family of Farjhem.

Runa: Leader of the minority opposition who rose up when the Senetat was created. Her execution is a symbol of strength for her followers, Runeans. She is often deified amongst her most devout followers. Her uprising is known as the First Runean War.

Runeans: Rebels. Those who oppose the Eldre Senetat are generally lumped together as Runeans (followers of Runa). Secretly, they have organized as the Dragon Brotherhood. Some in the Brotherhood are bloodthirsty and feel a call to action. Others are content to live quietly, off the grid of Empyrean society.

Scholar Saxon: The philosophy Scholar who carried out the execution of Mercy's parents after they were accused of heresy.

Scholars: A group of instructors selected by the Eldre Senetat to oversee the education of all Empyrean children. Their teachings often include propaganda-style support of the Senetat, and a fear-based deterrence of breaking rules. The Scholars spend a hundred years with Empyrean children.

Scholars' Temple: Place of instruction in Farjhem.

Second Runean War: Led by Erikr, the Runeans came together once more, in the spirit of Runa's beliefs, to overthrow the Senetat. As with the first uprising, they were squelched, and Erikr encased in a block of ice. This was the last large uprising of the rebels, who are now scattered and in hiding.

Senetat Sanctuary: Meeting place of the Senetat in Farjhem. Known for being sterile and devoid of any color excepting the crimson of their robes.

Shaman (Also: Healer): Another word for healer. There are varying degrees of shaman in the Deschanel family. Colleen Deschanel is said to be the strongest.

Sindre: Hails from the same Irish village as Birger, Astrid, and Eydis. A young elementalist who can conjure both fire and water, and often employs this skill to the hazard of others.

Skadi (Also: Skadi the Ruthless): The Brotherhood leader of Eastern Europe, residing in Bulgaria. She is known to be ruthless, cutthroat, and volatile to approach. She is remiss in her duties as a leader, in comparison to her peers, but is fiercely protective of her region.

St. Andrews, Finnegan: Husband of Anasofiya, father of Aleksandr. Born and raised in Maine to a normal, magic-free life. At his wedding, he accepted Aidrik's gift of Sveising, to grant him longer life and keener abilities. Recently learned he is descended from the Quinlans, and is a draoi, through this mother's side. Through his father, he is also descended from strong magic. Is a bestiakinetic.

St. Andrews, Ennis: Grandfather of Finnegan, father of Andrew, husband of Fiona. Lives in a protected, secluded clearing in the Scottish Highlands with his wife, who he keeps alive and young through potent magic.

St. Andrews, Fiona: Grandmother of Finnegan, mother of Andrew, wife of Ennis. Lives in a protected, secluded clearing in the Scottish Highlands with Ennis and is kept alive and young through his magic.

Starlight Awakener: An exceptionally rare form of necromancers said to "awaken the starlight," and employ the power of the heavens to occupy the living, and achieve immortality. Margarethe bred the family for centuries in search of a starlight awakener to come back through. Stella and Sebastian are starlight awakeners. Before them, the only known starlight awakener was Isabella.

Stian: A Brotherhood leader who chose Africa as his region because of the strife. He never stays anywhere for long, and is always moving around, helping where he can. As a terrakinetic, he can create a rift in the Earth, allowing a man to leave one place and appear in another, called a portail.

Sveising: DNA fusion unique to Empyreans. It is the process that allows multiple fathers for offspring, as well as the means by which Aidrik is able to save Anasofiya. Sveising can occur through sexual consummation (in the case of creating multiple fathers), but a mystic can also do it without consummation.

Telepath: One who can read the thoughts of others. Rare telepaths can read thoughts over long distances. Very few telepaths can also break a telepathic block. Tristan is a telepath who can reach across long distances and breach blocks.

Telepathic Block: A block employed my magic users to keep telepaths out of their head.

Terrakinetic: The ability to manipulate the spatial elements of Earth to your advantage. Example: a portail. Stian is a terrakinetic.

Thorvald: Brotherhood leader of Spain. He resides in the *Costa del Sol*, where he trains warriors and scouts in preparation for the inevitable war against the Senetat. Also one of the ancients, or earliest Empyreans.

Time Dancing (Also: Time Dancer): A skill unique to draoi. The time dancer can "dance" through time, a form of time traveling, but cannot change the past. Jacob is a time dancer.

Time Shaping (Also Time Shaper): An Empyrean skill that allows the individual to stop time and "reshape" it. The effect can be catastrophic if the caster is untrained, or if time stops for too long. Aleksandr is a time shaper.

Tribe: A group of Quinlans, usually descended from the same Tuatha tribe. All tribes have an elder, and a scribe.

Trygve: A Brotherhood leader, over Mongolia. One of the oldest Empyreans, having also been from the time of Runa, Brynja, and Einar, and has the markings of the ancients: exceptional height, dark red hair. Has one of the larger followings of the leaders. Known to be fair and loyal, but also quick to action and swift to justice.

Tuatha Dé Danann: Descended from Goddess Danu, early deities in Gaelic history, originating in Norway and later settling in Erin (Ireland). Ruled Ireland from 1897-1700 B.C. Many of the tales of faeries stem from their legends. There are four major tribes of Tuatha, each with a unique talisman of power. They hid in *Tir Non Og*, the otherworld, after Milesians drove them out of their lands. They believe strongly in reincarnation. Tuatha were the original druids, though modern day druidism became its own unique thing. The Quinlans descend from the four tribes of the Tuatha.

Ulfberht: A Viking sword produced between 800 and 1000 AD, made from Empyrean Steel (known to Man as Crucible Steel), known for its unusual combination of strength and flexibility. Though man believes this sword was crafted for Vikings, it was, in fact, created by Blacksmith, an ancient Empyrean metallurgist. The technology used to make Ulfberht baffles scientists to this day. Aidrik wielded one of the last of the originals, but gave it to Finnegan prior to his death.

Ward: A magical protection with unclear barriers, most

potent at its center. The ability to create wards came as a result of the alliance between Empyrean and Quinlan, and it was set forth that only an Empyrean (mystic) may create a ward, and only a Quinlan (draoi) can adhere it. Aidrik's ward is one such example, the center of it cast over *Ophélie* where it is most potent, with effects radiating out to protect other relatives. The protection diminishes the further out you go.

Yiva: Brotherhood leader of Southeast Asia, specifically residing in Thailand. Yields a body-length spear and is a powerful bestiakinetic. Known as the "she wolf."

ABOUT THE AUTHOR

Sarah is the USA Today and International Bestselling Author of over forty contemporary and epic fantasy stories, and the creator of the Kingdom of the White Sea and Saga of Crimson & Clover universes.

Born a geek, Sarah spends her time crafting rich and multilayered worlds, obsessing over history, playing her retribution paladin (and sometimes destruction warlock), and settling provocative Tolkien debates, such as why the Great Eagles are not Gandalf's personal taxi service. Passionate about travel, she's been to over twenty countries collecting sparks of inspiration, and is always planning her next adventure.

Sarah and her husband live in a beautiful corner of SE Pennsylvania with their three tiny benevolent pug dictators.

www.sarahmcradit.com